LORDS & LADIES
COLLECTION

Two Glittering Regency
Love Affairs

The Wedding Gamble
by Julia Justiss
&
Marrying the Major
by Joanna Maitland

The *Regency*

LORDS & LADIES

COLLECTION

The Regency

LORDS & LADIES
COLLECTION

Julia Justiss &
Joanna Maitland

MILLS & BOON®

*All the characters in this book have no existence outside the imagination
of the author, and have no relation whatsoever to anyone bearing the
same name or names. They are not even distantly inspired by any
individual known or unknown to the author, and all the incidents are
pure invention.*

*First published in Great Britain 2006 by
Harlequin Mills & Boon Limited,
Eton House, 18-24 Paradise Road, Richmond, Surrey TW9 1SR*

THE REGENCY LORDS & LADIES COLLECTION
© Harlequin Books S.A. 2006

The publisher acknowledges the copyright holders of the
individual works as follows:

The Wedding Gamble © Julia Justiss 1999
Marrying the Major © Joanna Maitland 2002

ISBN-13: 978 0 263 85106 9
ISBN-10: 0 263 85106 0

138-0806

*Printed and bound in Spain
by Litografia Rosés S.A., Barcelona*

The Wedding Gamble
by
Julia Justiss

Julia Justiss wrote her first plot ideas for twenty-seven Nancy Drew stories in school, and has been writing ever since. After publishing poetry in college, she worked as a business journalist for an insurance company and editor of the American Embassy newsletters in Tunis, Tunisia. She followed her naval officer husband through seven moves in twelve years, finally settling in the piney woods of East Texas, where she teaches French. 1997 winner of the Romance Writers of America's Golden Heart for Regency, she lives in a Georgian manor with her husband, three children, and two dogs. Find out more about Julia at www.juliajustiss.com

In memory of
Marsha Ballard
Critique partner and friend.
We shared the dream.

Prologue

"Just because that opera dancer got her clutches into you your first year on the town—" Edmund Stanhope paused to shoulder his creel "—doesn't mean all women are mercenary."

"You're dumber than a trout." Nicholas Stanhope, Marquess of Englemere, picked up his fishing rod and gave Edmund a mock-pitying look. "Take care, baby brother. A wench can bleed you dry faster than a Captain Sharp."

"Cynic." Shaking his head, Edmund kicked the hall door closed and set off across the rain-drenched lawn.

"Perhaps," Nicholas muttered as he followed in his brother's matted footprints. "Though I have excuse enough."

Rising sun gilded the grass and set off diamond sparkles among the dripping trees. They reached the lawn's edge, and leaving behind the stately bulk of Englemere Hall, turned onto a narrow wooded path.

Nicholas picked his way around the boughs strewing the trail, mute testaments to the violence of the previous night's storm. "About the wench," he continued, keeping his tone light. "Do try to remember, once she lands you, not to pay the trollop more than she's worth."

"She's not a trollop, and I won't have you speak of her so!"

Astonished at Edmund's vehemence, Nicholas nearly tripped over a fallen branch. Alarm coursing through him, he fixed his gaze on his brother. "'Tis a lady, then, who's caught your eye?"

"A lovely one, Nicky. Fair, blue-eyed and innocent as an angel." His earnest look faded to a frown. "Her father is the dupe of the Captain Sharps. Forever gaming, and never winning. I fear the debt-ridden bastard means to auction Angela off. I might have to bolt with her."

"You mean marriage?" Nicholas whistled. "All the more reason for caution, then."

Edmund opened his mouth as if to retort, then closed it. After a moment he said, "She's nothing like Lydia."

"Lydia was nothing like Lydia when first I knew her," Nicholas replied grimly. "I promise you, Edmund, no matter how enchanting her face, you'll never know what's really going on inside that lovely head. How can you be certain about her? Forgive me, brother, but you're rather young, and have hardly seen anything of the world yet."

"I've seen enough to know what I want," Edmund said quietly. "Besides, if I marry and set up my nursery, 'twould take the pressure off you."

"Don't be immolating yourself on the altar of matrimony to save my hide." Nicholas forced a smile. "I admit, since Lydia's death I've more or less handed over the duty of the succession to you. I'd not have you rush into it, though."

"I'm not rushing—I've thought carefully about this. Besides," he added, flashing Nicholas a grin, "surely you can't rest easy with only my poor mortal self standing between your title and Cousin Archibald."

"The Odious Archibald?" Nicholas shuddered. "Last time I saw him, he was swathed in lavender from head to toe. Tried to borrow some blunt from me too, the quiz. Indeed, if they distanced Archibald from Papa's honors, I might grow rather fond of a passel of grubby nephews leaving handprints on my Hessians."

They heard the roar of the river even before they reached the path's end. The Wey, flowing fast and full of floating debris, foamed high against its banks.

"Better not fish the point." Nicholas raised his voice above the din. "The stream's been undercutting that old stump."

"Growing cautious as well as ancient, my lord Englemere?" Edmund called back. "I always fish the point."

"Well, don't blame me if you sink up to your elegant thighs in muck."

Chuckling, Nicholas watched his brother straighten the creel on his back and slowly approach a jagged stump that jutted out over the stream. Reaching the edge, he sent Nicholas a triumphant smile.

A portion of the bank beneath the stump crumbled. Before Nicholas could even shout a warning, the old trunk shifted downward.

Clawing at the downed tree's weather-worn smoothness, Edmund scrabbled for balance. He twisted off his creel, teetered on one foot—and tumbled sideways into the water.

In the flash of an instant, Nicholas saw his brother's head strike the sharp stub of a projecting root. Saw blood against the dark hair before Edmund went under.

His heart stopped, then hammered in his chest. He threw down his fishing gear and raced toward the river.

Shedding his jacket as he ran, Nicholas slid and stumbled up the potholed bank beside the stump. More earth dissolved under him as he tugged frantically at his boots and watched for his brother to surface. When Edmund bobbed up, he jerked the second boot off and dived after him.

He came up sputtering, grit in his mouth and his eyesight blurred by muddy water. The current swept him blindly onward, scraping him against a hidden boulder as he dug at his eyes with his knuckles. Then his vision cleared and he spotted Edmund.

A whirlpool of swirling debris caught him. He fought free, battled downstream, grabbed Edmund and jerked the supine head out of the water. Clutching his brother's body, Nicholas let the torrent carry them over the rocks to the pool below, then struggled ashore.

Exhausted, he dragged Edmund onto the slimy bank, the wet-dog stench of soggy vegetation filling his gasping lungs. With shaking fingers, Nicholas turned the head to the side and pushed with all his remaining strength against his brother's chest. A trickle of muddy water drooled from the slack lips.

"Come on, bantling, help me!" Over and over he slammed his linked hands against his brother's chest, blew air into the unresponsive mouth. Long after any rational hope died he continued, his tired muscles burning and tears blurring his brother's face into a grotesque kaleidoscope of white skin, blue lips and river muck.

Sometime, moments or hours later, he pulled himself to his feet. As golden sun peeped over the treetops, he hefted Edmund's body onto his shoulders and stumbled toward the distant towers of Englemere Hall.

Chill wind whipped the scarf at Nicholas's neck and threatened to dislodge his curly-brimmed beaver. Pulling his greatcoat closer, he watched the slight, black-robed figure of his mother, the Dowager Marchioness of Englemere, as she arranged the bouquet of sweetbrier roses on the simple marble gravestone.

"Please, Mama, come along now. You'll catch a chill. Edmund wouldn't want that."

"In a moment, Nicky. Just one last prayer." The dowager dabbed at her eyes with a lace handkerchief. "By now—" she made a gesture toward the three graves flanking the dank raw earth before her "—one would have thought I'd be prepared for the uncertainties of life. Still, it is so hard to accept."

"If I'd reached him sooner," Nicholas replied, his throat tight, "maybe I could have—"

"Nicky dearest, you mustn't torture yourself!" She reached over to grasp his arm. "You did everything you could. I know that."

His jaw set, Nicholas helped her rise. "Come back to the Hall now, Mama. Your fingers are frozen. Martha will have a hot brick waiting."

"Oh, Nicky, don't fuss. I must go back, I know. I just wish that wretched Amelia would leave." She gave him a slight, sad smile that caught at his heart. "It's been ten days since the funeral, and still she lingers. With my Edmund barely cold in his grave, she has the effrontery to refer to that foppish son of hers as 'the heir.' It's almost more than I can bear, her snooping about, mentally rearranging furniture and redecorating rooms. Can you imagine, she told me the library would be much handsomer done up in puce. Puce! I cannot credit what possessed your uncle to marry that vulgar, jumped-up cit's daughter."

Nicholas smiled grimly. "The Odious Archibald already touched me for a loan. Wouldn't look right for the Stanhope heir to fall into the clutches of the cent-percenters, he said."

His mother's eyes widened, and he patted her cheek. "Don't fret, Mama, I have no intention of pensioning my cousin. Nor do I plan for him to remain much longer my heir." With a sigh, he turned his face away. "I may have been avoiding my duty these past four years, but only Aunt Amelia could be cloth-headed enough to think I'd eschew it."

The mittened hand on his arm tightened. He heard a rustle of silk, and knew his mother looked up at him. He couldn't bring himself to meet her concerned gaze.

"There's been so much pain in those years, for all of us. Give yourself time, Nicky. There's no need to rush."

He winced at the unconscious echo of his words to Edmund. Taking a ragged breath, he squeezed her fingers.

"What good would waiting do, Mama? No, 'tis time to go forward."

Gently disengaging his hand, Nicholas placed it on top of the hastily carved headstone. "I swear to you, by next Season's end, I shall bring home a bride."

Chapter One

Sarah heard the angry voices as soon as she entered the library hall. Or voice, she amended, frowning. Though she could not make out the words, the high pitch of the feminine tones warned The Beauty was in a rare temper. How could Clarissa be tiresome enough to quarrel with her fiancé on the very morning of their betrothal ball?

Coming around the corner, she nearly collided with a footman, his ear to the door and a grin wreathing his freckled face. Seeing her, he sprang back.

She raised a quelling eyebrow. "I believe Timms sent you to polish the silver, James. If that is complete, Cook needs you to help Simmons bring up the wine."

His face reddening, the young man bowed himself off. Sarah watched him retreat, thinking ruefully that the delicious details of Clarissa's latest outburst would be all over the servants' hall by luncheon.

Sighing, she grasped the handle in front of her. A smile pinned to her lips, she knocked lightly and entered.

In that first instant, she saw Clarissa's flushed face, Lord Englemere's back and a missile flying toward her. Instinctively she ducked. The object whizzed past to strike and shatter the vase behind her. As Sarah straightened, Clarissa stormed toward the door, thrusting aside her fiancé's outstretched hand.

"Beast! How could I have agreed to marry you? You're a detestable tyr-rant!" Bursting into tears, The Beauty brushed past Sarah and fled sobbing down the hall.

Sarah stole a cautious look at the man who had just been subjected—if the small sample she'd witnessed were any indication—to one of The Beauty's famous tantrums. Similar disagreements with Clarissa's mother normally left that unfortunate lady collapsed upon her couch. And afterward gained Clarissa whatever she wanted.

Her fiancé appeared made of sterner stuff. Evidently Clarissa had neither cowed him nor reduced him to red-faced embarrassment or white-eyed fury. He stood motionless, and Sarah could not glean from the sober face he'd turned to the window any hint of his thoughts.

Grudging respect stirred, followed by the reflection that if his lordship were as shrewd as he appeared, Clarissa was a looby to be flaunting her temper before the wedding ring was yet on her finger.

Uncertain how best to break the silence, Sarah knelt to tend the broken vase. She saw in the shards a glint of gold, and her fingers froze. *She couldn't have.* The large ruby winking up at her informed her Clarissa could indeed.

Fury displaced shock. Did that wretched girl expect her to smooth *this* over? When Sarah caught up with her—!

The polished boots beyond her shifted, jolting her back to the present. Swallowing her anger, she raked the rubble under the hall table and slipped the ornate ring beneath her cuff. Rising, she searched for the proper phrase. How does one tactfully return to a gentleman the betrothal ring his intended has just pitched at his head?

He turned and studied her, as if trying to assess her place. Even while anxiously weighing apologies, she had to appreciate what a work of perfection he was.

The coat of dark green superfine fit without a wrinkle over his broad shoulders, with nary a crease to show impatient hands had pulled at his immaculate sleeve. Nor had impetuous skirts dragged across the spotless Hessians disturbed their shine, or left a speck of lint on the tan inexpressibles molded over those muscled thighs.

The only sign of disorder was a lock of dark hair hanging upon his brow. She felt a ridiculous desire to brush it back, and almost laughed. The richest prize currently gracing the Marriage Mart, the widowed Marquess of Englemere had no need of *her* help.

When he smiled, as he did now, she had also to acknowledge him the handsomest man of her acquaintance. As she'd thought upon first seeing him years ago... She pulled her thoughts together and smiled cautiously back.

"Lord Englemere, I must apologize! With the ball, I'm afraid the whole household is rather...upset, and—"

"Miss Wellingford, is it not? I met you at Lady Rutherford's ball. Wearing something, ah, white." His smile deepening with a hint of humor, he bowed.

His unruffled composure, after what must have been an unpleasant scene with Clarissa, surprised her. She dipped a curtsy, her respect deepening as well. Perhaps more lay behind his typically bored aristocratic facade than she'd credited. Though if so, why had he offered for Clarissa?

Dismissing that disloyal and irrelevant thought, she nodded. "Yes, I remember. Lady Beaumont escorted us."

"Clarissa wore her usual flame red. 'Fire and Ice,' the ton calls the two of you. Having just been burnt, I could use some cooling. Is that what you were sent to do?"

Taken aback, she evaded his too perceptive gaze. She could hardly admit that Clarissa's abigail, lingering outside the door, had heard the quarrel and come flying to find Miss Sarah before her mistress did "something awful."

"Some 'cooling' refreshment, then, my lord?" she evaded. "Sherry? Or would you prefer brandy?"

"Brandy."

She poured a glass. "I was coming to fetch Clarissa, merely." She settled for a half truth as she handed the glass to him. "Lady Beaumont is a stickler for the proprieties. Until you wed, she must limit your time alone together.''

''You and I are alone. Will that cause gossip?''

She looked up quickly, but his face told her nothing. Surely he wasn't flirting—not with her. He wanted reassurance, she decided. ''Of course not. I am an old friend of your betrothed and a guest in her house. I—''

''There ye be, miss!'' A maid rushed into the room. '''Tis an uproar below stairs, and that's a fact. Wine in the cellar's two cases short, and Timms be shouting at James over it, and then the lobster for them patties were bad when Cook opened the crates, and she went into a swoon. Oh, and Ruddle says as Lady Beaumont's laid down on her bed with the headache and needs you to fix one o' them p-powders.'' Out of breath as she finished, the maid bobbed a belated curtsy.

''Oh, dear,'' Sarah murmured, embarrassed to have the household's problems blurted out in front of the marquess. ''You'll pardon me a moment, my lord?'' At his nod, she ushered the girl into the hallway.

Sarah kept her voice low. ''Lilly, tell Timms he must return to cleaning the ballroom, and I will handle James. Send Willy to Gunter's—inform them Lady Beaumont simply must have lobster, and counts on them to procure it. I shall return in a moment to make up Lady Beaumont's powder.''

She hesitated, fighting a craven desire to call farewell to the marquess from the hallway and retreat below stairs. The ring pressed her wrist with the heavy weight of Duty.

''Go along, Lilly. I shall be down directly.'' The maid eyed her uncertainly, then bobbed a curtsy. As the girl departed, Sarah forced herself to reenter the library.

''You said you are a *guest* in this house?''

''Why, yes. Oh, you mean—'' At his raised eyebrow, embarrassment flushed through her again. Evidently her voice hadn't been lowered enough. ''I'm very grateful for Lady Beaumont's sponsorship, and I do like to be useful.

Domestic details are fatiguing to one of her delicate constitution, she says, and I'm happy to spare her. I'm quite accustomed to managing a household.''

''You're Wellingford's eldest, aren't you?''

''Yes. With a houseful of servants and siblings, I have vast experience.'' She took a deep breath, her fingers clutching his ring. ''But with the ball tonight, you must forgive me for leaving you, after I—''

''Give back something that belongs to me?''

Again he surprised her. She'd sworn he'd not noticed her retrieving the ring. Feeling somehow guilty, she opened her hand, holding it out on her palm.

''I should return it. But I beg you, let me return it to Clarissa instead.'' She paused, seeking the most persuasive words. ''She is…high-spirited, I grant. Having lost her father when so young, she's been given her head much more than is good for her. When her temper cools, she will wish to beg your forgiveness. Will you allow her to?''

He looked at her steadily. ''Does she often fall into such, ah, 'high-spirited' freaks?''

Sarah stared at the ring in her hand, seeking some response short of blatant falsehood. ''Clarissa has the disposition often reputed to go with her coloring,'' she replied carefully. ''But she is also generous, courageous and loyal. Granted, her—exuberance—needs curbing. She should have learned that years ago, but no one ever troubled to teach her. The small effort of guiding so beautiful and accomplished a lady would be well worth the prize. Do you not agree, my lord?''

She dared not even contemplate Lady Beaumont's reaction should her appeal not convince him. Swallowing hard, she offered the ring again, praying he would not take it.

She didn't realize she'd closed her eyes until she felt his hand on hers. For a horrified moment, she thought he meant to gather up the ring.

''You may open those solemn silver eyes, Miss Wellingford.'' He curled her fingers back around the ruby. ''I will spare you the task of informing Lady Beaumont her daughter just jilted her fiancé, mere hours before the ball that was to present them to the cream of the ton.''

A vision of the piteous shrieks and burnt feathers that must have followed such a revelation shook her. ''Thank you, my lord,'' she said faintly. She looked up to see him smiling at the relief she hadn't managed to conceal.

Feeling better, she smiled back. ''I'm sure Clarissa will write you, wishing to meet before the ball to apologize. I must go, but please stay and finish your brandy.'' She held out her hand. ''Good day, sir, and again, my sincerest thanks for your understanding.''

He shook her hand, but to her surprise, retained it. ''Bear me company a moment longer, if you will.'' As she looked toward the open door, a protest on her lips, he continued, ''Your domestic crises will wait, and I dislike drinking alone.'' He turned on her his very charming smile.

When she nodded reluctantly, he brought her fingers to his lips for a brief salute. ''Thank you, my very cool and calm Miss Wellingford.''

His breath seemed to have ruffled the tiny hairs below her knuckles. She took the hand back, feeling less than cool and calm. Not at all certain it was the thing for her to entertain him alone, even with the door open, she seated herself at the edge of a wing chair.

He settled on the small sofa and grinned at her. ''I shan't ravish you, you know, and I'll send you off before there's any irreparable damage to your reputation.''

''Don't be nonsensical,'' she replied, nettled that he had perceived her unease. ''I'm hardly a green girl in need of a chaperon, and your passions are elsewhere engaged.''

His grin widened. ''All right, I'll behave. But after observing you fling yourself—quite decorously, of course— into the breach of a distressing scene and handle it so neatly, I admit a juvenile desire to see what might ruffle that calm veneer. Are you truly 'Ice,' Miss Wellingford?''

''Certainly not. I have a full share of all the warmer emotions. Wexley cursed us with that silly sobriquet before you came to London, and I hoped, since you've replaced him in Clarissa's regard, we might escape it.''

''Not if you continue to wear white gowns and Clarissa her red. With your fair coloring, and her fiery hair, the ton is constantly reminded.''

Sarah couldn't admit that new gowns were, for her, an impossibility, but with a trousseau to plan perhaps Clarissa could be persuaded. ''You might suggest you should like to see Clarissa in emerald, to match her eyes. She refuses to wear the so-called 'insipid pastels' generally required of girls in their first Season, but she's fond of bright hues.''

''Would she change from her favorite russet for me, do you think? I wonder.''

Before Sarah could frame an unexceptional answer to that leading remark, the marquess laughed. ''I'll ask no more questions that force you to choose between truth and loyalty. Clarissa has a good friend in you, indeed. But since you are, as you put it, not a green girl in her first Season, how did two such opposites as you become friends?''

''Do not men ever befriend their opposite? And we met as you probably met your closest companions, at school.''

''True, but my friends from Eton were of an age. You must be—four years older than Clarissa?''

''I'm three-and-twenty, my lord,'' she admitted. ''We were schoolmates at Mrs. Giddings's Academy for Gentlewomen.''

''And?''

Sarah looked up with a tiny frown. Surely he wasn't interested in schoolgirl reminiscences.

''I'm eager to learn everything about my betrothed,'' he said blandly.

''Of course,'' she replied, still puzzled.

"You were telling me how you came to be friends."

Wary, she took up the tale. "We met, as I said, at school. As you might expect with one of her commanding personality, Clarissa was her form's acknowledged leader. After several—incidents, we came to admire each other's strengths, and grew to be friends."

"'Incidents,' Miss Wellingford? You alarm me. What sort of mischief did my future wife brew?"

"Nothing significant." Sarah was sure Clarissa would not thank her for revealing details of her hoydenish youth. Even if he did wish—belatedly—to learn "everything" about Clarissa, she hardly felt it her task to enlighten him.

His lordship, however, continued to stare at her with a wide-eyed expectancy that positively begged her to impart all manner of ill-advised confidences. Well, she would not.

"We had a few, ah, disagreements over strategy, but resolved them. And later indulged in the normal sorts of high jinks schoolchildren enjoy."

"She was volatile, and you were the cautious one?"

"Something like that. I always favored the prudent approach, while Clarissa tended to be more adventuresome."

"Passion and Prudence, eh?" His shoulders shook. "What a pair you must have been."

"Oh, we did not long collaborate. The next year, things, ah, grew difficult at home, and I had to withdraw. We lost contact until we met by chance this spring at Lady Moresby's rout. Clarissa invited me to call, and I assisted Lady Beaumont with several trifling matters. Then—"

"Wexley made his infamous remark?"

"Yes," she said shortly, not wishing to pursue the point. The very day after Wexley's comment, Lady Beaumont invited her to reside with them in Grosvenor Square. Revealing that detail, however, might insinuate Clarissa resumed their friendship because their continued appearance together would give The Beauty a unique cachet to set her apart from the other Diamonds of the Season. Though Sarah privately suspected as much.

"As I was saying, learning I was staying with an elderly aunt, for Mama was too ill to sponsor me, Lady Beaumont graciously asked me to spend the remainder of the Season."

"Where you would be closer at hand to 'assist with trifling matters'?" Englemere asked dryly.

Sarah drew herself up. The fact that he echoed her own opinion merely made her more uncomfortable, for he must know she could never agree to so shockingly uncivil an assessment, regardless of its truth. "In this house," she replied stiffly, "I have been treated with every kindness, as a favored guest. If I have said anything to make you think otherwise, then I have expressed myself badly indeed." Rising, she nodded to him. "I must bid you good-day."

He rose too, rueful dismay on his face. "Now I have offended you. You *said* nothing, and I meant no disrespect, to you or your gracious hostess. I spoke out of turn, as I sometimes do among friends." One corner of his mouth turning up, he offered her an apologetic half smile. "Pray forgive me, Miss Wellingford."

A dimple creased the skin next to his mouth. She had the absurd desire to touch it, and gave herself a mental shake, annoyed both at his uncommon perspicuity and his effect on her. Of course he was charming, she told herself crossly. He probably practiced in front of his glass.

"Miss Wellingford?" he repeated, looking grave now.

She nodded shortly, but before she could reply, the maid reappeared at the doorway.

"I be so sorry to disturb you again, but, oh, please, miss!" Lilly gasped. Her expression as desperate as her voice, she stood on the threshold, breathing gustily and pleating the edge of her starched white apron.

"Yes, Lilly, I'm coming. My lord." Sarah curtsied.

As she rose, he once again caught her hand and brought it to his lips. "Thank you for the conversation, Miss Wellingford." Craning his head to ascertain the maid had already started down the hall, he added softly, "I must also apologize for being so—inquisitive. It was just borne upon me rather forcefully that the events of a Season don't allow one to gain a very clear insight into another's character. I was casting about, I suppose."

She drew back her hand, trying not to let the unexpected prickling sensation fluster her. "Indeed, my lord, I've sometimes thought all the busyness was expressly designed to *prevent* couples from getting to know each other." Belatedly realizing that was hardly a fortuitous remark, she looked up to catch him grinning at her.

Torn between exasperation and humor, she shook her head. "Now, before you trick any more impolitic comments from me, I must go."

"To make yourself useful?"

"I like to be useful," she said at her loftiest. His throaty chuckle followed her into the hall.

She'd brushed through that tolerably well, she decided as she hurried after the maid. Once she settled the household, she would search out Miss Clarissa. The peal she intended to ring over that damsel should echo in her flighty friend's ears for a week.

What a charming, intelligent woman, Nicholas thought as Miss Wellingford departed. Not that one could trust appearances, of course. He'd met her before, but she always seemed to withdraw into the background, and he'd not taken much notice of her.

Though she lacked the sort of vibrant loveliness that instantly captured masculine attention, her gray eyes and classic profile crowned with a coronet of white-gold braids were nonetheless attractive. And her womanly form merited much more than a second glance. Would that ice melt if one loosed those heavy plaits from their pins, fanned the silken strands free to play down—

In a wash of heat, he squelched his wayward thoughts. Best concentrate on the problem at hand.

The lady who'd just left him was about as different from his volatile betrothed as one could imagine. He'd chosen Clarissa Beaumont for her beauty, breeding and the fact that, of all the eager young misses crowding the Marriage Mart this Season, she alone didn't bore him.

He hadn't bargained on a chit of her tender years being already a hardened flirt. Or a shrew.

Nicholas swirled the brandy in his snifter and frowned. Should he have forbidden Miss Wellingford to give Clarissa back his ring? But how could he have resisted the appeal in those lovely silver eyes?

He recalled his fiancée's ugly tantrum, and shuddered. He'd better devise an effective plan, lest he spend a lifetime regretting that bit of gallantry.

Having sorted out the wine, smoothed feelings, succored Lady Beaumont and supervised the unloading of the new lobster, Sarah at last sought Clarissa. Her anger had cooled, but she still intended to give that rash young lady a thorough dressing-down. The task was, how should she deliver it so that the increasingly unmanageable Miss Beaumont paid her any heed?

Drawing, for the moment, a blank in that suit, her thoughts wandered to the marquess. She reviewed their conversation, wondering again why a man of his obvious wit would choose to wed a lady as self-absorbed as Clarissa.

Sarah shrugged. He'd not be the first gentleman whose powers of discernment diminished in direct proportion to the beauty of the lady. Besides, as a leader of London society, he would naturally prefer a bride who flourished there.

Her conscience smote her at that dismissive assessment. To be fair, she must admit she'd learned at first hand seven years ago that he was also a man of honor and compassion.

Remembering that incident inevitably recalled thoughts of Sinjin, and she flinched. With habit of long practice, she took a deep breath, waited for the ache to ease and forced her mind back to the marquess.

Were the widower not society's most famous gambler, as well as its most eligible bachelor, she might find him wholly admirable. But he did gamble. Indeed, Englemere's Luck was a byword throughout the ton.

Coming to London from Oxford with an exalted title and only a modest competence, in a few years at the tables he'd amassed a fortune reputed to be second only to Golden Ball's. It seemed, regardless of the wager or the game, the lord marquess could not lose.

Clarissa, along with the rest of the Upper Ten Thousand, considered his gaming prowess just another manly trait. Sarah could not.

She had seen her father when the gambling fever seized him, knew only too well the feckless optimism that, when Lady Luck frowned, convinced a man that surely the next hand, or the next throw of the dice, would find her smiling again. One reckless wager would follow the next until nothing was left, and heaven help any who depended on him.

Never would Sarah entrust her future to a gambler. Since Clarissa obviously didn't share her reservations, she could only hope, for her friend's sake, that Englemere's Luck would hold for a lifetime.

Which brought her back to Clarissa. As vexing as her friend sometimes was, Sarah truly wanted the best for her.

In addition to striking looks, Clarissa had a keen wit and a tempestuous spirit as often sunny as surly, as soon generous as toplofty. However, Sarah worried, having become the reigning belle, she seemed to forget that even for an incomparable there were limits. Limits, Sarah must make her recognize, that Clarissa could disregard only at her peril.

In offering their home and sponsorship, the Beaumonts had done Sarah a singular favor. Despite Englemere's insinuations, and her own reservations over Lady Beaumont's use of her, she owed them gratitude, loyalty—and an unbroken engagement.

Entering upon her knock, Sarah advanced into the chamber and stopped short. Standing next to the crocodile-legged Egyptian-style settee, Clarissa's abigail fluttered her hands and cast Sarah an apologetic look. Her charge reclined upon the settee, skirts drawn indecorously up above her ankles while she painted her toenails with silver gilt.

Despite her good intentions, Sarah's sorely tried temper snapped. "Heavens, Clare! Do you now plan to appear as an abandoned woman as well as a shrewish one?"

Harris gasped, but Clarissa laughed as she sat up, apparently in high good humor after her earlier pet. "I think it vastly becoming."

"Certainly, if you wish to look like a Haymarket whore. Not, I think, quite the thing for a marchioness."

"Oh, Sarah, you're so…fusty." Her temper miraculously unimpaired, Clarissa waved her hand at the abigail. "Bring us tea or something, Harris. Sarah's going to read me a scold, and I'd as lief not hear it with you gasping and moaning in the background."

By the time the chaperon exited, Sarah had her ire under control. "At least you've sense enough to expect a lecture. Thunder and turf, Clare, what possessed you to treat Englemere so? Are you all about in the head?"

Clarissa settled her skirts about her ankles and gave Sarah a suspiciously penitent look. "I shouldn't have lost my temper, I realize, so you may save yourself the scold. There, now you can't say I'm never reasonable."

"I'm glad to hear it. And I hope—" Sarah chose her words "—you'll take care to be sensible in future. Not just in your dealings with Englemere, but in general."

"Oh, I'm always sensible," Clarissa replied airily.

Sarah bit back a sharp retort. "I cannot call it 'sensible' to tool a curricle down Bond Street—"

"It was eight in the morning, with nobody about to see, and Montclair dared me!"

"Or to let Wexley take snuff from your wrist."

"Oh, that." Clarissa giggled. "He was saying the silliest things, and oh, his mustache tickled." Her grin faded, to be replaced by a frown. "I think it beastly of Englemere to take me to task for that, and for allowing Arthur both my waltzes at Almack's last Wednesday. 'Tis my first Season. Why shouldn't I kick up my heels?" Her tone turned petulant. "I've promised to become his dull marchioness at the end of it. Isn't that enough?"

"Don't you wish to marry Englemere?"

Clarissa studied her toes, moving them so they sparkled in the light. "I suppose so."

"He does gamble," Sarah allowed. "Dearest, if you harbor any doubts…"

"Oh, I don't! Not about his gambling—faith, all the world gambles, and besides, Englemere always wins." A small frown wrinkled the perfection of her profile. "It's rather that…well, he can be positively *gothic* sometimes, acting as though I should have eyes for no man but him. However, he *is* enormously wealthy, and the catch of the Season."

Clarissa picked up a hand mirror, a self-congratulatory smile on her face as she patted her glossy titian curls. "Did you know, in the four years since his wife died in that carriage accident, Englemere never once showed a hint of partiality for any woman—a respectable one, that is—until he met me? I can't wait until he makes the announcement tonight. The other girls will be positively green!"

"Will there be an announcement? I thought you just rather, ah, dramatically ended your understanding."

Clarissa looked startled, but then her face relaxed. "I expect I vexed him, but he'll come round. I'll send him a little note saying, oh, that I became distraught because he seemed disappointed with me, or some such rot." She smiled sunnily, oblivious to Sarah's gasp of outrage. "Gentlemen are so arrogant, he'll believe it. Even better, you write it. You're cleverer with words than I am."

"I most certainly will not!" Sarah retorted. "Engle-mere's no fool, Clare. You threw his ring back in his face! What makes you think you're still engaged?"

Clarissa eyed Sarah as if she were a perfect dunce. "A gentlemen never cries off."

"No? But you were the one, ah, crying off. What if Englemere doesn't take you back?"

Sarah watched intently, but the reaction she was seek-ing—horror, remorse, penitence—never came. Clarissa shrugged. "I'll marry someone else, I suppose. Wexley perhaps, or Montclair—he's so amusing."

"Wexley?" Sarah echoed faintly, shocked to realize Clarissa had not lost her heart to her betrothed.

"Or Montclair, but 'tis no matter. Englemere *shall* marry me," Clarissa announced before Sarah could re-cover. "And if he thinks to keep me under his thumb like some obedient schoolgirl, I'll soon set him to rights."

"You'll not convince him to allow you free rein by shouting at him or painting your toenails like a trollop," Sarah countered bluntly.

"Mrs. Ingram paints her toes."

Sarah's surprise must have shown, for Clarissa sniffed. "I know gossip says she's his mistress. Well, he'll not look at her again once he has me."

The slight change of tone, from confidence to bravado, revived Sarah's flagging sympathy. If Clarissa felt vulner-able, who could wonder? The woman identified by the ton as Englemere's current ladylove was no girl out of the schoolroom, but a mature, sophisticated beauty.

"Englemere may indeed admire spirit—even gilded toe-nails," Sarah said gently. "But you may be sure he never asked Mrs. Ingram to be his wife."

"Oh, stubble it, Sarah, you're getting to be a dead bore. Just be a dear, and write me that note."

"I will not," Sarah gritted out, once more holding on to her temper with an effort. "I warn you again, don't try to run a rig on Englemere. He'll not stand your nonsense."

Clarissa turned to face Sarah, ominous signs of impending explosion in her flashing eyes. "And how can you claim to know what Englemere will or will not 'stand'?" Clarissa's tone grew saccharine. "That must have been quite a little chat you had after I left. If it weren't beneath me to make such a comment, I might say you were jealous."

Sarah stilled, fixing Clarissa with a stony stare. After a silent moment, Clarissa's gaze wavered. She lowered her eyes, a faint blush staining her cheeks.

"It is indeed beneath you," Sarah replied in clipped tones. "You had better find other, equally vulgar things beneath you in future, if you don't wish to make yourself such a byword nobody will have you."

Clarissa dashed an angry tear. "That's unfair! I could never be! You're supposed to be my friend, and I think you're being horr-rid!" She turned away, her voice breaking on a gusty sob that promised more.

Sarah watched her, wondering a bit remorsefully if she'd overplayed her hand. After a moment, she pulled her weeping friend into her arms and patted her soothingly.

"Hush, now. Here comes Harris with your tea. Let her console you while your wasp-tongued friend goes to check on the household." Sarah pushed Clarissa to arm's length and studied her face. "We are still friends?"

Tears bejeweling her emerald eyes, Clarissa nodded a little doubtfully. The fit of weeping had turned neither eyes nor even the tip of her perfect nose red, Sarah noted with chagrin.

She turned to go, then halted. "I nearly forgot." Producing the ruby, she grinned. "You were right, he didn't cry off. You must write your own note, though. Mind you make it a good one."

Leaving her friend to the efforts of her abigail, Sarah walked out. At the end, she thought she'd reached Clarissa. With grave problems of her own to deal with, Sarah could only hope the impression would last.

Chapter Two

Sarah inspected the deserted supper room: platters, punch bowls, posies all in place. She nodded approvingly. The ball was a great success, Clarissa seemed on her best behavior, and Sarah had every reason to be pleased.

Glimpsing herself in the pier glass over the sideboard, she sighed. The stylish white dress fit well, but the color failed to show her to advantage. She looked, she thought as she inspected her mirrored image critically, like a ghost, or an ice maiden carved for a frost fair.

"So this is where you've hidden away." Englemere's voice interrupted her thoughts. "You should rejoin your guests." Smiling, he approached her. "The gentlemen will be missing you, for you look very lovely this evening."

She turned startled eyes toward him. His expression seemed sincere, and she frowned slightly. This must be gallantry, she concluded, since she'd just determined that she looked about as lively as a statue—

"You shouldn't wince at compliments."

You will not explain, the stern little voice in her head commanded. Sarah closed the mouth she had opened to do just that and pressed her lips together. Drat, what was there about the man that prompted her to almost unthinkingly respond to him? With—worse yet—honest thoughts, not the socially acceptable ones she believed she'd long ago learned to plaster over the genuine.

His lips curved in a smile. She realized she was staring—nearly as sorry a breach of decorum as candor. "Y-yes, my lord," she stammered, feeling like a perfect dolt.

"I wanted to thank you for a lovely party."

"Prettily said, but that compliment is due Lady Beaumont." She managed a reproving look. "As you know."

His smile widened to the twinkle-eyed grin of a small boy succeeding in mischief. "I have this lamentable urge to give credit where it's due. Reprehensible, I admit."

A gurgle of laughter escaped her. "If credit were always placed where it's due, society as we know it would crumble." Sobering, Sarah asked anxiously, "Everything is going well, is it not? Clarissa is—"

"—a paragon of decorum. This afternoon, I received an exemplary note of apology. Only four misspellings." He gave Sarah a penetrating look. "You must have delivered a thundering scold."

A little flustered, she replied, "I did speak with Clarissa, but she needed no prompting. She already regretted the, ah, incident. As her behavior demonstrates."

"You really must allow matters to run their course."

Though softly spoken, she recognized the reproof. He had every right to reject interference, but after all her efforts she couldn't help feeling resentful.

"I did not intend to meddle in a private matter," she said stiffly. "If you feel I have done so, I must apologize. Now, as you justly observed, I should return."

She started past. He caught her wrist. Once again, the touch of his gloved hand sent a tremor up her arm.

"I realize you intervene from a sincere desire to help." With one finger he caressed her wrist. "You aren't 'Ice' at all, are you, Miss Wellingford? 'Tis only right you detest the nickname."

Trembling, Sarah stepped back and withdrew her hand.

No wonder he'd won such a reputation with the ladies. His eyes held hers still; his compelling presence mesmerized.

Her mind skittered, locking on sensation: the throb of her pulse in rhythm with the distant orchestra...the mingled scents of beeswax, roses and shaving soap...the midnight of his eyes and broad, black-coated shoulders silhouetted against the dancing light of the sconces.

Coloring faintly, she turned to fiddle with the perfectly aligned flatware. "I should hope," she managed at last, "I am neither shallow nor easily shattered."

"Not at all." He replaced the fork she'd just moved a fraction of an inch. "If one must compare you to ice, I'd describe you as the solid kind on which one skates. Dependable, and a pleasure to be near. Now—" he took her hand from the table and placed it on his arm "—let me escort you back to the ballroom." In a lighter tone he added, "I expect several faithful swains await your return."

Gallantry again. More comfortable with that than his compliments, she replied, "I don't know about 'several,' but one or two might wish for a dance."

"Which one or two?" He wagged a finger at her. "You've solved my romantic difficulties—let us consider yours. You ventured to London to make a match?"

At her nod, he continued. "From what you've said, I gather you have no male relatives to screen your suitors. Perhaps I should take on the post."

She shot him a glance. Surely he wasn't serious. Nonetheless, she replied politely, "You're very kind, but I couldn't think of it."

He looked startled, as if he didn't understand her refusal. Not wishing to appear ungrateful, she added, "You are funning, I realize, but—"

"Not at all, Miss Wellingford. I'm quite in earnest. After all, who better to judge than an experienced older man acquainted with everyone in the ton?"

"'I being so young and green," she countered dryly. "'Tis most generous, but I wouldn't dream of imposing."

"No imposition. I should look upon it almost as…a duty to my fiancée." He drew himself up into a parody of a *pater familias*. "Come, Miss Wellingford. No secrets."

The absurdity of it—having that incomparable Corinthian, the Marquess of Englemere, pass her suitors in review—wrestled with proper reserve, and won. "'Tis ridiculous," she protested, laughing.

"Child, you wound me. Now, tell Uncle Nicholas everything."

For whatever reason—perhaps the same one that had led her to speak frankly before—after a moment's hesitation, she fell in with his game. Leaning closer, she said in confidential tones, "The first is rather young—Marshall Beckman, from Yorkshire."

"The coal magnate's grandson?"

"Yes," she replied, hoping she didn't detect a sudden coolness in his tone. "'Tis true, his grandfather was in trade, but his mother's family is unexceptionable. He's a nice lad, if a trifle…shy." As well he might be, she added mentally, with half the ton ready to cut him for his grandfather, and the other half mocking his tall, gawky frame and spotted face.

"I know nothing to his discredit, though I'd not judge him up to your weight. Who else?"

She chuckled. "The next is surely that! Baron Broughton must outweigh me by several stone. And though I suspect he's much more interested in a new mother for his six daughters than a wife, he has been attentive."

The marquess frowned with mock severity. "Family's acceptable, but for all his wealth, the baron is too fond of the green baize for unqualified approval."

She thought she'd masked her reaction, but Englemere laughed. "The pot calling the kettle black, you think? My dear, don't you know? *I* never lose. As for the baron, ru-

mor says he spends his winnings on—well, I should think
you would want more than a nursemaid's position.''

She gazed up at him appraisingly. "Do you think I look
for love, or some grand passion? I assure you, at my advanced age I've long since abandoned romantic notions.
Should he honor me with a proposal, I am certain the baron
would treat me with kindness and respect.''

"Paltry." Englemere dismissed the baron—or her sen-
timents—with a wave of the hand. "If not grand passion,
then devotion is a minimum requirement. I insist on it.''

One marble-perfect face flashed into her mind. "I would
rather dispense with the devoted one,'' she muttered.

"*Devoted?* Excellent. Who is this perceptive man?''

Sarah looked away, her enjoyment of their banter
dashed. She didn't wish to discuss Sir James. When possible, she avoided even thinking of him. Chastising herself
for having begun this silly recital of suitors, she reluctantly
replied, "Sir James Findlay."

Englemere's smile vanished. "Entirely unsuitable," he
said flatly. "Findlay's already buried two wives. Suicides,
rumor says. He's received—just barely—but no matron
worth her salt would let an unmarried daughter near him.
I'm astonished Lady Beaumont permitted it.''

"She's been busy, and he can be charming.''

"Perhaps, but I still think it a shocking lapse." He
looked steadily at her. "No more funning, Sarah—Miss
Wellingford. The man's a villain, and I say that based on
personal experience, not rumor. Dismiss him.''

Despite her reservations about Findlay, Sarah's independent nature bridled at the command. "I've heard the rumors, and I think it reprehensible that a man be condemned
on that basis. Sir James comes from an excellent family
and is, as you admit, everywhere received. To me, he has
been all that is correct.''

"Excuse me, Miss Wellingford. I didn't mean to dictate.
Please understand I spoke from genuine concern.''

Her resentment extinguished by his swift apology, she

felt foolishly churlish. "I do understand. Excuse *me* for flying into the boughs. And I must confess, for all that Sir James is handsome, well-bred and amusing, I cannot like him. Unfortunately, of my several suitors, he's by far the most persistent." Sarah sighed. "And he's very rich."

"They are all of them rich, aren't they?" he mused, as if just realizing the fact. "Is wealth *that* important?"

She sensed, rather than heard, the change in his tone. What matter if he thought her a fortune hunter. Was that not the bare truth? His disapproval should not have hurt, but it did. "Some of us do not possess the privilege of free choice," she said defensively.

"Naturally, one must choose jewels, and modish gowns, and fancy carriages," he replied, his voice sardonic.

"Jewels and gowns and carriages?" she gasped, truly stung now. "Try food, and clothing, and a roof over one's head!" She regretted the outburst the moment the words left her lips. Her face heating, she turned away.

"I had heard Wellingford was all done up." His quiet voice came over her shoulder. "Are things that bad?"

She was suddenly, furiously angry—at herself, for once again blundering into confession, at him for his well-heeled disdain. Even more, at that moment she hated Englemere for unleashing the burden of worry she struggled so hard to contain. Was it not enough that it haunted her dreams?

She turned back to stare straight into his eyes. "Lord Englemere, do you think me stupid enough to have thrown myself—a plain, penniless ape-leader—to the Marriage Mart wolves, were the case not *absolutely* desperate?"

"Tête-à-tête with Englemere? That will never do."

The mocking voice wafted to her from the doorway, and Sarah winced. *Not yet.* She needed to be at her best to deal with Sir James, and now her composure was in shreds.

"I wondered where you'd gone." Sir James strolled toward them. "Lady Beaumont sent you on another little errand, did she? I must return you to the party."

He took Sarah's hand. "''Evening, Englemere." He bowed. "I'm to wish you happy, am I not? Mayhap you will soon be doing the same for me." Sir James gave Sarah a significant look. "Come along, my dear. The next dance is mine."

Ushered out by Sir James, Sarah could do no more than nod a brief parting to Englemere. As he bore her down the hall, she found her voice. "'Twas presumptuous of you to speak so to Lord Englemere." She tugged at her hand. "You know quite well you have not asked, nor have I answered."

Sir James obligingly loosened his grip. Sarah felt a strong urge to remove her hand—and her person—from his presence, though she had no reason beyond an instinctive dislike to justify such rudeness. After a moment's inner struggle, she left her hand on his arm.

Smiling, as if in thanks, he patted it. "We both know I shall ask very soon. How much time have you left before the note comes due—ten days? I shall ask, and when I do, we both know what your answer must be."

Sarah glanced sideways at him, wondering not for the first time why she could not bring herself even to tolerate the undeniably handsome, elegantly dressed Sir James. Perhaps it was the coldness of that chiseled profile, which might serve as a sculptor's model for a Greek hero, or the disturbing light she sometimes caught flashing in his clear blue eyes. Or his irritating arrogance.

"You are not my only suitor."

"Sarah, surely you don't mean to compare my faultless breeding with that spotty-faced youth's. He's unworthy of you, my dove. In any event, I understand he's gone out of town—to Scotland, I believe. Inspecting a stallion."

"Indeed? He mentioned no such trip yesterday."

"Did he not?" Sir James shook his head. "Perhaps I'm mistaken, but I doubt it. 'Tis my stallion, you see."

A chill rippled through her. Resolutely she stilled it. "My resources are not quite exhausted."

"You refer to the corpulent baron?" Sir James smiled. "A sadly unreliable champion, my dove. Not only is he enamored of quite a different ladybird, he has a most unfortunate fondness for gambling." Sir James sighed. "It seems in recent days his luck has changed for the worse. From what I hear, he'll soon be barely able to afford that mistress, much less a new wife."

"I suppose he told you that?"

Sir James chuckled and tapped her nose with one finger, like an indulgent parent. "We gentlemen hear such things, in the wicked fastness of our clubs. 'Tis true enough, I vow. You do much better to have me, my dear."

Sarah pulled away. "I am not 'your dear' and certainly not 'your dove.' You will refrain from addressing me so."

An odd flash in his pale blue eyes sent a frisson of alarm through her. Then he laughed, leaving her to wonder if she'd only imagined it.

"But you *are* a dove, my dear. A lovely, fluttering dove dragging her wing across the ground to lead predators away from her nestlings. I shall save the nest—that is the bargain, is it not? Save Wellingford Hall and your brother's patrimony, and ensure your nestling sisters' dowries."

Before she could guess his intent, he brought her hand to his lips and kissed it. She jerked away, but he held on, his grip like iron. "My wealth I'll gladly expend to lift those burdens from your shoulders."

She tugged again and he released her, giving her wrist a quick, apologetic rub as if realizing he'd grasped it too tightly. "We shall deal well together. You will see."

"Perhaps," Sarah retorted, "but as you kindly remind me, I have ten days left. Mr. Beckwith may return from viewing *your* horse, or the baron's luck improve."

Sir James halted abruptly on the ballroom's threshold and gave her a long, slow smile. "I don't think so."

Mercifully, the movements of the dance separated Sarah from Sir James, precluding the need for conversation. For weeks she had suspected Findlay of toying with her, advancing, then retreating as he studied her other suitors with an amused and calculating eye.

Unease formed a little knot in her stomach. Twelve hours ago Mr. Beckman told her he was looking forward to this ball. Had Sir James indeed sent him to Scotland? Could he be gambling against the baron as well? Her attentive suitor was well-known to be infallible with the bones and unbeatable at cards, so much so that knowledgeable gamblers avoided him.

The music ended. She sensed Findlay's eyes on her. A sudden revulsion seized her, so strong she could barely prevent herself from bolting as he picked up her dance card.

"Baron Broughton's tardy," he announced after perusing it. "I shall claim his waltz."

"Sorry, Sir James." Lord Englemere materialized behind her. "You promised me this waltz in the supper room, remember, Miss Wellingford? You'll not object, Findlay."

He swept her away before Sir James could protest. She clung to him through the steps of the dance, as if the ballroom were a stormy sea and he the buoy keeping her afloat. Gradually, the lilting rhythm began to relax her.

"Much better, Miss Wellingford. Though I could not blame one suffering Findlay's presence from stiffening up, it is rather difficult waltzing with a board."

She laughed, if a bit shakily. "Thank you for the rescue, my lord. I have had a surfeit of his attention."

"Ah, we are to have conversation, too. Excellent! Then I am well rewarded for my bravery."

"In cutting out Sir James?"

"Findlay?" He dismissed the baronet in a voice laced with contempt. "No, 'twas my lady fair I feared. You left me with a look that would have melted stone. Though I was shaking in my slippers, I felt I must face your displeasure, if only long enough to apologize."

"You said nothing for which you need apologize. I must marry for money." She offered a smile that almost succeeded. "A fact no less true for being unpalatable."

"Too often the innocent suffer for the sins of the guilty," he said with an intensity that surprised her. "And I do owe an apology, to think even for a moment that you might marry for shallow or selfish reasons."

"Don't make me out a martyr," she murmured, tears pricking her eyes. "My predicament is all too common."

"One does what one must. But Sarah—not Findlay."

"Let us abandon such a dismal subject. Come, this should be a joyful night! Thankful as I am for your intervention, should you not be waltzing with Clarissa?"

"I'm afraid I'm in her black books again. Wexley." The marquess rolled his eyes in exasperation. "I objected to her marked partiality for that fop. Of course, she had to go off immediately and waltz with him." At Sarah's look of alarm, his expression lightened to ruefulness. "You didn't expect her to behave for an entire evening?"

The music faded, and the marquess led her off the floor. "There now, remove that troubled look from your brow." Englemere brushed a fingertip across her forehead as if to do just that. "Lady Beaumont is waving—she must require your assistance. I can handle Clarissa."

"I have no doubt. Yes, madam," she called, and turned back to him. "Thank you again for *your* assistance."

He gave her fingers a lingering squeeze. "You're most welcome. Good evening, Miss Wellingford."

Sarah walked over to Lady Beaumont, her mind in tangles and her hand tingling.

Thoughtfully Englemere watched Sarah go. He must hunt up his betrothed and escort her in to supper. Things in that line were progressing nicely, and once he had his own affairs sorted out, perhaps he should devote some time to Miss Wellingford's.

The idle conclusion startled him. He'd thought himself

beyond becoming interested in a woman toward whom he harbored neither carnal nor marital intentions. But, he realized, Miss Wellingford intrigued him.

No, she wasn't "Ice." He noted her response to him in the supper room, the flare of mingled interest and confusion that revealed her innocence even as it hinted of a hidden passion. Not that he'd be the man to uncover it, of course.

He'd immediately regretted the casual offer to review her suitors, but before he could retract it, she'd piqued him by refusing. In his experience no woman, be she countess or courtesan, ever turned down a chance to further her own interests. Upon the spot he decided to pursue the game, fencing with her until she acquiesced.

He liked the way she spoke frankly to him, with a man's directness rather than a woman's wiles. Those changeable silver eyes that glowed when he amused her, that throaty little gurgle of a laugh, charmed him.

He remembered her frown at the fulsome compliment he'd paid her, and smiled. He'd give a monkey to know what she'd been thinking behind those expressive eyes, what she'd almost said before a lamentable caution stilled her tongue. Damn, but she'd be wasted on the provincial Beckman or the pompous Broughton.

Then he recalled her shudder at Findlay's approach, and his amusement faded. Perhaps more than anything else, he admired the courage and sense of duty that propelled her, for the sake of family, to even consider wedding such a one.

To allow her sweet loveliness into the keeping of that scoundrel would be a crime. But how to prevent it?

He must review the ranks of his friends, he decided as he set off to bring his recalcitrant fiancée to heel. Surely one of them was ripe for the parson's mousetrap, and would prove a more fitting match for the quiet elegance of Sarah Wellingford.

Chapter Three

The warm parlor fire lulling her, Sarah let Lady Beaumont's bright chatter and Englemere's occasional polite replies wash around her like the babble of a country brook. The chiming of the mantel clock brought her up with a start.

Lady Beaumont cast a worried glance at the timepiece. "Clarissa wished to wear the charming new gown you commissioned. Emerald shows to such advantage on her, and I know she wants to look her loveliest—"

"I'm sure our patience will be well rewarded." Draining the brandy from his glass, Englemere walked over to lean against the mantel. *He displays well in evening dress,* Sarah thought sleepily, taking in the elegant black coat and trousers, the pure white waistcoat and snowy cravat. Elegant and annoyed, with Clarissa forty minutes late.

She turned to find Lady Beaumont glaring at her. Her ladyship refashioned the glare into a smile and said pleasantly, "Sarah, dear, why don't you go assist Clarissa?"

"With Harris and her maid both attending her, I'm likely to be more a hindrance than a help," Sarah protested. For Clarissa to be this tardy must mean she'd find above stairs a minefield of frayed temper and wrought nerves that she would as lief not enter.

"I'm told Harris took to her bed with a nervous spasm."

Lady Beaumont's voice conveyed her irritation at this blatant dereliction of duty. "Doubtless Lizette is having difficulty managing alone."

"I'll go at once, then." Sarah suppressed a sigh.

Lady Beaumont patted Sarah's hand and turned to the marquess. "Allow me to refill your glass, Englemere."

Sarah plodded up the stairs, puzzled that Mrs. Harris would have allowed herself to succumb on such an important evening. Invitations to the Dowager Duchess of Avon's occasional entertainments were jealously sought, and tonight's ball would be one of the Season's most glittering.

She hoped her erstwhile suitors would be there. In the four days since Clarissa's ball, she had neither seen nor heard from Marshall Beckman. Worse, rumor whispered Baron Broughton was indeed gaming against Sir James—and losing.

The news worried her. She'd not survived a gamester father to pledge herself willingly to yet another. And should the baron propose, would he be able to provide the staggering sum she required to rescue Wellingford?

Her recent chat with the banker confirmed she'd not be able to beg additional time. While expressing sympathy for her unfortunate circumstances, he informed her the full sum due must be paid by the stated date, or the bank would be forced, regrettably but unavoidably, to foreclose.

Six days left. Three, really, for even with a special license—her cheeks reddened to think of conveying the news that there'd be no time for a proper calling of banns—her hapless bridegroom would probably require another two or three days to gather the necessary cash.

Sir James, however, knew exactly how much money she needed, and when. She'd detailed it early on, thinking to discourage him, but the knowledge had seemed rather to pique his interest. If only she'd not made that miscalculation.

The vision that greeted her when she entered Clarissa's

room drove all other thoughts from her brain. Draped in emerald satin, Clarissa regarded herself in the pier glass while her little French maid beamed up adoringly. "Ah, *mam'selle,* is she not *magnifique?*" Lizette breathed.

Magnificent wasn't the first word that occurred to Sarah. She understood now what had caused Harris's attack of the vapors and why Clarissa had so delayed what would undoubtedly be an unforgettable entrance.

The satin material reflected the glow of the candelabra and hugged every curve of Clarissa's voluptuous body, outlining in a sensuous ripple of light the movement of her thigh as she tapped her foot. The merest suggestion of a bodice confined her full breasts, and Sarah could swear she saw the dark shadow of nipples below the gown's edge.

Clarissa had seemed troubled, but at Sarah's gape-mouthed shock, her chin rose. "Englemere chose the modiste and material. Harris has already scolded, wept and been sent to bed for her pains, so don't start."

Sarah knew she ought to do something to dissuade Clarissa, but she was too tired to summon the effort. Instead, she was struck by the total incongruity of such a gown being worn by a supposedly innocent young lady of quality.

Her lips twitched as she thought of the look on the stone face of Mrs. Drummond Burrell should Clarissa trip over the threshold of Almack's wearing this. As for the reaction of Clarissa's slavishly admiring courtiers—Wexley would probably walk straight into a post. A suppressed giggle escaped, and then she burst out laughing.

"Heavens, Clare." She gasped. "Do you mean to make your rejected suitors expire of jealousy?"

After a surprised moment, Clarissa's defensive face relaxed. "They should. Is it not wondrous sophisticated? 'Tis not the gown of some First Season mouse, and Englemere will see he cannot prose and criticize as if I were."

Sarah thought the dress would incite the marquess to more violent reaction than speech, but refrained from saying so. "Clare, surely he didn't approve this, did he?"

Clarissa fingered the gold and emerald choker that provided the only coverage for the otherwise bare skin extending to her cleavage. "We looked at fashion plates. But he grew 'bored with feminine twaddle—'" her voice shaded with pique over this unchivalrous remark "—and left for his club before I found the design. Madame Thérèse argued 'twas not suitable for one of my 'tender years,' but I knew I must have it." She patted the matching earbobs. "The bodice is a trifle…briefer than I expected."

"Why not have Thérèse alter it for tomorrow night?"

"I ordered it expressly for the Duchess of Avon's ball," Clare objected, her tone turning petulant. "Besides, Englemere has been carping at me every evening. With me wearing this gown—" she stroked her hips with a satisfied smile "—he shall see that though *he* may only complain and chide, quite a number of other gentlemen find much to admire."

The two friends looked at each other. Sarah could tell from the mulish set of her chin and her sparkling eyes that Clarissa had set her iron will upon this.

Dispensing with the useless, she rummaged in Clarissa's drawer and pulled out a thin shawl of gossamer gold thread. "This would set off the gown nicely," she coaxed.

Clarissa considered the shawl and, apparently satisfied with winning the rubber, conceded the point. "Yes, it will be pretty, do you not think, Lizette?"

The maid murmured approval and draped the shawl loosely about her mistress's shoulders. Sarah motioned her aside, wrapped the gauzy gold twice around Clarissa and tucked the ends under her elbows. "Do you think you can dance in it?"

Clarissa twirled. "I like it. Quite understated."

Sarah smothered a choke. *Heaven help us if it falls off,* she thought as she propelled Clarissa from the chamber.

* * *

The two friends entered the salon to silence, the desultory conversation Lady Beaumont had been maintaining having evidently expired in their absence.

Clarissa swept a deep curtsy. Relief lighting her face, her mother turned to them. Englemere walked over with no sign of impatience, though Sarah noted by the mantel clock they were now a full hour late.

"Mama, Englemere, I'm so sorry to have kept you waiting! Truly we don't value Harris as we ought. I had no idea it would take so long to dress without her."

"You look charming, dearest. Does she not, my lord?" Lady Beaumont darted a nervous glance at Englemere.

The marquess brought Clarissa's hand to his lips. "Doubtless worth waiting for. Emerald and gold with your glorious hair are stunning. I'll be accounted the luckiest man at the ball tonight."

"Thank you, my lord." Clarissa preened at his obvious admiration. "Ring for our cloaks, won't you, Sarah?"

Sarah nodded and walked to the bellpull. Clarissa made to follow, but Englemere caught her shoulder.

"The gown is delectable, my sweet." Englemere toyed with the trailing ends of the gold wrap. "Let me feast my eyes before I must share you with all the world." His smile teasing, he began to unwind the diaphanous cloth.

"Englemere!" Clarissa squeaked, catching his hands.

"My dear?" He raised one eyebrow.

Clarissa must have realized she could summon no reasonable objection. To her credit, she made no attempt to wriggle away or explain, but released his fingers and stood proudly silent. Sarah's hand clenched on the bellpull.

"Beauty unveiled!" With a flourish, the marquess pulled the drape free. Slowly his smile faded. The shawl slipped from his fingers and drifted to the floor.

"Cla-ris-sa!" Lady Beaumont wailed. Clutching her bosom, she toppled back against the sofa.

Galvanized by Lady Beaumont's cry, Sarah let go the

bell cord. For the briefest moment, she saw on Englemere's face a look of profound weariness, succeeded by—regret?

"Stunning indeed," he murmured.

Sarah fumbled through her reticule and pulled out smelling salts. While she patted Lady Beaumont's hand and waved the vial under the moaning woman's nose, she found her attention drawn irresistibly to the betrothed couple.

Clarissa, brave as Sarah had claimed, did not quail under her fiancé's scrutiny. Drawing her breath in sharply, a movement Sarah feared might drop the skimpy bodice to a truly indecent level, she stared with haughty defiance straight ahead.

"Any rumors you may have heard of my imminent financial collapse are grossly exaggerated, my dear," Englemere said at last. "I assure you there will be no need for my wife to earn her bread on the stage—or the street."

Clarissa stiffened. "You are offensive, Englemere." In one fluid motion, she scooped the shawl from the floor and flung it about her shoulders. "Do get up, Mama. Timms will be bringing our cloaks."

Englemere placed a hand on her collarbone. "No, 'tis you who offend, my dear." He ran his fingers up the bare skin to her chin and tilted her face toward him. "You've had your little joke, shocked your poor mama and made Miss Wellingford miss half the duchess's ball. 'Tis time to behave. You have twenty minutes to change into something suitable and present yourself back downstairs."

Clarissa set her teeth and glared at him. "The gown was commissioned for this ball and I mean to wear it. If you dislike the style, 'tis your own fault. You should have stayed at the modiste's until we made the final selection."

"You can't imagine I would have approved *this*." The marquess met her glare. After a fraught moment, and despite her obvious anger, Clarissa dropped her eyes.

"Twenty minutes. Considering how little there is of it,

'twill be no great piece of work to remove. Lady Beaumont, if you please, send Miss Wellingford to assist.''

Timms entered, the ladies' evening cloaks draped over his arm. The marquess turned to him. ''Have the housekeeper summon Miss Clarissa's maid—Lizette, is it? She is to be discharged immediately.''

Clarissa had been walking with sulky reluctance toward the door, but at this, she whirled around with a gasp. ''How dare you presume to dismiss my servant?''

Ignoring her, the marquess continued, ''Since 'tis already dark, the girl may stay the night, but I want her gone first thing in the morning. She may approach my housekeeper in Curzon Street for her wages.''

Clarissa stormed up to him. Englemere silenced her with one contemptuous look.

After the butler withdrew, he drawled, ''My dear, you can hardly expect me to nursemaid you through every social engagement. Since you've demonstrated so little sense of your own, you must have a proper dresser.'' He paused for a sip of wine. ''I cannot permit my wife to employ a maid lack-witted enough to send her mistress out dressed like a Covent Garden drab.''

Lady Beaumont moaned, and Sarah caught her breath in dismay. White-faced with fury, Clarissa stood stockstill, two bright spots of color burning in her cheeks. She made a movement with one hand. Englemere trapped her wrist.

''Don't even try,'' he breathed.

Clarissa jerked her hand free. Turning on her heel, she swept from the room and slammed the door.

In the hall Sarah heard the crash of splintering crockery. She wondered with numb detachment which of the Chinese vases had been sacrificed to Clarissa's wrath.

She started at a touch to her arm. ''We leave in twenty minutes,'' the marquess said softly, and Sarah was struck again by his air of weariness. ''If Clarissa chooses to stay home and pout, she may do so, but please do come down yourself." He gave her an apologetic flicker of a smile. "I shouldn't wish you to miss the ball entirely."

Quietly he moved to the sideboard. "Dear Lady Beaumont, you must need a restorative."

The door opened before she reached it, revealing a wooden-faced Timms and three footmen hovering in the hall. Jagged shards lay scattered about the marble floor.

Sighing, Sarah mounted the stairs once again. The state Clarissa would be in when she arrived didn't bear thinking of. Why could the marquess not have chosen to delay schooling his bride until *after* the wedding?

To Sarah's surprise, Clarissa completed her change with unusual speed, in even more unusual silence. However, anger radiated from her in palpable waves, and Sarah was unhappily certain that before the night ended, she would explode.

The marquess and Lady Beaumont awaited them in the entry, already garbed in their evening cloaks. As the two friends descended, Lord Englemere extracted a pocket watch from the folds of his cloak and made an elaborate show of consulting it. "So you can be punctual when you wish," he announced. "An encouraging sign."

Clarissa, engaged in adjusting the cape the footman had thrown over her shoulders, did not reply. Englemere strolled over to her. "Late as it is, shall we go?"

Clarissa looked through the marquess as if he weren't there. Ignoring his proffered arm, she walked past him to the door. Lady Beaumont and the footman both inhaled audibly, and even Timms's hands faltered on the door handle. Sarah thought she saw the flicker of a smile on Englemere's lips before he shrugged and gave his arm to Lady Beaumont.

The receiving line had long since disbanded when they finally arrived at the duchess's ball. Before they could attempt to find their hostess, a blond bear of a man accosted them.

"Thank God you're here, Englemere! Thought I'd mistaken the date."

"Sorry, Hal. Ladies, let me present my good friend Mr. Henry Mountbanke Waterman. Hal, Lady Beaumont, Miss Clarissa Beaumont and Miss Sarah Wellingford."

Clarissa turned on him a smile so radiant the young man's jaw dropped. "Charmed to meet you, Mr. Waterman. I'm in a positive *fury* to dance. Shall we?"

Before she could offer her hand, Englemere scooped it up. "Hal will be delighted to squire you later, my dear. First we must greet the duchess and settle your mama."

Clarissa tried, unsuccessfully, to pull her hand free. "Come along, my dear," the marquess said in the cajoling tone with which one humors a sulky child. He patted his friend's shoulder. "Hal, why don't you take Miss Wellingford for a turn? He looks ferocious," he said to Sarah with a smile, "but he's really quite tame."

Though Clarissa cast him a furious glance, the marquess bore her off. 'Twas one more match waved near a smoking fuse, Sarah thought as she smiled at the blond giant.

Mr. Waterman managed to cease gaping, but hadn't yet progressed to speech. With practiced ease, Sarah filled the gap. "I'm sure Clarissa will dance with you later."

Mr. Waterman shuddered. "No, thank you, ma'am! Don't like Beauties. Acid tongues, most of 'em. Like m'mother. Came to dance with you."

"Me?" Sarah echoed in astonishment.

"Nicky told us that bounder Findlay was making up to you. Said you needed some camfo—camfla—"

"Camouflage?"

"Yes, that's it. Nobody can see around me, you know. Avoid balls as a rule, but had to come. My best friend."

"Lord Englemere?"

"Why, yes. Did you think I meant Findlay? Bad man, that. Ought to avoid him."

With that sage advice, he led her onto the floor. "Big

lummox, but I dance well. No conversation, though. Nicky said you wouldn't mind.''

''There's no need to converse if you prefer not to.'' Sarah craned her neck up. Though his face and form were larger than an ordinary man's, her massive escort was quite handsome, once one adjusted to the sheer size of him.

If he were inarticulate, he also seemed kind. Curiosity got the better of her, and despite her assurance, she had to ask, ''Why do you avoid balls, Mr. Waterman?''

''Women. Girls, actually. Terrified of 'em. So little and frail. Afraid I'm going to step on a foot, or hold an arm too tight.'' He peered down at her in sudden alarm. ''You ain't fragile, are you? Nicky promised you wasn't.''

''I'm quite sturdy,'' Sarah assured him.

''Worse 'n that, they want to marry me. Oh, I know I'm not much to look at—or too much, rather.'' He smiled with self-deprecating humor. ''Don't matter, though. Least not to the mamas. Rich, you see.''

Sarah felt a rush of sympathy. ''Mr. Waterman, if you are pursued, I'm sure 'tis not for your wealth. I find you quite attractive, and I expect other ladies do as well.''

He missed a step and looked at her in amazement.

Sarah nudged him back in rhythm. ''Your manner is, ah, comforting, and I find your size very—manly.''

The tips of his ears reddened, but he shook his head. ''Nicky said you was a right'un, but that's doing it too brown, ma'am. Why, my valet's always complaining. Can't stuff me into any sort of fashionable rig. Sad disappointment to her, m'mother says,'' he added gruffly.

''How unfeeling,'' Sarah cried. Catching herself, she continued, '''Tis not my place to criticize, of course. I expect mothers always wish the best for their children. I'm sure I'm often a disappointment to mine.''

''Couldn't be,'' he returned firmly. ''Not much in the bone-box—'' he gestured to his head ''—but Nicky's a downy one. He likes you, and Nicky's never wrong.''

Suddenly Mr. Waterman stiffened. "Lord, m'mother! She'll try to push some little chit on me. Have to bolt."

He began to dance her rapidly to the opposite side of the room. "Promised Nicky I'd turn you over to Ned. Must go then. No offense taken?"

Sarah gave him her warmest smile. "Not at all, Mr. Waterman. Thank you for a lovely dance. And you're wrong, you know. You converse quite nicely."

"I do?" He looked startled, then a slow grin lit his face. "Tell m'mother, would you?"

"Why would Miss Wellingford wish to converse with your esteemed parent, Hal?" asked a quiet voice at her elbow. "Go on, introduce me," the man prompted.

Mr. Waterman grinned and bashed the newcomer on the shoulder. "Don't mind Ned. Always ragging me. Sir Edward Austin Greeves, Miss Wellingford. Guard her well, gallows-bait. Findlay's in the far corner." Nodding in that direction, he froze. "M'mother. Must dash. 'Servant, Miss Wellingford." With a speed unexpected in so large a man, he wheeled on one foot and fled.

Sarah froze too, and in spite of herself her glance went to the distant corner. As if waiting, Sir James caught her eye and made an elaborate bow.

Sir Edward grasped her trembling hand. "Shall we dance, Miss Wellingford?"

She stuttered something and followed him, taut as a bowstring at the knowledge of Findlay's scrutiny. The baronet simply stood, the mocking smile she hated fixed on his lips, watching them like a predator.

She forced herself to concentrate on Sir Edward. "Did Lord Englemere really send you? How singular of him."

"Nicky is a staunch friend, as I have good reason to know," he replied. "With his support, you need not fear—" his glance drifted briefly to Findlay "—unpleasantness."

In that instant she realized the full import of Mr. Waterman's terse words. Clarissa's quixotic betrothed had deliberately directed two eligible bachelors to attend, protect—and court her? A blaze of hope flared, as swiftly dying. Even had that been his intent, she had no time to ensnare a new suitor. Still, Englemere couldn't know that. Gratitude, regret and a simultaneous despair brought her close to tears.

"I don't recall seeing you before in London, Sir Edward," she said, forcing her mind to less dismal channels. "Do you, like Mr. Waterman, avoid balls?"

Sir Edward seemed to note her distress, and steered her so she could not see Findlay. "I don't trouble myself to attend often. At the risk of lowering what little credit I may have with you, I must admit I seldom spend the Season in London. I'm a simple countryman."

The last was said with the slightest touch of defensiveness, as if he expected her to take him to task for so unfashionable an admission. To Sarah, though, the country meant stability, security and peace. "How fortunate you are! I should thank heaven daily, could I but spend the rest of my life at Wellingford."

Her vehemence seemed to startle him, and she lightened her tone. "Where are your estates situated, Sir Edward?"

"In Kent. I breed horses and cultivate several thousand acres. But you can't be interested in that."

"But I am. Since our steward retired, I've managed Wellingford. Do you know anything of Mr. Coke's methods?"

"Why, I attended his fall session at Holkham just last year." His face lit with surprise and a dawning respect. "Shall I describe it?"

For the next few minutes Sarah drank in details of turnips and tares, barley and wheat, cattle-grazing and sheep. So absorbed was she that she forgot Findlay until she nearly collided with him at the edge of the ballroom.

"Miss Wellingford, good evening." Sir James bowed over her hand. "Our waltz awaits."

"The lady is thirsty, sir," Sir Edward interposed. "I am escorting her to the refreshment room."

"Then I shall take her, and claim my waltz after she is 'refreshed.'" The baronet extended his arm.

Sir Edward retained her hand. "Miss Wellingford and I are in the midst of a discussion. You may waltz later."

Instead of retiring, Findlay planted himself in their path and clapped a hand on Sarah's shoulder. "I, also, have much to discuss with Miss Wellingford. Our acquaintance being of longer standing, I insist on taking precedence."

Findlay's fingers bit into Sarah's shoulder until she winced. Sir Edward's gaze narrowed to Findlay's hand, and he took a menacing step toward the baronet. "If you choose to be impolite, sir, this is not the place to resolve the matter. I will be happy—"

"Please, gentlemen," Sarah broke in, indicating a gathering group of curious onlookers. "Let us not quarrel here. Sir Edward, I shall look forward to resuming our conversation soon. For now, I...I will go with Sir James."

"You need not," Sir Edward said quietly.

"At the moment, I think it—wiser." With reluctance, she withdrew her hand from Sir Edward's arm. Findlay's sardonic smile at her capitulation, though, provoked her to add, "I do thank you, Sir Edward, for the most interesting and enjoyable conversation I've had since coming to London."

He caught her hand and kissed it. "The gratitude is mine. When Nicky claimed he would present to me a lady I would find as intelligent as she was lovely, I bet him a monkey he couldn't. Never have I so thoroughly enjoyed losing a wager." He directed a hostile look at Findlay. "Your servant, Miss Wellingford, and do not hesitate to call upon me at *any time.*"

Findlay pulled Sarah from the room. In the relative solitude of the hallway, he extracted a lace-edged handkerchief and dabbed at his nostrils. "I never see that man without smelling the stables. I can't imagine what you could have found to converse with him about.''

''The stables.''

''How droll. No doubt you were secretly delighted by my rescue, then. 'Tis naughty of you to try to make me jealous,'' he said in a caressing tone that caused her teeth to clench. ''You nearly succeed, I vow. Though it is, you must grant, rather late for these last-minute champions.''

'''Tis all a game to you, is it not?''

''But of course.'' His smile became almost a smirk, and her fingers itched to slap it off his face. ''A game, my dove, I fully intend to win. Oh, yes, I remember,'' he said, raising a hand to forestall a protest. ''' 'I have not asked, nor have you answered.' Yet.''

His face darkened with irritation. ''For some reason, Englemere intervenes. 'Tis no matter. You couldn't truly consider either of his friends, even had you sufficient time to enslave them. The first, in addition to his inelegant bumptious self, has a mother who makes the shrew you call friend appear an angel of amiability, and Greeves—! I'm astonished the man knows how to open a door that doesn't lead to a barn.''

''I happen,'' Sarah grated out, ''to be quite fond of the country, and find Sir Edward knowledgeable and amusing.''

''Indeed? Perhaps a very long, bucolic wedding trip is in order. I find myself envisioning it with anticipation.''

Findlay abruptly steered her into a small antechamber.

Alarmed, Sarah halted. ''Sir James! You must not—''

''Compromise you, my dove? You closeted yourself with Englemere willingly enough. 'Twould never answer, you know. He's too slippery a fish to be caught by such tricks.''

''Compromise Englemere? I should never!'' Sarah protested hotly as she retreated from him, stopping before a pair of French doors leading into the garden.

Findlay nodded his head in mock approval. ''Wise of

you. Should Silence Jersey herself discover Englemere's hand up your gown, he'd not be trapped into wedlock.''

"How *dare* you—!" Sarah gasped, her cheeks flaming.

"Oh, I dare much for you, my dove. Have I not already sent two suitors packing?''

He pressed closer, until she felt the door handles against her back. Trapping her hands, he drew her to him. His glance traveled over her with insolent slowness, from her face down her bare throat to the modest décolletage of her gown. Deliberately he dropped his gaze lower, to rest on the breasts concealed under the thin veiling of muslin. "You are mine, and no one else shall have you."

Sarah held herself rigid, refusing to struggle. But when he raised a hand and traced her lips with a gloved finger, she had to fight the urge to flinch.

"No other man could appreciate you as I do. Your slender silver beauty. And that quick wit, my dove. One has only to suggest, and your nimble mind leaps to the accurate conclusion. I find the possibilities…arousing.''

He leaned closer still, his eyes glowing with unmistakable heat. She feared he meant to kiss her, and nausea coiled in her stomach. Though she knew she must not reject him, a desperate need to delay him seized her.

"Sir James," she choked out, "I find it fantastical that you go to such extraordinary lengths to pursue me, when you must know I, ah, cannot return your regard.''

"Love? Hate?" He shrugged one elegant shoulder. "They are but two edges of the same slim blade. I could slice from one to the other in a heartbeat." He smiled at her, and the chill struck bone. "I will teach you, little dove, and such pleasure it will bring us both.''

She pushed at him. "You flatter yourself.''

He laughed softly. "Of course I will please you. Without pleasure, there could be no shame." His breath quickening, he brushed his lips against her hair. "And I will teach you to please me." He dragged her resisting hand up, peeled down her glove and forced her wrist to his mouth. The hot wetness of his tongue stroked her naked skin. Her resolve forgotten in a mindless panic, she tried to wrest her hand free.

With surprising strength, he held the hand motionless, as if to prove he could effortlessly control her. With a groan of distress, she went still.

He smiled again. "Good—you learn to submit. Now you will learn to kneel before me, to pleasure me, with your fingers—" he forced her hand down the length of the hard bulge in his breeches "—and with your sweet pink mouth."

Revolted, she somehow managed to rip her hand free. Beyond caution or rational thought, she slapped his face with all her might.

As the crack of the blow echoed, they both froze. His expression incredulous, Findlay slowly reached up to touch his reddened cheek.

Then his eyes blazed with heat of another sort, and before she could think or move, he seized her. Clapping a hand over her mouth, he dragged her to the side table and pinned her against the wall.

"That wasn't wise, my dear. Now I shall have to punish you." Prying loose the hand he had kissed, he forced it against the burning chamber candle. She screamed, the sound muffled by his palm.

His smile returned. "Pleasure and pain. So swiftly can one become the other. Remember that, little dove." He turned his body and rubbed his hardness against her as he held her wrist to the flame.

Tears dripped down her cheeks and she bit the inside of her mouth, but she refused to cry out again. The pain was itself a blinding flame, blotting out all else and sucking up every reserve of strength. When it abruptly lessened, her knees nearly buckled.

Findlay relaxed his grip. She sagged against the wall, and though he supported her, he made no move to bring her close.

"I came tonight to tell you I'd be leaving town for two days," he said in a conversational tone, as if nothing untoward had transpired. "I must make preparations to receive you. And transfer funds. How much will I require?"

He meant to complete her humiliation, for he knew to the last ha'penny what was owed. Instead, she felt a rage that stiffened her spine. "Nine thousand eight hundred and fifty-six pounds," she spat out. Deliberately, she straightened and stepped away from him.

Findlay laughed. "Courage, too. Damn, but you make me impatient for our union. Until Thursday, then—and try not to gather too many new suitors. 'Twould be wearying to kick their carcasses aside when I return to ask that question."

She accorded him a cold nod. He bowed, and with lightening speed plucked her burned wrist and brought it to his lips. Rather than kiss it, though, he ran the rasp of his tongue over the raw flesh. Pain exploded, and Sarah closed her eyes, once more biting her lip to keep silent.

"Remember," he whispered.

Chapter Four

The pain subsided to dizzying waves. When Sarah opened her eyes, Findlay had gone. She leaned against the side table, for a moment incapable of thought or movement, while nausea roiled in her stomach.

Staggering out the terrace door, she managed to reach the shrubbery before she was thoroughly, miserably sick. When the retching at last subsided, she pulled herself to her feet and fled down the dimmest pathway.

She burst into a deserted clearing and stumbled against a low iron railing. 'Twas the river landing, she realized. A thick fog caught and diffused light from a pair of torchères, as if inside the smoked glass of a lantern. Welcoming the privacy, she sank onto a nearby bench.

She couldn't marry Findlay. Frantically she searched her mind for an alternative.

Marshall Beckman was gone, and the baron probably lost. Mr. Waterman would take years to gather the courage to make an offer, even were he so inclined. She'd been immediately drawn to Sir Edward. Could she possibly approach him?

"Dear Sir Edward," she imagined herself saying, "you begged me to call upon you at any time. Might you do me the small favor of marrying me, to save me from Sir James? By the way, I shall need ten thousand pounds the day of the wedding, which must be tomorrow.'' No, 'twas impossible.

Must she marry anyone? She could hire herself out as a housekeeper and have Aunt Sophrina launch Lizbet. With her beauty and gentleness, though dowerless, surely Lizzie would make a decent match. Later she might assist her sisters.

Her aunt could shelter Elizabeth and one or two of the other girls, but where would the rest go? A potential employer would balk at housing his new employee's penniless siblings. The modest wages Sarah might earn would never suffice to maintain Colton at Eton, much less provide the wardrobe to launch Lizbet's Season. And Colton— stripped of his estate, what future could he hope for?

Whereas, if she steeled herself to marry Findlay, she could see her sisters well dowered and well presented, free to accept worthy men of their choice. Colton could complete his education at Oxford, buy that commission in the Hussars he was always talking about or assume management of his acres. She could replant and tend Wellingford's fields, refurbish or replace its worn or sold-off furnishings.

Wellingford. The image of it, achingly dear, rose before her: the Elizabethan great hall, its half-timbered walls adorned with climbing roses…the graceful stone wings with their Palladian windows…the glass galleries flanked with lilac and flooded with morning or afternoon sun. Unless she acted, Wellingford would be lost.

If she acted, it would be hers always. Perhaps, if she didn't please Findlay, he could be induced to banish her there. A vain hope, she thought sardonically. Did she not please him, he'd be far more likely, given the relish he'd just displayed, to punish rather than banish her.

No doubt he wanted an heir. Though once, in Sinjin's arms, Sarah discovered the joy of closeness with a man she loved, she'd long ago accepted this joy would never be hers. But Findlay? She thought of his cold, white hands pulling her close, touching her intimately. With chilling clarity, she remembered how he meant to have her "please" him.

Gagging, she leaned into the shrubbery. When her already-emptied stomach stopped heaving, she grasped the iron railing and handed herself along it to the river's edge.

Below her, the stream flowed peacefully. How wonderful to feel inside the tranquillity of the river, how soothing to sink beneath its welcoming surface and be no longer tormented by terrible choices and a bleak future.

"Miss Wellingford! Why are you out in this fog?"

She started and nearly lost her balance.

"Careful, my dear!" Lord Englemere jumped over to steady her. "You're much too close to the edge. Why, you might have—" His scolding voice died as he gazed at her.

Sarah knew she must look like the wild woman she felt: hair in disarray, eyes and nose red, bits of shrubbery caught in the lace of her gown. Turning her face away, she tried vainly to summon up some light remark.

"You look upset, Miss Wellingford. I hope my friends were not importunate."

Sarah blessed him for providing so simple a conversational opening. "Indeed not," she croaked. "I found them charming. So kind of you to send them to dance with me. Delightful dancers. But all that dancing—so fatiguing. I had to get away and find some, ah, cool air."

His raised eyebrow as he surveyed their chilly, damp surroundings helped her stop babbling. In a more normal tone, she continued, "What brings you out?"

He gave her a penetrating look before replying. "My lovely betrothed persists in treating me like a leper. After greeting the duchess, she ripped herself free and latched on to Wexley like a limpet. Having watched that charming display quite long enough, I came out to blow a cloud. Yes, I know, a disgusting habit."

"I'll leave you in peace, then. Enjoy your nasty little cigar." Managing a creditable smile, Sarah turned.

Englemere stopped her. "It was Findlay, wasn't it."

"I should get back."

Nicholas didn't release her. "Was your papa so desperately under the hatches that you must consider him?"

At the mention of her father, all her anguish focused, and the remaining restraint in her overwrought mind seemed to snap. "My esteemed father wasn't 'under the hatches,'" she spat out bitterly. "Oh, no, he *sold* the hatches. And everything else he considered even remotely of value. The silver. The furniture. All the estate's and my mother's jewelry. You may see the portraits of my ancestors gracing the drawing rooms of a score of different cits."

Once started, she couldn't seem to halt the angry words. "He sold all the land he could and sucked every possible groat from what he couldn't sell, never putting back a penny. So when he was finally merciful enough to break his neck in some ridiculous hunting wager, we had nothing left. Or nearly nothing." She gave a mirthless laugh. "Fortunately he never realized books were of any worth. I financed this Season by selling off our library."

"The Season's only half over. Dismiss Findlay! You can't *wish* to marry him."

"Wish to!" This time, her laugh bordered on the hysterical. "It makes my skin crawl when he touches me. But Season's end or no, I'm out of time."

He frowned, and suddenly it seemed important that he understand fully, that he not again suspect she was merely weary of poverty, impatient with making do.

"You see," she went on, "when there was nothing left to barter, he borrowed nearly ten thousand pounds, secured by a mortgage on Wellingford."

"How could he? 'Tis entailed, surely."

"But it isn't. Some long-ago ancestor, incensed that his son supported Cromwell against the king, petitioned to have the entail broken. It was never restored." She looked out over the river. "We knew nothing of the debt until six

months after his death, when the bank approached our solicitors. Out of compassion, they gave us three more
months to avoid foreclosure. The time expires Friday.''

''Good Lord.''

''As gambling debts go, 'tis not so great a sum, but for
us, 'twas impossible. I hoped we could get by until my
sister Elizabeth came out. She's a true Diamond. But we
had so little time, it had to be me. Now there's no time,
so it has to be him.''

''Have you no other family to assist?''

Sarah shook her head. ''Both my parents were sole sur-
viving children. We've only Great-aunt Sophrina—and if
we lose Wellingford, she couldn't take in all of us.''

She inhaled deeply and straightened her shoulders.
''While there's breath in my body, I can't stand by and
watch my family beggared, parceled out to distant relatives
like—outmoded furniture. See my sisters denied any hope
of marriage and my brother stripped of his birthright and
his future. I can't! Could you?''

Nicholas met her fierce, anguished gaze with a troubled
look. ''No, I don't expect I could.''

''Then you understand.'' She ought to be shamed, now
that he knew the full extent of her family's degradation,
but instead she felt…comforted. ''I must go in. No, stay,''
she said when he moved to escort her. ''You've not had
your cigar, and it wouldn't do for us to walk in together.''

Reluctantly he halted. ''Go, then, but don't think I concede the point. There must be another way.''

''I appreciate your kindness, Lord Englemere. But
there's nothing to be done.''

''Tis not yet Friday.''

She smiled at that. He smiled back and took her hand.
As he lifted it, his fingers grazed the burn, and given no
time to steel herself, she cried out.

''Have you injured yourself? Let me see.''

Grimacing, Sarah tried to wriggle free, but his fingers

were so close to the wound that the slightest twist fired the burn back to white heat.

"That's what you get, stumbling about in the fog," Nicholas chided as he held her arm up to the flickering light. He froze, expression draining from his face.

Sarah saw the wrist as he must—the blackened edges of the unbuttoned glove, the red, weeping wound. "I—I d-dripped some h-hot candle wax on it." Even in her own ears, the excuse sounded lame.

Nicholas's face hardened. Cursing softly under his breath, he eased his grip. "Where did you leave Findlay?"

She stared back at him. "L-leave?"

"I'll escort you to Lady Beaumont. 'Tis time the baronet had a swift but punishing lesson in manners."

His curt words finally registered. "Oh, no, you mustn't!" Sarah cried in alarm. She dared not imagine what retribution Findlay would wreak on her later if Englemere confronted him. "I…I'm fine. Besides, in no manner can this be considered your concern."

He raised her uninjured hand and kissed it. "But my dear, 'Uncle Nicholas' always protects his own."

"'Twas but a foolish game! Please, my lord, if my desires mean anything to you, do not pursue him."

He stood utterly still for a long moment. "Very well," he said at last. "It shall be as you wish—for now."

"Thank you, my lord. I—I should go in."

He retained her hand. "You must not marry Sir James."

"I must," she said softly. "Despite my momentary weakness, I won't go meekly as a lamb to the slaughter. Nor shall I 'submit'—" she spat out the word "—or remove myself, as those other poor creatures evidently did. Sir James will find I've a stronger will than ever he imagined. And I'm a crack shot with a pistol." She smiled without humor. "If neither of us survives the honeymoon, at least Wellingford will be saved."

"Sarah—"

"There's no more to say. Thank you, my lord."

This time, he let her go. When she glanced back from the turning of the path, he stood staring after her, a lit cheroot glowing in the darkness.

Her wrist bandaged by a sympathetic housekeeper whom she fobbed off with a glib story of an overturned candlestick, Sarah proceeded to repair her glove. She had just finished that task when Lady Beaumont burst in.

"Sarah, thank heavens I've found you! Wherever have you been this age, child? You must come this instant!"

"Calm yourself, Lady Beaumont." Sarah sprang up to assist her. "Let me find your vinaigrette."

"Never mind that, I shall bear up somehow. Oh, 'twas dreadful! You must seek Clarissa at once!"

So, the shot had exploded at last. Sarah braced herself. "What happened to overset you, ma'am?"

"That wretched girl! What must she do but snub, absolutely snub, the duchess, and go hang herself upon Wexley's arm. Three dances—three!—with him, at the center of the ballroom for all the world to see, Wexley clutching her against him in a positively indecent manner!"

"'Twas unwise, truly, but their friendship is—"

"Friendship!" her ladyship shrieked. "I should like to strangle the blackguard! Bad enough that he led her into such indiscretion, but after the second waltz—the two of them still at the center of the room—he pulled off her glove and kissed her bare wrist. *At length!*" Lady Beaumont shuddered. "Countess Lieven was standing not three feet away. Of all moments, Englemere chose then to appear."

"He wasn't amused."

"I should like to strangle him as well. What was he thinking, subjecting my poor darling to such Turkish treatment tonight?" Lady Beaumont demanded, abruptly changing tack. "Small wonder she arrived at the ball in such a pucker, after the horrid things he said to her!"

Sarah made a sympathetic murmur. Lady Beaumont rushed on. "I know not what he said—'twas done so softly none could hear, but it must have been something equally nasty, for—'' she faltered and began shredding her lawn handkerchief ''—for then my darling reacted rather rashly.''

With foreboding, Sarah held her breath and waited. After a silent moment staring unhappily at the far wall, Lady Beaumont said, ''She slapped him.''

''Right there in the ballroom?'' Sarah gasped.

''Full on the face,'' her ladyship confirmed with a little sigh. ''I daresay he will have a bruise.'' That thought seemed to cheer her, for she smiled briefly, but then recalling her mission, she sprang to her feet.

''Englemere didn't say a word, but dragged my poor child off the dance floor.'' Lady Beaumont in turn pulled Sarah toward the door of the withdrawing room. ''And such a look on his face, he's like to murder her! You must go at once!''

Sarah caught the door frame. ''Lady Beaumont, they cannot want someone intruding upon such a…private moment.''

''My darling's safety is in danger! And her future, of course. Have I not sheltered and succored you?''

Almost, Sarah would have preferred to meet Sir James than to interrupt the quarreling lovers. But as Lady Beaumont continued to gaze imploringly at her, she heard again the clarion call of Duty. Why, she wondered as she straightened her shoulders and braced herself for the inevitable, was Duty so often unpleasant?

''I'll do what I can.''

''My smelling salts,'' Lady Beaumont moaned as she released Sarah and tottered back to the sofa. ''No, I shall find them. Go save Clarissa!''

Could anyone perform that melodramatic feat? Sarah wondered as she descended the stairs.

A number of curious guests loitered in the hallway. Shooing them away, she proceeded to the anteroom door.

"…suffer the sight of my intended making a spectacle of herself with that overdressed, underwitted fop."

"'Fop!'" Clarissa's voice cried. "He dresses far more elegantly than you. As for wit, *he,* at least, knows how to treat a lady."

"Kissing another man's fiancée in the middle of the ballroom? Gentlemanly behavior indeed. And I do know how to treat a lady—when I encounter one."

Groaning at that, Sarah entered. "Please, I beg you, restrain yourselves! At least, lower your voices."

She might have been shouting into a gale, for all the attention the pair paid her.

"By God, I've borne enough carping and insult! 'Tis not a ring you gave, but a ball and chain. Saddle some other unfortunate female with it!" Clarissa jerked off his ruby.

"I'm perfectly ready to take it back, I assure you."

Horrified, Sarah leapt over and trapped the ring in her friend's fist. "No, you mustn't! You are overwrought!"

"Stubble it, Sarah." Clarissa brushed Sarah's hand aside and dropped the ring on Englemere's outstretched palm. "Dear Lord Englemere, *devastated* as I am to disappoint you, I've discovered we shall not suit. I'm not at all partial to tyrants." With a regal nod, she swept to the door.

"Shrew," Englemere murmured without heat.

Sarah lifted her skirts to run in pursuit. "No, Clarissa, you cannot—"

Nicholas grabbed her. "Sarah, *don't fix it.*"

"But she will be so sorry, once her temper cools! And you've been no help at all, pushing her so hard all evening! Why, 'tis no wonder—"

She read Nicholas's expression and stopped dead. A niggling suspicion crystallized into certainty. "You complete hand," she breathed. "You *wanted* her to cry off!"

Looking shamefaced, he dropped his eyes. "Well, yes.

But before you take me to task, remember 'twas my future at stake. Desperate measures were called for.''

"Indeed?" Sarah choked out, still astounded.

"Had the deuce of a time of it, too. I was beginning to fear her lust for a title would outweigh her vanity."

"That's unfair, sir! Her character may need...polishing, but one cannot accuse Clarissa of coveting position. Why, the old Duke of Gresham has—"

"You're right, that *was* ungracious." Nicholas sighed and ran a hand through his hair. "Please believe, had I the smallest indication Clarissa truly cared for me, I should never have driven her to cry off. But 'twas obviously not my charming person she valued. So, seeing her reaction to that dress, I knew I had to end it."

Sarah's jaw dropped. "Do you mean," she asked slowly, "you *arranged* the green dress?"

He had the grace to blush. "I hadn't meant to admit that," he mumbled. "You will think me beneath reproach."

Sarah thought him rather ingenious, but wasn't about to let him off that easily. "You, sir, are a rogue. You conspired with Madame to fashion a totally unsuitable garment for your betrothed, just to judge her reaction."

"I needed to know we had at least some chance for happiness. If not—marriage would surely bring misery to us both. The deception was meant for the good."

"Equivocation, my lord. 'Twas a reprehensible act."

"Would you have worn the dress?"

"'Tis not my behavior in question, and at any rate—"

"Would you have?"

"Well, I...that is—"

"No, you would not. Nor would any modest woman of sensibility." He gave her a coaxing smile. "So you *do* think me justified, 'reprehensible' as I was."

She had to smile back. "All right, I feel some sympathy for your plight. Though that doesn't excuse you!"

His blinding, bone-melting smile seemed lit from within. "You forgive me, then. Thank you."

It seemed he valued her good opinion. That incredible realization robbed her of any further protest. "I must admit I never regarded you two as well suited. Though you must not think too harshly of Clarissa! She doesn't—"

"Spare me a recital of her virtues," Nicholas groaned. "She's a woman grown, and must answer for her own actions. Or her unlucky husband must, Lord help him."

Sarah sighed, knowing how truly he spoke. "Shall you take yourself off to savor your freedom?"

"I feel I've just wriggled out from under the Rock of Gibraltar." He laughed, the sound giddy. "I must remain in town, though. I shall have to begin all over again, you see."

"Surely you are not compelled to marry this Season."

He stared into the distance, rubbing her hand absently. "Mama took my brother's death very hard. It's time and past that I do my duty by the family." He looked back at her, his smile wry. "I can think of nothing that would cheer Mama more than dandling her first grandson on her knee."

"Shall I draw you up a list of eligibles? From *my* vast experience with the ladies of the ton," she teased.

"'Twould be very helpful, dear Aunt Sarah."

"Perhaps I shall. But not tonight. I expect you're anxious now to escape to your friends and your club."

"Excellent advice. Mayhap Clarissa has drawn the fire of the curious, and we can both slip by."

Sarah started. "Oh, dear! Lady Beaumont will be in a state. I must go to her."

"You'll not bear the blame for this fiasco?"

Sarah frowned as she pondered her sponsor's reaction. "Even Lady Beaumont must realize I can't work miracles."

"Are you sure?" He gave her another knee-weakening

smile and carefully clasped her injured hand. "Well, Miss List-Maker, is there nothing I can do for you?"

Her eyes followed his to her bandaged wrist. A wave of bleakness swamped her warm mood. Resolutely she slammed her mind shut against her worries and dredged up a light tone.

"If you *should* decide to gallop off on your white charger, you might ride up and fetch Mr. Beckman back."

He kissed her fingertips. "Perhaps I'll do just that."

With a curtsy and one last smile, Sarah left him. Euphoria swept through Nicholas as he collected his things and slipped out the entry. Free! Damn, he'd been terrified his beauty-blinded senses had lulled him into a blunder that would have blighted the rest of his life. This time, a merciful Providence had seen fit to spare him.

Perhaps he *would* take a trip to the country until the gossip died. He might even go in search of Mr. Beckman.

He recalled Sarah as she joked with him about Yorkshire, her worried face bravely light. His euphoria drained away, and he felt again the rush of fury that succeeded the shock of discovering her injury.

Had she not been so adamant he not intervene, he would have tracked down Findlay that very instant. *No, Sarah Wellingford,* he vowed silently, *you'll not wed Sir James, if I have to kill him to prevent it.*

Shooting Findlay wouldn't solve all Sarah's problems. She still needed to marry money, and she deserved better than the callow Beckman lad. Ned and Hal were both far preferable candidates—but how to get either to the sticking point before Friday?

He was halfway down the street when the answer came to him, so simple, so perfect and so blindingly obvious he wondered he hadn't tumbled to it immediately. No need to harry his friends: he would marry Sarah Wellingford himself.

Chapter Five

He stood stock-still, examining the decision from every angle. In one stroke, he could secure the wife he required and rescue a lady he admired from a difficult, possibly dangerous future.

A mature woman well beyond romantical illusions, Sarah Wellingford would be a skillful hostess, a capable manager, a congenial companion. Even better, they were friends. Their union could be grounded, not in some ephemeral notion of "love," but in the solid base of mutual respect.

Best of all, Sarah totally lacked the flirtatiousness that demands a permanent coterie of admirers, nor was her beauty the breathtaking sort that might entice men to rash or adulterous action. No, it required a discriminating man of considerable refinement to appreciate her subtle quality.

Skillful, capable, congenial—and *safe*. Since he was forced to gamble once again on a woman's honor, he felt better gambling on Sarah's than on that of any other woman he could imagine. Yes, 'twas perfect.

He didn't think himself conceited to assume Sarah would prefer his suit to Findlay's. Indeed, he couldn't wait to see her relief when he offered such a simple, safe alternative. Small wonder she'd looked worried tonight, weighed down by the prospect of falling into Findlay's power. He should go back right now and end her anxiety.

He swerved around to do just that, and halted once more. At the moment, she was no doubt tending a swooning Lady Beaumont, awash in burnt feathers and vinaigrette. Any attempt to spirit her away for a private chat was about as likely to succeed as an attempt to reform her father's gambling habits. He'd have to wait until morning.

Nicholas peered at his curricle from beneath shuttered lids. He waited for the high step, dancing in the disturbingly brilliant sunlight, to steady before hoisting himself up. That movement intensified the pounding in his head to a clang that rivaled Magdalen's carillon, and he groaned. Perhaps the last bottle of brandy had been unwise.

He'd met Ned and Hal at White's, broken the news of his fortuitous liberation and toasted his deliverance well into the night. Despite a gag-inducing mug of his valet's infallible morning-after potion, his head still throbbed, his eyes felt as if someone had lit a candle behind them, and his mouth hadn't tasted so foul since his last bowl of the noxious pap served as breakfast gruel at Eton.

Yet here he was, properly rigged for a call—at least he trusted he was, Baines being an efficient valet—having nobly abandoned his deathbed to totter off at a positively indecent hour, all to relieve Miss Wellingford's anxiety. Nicholas hoped she would appreciate it.

After crashing through the third crater that saw his stomach rise in proportion to the distance the curricle fell, he pulled up the horses. Damn, he cursed silently, why were London roads in such bad repair?

He handed the reins over to his grinning tiger. Informing the lad he would walk, he lowered himself gingerly to the street. Six blocks later, feeling he'd hiked six miles, he at last mounted the steps of Beaumont House.

The brass knocker dropped with a bang that made him wince. As the last reverberations echoed through his skull,

Timms appeared. Nicholas donned his most charming smile.

"Good morning, Timms. If I might—"

"My lord." Timms bowed. "The ladies are not in."

Before he could utter another word, Timms started to shut the heavy mahogany door. Nicholas just managed to shove in a foot before the portal closed on his soft leather boot. Eyes watering from the pain, he gritted his teeth and smiled gamely. "A moment, please, Timms."

The butler looked down to Nicholas's intruding foot and back up, his expression wooden. "Forgive me, Lord Englemere, but I have express orders to deny you the house."

"I appreciate that, but my message is urgent, and—"

"Your boot, my lord." Hands on the door handle, Timms cast another pointed glance at Nicholas's foot.

With a sigh, Nicholas dug a gold coin out of his waistcoat. "Admit me for a moment only, if you please."

After a brief hesitation, Timms pocketed the coin. He stepped back, allowing Nicholas barely enough space to pass. Wondering if his boot were past repair and envisioning Baines's swoon when he saw it, Nicholas limped through.

"Would you summon Miss Wellingford? She'll be quite willing to see me, I promise you."

"Miss Wellingford is not in."

Nicholas's smile died. "Not 'in'! Why, you thieving old rogue, I'll—"

The butler fell back, his hands raised as if to ward off a blow. "Indeed, my lord, 'tis true, I swear it! Miss Wellingford has gone out. To walk, she said."

The butler's alarm was genuine, and Nicholas saw no reason to mistrust his word. Irritation pulsed in time with his throbbing head. "When do you expect her?"

"She didn't say, my lord. I'm sorry, my lord."

Nicholas tried to make his spongy brain function. "Where did she go?"

"Miss Wellingford did not vouchsafe her destination."

"Have you any idea? Where does she usually walk?"

Timms knit his brow. "The park, I believe, my lord."

"The park. Which park?"

Timms looked aggrieved. "I'm sure I don't know, my lord." A faint noise emanated from above stairs, and Timms hastily reopened the front door. "Good day, my lord."

"Tell Miss Wellingford I called and must see her at once on a matter of the highest urgency."

"I'm not sure I can do that, my lord. My, ah, instructions, you know." Timms looked carefully past him.

Stifling a curse, Nicholas fished in his pocket for another coin. When the butler extended gloved fingers, he pulled it back. "Make sure she gets the message."

"Of course, my lord." Bowing, Timms plucked the coin.

His temper as foul as his breath, Nicholas stalked out.

After jolting about in various hackneys, all piloted by ham-fisted drivers with ill-matched nags, to Hyde, Green, and Regent's Parks, Nicholas concluded either Miss Wellingford didn't walk in the park, or he had missed her.

With ill-managed impatience, he gave up and went home for some luncheon to pacify his churning stomach.

He presented himself back at Beaumont House in the early afternoon, to be met by the intelligence that Miss Wellingford had accompanied the Beaumont ladies on a shopping expedition, but was expected back for tea. Returning a third time, he learned the ladies had encountered friends and were taking tea with them.

Pressed about evening engagements, Timms was induced, with the aid of a few more coins, to reveal the ladies planned to attend a musicale at the home of Lady Standish. Seething with frustration, Nicholas returned home to partake of a Spartan dinner and a stiff drink, and await his chance to finally corner the elusive Miss Wellingford.

* * *

Having seen Lady Beaumont settled and Clarissa whisked off by her friends, Sarah stole away to a dimly lit anteroom. She'd slept badly last night, awakening time and again to a surge of panic, quickly squelched but unnerving.

It must be done, so just do it, she repeated to herself. Almost, she wished the waiting over, so she might deal with fact rather than her hazy, awful imaginings.

"So this is where you're hiding."

Distracted out of reverie, she turned to see Lord Englemere at the doorway.

"You realize I've slunk through every antechamber in the house looking for you? Interrupted two sets of clandestine lovers and one dozing housemaid."

She shook herself, trying to clear her groggy mind. "I— I beg your pardon?"

"Blast it, woman, I've spent the entire day trying to run you to ground. Will you marry me?"

A shock jolted through Sarah and she came fully alert. Involuntarily, she looked over her shoulder. No, the room was empty but for herself and Lord Englemere. Incredulous, she turned back to Nicholas. "Wh-what did you say?"

Lord Englemere groaned and ran a hand through his hair. "What a clutch. No—no, I meant myself!" He closed the door and crossed the room to her side. "Miss Wellingford, pray forgive me. Trailing you about town today, and missing you at every opportunity, seems to have addled my wits. I collect Timms did not give you my *urgent* message."

"I've not seen Timms since this morning. I left—"

"No matter. Let me see if I can do this properly." He swept up her hand and dropped to one knee. "My dear, as I have come to know you, my respect and admiration have grown and deepened. Would you do me the honor of becoming my wife?"

Sarah stared at him. Like nonsense syllables babbled by a babe, his words didn't make sense. She must be hallucinating—lack of sleep and endless worry had affected her brain. That had to be the reason she thought she heard the Marquess of Englemere proposing to her.

"No, 'tis ridiculous. You can't be asking *me* to marry you."

"Nonetheless, I believe I just have. Twice, in fact. Though I admit, I made a botch of the first attempt."

"But why?"

"Why not? You need to marry, do you not? As do I. You are lovely, witty, well-bred, capable, and it would delight and honor me to make you my marchioness. Whereas I am sufficiently wealthy, reasonably personable, and I hope less 'ridiculous' a choice than Findlay."

"'Tis no comparison." Sarah tore her hands free and took an agitated turn about the room. "But it makes no sense! You could marry anybody. I would wager my lost inheritance there's not an unmarried lady in London who wouldn't leap at the chance to become your bride."

"I can think of one," Nicholas said dryly.

"A sensible one, then. Wealth, charm, beauty—there are dozens who would bring you far more than I."

"Name one."

"Well—Miss Rollins, for instance. Impeccable breeding, beautiful, good dowry—"

"A lovely witch who manages, in a sweetly confiding voice, to never say a good word about anyone."

"Lady Elizabeth Barnwell. Pretty, wealthy, biddable—"

"And whose entire conversation consists of 'Yes, my lord' and 'No, my lord,' and 'Oh, la, my lord.'"

Sarah smothered a chuckle. "'Tis true, I suppose, but what about—"

"What about Sarah Wellingford? Fine family. A kind and compassionate nature. Also honest, loyal, as brave as any man I know, and possessing one characteristic no other woman in London can boast."

She couldn't, wouldn't believe him serious, but amid the jumble of despair, shock and dawning hope, a strain of simple female curiosity won through. "What that might be, I can't imagine."

"I count her my friend."

"Oh." Inane and superfluous, it was the only comment she could manage.

Nicholas grinned. "Unusual in a marriage, I admit— friendship. Far as I know, though, there's no law *forbidding* it."

"No, of course not! I am honored, but a true friend must wish the best for you, and I cannot believe that is I." She frowned, troubled by a new insight. "You are concerned about my...situation, I know. Truly, you cannot consider it yours to rectify." She looked away, thinking of Clarissa and Chloe Ingram. "Especially not, to be frank, when you might later regret such chivalry. I'm...I'm hardly the sort of spirited, passionate lady you seem to prefer."

Nicholas shuddered. "Lord save me from 'spirited, passionate' women! You, Sarah—your calm, dignified loveliness—are exactly what I want in a wife."

Nicholas took her chin, lifting it so she met his eyes. "This isn't a spur-of-the-moment whim. I've considered carefully, and think this would be a perfect solution for both of us. True, we can't claim to be top-over-tails 'in love.' But are not mutual respect, admiration and friendship equally good bases for a marriage—perhaps better ones?" He gave her a deprecating smile. "Besides, consider the crushing blow to my self-esteem were you to prefer Findlay's suit to mine. I should go into a decline."

She smiled at his teasing. Despite her resolve not even to contemplate so unequal a match, a wild hope was licking through her veins. She tried hard to squelch it, to do the right thing.

"N-no, my lord. Your offer is amazingly kind, but I mustn't consider it."

"Sarah, do me the credit of believing I know my own mind. I want to marry you, and I will do all I can to make you happy. Will you not make *me* happy, and say 'yes'?"

"Oh, but you can't truly—"

"Sarah!" He put a finger to her lips. "Say 'yes.'"

He gave her a quick, encouraging nod and removed his hand. Could she seriously contemplate marrying Nicholas Stanhope—this surprising man who had somehow fashioned himself her champion? 'Twas unsuitable, impossible—and yet...to be forever free of worry, beyond Findlay's reach.

A euphoria of deliverance and relief swamped the last noble vestiges of self-sacrifice. "Yes," she whispered.

"Thank you." Nicholas grinned and led her back to the sofa. "I'll arrange for the special license and inform my mother. We can be married at her house, if you like. Shall I bring you by there tomorrow afternoon?"

Alarmed, Sarah swallowed hard. The dowager marchioness couldn't help but be stunned by her son's announcement. Yet if they were truly going to marry—fantastical as that seemed—she must certainly be presented to that lady.

She summoned up a brave smile. "Tomorrow would be fine." Memory stirred, and she gasped. "Oh, dear! Sir James is calling tomorrow! To make his proposal."

Nicholas smiled grimly. "Much as it saddens me, you will have to disappoint him." He lifted her injured hand, discreetly bandaged under its glove, and kissed the wrist. "Sweet Sarah, he shall never hurt you again."

A lump filled her throat and she blinked rapidly. Unable to trust her voice, she nodded.

"I must also send my secretary to settle the mortgage on Wellingford. What was the amount?"

The simple question hit Sarah like a rifle fusillade. She'd tossed the total off to Findlay with bitter bravado, but now, all the humiliation the baronet had meant her to feel rose up to choke her.

Though she knew the pride that shackled her tongue was false, and futile, still it took her two attempts to get it out. "N-nine thousand eight hundred fifty-six pounds."

"A paltry sum," Nicholas drawled.

"Paltry?" She gasped. "'Tis a fortune!"

"Hardly a fortune. Well, perhaps a smallish fortune. Certainly not a large one. Whereas *my* fortune is generally accounted to be somewhere between 'enormous' and 'obscene.'"

He grinned, and her discomfort slowly dissolved in a gurgle of laughter. "You are absurd."

He gave her a theatrically exaggerated look of reproach. "Absurd, me? Never. Arrogant, autocratic, spoiled, perhaps. You must work upon my failings."

"As if I should! You have been, as you well know, all that is noble. I can only promise to interfere in your life as little as possible, and to do my utmost—"

"If you thank me, sweet Sarah—" Nicholas once again stilled her lips with his finger "—I shall strangle you."

"I shan't tease you with gratitude, then," she replied when he removed his hand. "Still, I want you to know if…if you should come to your senses in the night, and wish to withdraw your offer, I shall perfectly understand."

"Sarah, Sarah," he admonished. "I promise you I shall not suffer second thoughts, cold feet, bridegroom's jitters or any other premarital malady you can conjure up. I shall come for you at Lady Beaumont's at noon tomorrow."

Her heart and mind churning with a riot of conflicting emotions, Sarah nodded. "Until tomorrow, then."

She started to rise, but Nicholas stayed her.

"Is it not customary to seal a betrothal with a kiss?"

While Sarah stared at him, mesmerized, Nicholas pulled her close. At first his lips gently brushed hers, tentative, questing. Then he deepened the kiss, and Sarah's stupor dissolved in a wave of remembered pleasure.

His touch ignited long-dormant desire to a flame that sputtered, caught and then blazed through her. Sighing, she opened her mouth and wrapped her arms around his neck.

He responded instantly, pulling her closer still until she felt the strong hard warmth of him down the length of her, felt the rapid beat of his heart against her own. His fingers caressed her back, curved toward her breasts.

He stopped abruptly, pulling away and leaving her bereft, every nerve afire with wanting. A little mewing sound of protest escaped her lips.

''Sweet Sarah,'' he whispered unsteadily, his eyes glowing with a heat she'd never seen in them before. ''I'm beginning to believe short engagements have much to recommend them.''

Nicholas tried not to grin as he awaited the return of his hat, cane and coat from Lady Standish's butler. After beginning a fiasco, this day had ended a complete success.

He relived the kiss that sealed their bargain, well pleased with her response. No reluctance or skittishness there. Marriage to Sarah was going to be a delight.

As he placed the beaver on his head and strolled out, the various sensory impressions suddenly coalesced into one startling realization. Someone had taught his spinsterish, on-the-shelf Sarah to kiss, and taught her very well indeed.

Chapter Six

For the fourth time, Sarah walked from her chair to gaze out the window at the deserted square. She glanced again at the mantel clock: five minutes to noon.

One daisy in the flower arrangement on the side table perched awry, and absently she plucked it out. 'Twas not until she returned from the musicale to the haven of her bedchamber that the shock, euphoria and confusion had diminished enough for her to realize the incredible truth. She, Sarah Ann Wellingford, had pledged her hand to the most notorious gambler in London.

Consternation seized her, and her first impulse was to dash back out to find Englemere and retract her acceptance. A moment's reflection squelched that notion. What could she say to Englemere, even should she run him to ground?

By society's standards, his was a brilliant offer. Despite his protests of their equality, Englemere surely recognized the disparity of the match. Her deeply rooted fear of gambling might be a valid concern, but 'twas also one she could hardly expect him to understand. As he had joked, to reject him would be to tender a humiliating insult. After his many kindnesses, such an action would be unconscionable.

But…marriage? Could she ever rest easy, knowing her

fate—and that of her eventual children—rested in the unreliable hands of a gambler?

There was Englemere's Luck, of course. But what would happen should it fail? Would he be able to toss down his cards and go home? What if he could not?

Even should that theoretical event transpire, the consequences couldn't compare to the immediate physical threat Findlay posed. Was she truly prepared to spurn Englemere's rescue and deliver herself back to the baronet?

For an instant, she felt herself again trapped against the wall while he forced her wrist into the candle's flame. No, she concluded, swallowing a wave of nausea, bankruptcy held no terrors worse than that.

Except for Englemere's gambling, she saw much to admire in him. Generous, intelligent, perceptive, he had been a kind and supportive friend. She enjoyed his company— and his kiss awoke her to desires she'd forgotten she possessed.

As for his late wife, she couldn't recall his ever so much as mentioning Lydia's name. If he still mourned, he kept his grief close. She could respect that.

He would remove the burden of debt from Wellingford and secure her family's future. With careful management, in time Wellingford could be restored to its former wealth and productivity. Having been willed to her brother, it would be there always—a safe haven beyond any gambler's reach.

So, she had concluded, she would marry Englemere. She might never be able to trust him enough to commit her whole heart—but he didn't want it anyway. She could offer what he did want: a well-bred, competent wife. And an heir.

Her mind skittered to the night of Clarissa's ball—the smell of his shaving soap, the warmth radiating from his tall body. And the betrothal kiss—her cheeks burned and a tremor spiraled down her spine as she remembered the hot velvet of his mouth, the liquid stroke of his tongue against hers. Marriage to Englemere might hold unexpected delights.

Assuming he still wanted her, of course. She looked down and realized she'd been methodically plucking petals from the daisy until only one silken bit remained. 'Twas nearly noon.

She'd advised Nicholas to think carefully, and think again. Sober reflection might well have convinced him the match was as unsuitable as she'd declared it. She thought of Chloe Ingram—violet-eyed, alabaster-skinned, voluptuous Mrs. Ingram. Why would a man sampling delicacies such as those want a tasteless pudding like Sarah Wellingford?

It appeared he wouldn't. The mantel clock began to chime the hour. As the last peal faded, Timms walked up. "Sir James for you, Miss Wellingford. Shall I show him in?"

Heart pounding, she nodded. She barely noted as the balled-up flower bits fell from her nerveless fingers, one lone white petal floating slowly to the floor.

Nicholas glanced at his pocket watch, cursing. Giving Jeb scarcely enough time to grab hold, he sprung the horses.

He'd had a devil of a time finding the bishop, and then the clerk who'd prepared the papers seemed to consider it a life's work. 'Twas already five minutes past noon, and he'd be willing to wager Findlay, that unspeakable cur, was probably never tardy. If the man so much as laid a finger on Sarah, Nicholas would beat him to a bloody pulp.

Narrowly avoiding two heavily laden carts and rounding corners with a recklessness that caused even his normally unflappable tiger to gasp, he arrived five minutes later at Beaumont House. He threw down the reins and took the steps two at a time, not slowing his pace until he reached the room to which an anxious Timms conducted him.

He entered and stopped short. Findlay had Sarah cornered on the sofa, his arms trapping her against its back, his head descending toward hers.

Stifling the urge to plant Sir James a facer, Nicholas said loudly, "Sorry I'm late, my dear."

Findlay halted and glanced at him. Surprise and irritation showed briefly before the faintly bored ton mask settled back on his face. "Englemere," he drawled. "Do you not realize you're decidedly *de trop?* Kindly pursue your red-haired vixen elsewhere."

While Findlay spoke, Sarah sat staring as if she'd seen a ghost. "N-Nicholas?" she whispered.

Englemere strode over and grasped one icy hand, pulling her up as he kissed it, and planted himself between her and Findlay. "I beg you'll not scold me for being delayed, darling. But I have the special license at last."

She nodded numbly. Nicholas turned to Findlay. "So, you are the first to offer us congratulations, Sir James."

Findlay looked from Sarah, who had retreated to the window, to Nicholas and back. "What farradiddle is this?"

Nicholas gave Sarah a mock-reproving look. "Did you not inform him, darling? How naughty of you! If you must dash a man's fondest hopes, you should do so quickly."

Sir James closed to a pace away. "I know not what your game is, Englemere, but enough joking. Miss Wellingford was about to accept my offer, so take yourself off."

"I'm afraid you're tardy, Findlay. Miss Wellingford has already accepted an offer—mine."

The two men locked glares. Sir James laughed harshly. "You? Marry the likes of Sarah Wellingford? I hardly think so." He cast her a dagger glance. "Your little jest does not amuse me, my dear. I fear you'll answer for it later. Englemere, if you'd be so—argh—"

Sir James gagged as Nicholas hoisted him off his feet by his neckcloth. "There'll be no 'answering,'" Nicholas hissed. He held the man suspended until Sir James's handsome face turned from white to blue, his arms windmilling as he tried to break free.

Nicholas dropped Findlay. "I fully understand your crushing disappointment. Naturally, you'll wish to take your leave. You'll excuse me a moment, my love?"

Nicholas clamped a hand on Findlay's elbow and propelled him toward the door. Coughing and clutching his throat, the baronet offered little resistance. In the hallway, the door closed, Nicholas released him.

Sir James fumbled with the limp folds of his ruined cravat. "Englemere," he croaked, "I'll—"

"You'll shut your vicious coward's mouth and listen."

Nicholas leaned toward Sir James until his nose nearly touched the shorter man's. "Neither you, nor any of your hirelings, will so much as approach my wife. Should you ever disregard those instructions, I'll do much more than wrinkle your pretty neckcloth."

Sir James did not retreat—Nicholas had to give him that much credit. "My, how bloodthirsty," he sneered. "Are you threatening to shoot me, Englemere?"

"I wouldn't waste a bullet on you. But rest assured, by the time I finished, you would wish I had shot you."

"So insulting. For that, and this atrocity to my person, I almost believe I should call you out."

"Name your seconds."

Anger blazed in the cold blue eyes, but Findlay was no match for Nicholas either with sword or pistols, and both men knew it. "I was speaking rhetorically, of course. So...violent you are, Englemere."

"You should know about violence."

Sir James brushed a spot of lint from his sleeve. "Indeed. You've crossed me before, Englemere. Remember the outcome of that little contretemps. I get what I want. Or no one does."

Nicholas held on to his temper, curbing the desire to finish strangling the baronet then and there. "Sarah's not

a horse I've outbid you for at Tatt's. You found a way to
have that colt garroted in his stall—''

"No evidence ever linked me to that unfortunate incident," Findlay protested, smiling. "Perhaps a careless
groom left the check-rein too tight. When fire broke out,
and the horse panicked..."

Nicholas gave him a withering glance. "You had best
pray my bride enjoys robust good health and suffers not
the most trifling accident. If anything at all untoward be-
falls her, you will pay for it. Remember that."

"Oh, I'll not forget. I'll not forget—*anything*."

The mocking tone frayed the tattered edges of his control. As the man stepped past him, Nicholas whipped one
limp end of the cravat around Findlay's neck and hauled
him back. Finely woven linen, he discovered when Findlay
gasped and clawed at his throat, made a rather crude but
effective garrote. "See that you do not," he said in Findlay's ear.

"Y—your things, Sir James." Timms's high-pitched
voice came over his shoulder. "If you please, Lord Englemere!"

Nicholas gave the cravat one last, savage twist, and had
the satisfaction of seeing fear flash briefly in Findlay's
eyes.

"It appears you win this round, Englemere." Settling
his hat on his head, he managed a laugh. "You, and that
ape-leader Sarah Wellingford. 'Tis almost amusing."

Before Nicholas could sidestep Timms to seize him
again, Findlay slipped to the door. "Good day, my lord."
With an insolent wave of his cane, he walked out.

Timms slammed the door shut, cutting off Nicholas's
pursuit. "Miss Wellingford awaits," he urged, so distressed he abandoned decorum and actually tugged on
Nicholas's arm.

Hands balled into fists, Nicholas took a deep breath and
willed himself to calm. Satisfying as it would be to hunt
down Findlay and horsewhip him like the scoundrel he

was, he had more urgent priorities. He'd savor that idea for some later time—and keep careful guard over Sarah.

She still stood where he'd left her. "I'm so sorry you had to deal with Findlay. The bishop was out, and his clerk was slow, and—"

He stopped abruptly. Sarah was paler than her gown, her silver eyes enormous, her face expressionless as she stood clenching and unclenching her hands.

Fury roughened his voice. "Did Findlay hurt you?" he demanded. She shook her head, displacing a tear that trickled down her cheek.

Her words from yesterday suddenly echoed through his mind. *If you should come to your senses…I shall perfectly understand.…*

"You didn't think I was coming, did you?" he asked incredulously.

She opened her lips, but they were trembling so badly she could not speak. She shook her head again.

He walked closer and saw she was trembling all over. Any urge to chide her for lack of faith evaporated. "Poor sweetheart, what a morning you must have had."

As he drew her into his arms, she threw herself against his chest and clung to him. Her hands dug into his shoulders and her body quivered with stifled sobs.

"'Tis all right, sweeting," he said against her hair. "He's gone, and he'll not trouble you again, I promise."

If he'd had any lingering doubts about the wisdom of wedding Sarah Wellingford, they were swept away as a wave of fierce protectiveness washed over him. Marrying her was right; having her in his arms felt right. He would guard her, and woe betide Findlay should he seek to do her harm.

At last the tremors eased and her rigid fingers relaxed on his shoulders. She drew herself back, though still within the circle of his arms. "I'm s-sorry. I detest w-weeping females." She swiped impatiently at a tear.

Nicholas stayed her hand and kissed away the droplet. "Let us get you ready to meet Mama." Seating her on the sofa, he produced a small box. "I wasn't sure of the size."

Looking bemused, Sarah watched him open it. The ring reposed upon a velvet bed, its large central pearl flanked by winking diamonds. Nicholas slipped it on her finger.

Sarah stared at it numbly. "'Tis not the ruby."

Nicholas laughed. "Did you think to have Clarissa's cast-off? No, I wanted something special for you—for my 'pearl of great price.'"

Sarah's eyes brightened, but she stemmed the tears. "'Tis beautiful, my lord. And how fitting. I only hope you didn't have to sell all your possessions to afford it."

"I've sufficient remaining. But when I arrived, you called me 'Nicholas.'" He pulled her back against him.

"Thank you...Nicholas."

As she whispered his name, he lowered his mouth. This time, she leaned up, parting her lips and winding her fingers into his hair. He deepened the kiss and she met him willingly in the sensuous dance of tongue with tongue, all the while caressing his neck with satin fingertips.

Completely absorbed in demonstrating his approval of her efforts, Nicholas was startled when she suddenly pulled away. Muttering a protest, he tried to draw her back and noticed her eyes were fixed on the doorway.

He turned to see Lady Beaumont standing stock-still on the threshold, jaw dropped, shock and horror on her face. "Sarah—Ann—Wellingford!" she gasped.

Nicholas looked back at Sarah. "You didn't tell her."

Sarah gave him a guilty smile. Moving apart from him, she reached up to smooth her tousled braids.

Sunlight flashed on the diamonds in her ring, and Lady Beaumont's gaze riveted on Sarah's hand. Her eyes widened farther, then rolled back in her head, and she fainted.

Clarissa helped Sarah revive and reconcile her prostrate mama. Though professing herself incredulous that Sarah actually *wished* to marry such a dull old stick as Englemere, she pledged eternal friendship and support.

After soothing Lady Beaumont, Sarah went to await Nicholas. To her mind, the worst was yet to come.

She recalled the unsmiling face of another highborn lady who had found Sarah Wellingford too poor and entirely unfit for the honor of wedding her son. Sarah struggled to banish Lady Sandiford's image and a sudden, searing longing for the tranquillity of her youth, her home—and Sinjin.

Nicholas's voice in her ear made her jump.

"I b-beg your pardon?"

"Calm yourself, sweetheart," he murmured. "Don't be imagining my mother an ogre. To be sure, she's quite astute." He chuckled reminiscently. "She'll see in a minute all your loveliness of character, and heartily approve my choice."

Sarah sighed. "And if she doesn't?"

"She will." He tipped her chin up so their eyes met. "But even should she not, *I* approve—and that's all that matters." Taking her arm, he led her into the hall.

Sarah rested her hand on his, marveling that it felt so natural to rely on one who a few short weeks ago had been a virtual stranger. Gradually in that time Nicholas had progressed in her regard from an amiable gentleman, to an admirable one, to the kindest of friends.

Yes, friends, she thought, the ache easing. Sinjin had grown up her dearest friend, the love she had always thought to marry. Then had come the debts of both their fathers, and the urgent duty to repair the respective family fortunes. Though she still wore on a chain around her neck the signet ring he'd pressed in her hand before leaving to join his regiment, she'd long known their union to be an impossible dream.

Reality was the enigmatic man beside her, whose thoughtful concern and careless kindness had saved her home, whose closeness even now soothed the ragged edge of worry.

She knew Nicholas didn't want words of gratitude, paltry payment in any event. In this moment she pledged instead to put away her doubts and give him unwavering loyalty, steadfast support—and the speedy birth of a son. *God keep you safe, Sinjin, love of my heart...goodbye.*

Waving aside the footman, Nicholas handed her into the carriage himself, a small courtesy that warmed her. *Careful, Sarah,* she cautioned herself. *Nicholas will never grow, as Sinjin did, from friend to lover. Accept his mistress, his preference for London life, and school yourself to be the "calm, dignified wife" he desires.*

Nicholas settled the carriage robe over her legs. "Now, when shall we tell Mama we wish to be wed?"

"Perhaps Friday evening would be convenient for her."

"'Tis not her convenience you need accommodate. Though I remain heartily in favor of the briefest of engagements—" he placed a lingering kiss on her palm "—there's no need to rush. 'Tis your day, sweeting. I know ladies put great store by weddings, and if you've always dreamed of a grand to-do at St. George's, with the usual crush of a reception after, I shall bow to your wishes."

"But—the mortgage!"

"Oh, that. I saw no reason to wait until after our vows to take care of it."

Nonchalantly he extracted a paper from his pocket and unfolded it: the mortgage on Wellingford, *paid in full* written in flourishing script across the top.

Sarah stared at that incredibly beautiful phrase, "paid in full," and then up at Nicholas. He gazed back, smiling faintly, tenderness in his eyes.

A swirl of strong emotion tightened her chest and forced her to blink rapidly. How compassionate he had been, teasing her out of her shame and pretending she was worth to him the considerable time, expense and trouble he'd gone to on her behalf. How compassionate now, to blithely hand back Wellingford and allow her to turn what she'd feared would be a hasty wedding into an event of taste and dignity.

"You could kiss me," he suggested, a glint coming into his eyes. "I know you wish to thank me, and I'm becoming quite fond of your kisses."

Carefully Sarah folded the precious paper and put it in her reticule. Placing her fingers on his cheeks, she caressed his face as she leaned up to him. She heard the hiss of his indrawn breath, then a muffled groan when she nibbled his lower lip and traced it with her tongue. He relaxed his jaw, inviting entry, and she slowly explored his mouth, until at last she claimed his tongue and stroked it.

With a deeper groan he bent her back against the cushioned seat. Once more the master, he devoured her lips and moved his hand lower, tracing her waist and the outline of her hip to her derriere. She pressed herself closer, letting desire flame beyond control.

As before, he pulled away first. For a moment, he simply held her, their hearts beating a staccato to the ragged whistle of their breath.

"Ah, sweet Sarah, that was the best yet. I've got the special license in my pocket. Do you think my coachman could marry us? No?" He sighed. "Call the banns, then, if you must, but I beg you, sweeting, let the wedding be soon."

Glendenning, a majestic silver-haired personage, announced them to the dowager marchioness and stood regally aside. Giving Sarah's hand a quick squeeze, Nicholas led her over to a slender brunette lady attired in black.

The dowager inclined her cheek for Nicholas's kiss, keeping her large green eyes, so like her son's, fixed on Sarah. She was much smaller than he, with a smooth skin and elegant bones that must have made her the reigning beauty of her day, and left her beautiful still. Her face showed no emotion beyond gracious courtesy. Sarah swallowed hard.

"Mama, may I present to you Miss Wellingford." He sent Sarah a warm glance. "My sweet Sarah."

"I'm honored to meet you, Lady Englemere."

"I'm quite anxious to meet you as well, Miss Well—Sarah," the dowager corrected at Nicholas's sharp look. "So, Nicky tells me you're to be married?"

"Yes, we thought to have the ceremony in a week, and the reception afterward at the home of her aunt, Lady Sophrina Harrington," Nicholas answered for them.

"I see," came the neutral reply.

With a quick glance at Nicholas, Sarah continued, "We envision a rather small gathering. Naturally, we should like to invite those of your friends or kinsmen whom you would wish to have present, if you would make me a list."

"Indeed."

A tense silence followed that monosyllabic utterance, deepening Sarah's unease. Then the dowager shivered.

"There's a chill in the air. Do you feel it, Nicky? Would you be a dear and fetch my shawl? I left it in the library, I believe."

She looked up at Nicholas with such bright entreaty he could hardly refuse, despite the blatant obviousness of her request. "Of course, Mama. I'll get it straightaway." Throwing Sarah an apologetic glance, he walked out.

"Now we can have a comfortable coze," the dowager said, with an edge to her voice that belied that warm prediction. "You've not known my son very long, have you?"

"Only a few weeks, ma'am."

"You've made quite a catch for yourself, young lady."

"Your son would be quite a catch for any girl."

The dowager inclined her head to that, and nerves already strained taut, Sarah lost patience with the subtle baiting. Better to just settle this for good and all.

"Your ladyship, let us speak plainly. 'Tis quite obvious your son could have done much better for himself than penniless Miss Sarah Wellingford."

The dowager showed no reaction. Taking a deep breath, Sarah continued. "I mean to make him the best possible wife. I don't wish to pull caps with you, but I can't change what I am. For your son's sake, I hope you will give us your blessing, regardless of any reservations you may have."

Head high, Sarah subsided into silence.

"Ah, there's Nicky," the countess murmured, after a long and rather uncomfortable pause. Indeed, Nicholas nearly flew into the room.

"Well, have you two finished shredding my character?" Though he smiled, his eyes looked anxious.

"Not quite yet," Sarah said dryly.

"Nicky, is Michael outside? Good." She turned to Sarah. "My dear, you must wish to freshen up before tea. Michael will show you to the blue bedchamber."

That stratagem was no more subtle than the shawl, but Sarah rose with graceful resignation. *Will she try to talk him out of it once I'm gone, or merely bewail his fate?* she wondered. As she started past Nicholas, he caught her hand.

"Though you look lovely to me, I suppose Mama must know best." Before the watching dowager, he gave her hand a lingering kiss. "Hurry back, sweeting."

A lump rose in her throat at his deliberate show of support. With a curtsy to the dowager, she left the room.

Nicholas's glance followed Sarah as she walked out. Though he could detect no distress in her composed face, he knew somehow the interview hadn't gone well.

"Are you sure you wish to be married so soon?"

He turned to his mama. "I should think after all the times you've urged me back to the altar, you'd be delighted at the prospect of seeing me riveted in a week."

"I don't think I ever precisely *urged* you," she replied. "When you broke the news last night, I was too shocked to respond, but it has since occurred to me there's no need

for the unseemly haste of a special license. Why not have
the banns read, and stage a proper wedding?''

"It will be a 'proper' wedding." Controlling his irritation, he tried for a lighter tone. "Given my broken engagement, any subsequent match is bound to set off the
gossips. Neither of us wants the circus of a large ton wedding. Besides, I don't wish to wait." He gave her a wink.
"Surely you can understand that."

She didn't smile, as he had hoped. Instead she continued
in a thoughtful tone, "Miss Wellingford gains access to a
great deal of wealth by this match."

Nicholas stiffened, as close to affronted as he'd ever
been by his mother. "True, Sarah's family is in straitened
circumstances, and I suppose mean-spirited folk might call
her a fortune hunter. But having met her, surely you don't
suspect her of that."

He was shocked to see cautious skepticism on her face.
"For goodness' sake, Mama, she's not some social-
climbing cit's daughter, like the insufferable Amelia!"

"I can't fault her breeding," the dowager admitted.
"But you've always preferred the most dashing beauties,
and she is rather plain." The dowager hesitated, as if sensing his growing anger. "Are you sure, once the pleasant
glow of knight-errantry has faded, you won't regret this
marriage?"

For a moment, he was too outraged to reply. "Sarah,
plain?" he choked out. "I happen to think her lovely."

He looked at his beautiful mother in disbelief, feeling
for the first time in his life that he didn't know her at all.
"I'm astounded after what we've been through that you,
of all people, would consider important the surface glitter
of appearance. Or that having met Sarah, you could fail to
discern the sterling character beneath her *plain* facade."

He broke off, fuming still, as Glendenning brought in a
tea tray. When the butler departed, Nicholas strode to the
fireplace, turning his back on his mother.

"I'll forgo tea. As soon as Sarah is ready, we'll proceed

to Lady Sophrina's.'' Over his shoulder he sent his mother a bitter glance. ''I trust her aunt will accord me a warmer welcome than you have offered my chosen bride.''

In an instant the dowager flew to the mantel. ''Oh, Nicky, do stay and let me apologize!''

He nearly shook off her hand before the words penetrated. ''Apologize?'' he repeated stiffly.

''Yes, I've been a tartar, and though the ploy succeeded beyond my wildest hopes, you put me in an absolute quake!''

He stared at her in total incomprehension. ''Ploy?''

The countess gave a musical laugh and tugged at his hand. ''Come drink your tea, darling, and let me explain.''

Confused but still angry, he followed her to the sofa.

''First, I shall tell you straightaway your Sarah seems to be all you claim, and I couldn't be more pleased! But I needed to discover for myself whether you both were entering this engagement—so scandalously soon after the termination of the old—for the right reasons.''

At his incredulous glance, she added defensively, ''Well, after Clarissa Beaumont, you must admit it was reasonable I entertain some doubts! Naturally, were I to just *ask* about your feelings for Sarah, you would give me the proper answers. I wished to see for myself.''

Relief coursed through him, and in spite of himself, his lips began to twitch. ''I take it I passed your test?''

''Oh, famously,'' she affirmed with a reminiscent shudder. ''I hope I shall never again see you direct me such a look.''

He laughed outright, and she frowned at him. ''You may say I deserved it, but I had to be sure. When you told me you meant to wed a lady I knew to be in rather desperate financial straits, I did fear that, in your haste, you might have been taken in by a fortune hunter. It required but a moment to alleviate that concern.''

Nicholas grinned. ''If you subjected my *plain* darling to

anything like the grilling you gave me, I expect you to offer her a most eloquent apology."

"I daresay you shall never forgive me that 'plain.'" The dowager sighed. "I *was* cool, but you would be proud of her response. She neither toadied nor explained. Nor, might I add, did she wilt under my supposed displeasure."

"I don't doubt it. I'd wager my stalwart Sarah calmly informed you that, though fully aware of the disparity of our union, she intended to make me a laudable wife."

"So she did." Hesitantly she took his hands. "From your spirited defense, I can dare hope she has truly engaged your interest. I'm so glad, Nicky! You're far too warmhearted to tolerate a mere marriage of convenience."

Nicholas stiffened. "Sarah is a dear and valued friend, 'tis all. We both need to marry. You may cease imagining some fairy-tale romance."

His mother remained silent a long moment. "Nicky dearest," she said at last, "don't let bitter memories poison your heart forever."

"Enough, Mama!" He pulled at his hand.

She caught his fingers and held on. "Call me foolish, with you a man grown, but to me you'll always be the darling son whose happiness I feel compelled to protect." The dowager smiled wistfully. "Perhaps now I can relinquish that role to your Sarah. She…she's nothing like Lydia."

"Thanks be to God," he said grimly. For an instant, the image of his late wife seized him—beautiful, vivacious, the undisputed center of attention as he looked on fondly.

Acid burning in his belly, he shook his thoughts free and kissed his mother's hand. "Thank you, Mama. I should marry her in spite of your disapproval, but I much prefer your blessing. You know, she reminds me of you."

"Rogue." The dowager made a face at him as she pulled back her hand. "What can I possibly do after such a tribute, than pronounce her perfect?"

* * *

When Sarah returned, Nicholas and his mother were tête-à-tête on the sofa. Suddenly she couldn't face any more sweetly barbed scrutiny.

She nodded to them and remained standing. "I don't wish to be discourteous, but I am rather tired, Nicholas. I should prefer to return to my aunt's now."

In a graceful swirl of black crepe, the dowager swept to her. "Sarah, you must not go until I apologize, as I already have to Nicky. I wished to discover for myself the true feelings each of you held about your union, and so I adopted that disapproving air. Do say you can find it in your heart to forgive a mother's concern."

Startled, Sarah looked at the dowager's hand clasping hers. As fatigued as she claimed, she found it difficult to grasp her words. "Of course," she murmured disjointedly.

"Thank you, my dear. Having raised only grubby boys—" she wrinkled her nose at her son "—I have always wished for a daughter to befriend. Now, thanks to my clever Nicholas, I have one." She caught Sarah in a scented embrace.

Over his mother's shoulder, Nicholas gave her a wink. Relaxing, she winked back. Perhaps becoming his marchioness wouldn't be so difficult after all.

Chapter Seven

Nicholas peered in the glass, straightened the white rose at his lapel and gave his cravat a quick tug.

"Nicky, if you fiddle with that cravat one more time, you'll ruin it." Ned's amused voice came over his shoulder.

Throwing his friend a black look, Nicholas turned from the mirror and moved to the small table before the mantel. Bowls of fragrant white roses flanked a gold cross, refashioning it into a makeshift altar. He repositioned the candles beside the cross and walked over to adjust a wing chair by the window, where bright afternoon sunlight filtered through sheer lace curtains.

"Leave it, Nicky, the room looks marvelous. Sarah's outdone herself." Ned indicated the neat line of chairs facing the altar, the white satin draping the mantel and doorway, the flowers on the mantel and side tables.

"Sit." Hal clamped one large hand on his shoulder and propelled him into the nearest chair. "Females'll be ready soon. You're wearing out the carpet."

Nicholas dropped into the chair but immediately sprang back up. Hal shook his head in disgust and Ned laughed.

Nicholas grimaced. Easy for them to mock. Bachelors both, they had no idea how quickly a wife could take a man's pleasant, well-ordered life and smash it. For one panicky moment, he considered calling the whole thing off.

Calm down, he ordered himself, taking a deep breath. His hands were sweating, and he wiped them on the chair's brocaded arm. He had chosen more wisely this time. And this time, he was on his guard.

He heard footsteps approaching. "That will be the priest. They must be ready at last, thank God."

Several moments later, they filed in formal procession back to the withdrawing room. Reaching his place by the mantel, he straightened his shoulders, and nearly tugged at his cravat again before he caught Ned's amused glance.

The opening chords of a Mozart piano piece startled him. The guests looked toward the doorway. His stomach doing a little flip, Nicholas's gaze followed theirs.

Sarah entered in a plain gown of gold satin. An airy breath of white net shot through with gold formed the tiny puffed sleeves, and a sash of the same glittering material tied at the high waist. Despite its simple cut, Nicholas detected the hand of a master, for the rich cloth clung to each curve of her body. The brief bodice, lower than any he'd seen her wear, offered a tantalizing glimpse of cleavage. Heat suffusing his face, he jerked his gaze up.

The glowing hue of the gown warmed her skin to cream and accentuated the delicate flush on her cheeks. Her coronet of braids was threaded through with wisps of gold net and circled by a ring of white rosebuds.

She raised her eyes, saw him waiting and smiled tremulously. By happy chance, at that moment a filtered beam of sunshine from the window touched her, gilding her fair hair and setting a thousand lights sparking on the sheen of her gown. She looked, he thought with a rippling shock, like a princess; she looked—beautiful.

Then she was beside him, a shimmer of gold in a scent of lavender, and the priest was intoning the ancient words of the marriage service. Sarah repeated her vows in a clear, firm voice, while, still shaken, he stumbled a little through his own.

Ned thrust the ring at him, he slipped it on her finger, and the priest proclaimed them man and wife. Sarah raised downcast eyes from their joined hands and gave him that shy half smile. He smiled back and leaned to kiss her.

Something twisted in his chest as he touched her soft lips with his own. Sweet Sarah, he thought, following the priest past the blur of guests. Sweet Sarah, *my wife*.

He had mastered himself by the time the other members of the wedding party signed the register, and penned his own name with a flourish. Sarah's fingers trembled on the quill. With a little frown, she steadied them.

"Gold becomes you," he murmured in her ear.

She glanced up, her solemnity softening into a mischievous look. "Well, 'tis certainly useful."

He chuckled and caught her chin. "When you joke like that, little flecks dance in those lovely silver eyes. You know what I meant. You look beautiful, sweet Sarah."

The pale apricot of her cheeks darkened. "More Spanish coin, my lord?"

"No, Miss Jokesmith. Except for one notable occasion—" he grinned, and knew she was also remembering Clarissa's ball "—I've always told you the truth—and I always will."

"Come along, lovebirds." Ned's voice interrupted. "Your well-wishers await."

Sarah gazed across the room to where Nicholas stood conversing with a cabinet minister, entirely at ease as he chatted with one of the foremost men in the realm. Several of Sarah's sisters hovered nearby, gazing up at him with incipient hero worship.

This handsome, charismatic man was her husband? So nonstop a blur of activity had this last week been, 'twas not until she'd begun to pen her name in the parish register, and realized after "Sarah Ann" she must now sign "Stanhope," that the fact of her marriage struck home.

In an instant of blind panic, she'd nearly fled the room. Then Nicholas had murmured in her ear, his warm voice steadying her. Nicholas the gambler, but also Nicholas the friend who rescued her from Findlay, who saved her family from eviction and want. Hand wobbling only a little, she'd signed the page.

Married a whole hour now, she shook her head and stifled a giddy laugh. Despite any lingering doubts, she felt like the Cinderella of the French fairy tale, wearing the most beautiful gown she'd ever owned, awaited by a prince out of a dream. Perhaps this was all enchantment, and would dissolve when the clock chimed midnight.

She looked at her heavy gold ring. No, this prince had really taken Sarah Wellingford to wife—and by midnight, should have made her his wife in fact as well as name.

Heat warmed her cheeks and sent a rush of prickly anticipation through her veins. She recalled the kiss in the carriage when, overwhelmed by the gift of the Wellingford deed, she'd abandoned maidenly restraint. Drawing upon instinct, she'd tried to give Nicholas back some corresponding measure of delight.

Chloe Ingram's image intruded, and her warm glow dimmed. What had she been thinking, to kiss him like the veriest lightskirt? Had he not told her several times what he prized most was her calm, well-bred reserve? "Lord save me from a spirited, passionate wife," he'd said.

She owed it to him to control herself and remember that preference. She also owed, and would bend every effort to give him, what Chloe Ingram could not: a son and heir. She sighed. Despite her best intentions, she suspected responding with well-bred reserve to Nicholas's touch was going to prove her hardest challenge yet.

Nicholas swung his mama through the last bars of the waltz. She fanned herself as he led her back to the table.

"No, Nicky, not another morsel! I declare, I've already stuffed myself outrageously."

"Sarah will be pleased you're enjoying it. She's been working like a Trojan."

"I daresay you don't know the half of it," his mother replied. "I talked with Lady Sophrina, and I'm amazed at what Sarah's accomplished. Do you realize none of these rooms have been opened for years, and just a week ago were shrouded in Holland covers? Half the furniture is hired—and the servants! She's been juggling three sets of them all week like a master acrobat at Astley's. My darling, you've not married a treasure, you've wed a miracle!"

"I'm beginning to believe that," he murmured.

Leaving her with a kiss, Nicholas strolled back to the dining room, where Ned and Hal awaited him.

Sarah appeared at the archway between the dining and dancing chambers, the gathering glow of the candles sparkling on the sheen of her gown. As the bride, she was the focus of all eyes, but she didn't demand that attention. Indeed, she seemed more the gracious hostess ensuring the comfort of her guests than the star of the festivities.

So modest and lovely, so serenely competent—everything he wanted in a wife. A mellow feeling of self-congratulation warmed him.

Ned looked in the direction of his gaze and smiled. "To think, someone once likened her to 'Ice.'"

"Not ice," Hal said. "Sunshine."

"She is indeed. Gentlemen, I'm a lucky man."

As Nicholas took another sip from his wineglass, he heard Hal's hiss of indrawn breath, and Ned's "Good God!"

Turning to see what had disturbed them, Nicholas choked on his wine. Before his astounded eyes, the midnight figure of Sir James Findlay led Sarah into a dance.

* * *

Nicholas leapt to his feet, upsetting his wineglass. ''The bloody bastard! I'll rip his arms off!''

Ned trapped the spinning goblet while Hal grabbed Nicholas's shoulder. ''Steady, Nicky! Can't mill the man down. Upset the ladies.''

''Lord, yes,'' Ned seconded. '''Twas appalling ton for Findlay to appear uninvited, but you can't brawl over it. Not at your wedding dinner!''

His body taut with rage, Nicholas tried to brush off Hal's hand. ''You don't know what he did to Sarah.''

''Sit, then, and tell us.'' Ned pulled his sleeve. ''Lady Jersey just noticed Findlay, and is looking straight at you. Don't offer her grist for the gossip mill.''

Nicholas sat. Briefly he related the incident at the duchess's ball. As Ned muttered a curse and Hal turned a stony glare on Findlay, Nicholas ended with his warning to his wife's former suitor.

''He thinks himself clever, the miserable cowardly bastard, certain I won't cause a disturbance at my own wedding feast.'' Nicholas clenched his fists, the urge to pulverize Findlay making it nearly impossible for him to stay seated. ''I must do something, surely you see that! 'Tis a clear challenge! I cannot let it go unanswered.''

''You're right, something must be done,'' Ned agreed. The three men looked toward the waltzing couple. A strained smile on her face, Sarah appeared to be holding the baronet off while he leaned close to murmur in her ear.

Ned's jaw set in a grim line. ''Something shall be done. But not by you.'' He rose and tapped Hal on the shoulder. ''That's why a man has friends, eh, Waterman?''

Hal nodded and stood, his hard gaze on Findlay while with one large hand he held Nicholas pinned to his chair. Growling in frustration, Nicholas leaned back.

'''Tis bloody unfair for you two to have all the fun, but I suppose I must bow to discretion.''

''That's the ticket,'' Ned said. ''Play the happy bridegroom. Hal and I will handle Findlay.''

Nicholas smiled grimly. "Don't kill him. I shouldn't wish my best friends to have to flee abroad. Short of that, you have my encouragement to deliver a memorable lesson."

"Bastard," Hal spoke up, startling them. His unblinking gaze never left the baronet. "You distract Sarah. I'll take Findlay."

Ned's lips curved in a slow smile. "Be gentle with him, Hal—for now. You sometimes forget your own strength."

"Time he tangled with someone *stronger*."

Despite his friends' wise counsel, Nicholas could not relax and mingle with the company. Wine, guests, music forgotten, he focused on the drama unfolding before him.

While Ned bowed and inclined his head to Sarah, Hal surreptitiously clamped a bearlike hand on Findlay's elbow and marched him toward the hall. Ned caught the sleeve of an Oxford friend, passed him Sarah's hand and motioned the couple to dance. Then he followed Hal.

Had Nicholas not been watching closely, he would never have noticed that while Hal bent down, seeming to offer a solicitous ear to some vehement comment Findlay was making, he delivered a vicious left hook to the baronet's stomach.

Behind the animated figure of Ned, who was playfully batting the shoulders of a friend he'd hailed, Nicholas saw Findlay crumple like a folded greatcoat over Hal's arm. Hal scooped the smaller man off his feet and bore him away.

Satisfaction warmed Nicholas, to cool at the memory of Sarah's distressed face. As soon as she finished this dance, he would escort Sarah off the floor, perhaps spirit her away to enfold her safely against his chest.

At last the music ended. As he walked to fetch his wife, a group of Wellingfords approached. Trying to recall last night's introductions, he decided the older girl must be Sarah's next eldest sister, Meredyth, and the younger two...? No, not the dazzling Elizabeth. Probably the six-teen- and fifteen-year-old lookalikes, Cecily and Emma.

"Lord Englemere, you must have some of this ice Timms just set out," one of the girls—Cecily?—cried.

Blue eyes starry, her twin—Emma?—made a sweeping gesture. "So much delicious food, the lovely music, and such elegant ladies and gentlemen. Surely not even Al-mack's or—or the prince's court could be any finer!"

The elder girl laughed and shook her head. "You must remember, Emma, Lord Englemere has doubtless tasted any number of ices from Gunter's, and probably visits of-ten at Carlton House. Our reception is not nearly so grand."

"Perhaps, but 'tis undeniably more elegant," Nicholas replied. Noting out of the corner of his eye that Sarah was being led into another dance, he accepted the bowl and waved them all to a seat. "'Lord Englemere' makes me sound old and cross. Why not—" the memory it brought back set him grinning "—call me 'Uncle Nicholas'?"

One sister gasped, and both turned round saucer eyes to Meredyth. "Might we dare?" Emma breathed.

"Are you sure, my lord?" Meredyth asked. "'Twould seem rather forward."

Nicholas shrugged. "I see no reason not."

"Capital!" Cecily clapped her hands. Emma giggled, blushing, and lowered her eyes.

"Here, Colton." Cecily waved to her brother. "Only listen, Lord Englemere has said we might call him 'Uncle Nicholas.' Is he not vastly condescending?" She turned sparkling eyes back to Nicholas. "I'm so glad Sarah mar-ried you instead of that nasty Sir James!"

Nicholas started as Meredyth murmured a reproof. How did the girls know of Findlay?

"Well, I am," the irrepressible Cecily was replying, "and you must be, too. He's just as rich, and surely nicer, and much handsomer, I dare swear."

"'Tis most unbecoming for you to discuss him so."

Meredyth gave Nicholas an apologetic look. "The girls need taking in hand, I fear. Sarah schooled them after we let—after our governess left, but I'm afraid in her absence their education has been rather neglected."

"That bang-up bay team is yours, is it not, Lord—Uncle Nicholas?" Colton asked as he joined them. "And the shiny black phaeton? Oh, to drive such a rig!"

"As if he'd let a cow-handed bantling like you handle them," Cecily muttered.

"Children!" Meredyth protested, her face flushing. "What must Lord Englemere think, to hear you brangle so?"

Nicholas smiled at Colton. "Perhaps we'll have a go at the ribbons sometime later." Suppressing a grin when Colton leaned behind Meredyth to stick out his tongue at Cecily, he continued casually, "I'm flattered you all prefer Sarah's final choice. Had she written you about Sir James?"

"Oh, no, Sarah never mentioned him in her letters," Cecily chimed in. "Lady Sandiford told us."

"Lady Sandiford is our neighbor," Meredyth explained. "Although she resides mostly in the country now—"

"No blunt," said Colton.

"—she has many good friends in town, who send her all the news," Meredyth concluded, frowning at Colton.

"Yes, and when her friends wrote her Sarah was about to make a match with a wealthy man, she came straightaway to tell us the good news," Emma expounded. Her brow crinkled thoughtfully. "Although she hardly called on us at all before, these three years since Sinjin left."

"That's her son—Viscount Sandiford, a captain in the Tenth Hussars," Colton inserted.

"And so handsome in his uniform," Emma murmured.

A handsome soldier. Nicholas's smile faltered.

"I don't think she was happy for us at all," Cecily objected. "Leastwise, not for Sarah. Why else would she tell us what a good match Sir James was for a plain, penniless girl, despite his *tarnished* reputation? And the things she hinted about his dead wives! Even if 'tis uncivil to say so—'' she glanced at Meredyth ''—she was always mean to Sarah, and that's the truth.''

"She likes Elizabeth," Emma put in. "When we called on her together, Lady Sandiford was always quite gracious."

Cecily snorted. "Only if Sarah had just gotten a letter from Sinjin, and she wanted to pump you for news."

"The grandest letters—calvary charges in the thick of the action." Colton sighed worshipfully.

"No, she truly likes Elizabeth." Emma returned to her point. "Don't you remember she said how marvelous it would be if Elizabeth and Sinjin made a match of it?"

"Piffle," Cecily retorted. "Just shows what a looby she is, when everyone knows Sinjin really loves—ouch!"

In the sudden silence, Cecily's small exclamation rang in his ears. His stomach lurched, and only with difficulty did Nicholas keep the polite smile plastered in place.

"Lord Englemere can't be interested in country gossip," Meredyth said quickly. "Come along, children." She slanted him a glance. "They are such chatterers. 'Tis quite…overwhelming, when one isn't accustomed."

"I expect," he managed to choke out.

"Colton, you must fetch Faith, if she is to have some ice." Dipping a curtsy, she motioned her siblings away.

Nicholas leaned back against his chair, the celebrated ice melting to a sugary dribble in his bowl. Sarah's neighbor a handsome soldier—a handsome soldier who loved her, if the impetuous Cecily's unspoken assertion could be credited. God in heaven, this couldn't be happening.

Numbly he rose and stumbled past the chatting guests, down the stairs, into the garden. This time, he couldn't fend off the searing memories.

Lydia, the radiant bride reveling in the attention of the entire Upper Ten Thousand who gathered to celebrate their nuptials. Lydia, whose sweetness soured and whose pettishness grew week by week as she increasingly complained that he was neglecting her for his fusty papers, his friends, his library, his meetings with the solicitors.

Business compelled him to remain in town after the Season, and weary of the constant harangues, he rented her the town house in Bath for which she pleaded. And found when he joined her there, a week earlier than expected, not his beautiful, pouting wife, but a note she'd left with the butler a bare half hour before his premature arrival.

Recalling the words it contained still made his hands sweat and his stomach turn over.

I never loved you.... I go to one who truly cherishes me, an officer of the king's Guards and a real gentleman.... Don't try to pursue us.

He had pursued her, of course. And perhaps sensing that pursuit, she must have driven recklessly along the twisting road that led from the city to the military encampment. He'd come upon her phaeton, one wheel off and its body smashed against the pale Bath stone of the sharp curve she'd not quite managed to negotiate. Arrived too late to arrest her flight, too late to beg another chance for their marriage. Like a fashion mannequin propped on a shelf, she sat among the ruins, her lovely neck lolling at an angle, her open eyes staring. *"I never loved you...."*

He realized he still gripped a glass of champagne and downed it in a gulp. *Be sensible,* he rebuked himself.

He should hardly find it surprising that Sarah once had a beau. She was too remarkable to have escaped the notice of some discerning gentleman, even buried as she'd been in the wilds of the country.

Had he not suspected some romance gone awry after she kissed him with such practiced skill? 'Twas an indigent viscount with a disapproving mother who'd schooled her responses, apparently. And then gone for a soldier.

But he'd loved Sarah, this dashing young hussar in his fur-trimmed blue coat. Had Sarah loved him as well?

Sapskull, he admonished. Why should Sarah have confessed a former love? After all, he'd not vouchsafed to her any details of his own disastrous entanglements.

She'd come to London to find a husband, was nearly pledged to another when he rescued her. Whatever her relationship with the soldier, 'twas clearly over now. To start suspecting deception behind her words, betrayal in her actions, would be unfair to Sarah and would sound a death knell to any chance of future happiness.

I will lock away the memories, he vowed, *and never compare Sarah's behavior to Lydia's.* 'Twas the only honorable course—not to mention the only path that would preserve his sanity. Nonetheless, he uttered a swift, fervent prayer that a certain hussar remain safely posted in the farthest reaches of the Peninsula.

Several hours later, Sarah stood in Aunt Sophrina's entryway in her smart new turquoise traveling dress to offer her family a final hug. In a shower of good wishes, she and Nicholas entered the carriage that would take them to the little cottage outside London Ned had lent them for their honeymoon.

Sitting beside Nicholas, his thigh warm and hard against hers as the rumbling carriage jostled them together, she thought with a shuddering thrill of the night ahead. This time, fear curdled the excitement. Her handsome husband was so powerfully male—and so very big.

Put Findlay's nasty words out of your head, she ordered herself. *He said them for naught but revenge, the wretch, knowing you couldn't pull away in the middle of a dance—*

She jumped when Nicholas patted her hand.

"Turquoise becomes you, too, my lovely wife. And as I know of no realm that employs currency of that hue, you can't possibly misconstrue this compliment."

She laughed nervously. "Th-thank you, my lord."

"My friends call me Nicky," he said softly, "and you may if you wish. But I rather prefer the way you say 'Nich-o-las.'" His fingers caressed her cheek as he tilted up her chin. "You make my name sound like music."

A deep peace settled over her. How could she fear this man, who had shown her naught but gentleness and affection? She might distrust his gambling, but she knew beyond question he would never harm her. Willingly she leaned up to meet his lips.

He didn't try to deepen or prolong the kiss. Ending it, he merely held her close. "You've had an exhausting week, sweeting. Rest now. I'll wake you when we arrive."

She ought to engage him in some pleasant conversation to while away the dull, dark minutes. But his arms about her were so comfortably warm, his shoulder so broad and inviting a pillow, that even as she murmured a protest, she felt her heavy eyelids descending. In an instant, she was asleep.

His hands cradling the brandy glass, Nicholas waited for his wife's maid to prepare Sarah for bed. His previous experience with initiating a gently bred virgin into the duties of matrimony had been distinctly unpleasant, and he frankly dreaded the task ahead.

Lydia had been all seductive enticement until the fatal moment. Apparently shocked by the pain, she pleaded with him to stop. Concerned and utterly frustrated, he had done so. Despite his efforts over the next few days to soothe and prepare her, she remained skittish and moody. After she finally permitted him to finish the deed, she wept. And kept her bedroom door locked for a week.

Well, this time he would go slowly from the very beginning. Fortunately, he'd noticed no signs of missishness in Sarah. Indeed, her kisses seemed to promise a rather receptive welcome. The thought cheered him, until he remembered her obvious nervousness during the drive.

'Twas only the natural trepidation of a virtuous maiden on her wedding night. Or was it? an insidious little voice asked. *"Everyone knows he really loves—"*

Uneasiness stirred. Might Sarah's distress have been, not bridal nerves, but the anxiety of a new wife who feared to be discovered less a maid than she should be?

Nonsense, he told himself, annoyed that he'd once again slipped into comparisons, and even more annoyed at the invidious suspicion. Sarah would never have offered herself on the Marriage Mart, were she less than a virgin. He was quite certain of it. With that reassuring conclusion, he downed the brandy and strode purposely from the room.

Sarah's nervousness returned later that evening as Becky, the sisters' former nursemaid, helped her into the shimmering gold nightrail and began unplaiting her hair.

A quick knock sounded. Clad in a satin-frogged dressing gown, Nicholas entered.

Becky curtsied. "My lord, let me but untangle—"

"Allow me." Nicholas reached for the brush.

Becky cast Sarah an inquiring look. Her stomach in knots, Sarah returned a short nod.

Becky handed him the brush and bowed herself out.

Acutely conscious of a partially clad Nicholas behind her, Sarah opened and closed her mouth, unable to dredge up a single conversational topic.

Meanwhile, Nicholas separated her thick braid into individual plaits. "Lord, Sarah, what glorious hair you have," he said, his voice a husky rumble. Slowly he combed his fingers through it to untangle the full length.

She shivered when he ran his thumb down the back of her head, parting the hair in two. Then he pulled the tresses forward over her shoulders and let them fall to her lap.

Stray strands brushed silken across her jaw, setting her nerves tingling. The tips of her breasts burned at the cascading caress of hair over satin.

Nicholas groaned deep in his throat. "Glorious," he breathed, and pressed his lips to the bare nape of her neck.

Sarah's heart leapt in her chest, and despite her best intentions, she stiffened.

Nicholas straightened. She gasped when he wrapped his arms around her, but he merely slid her over on the bench and seated himself beside her.

"What is it, Sarah?" He took her hand and looked closely at her. "You've been skittish as an unbroken colt all evening—and your fingers are like ice."

"'Tis n-nothing," she stuttered. Her obvious cowardice disgusted him, she thought miserably. She cast about for some calm, confident reply, but no words came.

The warmth seemed to leave him and his eyes narrowed. "Troubled thoughts, my dear?" he drawled, his tone slightly mocking. "Surely you don't fear what this evening will reveal? Or dare I hope 'tis delight makes you shiver— anticipation of the treats Findlay whispered about today?"

Sarah shuddered, closing her eyes as those far-from-delightful predictions once again assailed her. She felt a scarlet tide of shame and embarrassment mount her cheeks. Then Nicholas's hand under her chin lifted her face to his.

When she reluctantly opened her eyes, an arrested expression had replaced the coldness on his face.

"*Did* Findlay speak to you about tonight?" he demanded.

She stared at him, her high color making it pointless for her to deny it. With a sigh, she nodded.

"Bloody bastard!" His eyes blazed, but when he met her anxious gaze, the fierceness left him. He took her chilled hands and chafed them gently. "I hate that he upset you, sweet Sarah. What did he say to frighten you so?"

"I'm s-sorry, Nicholas!" she cried, still mortified by her cravenness. "I'm not frightened, truly!"

"Oh, no." He grinned at her, looking inexplicably relieved. "You always go round with frozen limbs and cringe when I'm near, as if an ogre were about to attack.'' With a mock growl, he nibbled her fingers.

She had to chuckle. ''He did say some…distressing things,'' she admitted, ''but I dismissed them.''

''I can see you did.'' Wrapping his arms about her, he drew her close. ''What did he tell you, Sarah?''

''I'd as lief not discuss it.''

He shook his head, adamant. ''I think I need to know.''

She exhaled in an unhappy little rush. ''He said you would not—'' she flushed and turned away ''—you would not have a, a care for me, that you would…'' Heavens, she could hardly tell him Findlay had warned Nicholas would be as quick as possible about the business, the faster to return to his beautiful mistress. Nor could she bring herself to utter the ugly, explicit words in which he described how Nicholas would go about it.

''That I would…?'' he prompted.

She opened her lips, then firmly closed them. After a moment, she said, ''I'm sorry, Nicholas. I couldn't possibly repeat the rest.'' Straightening her shoulders, she willed her body not to tremble. ''He meant to spoil my wedding night, but I shall not let him. I'm ready, truly.''

''You're not afraid of me, are you?''

''Of course not.''

He smiled at her unhesitating response. ''Thank you for that. Then believe me, sweet Sarah, I would never hurt you. You do believe that?''

She nodded, unable to pull her gaze from his.

''You know what happens between a husband and a wife?'' When she nodded again, he continued. '''Tis unreasonable to expect to go from friendship to such intimacy in an instant. We have Ned's little house all to ourselves, for as long as we want. There's no need to rush.''

''But I wish to be your wife now, tonight!'' she cried. Heavens, waiting wouldn't ease her anxiety, and besides, perhaps this very night she might conceive a son. ''Nicholas, please.''

"Are you sure?"

"Oh, yes!"

A slow smile lit his face. "Far be it for me to refuse a lady."

Chapter Eight

Sarah smiled back tremulously, determined to yield to him with no more ridiculous missishness. But he didn't lead her to the bed. Instead he took up the hairbrush once more.

Her surprise must have shown, for he chuckled. Slowly he pulled the brush through her unbound tresses. "What happens between a man and a woman takes many forms, and is quite delightful, sweet wife. Being a greedy sort, I like to make it last."

She'd always loved having her long, thick hair brushed out. Sighing, she relaxed into the soothing strokes.

She was near to drowsing when Nicholas dropped the brush and began combing the heavy strands with his fingers instead. "I'd guessed your unbound hair would be like this," he whispered, "the sheen of satin with the feel of silk. I didn't dream it would be so beautifully thick and long, falling all the way—" his fingertips traced through the tresses from her collarbone down her chest, over her tautened nipples, her waist, her thighs "—to your knees."

He grasped a few strands and gently pulled her face to his. This time, it was she who made the first sound, a little shuddering moan as he kissed her forehead, the tips of her earlobes and finally her lips.

He made it last, just as he'd promised. At first his mouth

merely brushed hers. Then with his tongue he slowly out-lined the slender, sensitive ridge where skin becomes lip. Deep within her, a hot, breathless tension coiled.

She was warm, so warm. Her nipples seemed to swell and ache, each gossamer touch sending a tingle of sensation to them, and lower.

She needed more of him, closer. Carried away by the liquid fire coursing to every vein, she opened her mouth.

His hands on her shoulders clenched and his tongue swept inside, probing deeply. Then his grip eased and he slowed to trace her tongue with light, quick touches.

The tension within her grew, her pulse throbbing to the teasing advance and retreat. The taste of him, wine-sweet, his scent of maleness and sandalwood, made her dizzy. She felt perspiration along her back, between her breasts.

She stretched toward him, craving the touch of his hands, the feel of his body against hers.

Kissing her more deeply, Nicholas carried her to the bed. He raised the hem of her nightrail, his hands tracing spiral circles of wonderment along her ankles, her shins, her knees. "Are you sure, sweeting?" he whispered hoarsely.

Her body burned, the very core of her molten with heat and pressure, like lava rising. "Y-yes, please!"

In one swift movement he pulled off her gown. Modesty abandoned, she parted her legs and urged him toward her.

He made a sound deep in his throat, half chuckle, half growl. "Not yet, sweeting." Capturing her hands, he drew them from around his neck, brought them to her sides and reclined his body beside her. Slowly he slid his fingers over her bare hip to cup her breast.

"Beautiful," he murmured, and bent his head.

His tongue circled her nipple, tasted it. She cried out, unprepared by anything she'd experienced for the surge of exquisite sensation that flooded her as he suckled.

His hand caressed the ridge of her hipbone, moved lazily

across the smooth curve of her belly, dipped to touch the warm, moist center of her parted thighs.

''When I come in you,'' he whispered against her breast, ''I'll come here.'' He slid a finger into her intimate passage. ''Are you ready, sweeting?''

She must truly be melting, for she felt herself wet against him. Beyond speech, she moved with him as he withdrew, pushed deeper. ''R-ready,'' she answered unsteadily.

At some point he must have removed his own robe, for when he swung his body over her, his hard man's part probed where his fingers had been. He thrust down.

A clear flame of pain seared her, and she gasped.

He stilled, his rigid shaft a stretching, tearing pressure at her core. Murmuring soothingly, he braced himself on his arms and bent to lave one nipple.

Pleasurable sensation rippled through her faintly, then stronger. She sighed, her muscles softening.

His tongue laving first one breast, then the other, then drinking of her lips, he slowly eased himself deeper. The harsh burning within her subsided to a throbbing ache. As she relaxed, the coiling tension, momentarily suspended, started to build once more.

He began to move, and she learned his rhythm. The ache lessened, submerged under a simmering urgency.

His breath shortened, the muscles of his arms knotted. Then he cried out, his whole body tensing. After a breathless moment, he exhaled with a shudder. Holding her close, he rolled them over and settled her against him.

Sarah lay listening to the sound of their breathing as it steadied and slowed. She felt at once strangely dissatisfied, and elated. She was truly his wife now. And it had been nothing like Findlay predicted.

She thought of the gentleness Nicholas had shown, how he'd waited for her body to accommodate his. With a thrill that sparked her breasts and thighs to renewed throbbing, she remembered the incredible reactions he'd drawn from her with mouth and hands and tongue.

Nicholas pressed his lips to her shoulder. Propping himself on an elbow, he smiled down at her.

She smiled back. "Oh, Nicholas," she whispered, "that was wonderful!"

He chuckled and kissed her on the mouth. "Are you sure? I swore I'd not hurt you, but I know I must have."

"Only for a little. As for the rest—ah, 'twas as marvelous as you said."

He kissed her again, his tongue twining with hers as if to demonstrate gratification at her approval. That heated tension within her, which had subsided as she lay quiescent, began to build again.

"'Twill become more delightful still, sweet wife. For the lady, 'tis always better after the first."

His fingers played with the ends of her hair, feathering light touches across the insides of her thighs as he did so. The pressure grew more urgent.

"I can hardly c-credit it," she stuttered, the motion of his hands somehow hindering speech.

"Ah, I knew you were of scientific mind," he murmured. He moved his hand higher, dallying with the thicker, tighter curls nested there. "I think we should test the theory."

His fingers slid to her passage, now dewed with her essence and his. She moaned. Taking that for assent, he put his lips to her breast.

She shuddered and arched into him. This time, he traced with his tongue the pebbly edge of her nipples, holding her still when she would have moved. Against his exploring fingers she felt herself liquefy.

Instead of plunging deeper, he withdrew a finger and slid upward, painting her inner lips until he touched— there.

She jumped, even his slight pressure on that small, rigid

spot unbelievably acute. Murmuring, he suckled her harder and rubbed his slick fingers against it.

Over and over he stroked her, his fingers dipping to her throbbing wet passage and then back, the feel of it so piercingly exquisite she felt she must surely shatter. When the stroking suddenly ceased, she felt bereft.

He stifled her protest with a quick kiss, then moved his mouth to the place his finger had stroked.

If the sensation had been intense before, 'twas doubly so now—the soft pressure and liquid heat of his tongue sparking fire against her tender nub, and then lower as it slid into the passage his manhood had probed. Compelled to move, she broke free of his restraining hold and arched up at him, instinctively finding the rhythm.

She heard strange, feral sobs and realized they were her own. The deeply buried regret that it was not Sinjin who kissed her, Sinjin who loved her, flamed to cinder and disintegrated.

Nicholas entered her, his movement within this time all pleasurable friction and smooth, slippery delight. His body sheened, his breathing a harsh gasp, he filled her completely, advancing and retreating in urgent cadence.

In the next instant, he plunged deep and cried out. The world exploded around her into brilliant shards of sensation that shocked along her nerves for long, exquisite moments before dimming and slowly, slowly subsiding.

Sometime later, she opened her eyes to find Nicholas inclined above her. He held his weight on his hands, but his hips pressed hers intimately where their bodies still joined. She could feel the thunderous beat of his heart.

"Better?" he whispered hoarsely.

"Better," she breathed.

"Good." He bent and kissed her gently. "Sarah, my sweet wife," he murmured, the words a caress.

In the vicinity of her heart, her chest tightened.

Once again, he rolled to his side and pulled her against his chest. With a long, deep sigh, he nestled into the pillows. A few moments later she heard his slow, even breathing and knew he slept.

Awe and wonderment grew in her. He had taken her tenderly, given a pleasure as unexpected as it was profound. Even now, the miracle of that possession might be transforming itself into the miracle of new life.

'Twas no going back now. Though they had not exchanged words of love, the language spoken by their bodies had sealed a bond that for Sarah was permanent and irreversible.

A profound tranquillity settled within her. A scientific mind, Nicholas had said? She lifted a hand, tempted to trail it along the beauty of muscle and bone that lay beside her, see if she could uncover for him unexpected wonders such as those he had revealed for her.

Then her hand stilled. *Lord save me from spirited, passionate women.* No, he had married her to create a bond of flesh—the second miracle, not the first. She must remember that, and the fact that, as riveting as this experience had been for her, 'twas not the same for him.

He had known others before and might again. Though at this moment, suffused in the marvel of their joining, her mind refused to acknowledge that possibility in more concrete detail.

She moved her hand from the enticing curve of hip, instead brushing back the lock of hair that had drifted onto his brow. She must remember her place, and her duty.

This marriage, she thought sleepily as she snuggled her cheek against the fragrant velvet pillow of his shoulder, might be worth the gamble after all.

Smiling, Sarah seated herself at the desk in her sitting room, poured herself some tea and turned her face into the pale sunshine. Nicholas was in the library, but would be up shortly to escort her to yet another fitting. It seemed, at her husband's urging, she'd done nothing since returning to London but acquire the enormous wardrobe that he assured her was required for a lady of her position.

She sighed. She'd much enjoyed her more lowly position as temporary chatelaine of Ned's little cottage. Though Sarah had been the one to end the idyll of their honeymoon, reminding Nicholas of Lady Jersey's upcoming ball, she had been most reluctant to do so.

For idyllic it had been. They'd spent a profusion of lazy sunlit hours exploring the countryside, fishing poles and picnic basket stowed on their saddlebags. Rainy days they whiled away at billiards or chess. In the evenings they read aloud, or she entertained him with her repertoire of piano. They had even played cards.

Nicholas had at first suggested they wager chicken stakes. All her defenses springing to the alert, she sharply declined, replying if they played at all, she would prefer it to be merely a test of skill.

He countered by proposing they wager something more interesting than guineas. And proceeded to disarm all her apprehensions by suggesting, with a naughty-boy smile, that they play for kisses. By the time he demonstrated his expectations of what losing a point would entail, she could hardly recall which cards she held. She lost the first game with embarrassing swiftness, and he claimed his forfeit with such skill that cards were abandoned for the night.

Ah, yes, the nights... Her cheeks grew hot and a spiraling warmth uncurled in her belly at the memories.

She caught her wayward thoughts. However wrong he'd been about Nicholas's initial treatment of her, Findlay most likely spoke the truth when he predicted that, once she got with child, Nicholas would reduce his nocturnal visits.

Perhaps 'twas as well, for she found adhering to their bargain more difficult than ever she'd imagined. It had been all good and well to promise a calm, ladylike reserve in intimate matters while wholly ignorant of what that promise entailed. But now...

The powerful response he evoked made her burn to cry aloud at his touch, ache to follow his lead and to let her own lips and fingers explore his beautiful lean body.

Well, she would just have to manage it. She'd given her word, and she never went back on a promise.

Firmly redirecting her thoughts, she came across a note from the old steward's son she'd left in charge at Wellingford. Jenkins wrote of the repairs he'd effected over the winter and the preparations for spring planting. He'd do his best possible to stretch funds, he promised, but might she have available any additional monies?

A familiar mix of longing, frustration and shame filled her. Wellingford's land held such potential, could she but scrape together the funds to exploit it. She might apply to Nicholas—but no, she absolutely could not ask him for another groat. The quarterly allowance he allotted her was already more than generous.

With a tremor of excitement she straightened. A considerable sum still remained from that allowance, and her wardrobe was already stuffed to repletion. Why not send the rest to Wellingford?

Swiftly she estimated the amounts required for additional seed, roofing and tools. She set down the pen, her heartbeat quickening. She could do all, or much of it.

This very afternoon she would visit the bank. Taking up her pen, she mentally reviewed the instructions she must send Jenkins. But where did one obtain the rapeseed and the new curved plow Sir Edward had described?

Ned would know. Surely he would be willing to share his expertise. She'd write Ned first.

Her pen flew through the note, her mind whirling with images of Wellingford renascent. Not until she sealed it did a tremor of doubt trouble her.

The allowance was given her to fulfill her role as Marchioness of Englemere. But then, hadn't Nicholas several times assured her it was hers to spend as she liked? Besides—a gambler's passion had nearly lost her Wellingford. Wasn't it somehow fitting that a gambler's winnings rescued, and might now begin to restore it?

True, Nicholas might not appreciate her plowing yet more of his blunt into a farm—if he knew. Not that she'd dissemble, but she doubted he'd ask how she spent the funds, and couldn't imagine him troubling to inspect account ledgers. In a few short weeks, she'd have another shamefully extravagant sum to draw upon. Meanwhile, the sums she borrowed would buy a whole growing season's benefit for Wellingford.

Hours later, Sarah stood at the edge of Lady Jersey's ballroom as a teeming swirl of the haut ton passed by. She thought wistfully of Ned's cottage just an hour's drive away. Why ever had she urged Nicholas to return to London?

After one dance, she'd released him to make the rounds of his friends, while she sought out Clarissa. When Wexley claimed that lady, Sarah wandered back to the ballroom. Nicholas wasn't present, though, and Sarah wondered if she'd see him again tonight.

"The fair maiden doesn't dance? How can this be?"

She whirled to find Nicholas behind her. He caught her hand for a lingering kiss that sent a shiver of sensation from her fingertips to her toes.

She could feel her cheeks flush, and blessed the relative shadow of this alcove. "You found your friends well, I trust. And caught up on the latest *on-dits?*"

To her surprise, he threw back his head and laughed. "Indeed. Including this interesting tidbit. It seems a certain young lady, observing that her fiancé had fallen unaccountably but desperately in love with her companion, ended their engagement so those two persons might wed."

Sarah gasped. "She didn't! Oh, that wretched girl! Clarissa mentioned such a silly scenario, but I never—"

Nicholas put a finger to her lips. "Come, do you not find it amusing to figure in this affecting little tale?"

"But 'tis entirely untrue, and unfair to you, as well! As for your falling in love with me, 'tis a notion too preposterous for anyone to entertain."

"Ah, but entertain it they do. No less than three of my friends asked, in strictest confidence, if 'twere true."

Upset now, Sarah gave a helpless shrug. "What can I say, but assure you again how sorry I am."

"Don't let it trouble you, sweet Sarah. I did in fact abandon her—with no regrets. And I've been an object of gossip since the moment I inherited. Besides, I rather like the role of dashing knight discovering his one true love." His voice softened. "Do you not wish to be my lady fair?"

"I should be honored! But never would I wish to embarrass you."

"Then I must convince you this is ardor."

He peeled back her glove. With lips and tongue he slowly caressed each rounded pad of her exposed palm.

Sarah's heartbeat stampeded. "My lord," she said, gasping. "Have a care, else I shall start to believe it myself."

He nibbled the swell of her thumb before releasing it. "Would that be so bad a thing?"

"Shame on you, Englemere!" Lady Jersey tapped him with her fan. "'Tis bad ton to dance attendance on your wife—despite the interesting rumors I hear."

She cast them a shrewd glance. "Go along now, and let me chat with Sarah. Several ladies present tonight, I know, are dying for a dance with you." With a private little smile, Lady Jersey motioned him away.

Nicholas bowed and walked off, then turned to gaze back at his wife. The emerald of her gown accented the gold of her pale hair and seemed to set off jade echoes in her silver eyes. After a month, her subtle beauty still startled him, as it had dazzled him the unforgettable moment he'd first seen her in that gold wedding dress.

Their honeymoon had been emphatic proof of his brilliance in choosing her. Sarah never kept him waiting to fuss with her gown, or chattered at him over the breakfast table, or pouted if he left her alone to tend his accounts. Even better, with her ready wit and her many mannish accomplishments, she was…fun.

He'd expected her to be a bruising rider, but hadn't anticipated needing to use every trick to best her in their races. At their first billiards game, he deliberately missed a ball and found himself royally trounced before he could recapture his cue. And, he recalled with a grin, she was just as good with a pistol as she claimed.

She was also unexpectedly, delectably good at other things. The vein of sensuality he'd suspected beneath the calm exterior ran deep and pure. From their wedding night onward, Sarah entranced him with her delight in each touch, every sensation. 'Twas as if, he reflected in bemusement, her eager wonderment was scouring away his layers of jaded experience, making everything new for him—as if he, too, were exploring intimate pleasure for the very first time.

Equally amazing, she attempted none of the manipulation he'd come to believe inevitable in the sensual waltz of a man with a woman. Never did she entice and then refuse him; never did she hint that intimacy hinged on a gift or favor. She was just—Sarah, unaffectedly natural and willing.

Still, he sensed a banked passion smoldering behind a remnant of maidenly reserve. Though he was thoroughly pleased with the physical bond that already existed between them, it had become an intoxicating game to try to draw still more active a response from her. Faith, with a wife as arousing and arousable as Sarah, what need had he of a mistress?

The unexpected thought shocked him, his cautious head reining in his impulsive heart. 'Twas early yet, too soon for so far-reaching a decision. For now, he meant to just enjoy a marriage far more pleasant than he'd dared expect.

A wicked idea occurred, and he grinned. Damn, how long until they could leave this dull party?

"I should be delighted if I believed that—satisfied—smile sprang to your lips at the prospect of meeting me," a low voice murmured. In a swath of black silk cut low over her sumptuous breasts, Chloe Ingram glided to him.

"I'm certainly glad to see you, Nicholas, after all these weeks." She reached out a hand, then stopped. "That is, if you're still greeting your old...friends?"

It was a perfect opening, and for an instant he nearly seized it. But he and Chloe had been friends, as well as lovers. He owed her more than a cut direct in a ballroom.

"Of course I'm greeting old friends." Glancing past her as he brought one perfumed hand to his lips, he noted Sarah and Lady Jersey nowhere in sight. "Ladies dying to dance with him," indeed.

This explained Silence's cat-licking-the-cream-pot smile. He bet Sally Jersey would never send Chloe vouchers to Almack's, yet she'd included the lady in her ball tonight. A score he'd settle with the mischievous Sally later.

"You're looking exceedingly lovely." He dropped the compliment smoothly and looked back to Chloe.

"Flatterer." She made a moue at him and leaned closer. And thereby offered him, he realized critically, a better view down her brief bodice. He could easily make out the shadow of nipples barely covered by dusky silk.

She noted the direction of his eyes and drew a deep breath, swelling her ample bosom toward him. "London has been dreadfully dull. Indeed, I'm quite overwhelmed to see you again." She swept her glance down, like his, to her breasts, and her nipples under their silk veiling hardened.

In the past, he had found such innuendo about her passion—and its physical evidence—highly arousing. He thought now it was a cheap whore's trick. Surprised by that harsh judgment, he said brusquely, "Oh, I daresay you had much to amuse you."

He thought he saw a flash of pique in her eyes. Then, perhaps sensing his thoughts, she slipped out of the seductive pose. "I've been so lonely I fear I've been unwisely amused. Everly begged me most particularly to come to his party...." She sighed and cast him a look of appeal.

Lord Everly, the wild youngest son of an earl, hosted raffish affairs where, attracted by the possibility of casual liaisons and high-stakes gambling, one might find mingled both the haut ton and the demimonde. The beauteous Chloe had a weakness for gambling.

"Dipped again, Chloe?"

"I'm afraid so. Who could have believed that wretched ball would continue to favor the red?"

He shook his head at her. "Surely you know by now never to trust Lady Luck."

All wiles seemingly suspended, she showed him the repentant face of a schoolgirl. "I know, but I can't seem to help myself. I can still count on you—can't I, Nicky?"

The beautiful violet eyes looked at him guilelessly. She might only be asking about his readiness to stand her a loan—perhaps. Unwilling to be forced at this moment to decide Chloe's future, Nicholas chose his words with care.

"Send my secretary a note. But have some sense, Chloe. I may not always be able to rescue you. On the income Ingram left, you shouldn't game so freely."

She stiffened, and her eyes flashed. "'Tis easy for you to preach, circumstanced you are. Or has your little wife been preaching puritan restraint? Quite a prim and proper miss, I've heard."

Nicholas drew back. He supposed Chloe was angered by his marriage, but she should have been clever enough to realize he would never elevate a mistress to be his countess. Nor could he permit her to gossip about his wife.

Before he could deliver a set-down, Chloe put a hand

to one rouged cheek. "Oh, Nicky, forgive me! You are right, I am unwise, but it frightens me to consider the future…to think of being abandoned." Her voice wobbled on the word and her eyes looked suspiciously bright.

That concern at least was unfeigned, for Ingram had not left her well circumstanced. A fact that, Nicholas suspected, had weighed as much as his manly charms in deciding her to take him to her bed. Compassion stirred.

"Chloe, surely you know I never abandon my friends."

She swiped at the corner of her eye. "Of course. I'm just being foolish. You have ever been all that is kind."

She gave him a tremulous smile and put a gloved hand hesitantly on his arm. When he patted it, her smile warmed to brilliance and she squeezed his wrist.

Nicholas glanced up from that possessive little gesture to find Sarah's eyes resting on them, her face impassive. Swiftly he withdrew his arm, but at the moment he sensed her gaze, Sarah closed her eyes. As if blotting out some unpleasantness, she turned aside.

Nicholas simply stood as Sarah walked away. That she knew—or would be shortly informed—who Chloe Ingram was, he had no doubt. Cursing his luck, he wondered whether he should pursue her immediately, or let the matter rest. After all, a bit of jealousy never hurt.

At the far side of the room, Sarah stopped abruptly. Clapping a hand to her lips, she cried out and threw herself into the arms of a tall blond man in a hussar's blue coat.

A lightning bolt of shock immobilized Nicholas. As Nicholas watched in numb horror, the soldier hugged his wife tightly and rubbed his cheek against her hair.

Sensation returned in sharp tingling waves and nausea roiled in his gut. So much for the wilds of the Peninsula.

Chloe and the dancers forgotten, he strode across the ballroom. He was, he knew with a sour taste in his mouth, about to meet the man who had taught his wife to kiss.

Chapter Nine

Nicholas reached them in a moment. Apparently realizing what a spectacle she was presenting, Sarah stepped away from the soldier. "Sinjin, 'tis marvelous to see you! Why didn't you write you'd gotten leave?"

Then she saw Nicholas, and with a smile, led the officer over. "My lord, let me introduce my neighbor and dear friend, Captain St. John Stafford, Viscount Sandiford. Sinjin, this is Nicholas Stanhope, Lord Englemere, my husband."

The captain stopped short, friendliness draining from his face. "Husband?"

Her glow dimmed. "Yes, we've been wed this month and more. I wrote you, Sinjin. Did you not get the letter?"

In the ensuing silence, polite words of greeting stuck in Nicholas's throat. The best he could manage, his pulse still pounding and every nerve alert, was to twist his lips into what he hoped might be taken as a smile.

For a long, uneasy moment, the captain stared at him, his sunburnt face unreadable. Then he looked down at Sarah. "You know how uncertain the mails are. The last letter I had from you said you'd gone to London, for—urgent reasons. I demanded leave immediately, but we had some nasty set-tos with Soult before I could get away."

"Oh, Sinjin," Sarah murmured.

Finally managing to force the ritual of civility, Nicholas stuck out his hand. "Pleased to meet an old *friend* of Sarah's. I've heard of your gallantry, Captain."

"You have?" Sarah looked startled.

"Colton particularly lauded his abilities under fire."

Seeming to recover as well, the captain gripped Nicholas's hand. "Forgive my deplorable soldier's manners. Your servant, my lord. I'm sure whatever account you got from Colton was highly exaggerated." He tossed Sarah an amused glance. "The scamp's army-mad."

Nicholas found the captain's easy familiarity grating. And must the fellow be so tall, well-muscled and handsome? He looked across into blue eyes that, behind the smile, were as frosty as he suspected were his own.

"You're on leave from your regiment, then, Captain. Do you make a long stay in London?" He pushed the conventional pleasantry through tight lips. "You must call on us."

"Yes, do, Sinjin," Sarah echoed. "I should like you two to become acquainted, and we have—much to discuss."

For another long moment the hussar studied Sarah. A ripple of emotion crossed his face.

His tone, when he at last replied, was unexceptional. "So it seems. Yes, I shall certainly call upon you."

Lady Jersey descended on them in a flutter of pink satin. "Sarah, dear! Who is this dashing stranger you induced to visit my ball—and greeted with such warmth?"

"'Tis my wife's neighbor, Captain Lord Sandiford, just returned to London from the Peninsula," Nicholas answered.

The captain made her an elegant bow. "Forgive me, Your Ladyship! Even in the wilds of Portugal, my army mates traded tales of your beauty, wit and fascinating entertainments. How could I help but present myself? Raff Peterson assured me you'd greet an old soldier kindly."

Lady Jersey tinkled a laugh and preened herself. The

captain had taken her measure at a glance. Nicholas wasn't sure whether to be relieved or annoyed at his perspicacity.

"Marcus Rafferty Peterson, that devilish scapegrace? Well, if you are one of Raff's friends—as well as Lady Englemere's," she added with a penetrating look at Sarah, "then certainly I must bid you welcome."

Chloe Ingram stepped out of the crowd, startling Nicholas. Drat the woman, she must have trailed him.

She startled him even more by boldly inserting herself between her hostess and the newcomer. "You must present him to me, your ladyship," Chloe said. "I have a brother in the army, Captain. Mayhap you know him."

Someone gasped. The small circle about Nicholas seemed to hold its collective breath. Would the great queen of society punish or tolerate this intrusion?

Lady Jersey chose to be amused. After an ironic glance from Sarah to Nicholas to the hussar, she turned to Chloe. "Captain Lord Sandiford, may I present Mrs. Chloe Ingram. Certainly one of our, ah, loveliest London widows."

The captain bowed, and Chloe swept him a curtsy. "Chat with me, Captain. I believe we have much in common."

Lady Jersey trilled another laugh. "Oh, without doubt. Mrs. Ingram will lead you to…refreshment, Captain. Sarah, dear, let me steal your handsome husband. 'Tis my own ball, and I've not had a dance with him all evening."

The musicians were striking up a waltz. Avid curiosity lit her ladyship's face, and Nicholas knew he was about to be mercilessly quizzed. Bowing to his hostess and the inevitable, Nicholas offered an arm.

"I'd be honored, Sal. You must promise, though, if the gallant to whom you've bespoken this waltz calls me out, you'll leave flowers on my grave."

"Rogue," Lady Jersey reproved, and turned to Sarah. "I'll send him back intact, my dear. As for you," she said, placing her hand on Nicholas's sleeve, "should it come to grass for breakfast, I'd wager my blunt on you."

Nicholas cast a narrowed glance at a retreating blue-coated back. Fury sizzled through him. He felt a primitive urge to strike down the handsome captain here, now, in this very ballroom, to prevent with a preemptive blow even the possibility that the soldier might seek to wrest from Nicholas what was his.

The intensity of that battle instinct shocked and disturbed him. Like a blind man groping his way through unfamiliar landscape, he struggled to remember the place and time, to recover the normal pattern of behavior.

The matter of the dashing Captain Viscount Sandiford's untimely return couldn't be settled by fisticuffs in a ballroom. Though deal with it he must, and soon.

At a very late hour, Nicholas escorted Sarah back to Stanhope House, where a yawning footman admitted them.

The rest of the ball had passed uneventfully. The captain danced with Sarah only a proper two sets, after first honoring Chloe, his hostess and several other ladies. When Nicholas claimed Sarah's hand for the second waltz, she chatted amusingly and not once mentioned Sandiford.

He was thus unsure whether to be pleased or sorry when she asked if he would come speak with her before he retired. Though a discussion of the captain was undeniably necessary, once out of the man's troubling proximity Nicholas had half hoped to postpone it.

He smiled ruefully as he knocked at the dressing room door. He should know if difficulties loomed, in Sarah-fashion she would want to attack them head-on.

Sarah stood warming her hands at the hearth, her hair, in a loose braid down her back, gleaming in the firelight.

Nicholas tangled his fingers in the plait and leaned to kiss her. "Later," she murmured. A gleam of promise in her eyes, she urged him onto the settee behind them.

"What did the children tell you about Sinjin?"

His ardor vanished. "Does it matter?"

"I just wondered, that I might not bore you repeating

what you already know. After my rather—demonstrative greeting tonight, I thought you entitled to an explanation.''

"It did seem a trifle excessive," he said dryly.

To his surprise, she flared up. "I'll not apologize for that! For forgetting myself in such a place, I do beg pardon—that was not well done. But Sinjin has been my dearest friend for as long as I can remember. His regiment is fighting in the Pyrenees, the journals say, and I knew he'd be in the thick of it. I was overjoyed to see him return uninjured. Just as you would be, should someone dear to you escape from that action.''

"Probably," he admitted. "I wouldn't kiss him in a ballroom, though.''

She laughed, her heat dissipating. "I didn't kiss him, merely gave him a hug. Let Sally Jersey make what she likes of it! The children told you, I expect, that his land marches with ours and the families have long been intimate.''

She looked up at him, waiting. With resignation, he prepared to offer up what else he'd learned.

"Yes, they said as much. After Cecily voiced her approval of your choice in husbands." He grinned.

"That child needs a curb bit," Sarah said, shaking her head. "What other indiscretions did she let slip?''

"Apparently Lady Sandiford kept them informed of your, ah, progress in London. Cecily claimed the viscountess disliked you—" Sarah groaned "—but Emma insisted she had a fondness for you all." He paused, watching her. "So much so that she favors a union between her son and your sister Elizabeth—now that she has a dowry, of course.''

If pain crossed her face, he didn't see it. "'Twould be a good match. He would make her a kind husband. And he could wish for no finer a wife.''

"Could he not?''

She studied her fingers. "Not any longer.''

After a moment she continued. "'Tis true, we expected

to marry, though his mama never truly approved.'' A brief smile touched her lips. ''How could I blame her? She wished a beautiful heiress for her son, and I was hardly that.''

Nicholas instantly extended his dislike to encompass the captain's mother.

Sarah sighed, her gaze on the dancing firelight. ''In any event, our fathers were fellow gamesters. By the time I was old enough for a come-out, both estates were heavily in debt. We knew duty compelled us to marry elsewhere.''

''Did you? Sandiford seemed shocked to find you wed.''

''I had vowed never to marry. But one does what one must.'' She looked up at him, her eyes warming, then took his hand and kissed it. ''Never has a woman been so bountifully rewarded for doing what she must.''

A tightness gathered in his chest and he drew her into his arms. He'd been about to ask if she had loved her soldier friend. Why, he couldn't imagine. It didn't matter now, and quite frankly he would rather not know.

Despite these self-assurances, the tension in his gut continued to build. He discovered with dismay that it did matter, rather desperately, whether his wife had cherished a *tendre* for another man. Damn, he vowed, he'd bite off his tongue before he'd ask such a useless, green-sick question.

''I did love him,'' Sarah admitted. ''As the eldest of so many girls, Papa treated me almost like a son, and it was always Sinjin who challenged my skills at riding, shooting, hunting. The change from tomboy companions to youthful lovers came as natural as breathing, I suppose.''

I did love him. He barely prevented himself physically recoiling. Prickling shards of memory gouged at old wounds.

''I had hoped you were happy with me, Sarah.''

Her eyes widened. ''I have been happy! How could you think otherwise?''

The pressure in his chest eased a little. ''I'm glad for that. It has been a splendid month. But...now?''

"I'll not receive him, if you prefer."

The offer, freely given, loosed the tension still further, and he was vastly tempted to accept it. But he knew society too well.

"That wouldn't serve. Too many people observed us tonight. 'Twould be better for us all to be on cordial terms, as befits old friends." His smile twisted. "But only cordial. Though I would suffer much for your happiness, there are some things I simply could not allow."

She didn't pretend to misunderstand. "You must not worry the sudden reappearance of a former—friend— would make me forget my place, or my duty. Before ever I came to London, I set old loyalties aside. And now— you have treated both me and my family so generously, how could I think to look elsewhere?"

Her avowal helped, but couldn't completely reassure him. "Duty is a rather cold companion," he said gruffly.

Before he could look away, she reached up to cup his face in lavender-scented palms. "We may not be able to choose our fate, but we can make our own happiness. If I ever doubted that, this past month has convinced me."

Swiftly she encircled his neck, surprising him with a kiss. It was one of her best Sarah kisses, starting soft, then deepening as she parted his lips to tease his tongue and stir the smoldering embers of desire.

"You have brought me so many blessings," she murmured. "I only hope I may bring you half as much."

His turmoil flamed into another need. *Mine,* it said. *Now and always mine.*

"You will," he promised, and pulled her into his arms.

Sarah sat at the dressing table, inspecting herself in the glass. Her morning gown of deep blue, with its slashed rouleau puffs at the shoulder and gold military braid, was perhaps the most stylish of all her new gowns.

After their appearance last night, the news that Lord and Lady Englemere had returned from their honeymoon would by now have swept the ton. She expected a steady stream of the curious to come calling on his lordship's new bride.

When they breakfasted, Nicholas told her he must meet his solicitor over some matter that could not wait, and asked her to make his excuses to any callers. With his usual perception, Nicholas must have taken Sinjin's measure and known he would lose no time seeking her out for a full explanation. How thoughtful Nicholas was, to have arranged so unexceptional an excuse to allow them a private meeting.

How understanding as well. Until Sinjin's unexpected return shocked her into that emotional greeting, she'd not thought it necessary to inform Nicholas of her unhappy love affair. 'Twas past, and in no way affected him.

Last night she'd known she must acquaint Nicholas with the bare facts and reassure him of her commitment. After all, any husband must feel unsettled by such a public demonstration of his wife's feeling for another man. Even one, she thought with a sigh, whose heart was not engaged.

Some men might have berated their errant wives for such a lapse, but he barely reproved her. He even said, she recalled, that he wanted her to be happy. And demonstrated his trust by allowing her to meet her former love. Gambler though he were, she could not have asked for a more generous, considerate husband.

At the idea of meeting Sinjin her nervousness returned. Though the hour was too early for callers, she knew her childhood friend well enough to suspect he would call when he could anticipate finding her alone.

Almost upon the thought, a knock sounded. The footman announced a caller below.

Her stomach fluttered as she caught up a shawl. Downstairs she would see Sinjin alone for the first time in three years. 'Twas the moment she'd dreaded ever since steeling herself to the necessity of London, and marriage.

He said he'd gotten the letter detailing her plans, yet

he'd clearly been shocked to discover her wed. She feared he was not going to be as understanding as Nicholas.

Sinjin was gazing out the window, sunlight glinting on the gold of his epaulets, when Glendenning announced her.

"Some sherry for the captain," she instructed the butler. "And let Lord Englemere know we have a caller, that he might join us when he returns."

Betraying not a flicker of the curiosity he must be feeling at leaving his mistress alone with this stranger, Glendenning bowed. "As you wish, my lady."

Not until the butler departed did she turn, palms moist and heartbeat quickening, to greet her former love.

He had turned toward her as well. The bright light from the window illuminated every feature as the wavering candlelight last night could not. Her polite words of welcome dried on her lips.

He looked achingly familiar and yet changed. His tall frame was thinner than she remembered, his skin bronzed by a harsher sun than England's. A jagged scar running from temple to cheekbone showed whitely against the mahogany of his face. Tiny lines webbed the corners of his blue eyes and the edges of the firm, taut lips.

He'd left a boyish young man, but naught of youth remained. An aura of command surrounded him, the air of a man accustomed to giving difficult orders and being obeyed. His once-laughing eyes were hard, as if he'd met danger, privation and suffering, and conquered them all.

Then he smiled. Dimples creased the lean cheeks—the same dimples she traced with a finger before she kissed them, that happy summer she planned to be his bride.

"God, but you're beautiful, Sarah," he said huskily.

A bolt of pure joy shot through her, and she instinctively stepped toward him. At the last moment, some shred of sanity penetrated. She stopped just short of once again flinging herself into his arms.

Her heart pounding, she turned aside, aghast at the intensity of her emotions. After long bitter years, she thought she'd tamed the tumultuous love she once felt for him, toned it down to the limits permissible between friends. Yet it took every ounce of her control to keep her hands at her sides and her feet motionless. A great gash of pain tore through her heart.

Mercifully he made no move toward her. She thanked God for that and for Glendenning's swift return with the sherry. Uttering what she hoped were appropriate words, she went to pour, willing her hands not to rattle the glass.

By the time she dispensed his sherry she was calmer. Careful not to touch his hand, she gave it to him.

"You're looking well, too, Sinjin," she said, relieved her voice was steady. "Older, of course, but very handsome and commanding."

He raised his glass, took a sip and sat silent, twirling the fragile stem in his fingers. With a twisted smile, he looked over. "Obviously not handsome enough."

She winced as another shaft of pain lanced through her. "Surely you were expecting as much. I clearly remember writing you I could no longer honor my vow. That I must find a wealthy husband with all speed, lest we lose Wellingford—lose everything. You did get that letter."

"Yes, I got it. Indeed, I reread it so often I can still recite it, long after the paper fell to shreds. 'I have racked my brain, but can come up with no honorable way to meet our obligations save marriage to a wealthy man. Thus, I must break my vow and go to London. Repugnant as the idea is to me, the alternative is to lose Wellingford, and that I can never permit....'"

He turned to the window. "Was the idea truly repugnant? Or after three lonely years did you begin to yearn for marriage after all?"

She stared at him, not comprehending. "No, I had no wish to marry elsewhere! How can you think that?"

He turned back, his face impassioned. "If 'twas only to save Wellingford, why not launch Lizbet instead? She's old enough, and if she's grown as beautiful as she bade fair to do, should have met great success. Why seek a husband yourself—unless you truly wished one?''

"Oh, Sinjin, you have no idea how things stood, to accuse me of that!" Angered, she rose and paced the room. "Beautiful she may be, but you know the way of the world. With neither dowry nor important connections Lizbet could scarcely hope to attract the more desirable gentlemen. How could I bear to see that gentle loveliness bestowed on someone whose sole qualification was sufficient wealth? Sinjin, you know her. Of all my sisters, she would suffer most from a union in which affection played no part.

"No, if one of us had to endure a loveless marriage, I knew it must be me. I'm the eldest—'twas only my duty.'' She halted her restless pacing before the mantel and sighed. "Even had I determined to sacrifice Elizabeth, 'twould not have answered. You cannot image how little coin we had. I could not have come to chaperon her.''

She turned to face him, cutting him off before he could speak. "Surely you realize I couldn't let her go about London with only nearsighted Aunt Sophrina to guard her! Let us speak plainly. There are those who, seeing such a beautiful innocent unprotected, might seek to force her into something less than marriage.''

At length he slowly nodded. "I suppose you are right."

"Then you understand why I came myself—regardless of my *inclination*," she concluded with caustic emphasis.

He stepped toward her, his hands outstretched. "I'm sorry, Sarah, I meant no insult. But the shock of finding you married! And to one I believe you might well choose.''

"I was lucky." She thought of Findlay and shuddered. "The man I was nearly forced to marry is an altogether different sort. During the course of the Season, Nicholas and I became friends. When the mortgage came due, and he learned I intended to marry Sir James in order to pay it off, he proposed a marriage of convenience.''

"Kind of him."

At Sinjin's mocking tone, Sarah fired up. "It was indeed kind! You cannot know society if you do not realize how far above my touch is the Marquess of Englemere! Not only did he condescend to the match, but he expended a great deal of blunt over it as well. He has been everything generous, even allowing me to see you privately that I might...explain the circumstances of my marriage."

"You mean that you would not have received me, had he not given permission?" He seemed to choke on the word.

"Certainly not. Not alone, at any rate. Despite our long friendship—mayhap because of it," she inserted with a tinge of sadness, "'twould have been most improper."

He stared at her. "You would be that obedient."

"Of course. He's my husband, Sinjin."

He looked dumbfounded, as if, despite the knowledge of her marriage, the reality of what it meant to her—and to him—only at this moment sank in. He sat down abruptly.

Sarah seated herself as well. Done, she thought with relief, her obstreperous emotions once more well in hand.

"Will you be remaining in England, or must you return to your regiment?" she asked, breaking the silence.

"I've a month's leave, though my business may take longer. I shall certainly rejoin my men after that. In good conscience, I can't sell out until Boney's routed."

"I see." Fear for him shook her, but she swallowed the words. "We must make your brief stay pleasant, then. A number of young ladies at the ball last night are both eligible and wealthy. I dare swear they would be only too eager to meet a dashing young captain." Though the words nearly choked her, she added, "And Elizabeth—"

"Don't, Sarah!" After a visible struggle, he seemed to master himself. "Having so successfully managed your own, do you think to play matchmaker for me? I've no interest whatsoever."

"Sinjin, what's done is done. We must go forward."

He walked to the window and stood, tilting his glass and watching the play of light on the amber liquid. "Yes," he said at last. "When one path closes, we find another."

"Yes," she echoed, relieved he seemed to understand. "Your mama would be pleased should you plan to wed. Have you seen her yet?"

"No." He tossed down the sherry. "I shall have to post down to Sandiford, I suppose, though I'd rather not. Seeing her brings it all back." He turned to Sarah, his face hardening. "Had she not been so opposed to our marriage, had she not harped so endlessly that I owed it to my family to marry an heiress with the means to restore our fortunes... Unable to marry you, unable to remain and resist you, the army seemed the only way out."

Sarah fought the memories his words recalled. "At least you got away! I used to pray I might find somewhere— anywhere—else to go. Anywhere but home where the walks, the glens, the very barns teemed with—"

His gaze shot back, and too late, she fell silent. She knew he was recalling, as she was, their last day before he went off to war.

They rode together as the sun was setting, and he walked her back to Wellingford's shabby parlor. They said their goodbyes under her mama's eye, exchanging proper expressions of mutual regard, and one chaste kiss.

But later that night, wild with grief and despair, Sarah stole out of the house and rode to Sandiford. She threw a pebble at his window, as she had in childhood when she'd bidden him to sneak out, and as in childhood, he came.

He met her in the stables, but unlike the many times before, she'd not had his horse saddled and ready. Instead, she threw herself in his arms, weeping, and covered his face with kisses. He laid her back against the sweet-smelling straw, and she molded herself to him, as if to burn into her skin forever the feel of his body against hers.

"I could have taken you that night, couldn't I?" Sinjin

said softly. "You wouldn't have resisted. I think perhaps you wanted me to. It would have changed everything, wouldn't it? And you knew it."

He laughed, the tone a travesty of humor. "But I was too noble—or stupid. I could envision no honorable choice but to leave, and how could I have ridden away, knowing you might carry my child?"

Sarah said nothing. She concentrated all her energy on drawing air in smooth, even drafts, lest dizziness overcome her or the agony in her chest rob her of breath.

Sinjin's expression harshened. "Damn, but I wish I'd not been so noble. Regardless of what happened after, I know one thing for sure. Had I taken you then, you would never have come to London—would you, Sarah?"

"Stop!" Sarah cried out, unable to stand it longer. "It makes no difference now! 'Tis long past and done."

Sinjin sighed heavily. "I thought to buy time when I rode away, time for—something—to happen. But in the end, love was not enough. You're lost to me—by your own choice."

Her torment exploded in fury. "*My* choice? How dare you talk to me of love, or choice? Yours was the first choice, Sinjin—and it wasn't me! I would have married you with us penniless both, worked happily my whole life to restore my home and yours. *You* chose to ride away."

He flung himself at her. "Sarah, how can you think—"

She held up a hand, halting him. "I'm sorry, Sinjin. That wasn't fair. Your choice *was* the honorable one, perhaps the only one. As was mine, when I had to make it three months ago. We can only live with both of them now."

"Then there's nothing left for us? I will not believe that! You still love me, Sarah—I know it. Surely we can work out something." His voice dropped to a hush. "I cannot live the rest of my life without you."

A lead weight seemed to bear down on her, hampering thought and making breathing difficult. "You must. Oh,

Sinjin, can you not understand? I'm Nicholas's wife now. He rescued my family and has treated me with such unfailing courtesy I would tear out my heart, if I must, before I would dishonor him.''

''And mine?''

''And y-yours,'' she whispered, her voice breaking.

His fierce face softened and he leapt to her side. ''Ah, sweetheart, don't weep.''

His fingers barely grazed her shoulder, but she sprang back as if his gloved hand held burning coals.

''Don't touch me!'' she cried. ''You must never touch me. How can I bear it, else?''

Sinjin froze, his hand still outstretched, his face bereft and pleading. Slowly his hand fell to his side.

Leaving him standing in the middle of the room, Sarah stumbled to the window seat. With an inarticulate growl that might have been anguish, or anger, or both, Sinjin walked over and dropped onto the sofa.

Sarah hugged herself, as if by holding on tightly she could contain the ravaging pain. She had thought in these three years she had learned every nuance of wretchedness heartbreak could offer, but she'd been wrong. Nothing compared to the soul-searing agony she felt now, her heart bleeding with love for him, half her instincts screaming for her to fly to him, and the other half telling her 'twas too late.

Desperately she listened to the faint voice of reason. Anything less meant scandal and dishonor. She would not—*she would not*—allow the love that had burned so purely in her for so many years to end like that.

''Glendenning said we had an early caller, my dear.''

Sinjin drew in his breath sharply, but Sarah could not even trust herself to glance up as her husband strolled in.

Chapter Ten

Taut with trepidation, Nicholas paused at the morning room door. He'd barely been able to mask his outrage when Glendenning informed him a Captain Viscount Sandiford had called on his wife.

He never dreamed the soldier would make a move so quickly. Telling the butler he'd announce himself, Nicholas dismissed him—and two loitering footmen.

What were they doing there, behind closed doors? Was Sarah merely filling in the captain on the circumstances of her hasty marriage? Or, if he were to walk in unannounced, would he discover his wife in another man's embrace? Sickness churned in his gut.

Hands sweating, he raised a fist to knock, paused, lowered it. If the worst were going to occur, better to find out straightaway. Taking a deep breath, he thrust open the door and strode in.

When he saw Sarah at the window, the captain seated on the sofa, he went almost dizzy with relief.

"Good day, Sarah," he called. "And—Captain." He couldn't bring himself to add "welcome."

The viscount rose lazily to his full height. "Lord Englemere." He sketched a bow. "Sarah's been telling me what a timely—*rescue* you made in marrying her."

The words, though polite, held an edge. Nicholas suppressed an urge to smack the slightly mocking smile off the captain's bronzed face.

"We rescued each other." He strove for a polite tone while he poured himself a badly needed sherry. "Despite the pleasure of greeting old friends, after your experiences London must seem rather tame. Do you make a long visit?"

That was direct probing after a bare minimum of greeting, but Nicholas couldn't help himself. The captain seemed aware of it, for the mocking smile deepened.

"I'm not sure as yet. My business here is—complex. It could take some time to resolve."

So the captain did not intend to fade away gracefully. What gall the man possessed! Nicholas's ire refueled.

And like a distraught parent whose anxiety over a missing child transforms, once the child is found unharmed, into anger, he fixed a furious gaze on Sarah.

Who had yet to glance up or utter a word. Whatever had possessed her to grant the bounder a private interview? Didn't she know the servants would be whispering? Just how warmly had she welcomed the brazen hussar?

Eyes narrowing, Nicholas crossed to the window. "I trust you've spent a pleasant morning, my dear?" he asked with barbed intent as he carried her hand to his lips.

As soon as he touched her, though, his anger lessened. Her fingers were chilled, her body rigid, and her eyes, when she finally looked up, spoke of an anguish too deep to hide. As she must have realized, for she quickly averted them.

"Oh, quite," she replied, her voice unsteady. "Sinjin and I caught up on old times. We mustn't keep him, though. Having just returned to England, I expect he has many friends to see and much pressing business."

Whatever was distressing her, she didn't want the captain to linger. Relief rippled through Nicholas.

"Yes, I mustn't outstay my welcome," said the captain, his lips twitching at the irony. He made them a bow.

"Sarah, Lord Englemere. It was truly good to see you, and I hope to enjoy your hospitality again."

Sarah remained at the window after the captain departed. She held herself stiffly, her eyes fixed straight ahead, as if she might shatter if she moved.

Nicholas stood hesitant. Distrust, fury and irritation at her indiscretion battled with compassion. His instinct to comfort, however, strengthened every moment he gazed at her obviously distraught figure. Finally, with a sigh, he drew her into his arms.

She shuddered, then clutched his shoulders and laid her head against his chest. His heart twisted. The remnants of his suspicious anger dissolving, he hugged her close.

After a moment she disengaged herself. With shaking hands, she smoothed her skirts.

Dimly he heard the clock strike. At any moment they might receive morning callers. Looking at her still-trembling figure, he knew she wasn't ready for that.

"Is a headache troubling you, sweet Sarah?"

"No, my lord." She managed a wan smile. "I'm quite well, thank you."

Her face was ashen and her lip bled where she must have bitten it. "Well" indeed. His smoldering anger toward the captain revived. Just how harshly had the man grilled her?

"I suspect the curious will be anxious to bedevil us this morning—especially after Clarissa's rumor. An appalling prospect," he said with an exaggerated shudder. "Shall we cry craven, and deny ourselves?"

"Would that not be dreadfully impolite?"

"You're looking pulled, sweeting. We've only just returned to town, and are unaccustomed to late hours. At least—" he winked "—late hours in a ballroom."

A genuine smile rewarded that quip. "I should like to rest," she admitted.

"I'll escort you up, then."

As they crossed the hallway, he told Glendenning to

deny them. Once inside the privacy of her chamber, he again embraced her.

"Rest well, sweeting. I'll look in on you later."

"Please, stay. I haven't yet properly thanked you."

"Thanked me?"

"For inventing that errand this morning. Somehow you guessed Sinjin would take the first opportunity to seek me out. We have been friends so long, I owed him at least a full explanation. You knew I could not have received him in private to give it, had you been at home."

He stared incredulously into her clear gray eyes, but he could find no guile there. Either she was the best actress he'd ever met, or she believed what she'd just said.

"You give me too much credit," he managed at last.

"You give yourself too little. Most gentlemen, I dare swear, upon anticipating a visit from a wife's former— friend, would forbid him the house."

Unable to invent a response, he simply stood silent. Should he confess that, had he in truth even suspected the captain might have the temerity to call, he would have locked her in her chamber and barred the front door?

"Thank you, Nicholas, for trusting me."

The simple words stabbed in his gut like a dagger. She seemed to believe him a better man than he was. The knowledge awed—and shamed him.

"You...you are welcome," he stumbled.

She studied him, and for an instant he feared she suspected the truth. Then she said softly, "What a puzzle you are." And kissed him.

Guilt, and a primitive urge to reestablish his claim on her, impelled him to respond. His original intent to leave her in solitude wavered, then evaporated altogether as with unprecedented boldness, she slid her hand under the linen of his shirt to stroke the bare skin beneath.

His last thought, before he abandoned all other efforts to free the excessive number of buttons on her bodice, was fierce and comforting. In her distress, she had returned not to her former lover's arms, but to his.

Several mornings later, as Nicholas worked at his desk over a dossier of papers, Glendenning interrupted him to announce a caller—Captain Lord Sandiford.

His first impulse was to deny himself. But for form's sake he really must attempt to be friendly to Sarah's dearest...neighbor. Even though he could barely stand the sight of the man.

"Show him in, Glendenning. And bring us some sherry."

He rose as the captain entered, looking splendid in his regimentals, drat him. "Sandiford, I trust you're enjoying your London sojourn. Can I do aught to assist?"

"To shorten it, you mean?" the captain suggested.

Nicholas pressed his lips together. He would not, he vowed, let this insufferable man annoy him. "You've missed Sarah, I'm afraid, but do stay if you like. Some sherry?"

The captain merely grinned. "You are too gracious, my lord. Yes, sherry would do nicely. And I waited until Sarah left. I wish to speak with you privately."

Nicholas tried not to let his surprise show. Uneasiness stirred as well. "Indeed? How may I serve you?"

The captain deposited his lanky frame in a leather wing chair opposite. After a sip, he looked up at Nicholas.

"First, it appears I owe you thanks. You've saved me the killing of this Sir James Findlay, who, by all accounts, is an out-and-out villain. I plan to return abroad in any event, but it will be more pleasant to leave England without a cloud over my head. Though I must admit the idea of Sarah being a widow has a certain appeal."

Nicholas choked on his sherry.

Seeming unaware, the captain continued briskly. "I must compliment you also. It seems your friend—a Mr. Waterman, is it?—did a highly satisfactory job of rearranging the bastard's face. Though he's left London, I understand, you might have a care. He's found himself another tool—a weasel-faced society fribble named Lord John Weston. Paid his gambling debts, which I hear were considerable, and now the man toddles back and forth from London to Findlay's country home. He'll bear watching.''

Nicholas shook his head, hostility battling with astonishment. ''You seem amazingly well informed, Captain.''

The hussar shrugged. ''One of the benefits of a military education. Gather intelligence poorly, and you die—or your men do. The skill has its uses.''

The frosty blue eyes met his. Nicholas had the feeling he was being sized up by one who'd learned, under fire, to judge men quickly and well.

Instinctively he straightened. ''Perhaps we should come to the point. I am not, you will find, a 'society fribble.' And I must ask—'' he kept his voice even but could not hide its animosity ''—what your intentions are regarding my wife.''

The captain smiled grimly. ''As well you might. Yes, let us dispense with further social niceties.'' He crossed one booted leg. ''I admit, my first thought after the horror of finding Sarah married was to carry her off to Spain.''

Before Nicholas could recover from that announcement, the captain had the incredible gall to laugh. ''What a splendid soldier's wife she'd make. I can see her now, babbling Portuguese as she ordered billets and saw to the wringing of chickens' necks.''

His fingers clenching at the thought of another neck he'd like to wring, Nicholas took a long sip of sherry. ''You have the audacity to think she would go?''

The captain grinned. ''I'd have to drug her, probably. Once I had her abroad, and she saw scandal would make it impossible for her to return, she'd come round. She loves me, you know—always has. I'd make her happy. To be sure,'' he admitted with an offhand gesture, ''she'd be upset for a while. She has such a powerful sense of *duty*.''

Nicholas winced. The captain saw it, and one eyelid flickered in triumph.

You conscienceless bastard, Nicholas thought, rage filling him. He envisioned swords, pistols—

"Like to spit me on your sword, would you?" the captain said with unimpaired good humor. "Can't say as I blame you. No doubt I'd feel the same, did I stand in your boots."

Nicholas took a deep calming breath. "Unlike you, Captain, I adhere to certain rules of morality. Which do not include, regrettably, murdering a guest in my library, no matter how much he might deserve it."

"Doubtless you are correct," the captain replied. "One of the drawbacks of war—it tends to blunt one's sensitivity to conventional moralities."

"Such as stealing another man's wife?"

"But for a mischance of the mail and a stubborn French general, Sarah would be my wife now, not yours."

Steering away from that shoal, Nicholas turned his attack. "Are you so certain you'd win her, despite your arrogant presumption? After all, you left her more than three years ago. And I can be rather charming."

The captain gave him another measuring look. "Would you choose to make yourself so? You prate of morality, but that seems shabby to me—to make Sarah love you, then slip away to Manton Street and the arms of Mrs. Ingram.

"I know," the captain said, waving a hand as Nicholas started to sputter, "you've not visited her since your marriage. Gallant of you to abstain for a whole month. However, the liaison is, I've discovered, of long standing. Judging by the ruby she sported when we talked and the fact that, just yesterday, you discharged a large gambling debt for the lady, I take it you've no intention of giving her congé?"

Nicholas found his voice at last. "Captain, you reach the limits of what I can tolerate, even of a guest in my home. That you investigated Sarah's activities is offensive enough, but to pry into my personal affairs—''

"Reprehensible, I agree. I've no real interest in your doxies, though I must say I've not seen such a coarse display of womanly charm since leaving Spain. 'Twould hardly tempt me—if I had Sarah.''

"Curious. It was my understanding you might have married Sarah. And declined the honor.''

The mockery left the captain's face and he flushed. Nicholas felt a savage surge of triumph.

"I cannot deny it,'' he said quietly. "'Twas the worst mistake of my life, though at the time I thought I was doing the right, nay, the only *honorable* thing.'' He punctuated the word with a savage look and flung himself to his feet.

He paced for a moment, then turned. "Yes, I spurned the fair lady and rode off to assuage my grief by dying gloriously in battle.'' His tone was self-mocking now, and his face bitter as he stared sightlessly at the bookshelves. "It took but one battle to discover there's naught of glory in dying, and naught to battle but dirt, anguish and fear.

"I must say this about it.'' He turned with a twisted smile. "There's something about standing surrounded by smoke, the roar of guns and the screams of the wounded and dying that clears the mind. Land, titles, wealth—none of that matters,'' the captain finished softly. "Only people do. And Sarah matters most of all.''

Did he speak of any woman but his wife, Nicholas might have sympathized. Before he could reply, Sandiford continued, "Had Sarah's letter reached me sooner—had Soult not caught us in the mountains, I should have reached England weeks ago, and we would not now be engaged in a conversation that cannot but be distasteful to us both.''

Nicholas raised an eyebrow. "You think so? Wellingford came at a rather high price.''

The captain shrugged. "I'd have sold off some land.''

"Land doesn't fetch much just now."

"Then I'd have touched up one of my wealthy army friends, or gone to the cent-percenters. Whatever it took to save Wellingford, and Sarah."

There could be no mistaking the sincerity of his words. Nicholas felt a reluctant tug of sympathy.

"But wishing cannot turn back the clock." The captain took another sip of sherry. "That is, I assume you wouldn't consider an annulment?"

Nicholas's infant empathy expired. "No."

"Divorce?"

"Absolutely not!"

"I feared as much. So, we come to the proposal that brought me here today."

Nicholas looked at him coldly. "The only proposal I expect to entertain is the one that tells me courtesy forbids my kicking your insolent ass down my front steps."

"Hear me out first," the captain persisted. "Yours was a marriage of convenience, not a love match. You take your pleasure elsewhere, and intend to continue doing so. I see no reason why we cannot both be accommodated. After Sarah does her duty by you, send her to me."

Through the sudden roaring in his ears, Nicholas stared at him. "You cannot have said what I think I just heard. You want me to keep Sarah as my wife until the succession is secured, and then—" he nearly choked "—let her go to you? By God, I should run you through where you stand!"

"Whatever for? Outraged vanity? True, she's your wife, and let no man poach on your preserves. But by God, she's more than that! Can you claim, as I can, to love her? Can you pledge yourself to making her happy?"

He gave Nicholas no time to reply. "Of course you cannot. You go your own way, as our society permits. As long as she satisfies convention, why not let her do so as well? For the sake of pride, would you deny her any happiness?"

Too incensed by now even to formulate words, Nicholas clenched his fists, restraining by force of will the impulse that shrieked at him to lay the captain out flat. Somehow he managed to hold himself motionless.

The captain ran a hand through his burnished hair. "Do you think I like the idea of taking to mistress the only woman I've ever wanted for a wife? But short of your demise, which I doubt you'd be willing to arrange despite my most fervent encouragement, that's all that's left to me. I'll take whatever I can get—another attitude war inspires."

He leaned his hands on the desk, fixing on Nicholas blue eyes burning with intensity. "Don't dismiss the idea out of hand. 'Tis no secret you're a creature of London. Sarah prefers the country. If you lived separately, 'twould cause little comment. And we would be discreet."

From the midst of Nicholas's fury an incredible, galling suspicion bubbled up. Sarah's distress on the morning of the captain's visit: had it been the anguish of tearing open old wounds—or unhappiness at the idea of waiting for her lover? Had she come to his arms for comfort, or out of guilt? Red spots danced before his eyes.

"And did Sarah agree to this charming little arrangement?" he asked through gritted teeth.

"Lord, no!" The intensity left the captain's gaze. "I wouldn't dare propose such a thing to her. She'd probably put a bullet through me for so maligning her honor." He laughed. "An impulsive lass she can be, as I suppose you've discovered. She'll take a deal of convincing. 'Twould be easier if I could tell her you approved."

"On a snowy day in hell," Nicholas retorted, though his anger cooled a fraction at discovering Sarah had no hand in this. "You must be a bedlamite to think I'd consider it."

"If you loved her as I do, you'd consider any alternative."

"You had your chance, Captain. I don't feel any obligation to provide you with another—certainly not the tawdry, illegitimate little arrangement you've proposed."

"You can't offer her love, or even fidelity. So give me no pious tripe about the sanctity of marriage."

Nicholas clenched his jaw to stifle a vicious retort and crossed to the bellpull. "I consider the subject closed. Thank you for your...*illuminating* visit, Lord Sandiford." He gave the embroidered cloth a ferocious tug. "I shall be cordial in public, but pray do not call again."

"My pleasure, though the matter isn't closed, merely pending. I've a score yet to settle with Boney, but when I return..." The captain smiled grimly. "You may hope some Frog marksman relieves you of my presence. The odds are with you."

"Never before have I favored the French."

The captain made an exaggerated bow. "Henceforth, I'll restrict my calls to Sarah. Quite conventional ones, I assure you. She thinks to make me a list of potential brides, and I'm willing to humor her." His voice softened. "I don't wish to hurt her more than I already have. Good day, my lord. Take care of her for me."

Nicholas gasped. "First you fit me for a pair of horns, then you instruct me to care for her until you choose to make me wear them! By God, Captain, you have gall!"

"A useful attribute in a cavalry officer, my superiors tell me. Your servant, sir."

As Nicholas escorted him to the door, an opening occurred, and he seized it. "A delightful business, this getting of sons. Chancy, though. One may end up with any number of daughters first. And as you so thoughtfully reminded, Sarah will do her *duty*." He let a lascivious smile play at his lips. "I promise you, Captain, I take great pains to ensure she enjoys it."

With an ignoble but satisfying rush of pleasure, he watched this shot strike target. The captain's mocking expression vanished, a muscle twitched in his cheek and the blue eyes blazed with rage.

But Sandiford hadn't been battle-tested for naught. Though his sword hand clutched at his side and his other hand balled into a fist, he made no move. Nicholas wasn't sure whether to be disappointed or relieved he'd failed to provoke a guest to brawl in his own library.

"Why not meet me at Jackson's?" The captain looked Nicholas up and down. "For a useless society fribble, you might strip well."

"Nothing would give me greater pleasure than beating your pretty face to a pulp. But then, I should hate to jeopardize Sarah's matchmaking plans."

Glendenning appeared at the door. "Show Lord Sandiford out," Nicholas snapped. With the barest of bows, he turned his back on the visitor and stalked to his chair.

Nicholas stared at his paper-strewn desk and counted to one hundred, then two. Fury, outrage and a brace of other strong emotions he'd not put a name to elbowed for room in his mind like noisy spectators at a cockfight.

Send him Sarah, indeed! he fumed. Rifle fire must have rattled the man's brain. How dare he suggest such a thing, or question Nicholas's fitness to be Sarah's husband. He really should meet the captain at Jackson's and pummel some of the effrontery out of him. The very idea of her in the arms of that hussar sent a shaft of torment through him.

He had never learned for sure if Lydia actually betrayed him. After the accident, her hysterical maid disclaimed all knowledge of the nameless soldier, and not wishing to arouse more speculation among the servants, he hadn't investigated further. Knowing that Lydia had always preferred wooing and gifts and pretty speeches to the physical act of love, he suspected she might have gone to her grave still technically faithful.

In truth, Lydia had always been somewhat chilly, especially before that ill-fated sojourn in Bath. Unlike his eager, sensual Sarah—Sarah, who even after an obviously wrenching scene with her former love, sought out rather than rebuffed his embrace.

He reviewed the encounter in fond detail, finding reassurance in each kiss, each sigh. If loving would keep her close and content, he was more than happy to provide it.

What else was it Sandiford said—that Sarah would shoot him for maligning her honor by suggesting an adulterous relationship? If Sandiford, who—God rot him—had known Sarah longer than he, discounted the possibility of her abandoning her marriage, why should he worry?

He wouldn't. He would forget the whole distasteful interview. Sarah would never consider such a sordid arrangement. In turn, he vowed, he would ensure she never regretted her loyalty. After all, contrary to the opinion of that fur-pelissed popinjay, Sarah's happiness *was* of great concern to him.

So why was he still troubled? The answer trembling at the edge of his mind unsettled him. Surely he wasn't such a coxcomb that he demanded both his wife's fidelity—and her love—without being willing to pledge his own.

Love. He'd thought he loved Lydia, that she loved him in return. But she claimed in her farewell note he couldn't have loved her and neglected her so—then abandoned him.

All he knew about for sure, he concluded bitterly, was the devastation of betrayal. And the simplicity of more businesslike arrangements.

From beyond the stack of musty ledgers where he'd relegated it, the cloying scent of a perfumed letter reached him. Twitching his nose in distaste, he picked it up.

Chloe's missive thanked him prettily for paying her gambling losses and hinted she lay ready at any time to offer thanks of a more intimate nature.

He stared at the letter, frowning. Despite Lydia's quixotic bedroom behavior, he'd never taken a mistress during their marriage. The captain's harangue on the subject pricked at him.

A "coarse display of womanly charm," the captain had

uncharitably described Chloe. Truth be told, of late he was beginning to share the captain's opinion.

He could pen a cordial note assuring her of his regard, but terminating any future relationship. And yet…

He rolled the quill in his fingers. After Lydia, he had been relieved to settle on a straightforward exchange of cash for services rendered. Intimacy with Sarah was so sweetly different.

As friends, as lovers, they had grown close enough to make their marriage a comfortable and pleasant arrangement. Without Chloe, it would be all too easy to become— rather devoted.

The old, sick feeling stirred in his belly. Once he had thought Lydia devoted. Were he to be wrong again, he wasn't sure he could bear it.

His head was beginning to throb. With a growl he set the paper aside and stood up. Damn the hussar for reviving all his doubts.

No one would force him into a decision about this now, he vowed as he stalked from the room. Not Chloe, not Sarah and certainly not an obnoxious, adultery-minded captain.

Chapter Eleven

After a highly satisfactory visit to the factor, Sarah sat at her desk reviewing the agricultural supplies she'd ordered. There'd be a bountiful harvest at Wellingford this year—thanks to Nicholas. Perhaps she *should* tell him. 'Twas such a wonderful prospect, surely he would share her delight.

Her enthusiasm cooled. Perhaps she should tell him before someone else did.

After shopping for the usual fripperies with Clarissa, she'd intended to slip away to the agricultural factor. Scenting a secret, Clarissa had insisted Sarah reveal her mysterious destination. When she'd reluctantly confided her plans, her friend dissolved in laughter. Sobering, Clarissa swore not to divulge a word. Englemere would be a laughingstock, she declared, if the ton ever discovered his wife had spent her quarterly allowance on a farm.

Entering upon her knock, she found the library deserted. She paused, frowning. She could inform Glendenning she wished to see Nicholas when he came in. But no, she'd as lief not offer the servants any cause for speculation so soon after her meeting with Sinjin.

Write him a note, she decided. She walked to his desk, thinking to find paper and a pen.

The pale pink vellum scribed in a childish hand was

tucked in his blotter. A sheet of paper poised beside it, as if he were about to reply. Even at the distance of several feet, she could smell its cloying scent.

Something tightened in her chest. Even as instinct urged her forward, she retreated. No, she'd not stoop to reading letters from his mistress.

All thoughts of a note forgotten, she sped from the room. Not for anything would she want one of the servants—or worse yet, Nicholas himself—to discover her snooping.

When she got to her room, she found her fingers still trembling. Though she'd accepted Mrs. Ingram's position before she married Nicholas, lulled by the harmony of their honeymoon, she'd put the woman out of mind. She was, she discovered with mingled irritation and chagrin, woefully unarmed for the evidence of their continuing liaison that now sat conspicuously displayed on Nicholas's desk.

Don't be an idiot, she scolded herself, swiping at a tear that had the temerity to produce itself unbidden. *You neither asked for nor expected fidelity of him. How can you be foolish enough to hurt for it now?*

Her heart had an answer, and she didn't like it. Angrier still, she picked up a china shepherdess from the side table and hurled it toward the mantel.

The satisfying crash as it shattered brought her back to earth. Embarrassed, she hurried to gather up the pieces. *Let this be a warning,* she rebuked herself as she bundled the fragments.

True, her husband was kind and generous. Finding her closeted with Sinjin at that awful meeting a few days ago, he could have assumed the worst. Instead, he trusted her, comforted her, loved her so sweetly he brought more balm to her shattered heart than he would ever know.

But theirs was not a love match. In her need to distance herself from Sinjin, she must be wary of turning to Nicholas. She could never preserve the well-bred, unemotional facade Nicholas required of her if her affections became truly engaged.

Besides, she reminded herself, though he'd so far displayed only a milder form of the addiction, he was still a gambler and not to be trusted.

Could there be anything worse than losing her heart to one who not only didn't want it, but who with a toss of the dice could lose everything she possessed as well?

Lord above, help me to be wise. She sent the silent prayer heavenward. *Have I not known heartache enough?*

Nicholas sat in the parlor sipping sherry. Hal was joining them for dinner, after which they'd go on to the rout at the Sheffingdons'.

Restless, he glanced at the mantel clock, but instead of Roman numerals on a silver ground, he saw a gold-haired man in royal-blue regimentals.

No doubt they'd encounter the resplendent captain tonight. Since that first morning call Sandiford had been attentive but not overly familiar with Sarah, cordial and straightforward to Nicholas. Had the captain not paid him that incredible visit, Nicholas might have come to view his wife's neighbor as an admirable man, a valiant soldier who had rendered great service to his country.

But Sandiford had called, and Nicholas could never forget the look on his face when he said he would consider anything that would keep Sarah in his life.

'Twas better to be forewarned. Still, though Nicholas doubted the captain would attempt to fly with Sarah, and dismissed completely his absurd future plans, he could not shake a smoldering unease.

Damn, he didn't wish to think of the man. He'd go fetch Sarah. In the hall, he came upon Sarah's maid.

"Her ladyship'll be that happy to see this," Becky said as she took a letter from the butler. He got a glimpse of Sarah's name written in an unmistakably masculine scrawl.

The maid glanced up. Looking startled—and guilty, he wondered?—she hastily tucked the missive in her sleeve.

"Mistress will be down directly, my lord," Becky said, dipping a curtsy. "I had to match a thread on her shawl, but 'tis finished, and I'll take it right up to her."

Which, the shawl or the letter? Nicholas thought. A tremor of anger rippled through him. Was Sandiford sending Sarah letters, the blackguard? Did the note contain an avowal of undying love—or just the man's reactions to a list of the potential brides Sarah was supposedly compiling?

He turned on his heel and went back to the parlor, poured himself a brandy, and stared moodily at the clock.

"Sorry to have taken so long, Nicholas," Sarah said as she entered a few moments later. "I half expected to see Hal already arrived."

Did you linger to read his letter? he wanted to ask. "Collect any oddities on your shopping trip, my dear?"

For a moment she looked startled. "Only the ordinary," she replied at last. "Though it never ceases to amaze me the fripperies Clarissa finds she cannot live without."

"I hope you've avoided her example and retained some blunt," he said, forcing a smile. "Mama will be returning next week. You'll want to commission something suitable."

Sarah looked at him blankly. "Commission something?"

"Do you not recall?" He handed her a sherry. "Mama said since we'd had no engagement ball, and so small a reception, she must hostess a presentation ball—to properly introduce my wife to the ton."

Sarah choked on the sherry. "Good gracious! I'd forgotten all about it."

"Mama's so delighted with her new daughter she's happy to do this. You have only to select a gown splendid enough for a marchioness, and look lovely."

His words didn't seem to encourage her. "Nicholas, I,

ah, I've ever so many gowns. Surely I don't need another.''

"Nonsense, my dear. You're a marchioness now, and must dress the part, especially on such an important occasion." He patted her hand. "At the risk of putting you off completely, I must confess you should expect to greet most of England's nobility, from Prinny and his advisers on down. Something in gold and diamonds should do the trick."

"Diamonds?" she repeated, moistening her lips.

"Is something amiss? Not run off your legs already, I trust." Nicholas grinned at her.

"I'm afraid that's rather the case." She gave him a nervous smile. "I was going to inform you, but I'd not yet had the...opportunity."

"Well, I daresay dressmakers' bills are more expensive than I remember," he allowed.

"I didn't spend the money on gowns, Nicholas. It was something quite different, something I doubt you'd guess."

Whatever could she have purchased? Nicholas wondered. Articles so extravagant she suspected he'd disapprove them, if that troubled look was any indication.

A thought popped into his head, too outlandish to credit. Sandiford had as much as admitted he was short of funds. Had Sarah lent him money—Nicholas's money? Was the letter he'd seen Sandiford's note of thanks?

No, 'twas preposterous. Nonetheless, all his simmering anger reheated.

"Perhaps you'd better tell me the whole."

"Hope I'm not late, Nicky." With a genial smile, Hal Waterman walked in. "Famished. Shall we dine?"

Nicholas grimaced. There'd be no answers now.

"Evening, Hal. Certainly we'll dine. Escort Sarah, won't you?" He gave his wife a curt nod.

Nicholas watched Hal take Sarah's arm. With a light remark, she set him laughing. Moodily he followed.

Oh, she was good at nurturing, his lovely bride. He thought of the letter, and set his teeth. Just who else did she think to nurture?

Nicholas stared at the window and tossed the coin up again. He'd wandered into the Sheffingdons' gaming room to join in a hand of whist while awaiting his waltz with Sarah. But what tepid interest he'd managed to summon up for the game had already evaporated.

He simply hadn't been able to stomach any longer watching the country dance into which the captain had led his wife. Wasn't the man letting his hand linger on Sarah's? And Nicholas wasn't imagining the caressing look on the captain's face as he followed Sarah's movements, an expression far removed from brotherly regard. Had anyone else noted those all-too-fond glances?

Impelled by some sixth sense, he turned to see Sarah framed in the open doorway. The smile that automatically sprang to his lips died as he took in her appalled face. Before he could move or speak, she whirled around and fled.

Fear rocked him. Nearly running, he crossed the room, but by the time he reached the hallway she had disappeared.

He stood, perplexity and alarm coursing through him. If she were in trouble, why had she not waited for him?

Unless it were not he she'd been looking for. Unless she'd been rushing to rendezvous with another, and he was the last person she wanted to see.

Surely not. Had he not just left them in the ballroom?

He hesitated, then strode to the crowded dance floor. Neither the captain nor Sarah was among the revelers.

Acid burned in his belly. Pasting a society smile on his face, he set out to hunt for his wife.

Twenty minutes later Nicholas paused, trying to curb a rising outrage. He'd checked the refreshment room, the card room and several antechambers. That he was forced to progress slowly, speaking to the friends he encountered and maneuvering glibly to evade the invitations they pressed upon him to eat, chat or dance, only exacerbated his ire.

There was no sign of either his wife—or the captain. Wherever had they vanished? The only rooms he'd not checked were the ladies' withdrawing room—and the bedchambers.

Between the barely contained fury smoking in him and the sick churning in his gut, he had no taste for food or conversation. The waltz was long past, and by now he was too angry to face Sarah.

He'd go to his club, he decided. Perhaps after a bottle of brandy, he'd be calm enough to discuss this.

He went to the foyer and called for his greatcoat. He'd leave word for her to go home with a friend.

The image of Sandiford rose before him. Ah, yes, the captain would be only too willing to escort her home—and settle her in bed. A red mist of rage clouded his head.

Better make that two bottles of brandy, he told himself savagely as he awaited his coat.

Sarah sat in the ladies' withdrawing room, mopping her cheeks as she tried to make sense of what had just happened.

She'd gone to find Nicholas after the dance with Sinjin. He'd signed her card for the waltz, but she'd decided to ask him to slip away and talk with her instead.

She'd been berating herself for her stupidity in forgetting the presentation ball and her poor judgment in not consulting Nicholas about the Wellingford purchases.

Though well deserved, his coldness during dinner struck her like a chill wind, destroying her comfort. She suddenly realized how, in just a short time, she had come to rely on his kind and steadfast support.

She would make a full disclosure, endure his scold and pray all would be right between them again.

Pausing on the threshold to survey the occupants, she spied Nicholas across the gaming room and was about to approach him when a small movement caught her eye.

Nicholas was staring toward the darkened window, a troubled look on his face, while with one hand he tossed up a gold guinea, caught it, threw it up again.

The breath stopped in her throat. She stood riveted, unable to tear her gaze from the tumbling dance of the bright coin winking in and out of his fingers.

The image before her blurred, and she saw a slighter man, gray at the temples, standing before a darkened window at Wellingford, tossing and retossing a single coin. "I've lost it all, Sarah," her father said. "I've lost it all."

Beyond rational reaction, she fled blindly down the hall. Even now, recalling the scene made her stomach heave.

She mopped her brow again. *Calm down.* She was an idiot, letting a ghost of the painful past spook her. 'Twas not the disheveled wreck of her father who stood there, not the vacant stare of a man who'd gamed away everything.

But Nicholas gambles! her frantic heart replied. Maybe 'twas not him tonight, but it could be. Maybe tomorrow night. Maybe next year.

She dipped the cloth again in cool water. Yes, Nicholas gambles. Mostly, he wins. Should he lose, he's wealthy, much wealthier than Papa ever was. And even should he lose everything, there will be Wellingford.

Yes, Wellingford. A refuge for her—and her son. She put a protective hand over her stomach.

Should she tell him? No, right now she had a different confession to make. She'd best get hold of herself and find Nicholas.

She smoothed her braids and turned to leave.

Just then Clarissa tripped in. "Sarah darling, you simply must hear this! Oh, and could you help me with my lace? Wexley trod on it during our last waltz, the oaf!"

Resigning herself to the delay, Sarah pinned up the torn

bit, half listening to Clarissa's latest *on-dit* while in her mind reviewing her explanations to Nicholas.

Ten minutes later, arm linked with Clarissa's, Sarah at last strolled down the hall to the refreshment room. She would escort Clarissa back to her courtiers and then seek out Nicholas.

The first couple they encountered stopped chatting as they neared. Sarah thought the lady, one of the Season's Marriage Mart hopefuls, intended to speak, and smiled.

The girl turned aside and whispered to the young man. Both burst out laughing.

Sarah frowned and glanced at Clarissa. Her friend's chatter continued unabated.

When they reached the crowd outside the ballroom, a hush fell. Half the people in the milling throng looked toward Sarah and, avoiding her eyes, quickly turned away. Titters behind fans and ill-concealed chuckles followed.

This time Clarissa noticed, stopping her recitation in midsentence. A deep foreboding engulfed Sarah.

Clarissa bristled. "What the devil is going on?"

A slight, narrow-faced young man in a puce jacket and bright saffron waistcoat sauntered toward them. Sarah recognized the sharp-tongued Lord John Weston.

"Well, if it isn't the Farmer Bride. Did you leave the cows at home tonight, or do they await you in the street?"

Farmer. Cows. Alarm coursing through her, Sarah rapidly reviewed the passersby near the agricultural factor's shop. Surely this fribble hadn't seen her.

Lord John smiled, a thin curve of lip with no humor in it, and turned to several young fops by the wall. "We must watch our step after she passes, gentlemen. Something other than straw may still cling to her shoes."

She heard Clarissa's gasp, and several bystanders tittered. Sarah stiffened, anger replacing her chagrin.

"Lord John." Sarah nodded, head high and voice imperious. "And—gentlemen?" She invested the word with every bit of scorn she could muster.

Lord John swept her a bow. "How kind to acknowledge those of us so far beneath you." He gestured to the lounging men. "Alas, you think us a poor lot. All of London society, in fact. From the nouveau-riche hangers-on to the greatest hostesses, we are naught but a passel of idle gossips and mindless, pleasure-seeking dandies."

For a second, she was tempted to agree, adding sweetly he was the worst of the bunch. Good breeding prevailed. "Certainly not. I'm vastly grieved you could have invested me with so uncharitable a thought." Nodding her head once more, she gripped Clarissa's arm and swept past them.

More titters, though fewer this time. Then, in the silence that followed, she heard Lord John's voice. "Pawk, pawk, pawk, pawk."

Anger sizzled through her—not at his goading, for she cared naught for his opinion. But it rankled her that this worthless man should mock the humble farms whose revenues made his dissolute London life possible.

She turned her head back. "Chickens don't sound like that." She gave him a condescending smile. "But then, you wouldn't know. Being better acquainted with swine."

Squeezing Clarissa's arm, she resumed walking. By mutual, unspoken consent, they traversed the ballroom and proceeded out onto the terrace beyond.

Finding an unoccupied corner, Sarah let go Clarissa's arm and leaned wearily on the balustrade.

Clarissa slashed her fan again a pillar. "'The Farmer Bride' indeed! What a detestable worm! Oh, were I a man, I'd run him through for that."

Sarah laughed without humor. The Farmer Bride. Little as it meant to her, she knew Nicholas wouldn't be as sanguine. What the ton said of her would matter to him.

Then she remembered his angry face in the card room. Shock sizzled through her. He must have already heard it.

"Someone must have seen me at the farm goods emporium," she said with exasperation. "Damn and blast!"

"Perhaps, Sarah," Clarissa said, tears glittering at the tips of her long lashes. "But I-I'm afraid I mentioned something to Wexley."

"Oh, Clare."

"He complained his factor was taxing him over some matter about his estate, and how dare the man bother him while he was in agonies deciding whether to commission a waistcoat in daffodil or saffron? I scolded him, and told him some people not only listened to their agents, but sent them funds. When he swore it could not be so, I..." Tears slid down the porcelain cheeks.

Trying to stifle her annoyance, Sarah patted Clarissa's hand. Wexley was one of the worst rattles in the ton. Nicholas was going to be livid.

Clarissa straightened. "You trusted me, and I failed you. I shall make it right, Sarah, I swear it."

She took a few restless steps. "I shall cut Wexley completely. He swore he'd keep the news in strictest confidence, and surely realized what would happen if he whispered it." She gave her titian curls an angry shake. "He cannot hold me in much esteem, to injure my dearest friend. And I shall give the cut direct to anyone who dares call you that dreadful name, or so much as giggles in your direction. Let the despicable Lord John deal with that."

Sarah frowned. A public vendetta between Clarissa and Lord John would stir up just the sort of dust to fuel the gossips—and Nicholas's ire—for the longest possible time.

"Cut Wexley if you will, Clare, but leave the rest to me. The best way to deal with this is to ignore it. I am a marchioness, am I not?" She straightened and gave an imperious look. "What care I for the chatter of inferiors?"

Clarissa sighed. "Very well, I shall do nothing. Except—" her eyes glittered with anger "—deal with Wexley."

"What's done is done," Sarah said, trying to sound unconcerned. "We should get back."

"Yes." Clarissa unfurled her fan with a snap. "And if you'll excuse me, there's a gentleman I wish to see."

Silently they reentered the ballroom and scanned the dancers, Clarissa stiffening as she identified Wexley. Giving Sarah a militant nod, she set off.

Nicholas was nowhere in sight. Her chest tight with apprehension, Sarah left the ballroom.

As she crossed the landing above the entry, she saw a familiar figure collecting his greatcoat and hat.

"Nicholas," she called.

He looked up, his face hardening when he recognized her, and raised an eyebrow sardonically. "Madame." Making an elaborate bow, he settled his hat and stepped to the door.

His glacial tone shocked her nearly as much as the fact that he appeared to be quitting the rout without so much as a word. In a rustle of skirts, she flew down the stairs.

"You are leaving?" she asked, her cheeks pinking under the gaze of the butler and several hovering footmen.

"You have some objection, my *lady* wife?"

At his savage emphasis, her heart sank. Without doubt he had heard the story, and he was most definitely livid. So livid he intended to leave his disgraced wife to face a disdainful crowd alone. *Nicholas, how could you abandon me?*

"N-no, of course not. The evening is yours to command."

"At least something is," he muttered. "Don't let me keep you from your *admirers*." With another overcourtly bow, he turned his back on her and strode out the door.

Sarah swallowed the tears that clogged her throat. Damping down hurt and a burgeoning anger, she lifted her chin. If Nicholas did not wish to support her, so be it. Had she not always relied solely on herself? Perhaps 'twas only right. She'd gotten herself into this mess. She'd just have to get herself out of it.

Setting her head high, she made herself reenter the ballroom. And nearly bumped right into Sally Jersey.

Before Sarah could utter a word, Lady Jersey took her hand and tucked it under her arm. "Stroll with me a moment, Sarah darling. My, you do manage to get yourself talked about. Now, what's this I hear about a farm?"

Ignoring the queasiness in her stomach, Sarah raised an eyebrow. "Is something being said? If you'll tell me what you wish to know, your ladyship, I'll be happy to enlighten you. Though quite frankly," she added, trying to invest her voice with just the right note of boredom, "I can't credit you've any interest in a *farm.*"

Lady Jersey eyed her sharply. Sarah held her gaze, maintaining a look of faint hauteur. After a moment, her ladyship's lips twitched.

"Very good, my dear." She patted Sarah's arm. "Despite your denial to Lord John, the ton does possess some dreadful gossips. Yes, Mrs. Drummond Burrell was standing by the hallway, and heard all. You're quite right. That Weston boy is a swine."

A vibrating hum in Sarah's ears muffled the rest of her ladyship's speech, and she felt faint.

Mrs. Drummond Burrell witnessed the encounter! Praise heaven she'd not succumbed to the temptation of seconding Lord John's assessment of the ton. Had that haughty woman—perhaps the greatest of London's great hostesses—overheard it, by night's end, her name would have been cut from the invitation list of every person of social standing in London. She dared not even contemplate Nicholas's reaction to such a catastrophe.

"...thought I saw Nicky sneaking away," Lady Jersey was saying. "How like a man to hie off to his club, just when one most has need of him. Well, never you mind." She gave Sarah a conspiratorial smile. "I shall support you."

And she did. Lady Jersey made a determined stroll through the entire ballroom, chatting as they went with various of the highest-ranking, most socially prominent people present. Any lurking sniggers vanished as Sarah approached on the arm of the queen of society.

At last they reached the ballroom doorway. "I expect you're ready for refreshment, Lady Englemere," Silence said as she released Sarah's arm.

"Since her husband has already gone—no doubt seeking refreshment of a more intimate nature," remarked a voice beyond the doorway.

A mocking smile on his face, Lord John stepped into the room. He stopped short, his expression changing to dismay, and bowed hastily. "Ladies."

Lady Jersey's eyes flickered over Lord John without acknowledgment. "I dare swear, my dear Sarah, one is continually astonished by the low sort of person one encounters at these parties. Whatever can the Sheffingdons be thinking of? Perhaps I must cut the connection.

"Christopher, darling." Lady Jersey plucked the Earl of March from the gaping onlookers, "you simply must accompany Lady Englemere." She wrinkled her nose in the direction of the frozen Lord John. "'Tis suddenly so *close* in here."

The captured peer dutifully escorted Sarah and remained with her, chatting pleasantly over a glass of champagne. By the time they returned to the ballroom, Sarah could sense the change in the atmosphere. Cordiality reigned now.

Though all she wished to do was return home to await Nicholas and the explanation she vowed she would not sleep until she had delivered, Sarah remained at the ball. 'Twas best to firmly face down the rumors.

Why Sally Jersey had chosen to help her, Sarah couldn't imagine, but she could only be grateful. Catching the lady's eye across the crowded ballroom, she sent her a nod of silent thanks.

At last, feeling she'd aged two years in as many hours, Sarah departed for the blessed solitude of Stanhope House.

* * *

Sighing, Sarah dismissed Becky, found a book and ensconced herself in a chair beside her bed. 'Twas no telling at what hour Nicholas would return.

Was he in fact at his club—or enjoying "more intimate refreshment"? A pain shot through her.

She seemed unable to summon up the explanations she'd used before to dismiss the matter of Nicholas's mistress. She was simply too weary, she told herself. Opening the book, she settled in to wait, and forced from her mind the searing image of Mrs. Ingram in Nicholas's arms.

Chapter Twelve

A banging in the hallway startled her. She must have dozed off, for her book had slipped to the floor and the candle at her elbow guttered. Unsteady footsteps clomped past to the adjoining bedchamber.

She crept to the door and put her ear to it, listening until Nicholas dismissed his valet. Then she knocked.

Eyes closed, Nicholas lay back against his pillows. He blinked them open as she approached the bed.

"I'm sorry to disturb you, Nicholas, but I should have spoken much sooner, and don't wish to wait any longer."

He put a hand to his temple and groaned. From the pungency of the alcoholic odor emanating from him, she could well believe his head hurt. "I'm in no state for confessions now. Leave me to my bed."

Resentment boiled through her apprehension. If he'd not abandoned her, she'd have finished this task much earlier. "'Tis but a moment I would have. As I've not seen my bed tonight either, surely you can spare me that."

He glanced up then, albeit slowly, a calculating look in his bloodshot eyes. "No bed at all, sweet Sarah?"

"No. I knew you were angry with me, so after Clarissa brought me home, I waited up for you."

"Clarissa brought you?" His eyes opened wider. "And you've been waiting for me since? Alone?"

She wrinkled her brow. Whomever would she have waited up with? "Y-yes, I sent Becky to bed."

"I suppose your maid or the butler can attest to that?"

She tilted her head, exasperated. He didn't seem to be making any sense. Perhaps he was more castaway than she'd thought. "You may have Glendenning inventory the tallows I expended whilst reading, but—"

"No, no." With another groan, he hauled himself up onto the pillows and folded his arms across his chest. "You've courage, to brave the lion in his den. Proceed."

She took the chair beside the bed. Now that the moment had arrived, her stomach was doing more leaps than an unbroken colt put under his first saddle. "I wanted to apologize. I'm fully aware I've been the most miserable sort of wife. First Clarissa's rumor, and then to have forgotten your mama's ball! Anyway, before spending what is, after all, your money, I should have consulted you."

"You wanted to apologize about *money?*" he asked, his tone sardonic. "'Tis of little moment. Your allowance is yours, to do with—" he grimaced "—what you wish."

She stared at him, trying to gauge the depth of his displeasure. If only she could bring him to appreciate her goals, she might make him sympathize. "Oh, Nicholas, the money will bring such benefit to Wellingford! Surely you cannot begrudge the poor tenants that."

"Tenants?" He opened his eyes wide again. "Wellingford? What have they to do with this?"

"Did whoever told you the—the rumor not tell you about the seeds?"

"Seeds? Rumor? What the devil—?" Hand to his head, he sat up straight. "Sarah, are you trying to tell me you spent that allowance money on seeds?"

"You did not know? When I saw you in the card room looking so displeased, I was sure someone had told you."

His intent gaze devoured her. "You ran away before I could speak with you—because you thought I was angry?"

"Y-yes. I wanted to explain, but after I'd composed

myself, I couldn't find you. And then you left, so I...I waited up for you,'' she finished in a small voice.

He flopped back against the pillows, looking dazed. "You thought I was angry. About seeds."

"Well, there were also plows, and roofing thatch—''

As she spoke, a smile lit his face, then his lips twitched. Finally he threw back his head laughing.

Her words trailed off. She gazed at him first in wonder, then with growing resentment.

He seemed to be deriving great amusement from her expenditures, she thought grumpily. She was just about to retreat with injured dignity when he seized her, and laughing still, dragged her onto the bed.

"S-seeds," he stuttered between gasps. "Oh, Sarah, if you only knew what I thought—! God's blood, what an idiot I am!'' Fiercely he pulled her into an embrace so tight she could scarcely breathe.

All her disgruntlement dissolved as he clutched her to his warm chest. After the miserable evening she'd endured, the sound of his laughter and the feel of his strong arms were a precious gift.

Then a dismaying fact struck her. "But—if you didn't know how I spent the money, then you couldn't have heard—'' She drew away, consternation flooding her.

"Heard what?'' He kissed the tip of her nose.

"Oh, Nicholas,'' she whispered. She detested having to jeopardize the blessed sweetness of their reestablished rapport by telling him the rest, but he must know.

"You're going to be truly angry with me now. You see, Wexley found out I spent my allowance on estate needs, and thinking it vastly amusing, spread the story all over town. Some...wits have started calling me 'The Farmer Bride.'

"I've ignored them,'' she went on quickly, "and Lady Jersey was kind enough to stand by me, though I believe she more than half suspected 'twas true.'' She sighed. "Even so, I very much fear there will still be whispers.''

Unable to bear his scrutiny, she covered her face with her hands. "I'm so sorry, Nicholas. Rumor upon rumor! What a sorry bargain I've been as a wife."

"Hush, sweeting." Gently he pried her hands away and kissed them. "What matter to us what the gossips say?"

"I care what they say about your wife," she said in a low voice. "For once, I should like to be a source of pride rather than an embarrassment."

"I am proud of you. Did you not use your pin money to better the lot of some distant tenants? No other lady I know would have done so." He chuckled. "My farmer bride."

She shuddered.

His face sobered. "'Tis almost nothing you could do that would truly anger me, Sarah. You can't imagine the start you gave me when I saw you in that doorway looking so distressed. I followed you, searched everywhere, and when I couldn't find you I was...beside myself."

How like a man, to translate upset into anger, she thought, touched by his concern. "Clarissa cornered me in the withdrawing room begging help in repairing her torn lace. I'm so sorry you worried."

He took her hand and kissed it earnestly. "Promise me, Sarah, you'll never run from me again."

The image of her papa with his coin recurred. Should she confess the whole? Perhaps he might understand.

"You were in the game room, if you'll recall, flipping a guinea?" When he nodded, she continued. "The night Papa lost the rest of our capital, our dowries, everything, I found him staring out the library window, tossing a single coin. Oh, 'twas foolish, I know, but seeing you do that brought it all back. Gaming—frightens me so, Nicholas."

He looked at her gravely. "I'm not your papa, Sarah. I've worked too hard for my fortune to throw it away."

"But you like to gamble! You cannot continue to risk, and expect always to win."

"Yes, I enjoy gaming—specifically, games in which I

can calculate the odds and pit my expertise against that of other players. I do not play those that depend solely on chance. But you mustn't fear that enjoyment will land us on the parish. Though I tremble to confess something so unfashionable, I'm afraid most of our income comes from deplorably bourgeois business activities.''

''Business?'' she echoed.

She must have seemed incredulous, for he chuckled. ''Ah, yes, you're thinking of Englemere's Luck. Though I've never made any secret of my activities in the city, the ton seems to prefer perpetuating the image of me as a wildly successful gamester. 'Tis partly true—I did have a phenomenal run of luck when I first came to town. Fortunately, a friend of my father's advised me to put most of my winnings into investments. My dear, we currently own shares in shipping, coal, canal projects—we've even thrown a bit into Mr. Trevick's horseless carriage experiments.''

Her immediate surge of relief quickly faded. ''Shipping and canals and horseless carriages? But are not such investments even more risky than the tables?''

''True, there are losses. A cargo of East India spices here, a coal shipment there may founder. The trick is not to sink all your capital in any one venture. Those that do succeed usually bring a handsome profit.''

His face lit with enthusiasm. ''Assessing the potential value, weighing the probability of success, choosing which projects to fund and which to refuse—ah, that is even more fascinating than gaming.''

Sunken cargo here, lost shipments there? Sarah blanched. 'Twas only the thrill of risk-taking translated to a different environment. She could see the gambler's fever she so feared glowing in his eyes as he spoke.

His excitement faded as he gazed at her. ''You don't trust me, do you?'' he said at last.

He looked more hurt than affronted. She opened her

mouth, closed it, searching desperately for words that were softer than the truth and yet not a lie.

He sighed. "I suppose 'tis not remarkable, after what you and your family endured. Sarah, I would never gamble with our security."

"I know you will do what you feel is right." That, at least, she could say honestly.

He smiled, the warm light she so loved back in his eyes. "And what would you sink our capital into, little Puritan? Land, I suppose?"

"'Tis ever there, Nicholas," she said fervently. "No flip of the dice or shipwreck can make it disappear."

"But land lying fallow earns nothing. You must harvest salable crops. How many years has the corn or wheat failed? All life is a risk, Sarah, none more so than farming."

She yearned to dispute that, but memories of the lean times came back all too vividly. "True, land may not always be profitable. But still it remains, with its potential for next year and the year after. Land remains to pass on to your children and grandchildren."

He laughed shortly. "My father passed all the Stanhope lands to me. And almost nothing in cash, having ever put his money back into his properties. After his death, when the price of grain plummeted, I could barely keep the household in coal and tallows." He shook his head. "That's a position *I* never wish to be in again."

She couldn't dispute that either. The image of wealthy, successful Nicholas in want of anything was so novel she could hardly credit it.

He grinned at her. "We shall make a bargain. I will teach you about investments, and you can instruct me in farm management. Deal?"

She winced. Even now, he used gambler's terms. "I shall try, Nicholas. It's just—oh, you cannot imagine what 'tis like to suddenly have your familiar world, your very

future, collapse in the space of an instant into unsalvage-
able ruin!''

"Can I not?" he said, an odd note in his voice. A
strange, bleak expression crossed his face before he took
her hand. "Sarah, I will never risk our children's inheritance. Can you trust that?"

'Twas an honorable bargain. "As you have trusted me.
I shall do better, Nicholas! I shall apply myself to all my
duties, be a model wife and never embarrass you again.''

"And so shall I do better, Sarah, I swear it. Now, about
those 'duties,''' he murmured, his fingers going to the sash
of her dressing gown. "You can begin right now.''

Three weeks later, Nicholas sat with Hal at White's,
sharing a convivial bottle of brandy after dinner.

"Excellent meal, Hal. Thank you.''

Hal nodded. "Pleased to host you. Don't see you here
much. Married, an' all.''

"Married indeed," Nicholas said with a sigh and
drained his glass. "I'm off to fetch Sarah for a party. Not
that I can complain—I should have dined with her at the
Dowager Duchess of Arundel's first.''

Hal shuddered. "Good you shied off. Dreadful
woman.''

"Sarah got me out of it, actually." He smiled wryly.
"Another of her courtesies.''

At Hal's baffled look, he continued, "First it was the
rumor about our star-crossed love, and then that silliness
over the 'Farmer Bride.' Was Sarah upset over that!''

"You miffed about it, Nicky?''

"Devil a bit." Nicholas laughed. "Sarah's much more
concerned about my consequence than I am." His humor
faded. "So much so, she's throwing all her energies into
being the perfect marchioness, the perfect chatelaine of my
household and the perfect wife. To make it up to me for
the rumors, she said." He groaned. "I'm being 'perfected'
to death.''

"Fretting you to flinders, eh?"

Unable to resist the temptation of unburdening himself, Nicholas poured another glass and eased back in his chair.

"You don't know the half of it. Take this function to-night. I doubt I'll manage half a dozen words with Sarah. She'll be too busy chatting up every dowager and dragon in the place—doing her 'duty' as a marchioness, you see."

Hal blinked. "It is?"

Nicholas sighed again. "I suppose. Mama does it, but then damn it, she's a dowager herself. I suspect she detests it—Sarah, I mean—but she still keeps on, function after function. I can scarcely drag her away for a waltz."

Hal gave an understanding nod. "Makes her testy."

"No, it isn't that. She does it cheerfully enough, and when I ask if she's enjoying herself, she assures me she is, now that the Farmer Bride business has blown over. Thanks to Sally Jersey, which—" he paused for a sip "—about evens the score with Sal for inviting Chloe to her ball."

Hal chuckled. "Manages doxies, too."

"Sally? She can't resist the urge to manage everyone."

"No, Sarah. At the Jerseys' ball. Heard her."

"She talked with Chloe at the ball?" Nicholas gasped.

"Not with the doxy. Weston." Hal chuckled again.

Exasperated, Nicholas nearly snapped at him. Willing himself patience, he tried to decode that cryptic utterance.

And gave up. "You mean Lord John Weston? What has he to do with this?"

Hal recovered from his mirth. "Bounder. Saw Mrs. Ingram enter. Went over to Sarah. Asked her how she liked being married to a chap with so beautiful a mistress."

"He *what!*" Nicholas exploded. "I'll wring his neck, the bloody bastard!" Suddenly he remembered Sandiford's warning—that Weston was Sir James's tool. Hadn't Sally also told him the man was responsible for that "Farmer Bride" epithet as well?

"Cool as you please, though. Sarah. Married handsomest and most accomplished man in London, she says. 'Course he has the most beautiful mistress.''

Nicholas's jaw dropped. Not a word had Sarah mentioned to him of the incident, or uttered a hint of reproach.

'Twas the response of a true lady of breeding, and more. 'Twas a clever deflection of someone's intent to wound. Anger stirred—and regret. He'd not considered others of malicious mind could use his liaison with Chloe to hurt Sarah. He really should end the relationship.

''She's the best of good wives, 'tis certain. I just wish she wouldn't overdo it.''

''Overdo?'' Hal looked puzzled.

''For instance, I said 'twould be nice to have macaroons with tea. Next day, the biscuit box was full of 'em. And every day since. If I see another macaroon, I'll puke.''

''Invite me to tea. Like macaroons.''

''Try this. I babbled something about Baines bringing me the wrong boots. She made the man take my wardrobe apart and reorganize everything in it. He sulked for a week.''

Hal frowned. ''Shouldn't truck with one's man.''

''Quite right,'' Nicholas agreed with feeling. ''I tell you, Hal, I'm in a quake every time I return home, worrying that she's seized on some chance remark and turned the house upside down. I swear, were I to express an interest in squid for breakfast, there'd be a damned rasher of 'em next to the bacon come morning.''

''Couldn't. Come from—'' Hal knit his brow ''—some foreign place. Impossible.''

''You underestimate Sarah. Did I breathe the word, I bet you a monkey I'd find them on the sideboard within a week.''

''You're on.''

''Well—'' Nicholas sputtered ''—I didn't actually—''

''What's this, a wager?''

At the vaguely familiar voice, Nicholas looked over his

shoulder. Lord John Weston lounged behind him, smiling. "Waiter, bring the book."

"Just a minute!" His grievances against the man sparked him from exasperation to anger in a heartbeat.

"Yes, bring the book." Hal motioned to the servant. "Sarah's a game 'un, but nobody'd do that. Saw 'em once—nasty things." He shuddered. "Got eyes on little sticks."

"Hal, I didn't really mean—"

Weston's loud halloo drowned out Nicholas's protest. "I say, gentlemen. A wager!"

Nicholas watched in consternation as, in a babble of voices, half a dozen club members ambled over.

"What's the bet?"

"I'll back Englemere, whatever the odds."

Nicholas cast Lord John a fulminating glance. Had the bastard been eavesdropping? 'Twas the worst of bad ton to make his own wife the subject of a vulgar bet—a recorded bet at White's, no less. But trying to explain to Hal, never nimble-witted, in the midst of this attentive crowd that he never intended to make a wager, would probably cause more gossip than letting it stand.

Damn Weston for trapping him like this—and his master, Findlay. Reluctantly Nicholas watched Hal scrawl a note.

"Squid by Friday, eh? Monkey says you're wrong."

"A monkey, then," he mumbled. It might be interesting to see if Sarah would really go that far. At least he'd have reason for once to anticipate with amusement rather than dread the results of a casual remark. And yet...

Hadn't he done Sarah enough disservice already? Hating himself, but driven to do so, after her midnight confession he'd made some casual inquiries at the club and verified Captain Sandiford's departure from the Sheffingdon rout immediately after his dance with Sarah. Having confirmed that, in a euphoria of relief—tinged with shame—he'd vowed to banish for good his ignoble, unworthy suspicions.

Sarah had been all that was honest and honorable. He owed her no less in return. After this, he swore with a dagger glance at Weston, he'd be on his guard.

The image of squid in a cooking pot, though, set him grinning. "Faith," he said with a chuckle. "Cook'll have palpitations."

A week later bedecked in a dressing gown, Sarah sat at her dressing table in the pale dawn light, the large cask containing the Stanhope jewels before her. Nicholas's mama had brought them, insisting rightly enough they were now Sarah's. She should choose something to match her gown for the presentation ball tonight.

Fumbling in her own small cask for the key to the larger one, she came upon Sinjin's signet ring.

Her chest constricting, she stared at it. She'd not worn it since the day she accepted Nicholas's offer. She should have returned it the morning Sinjin called, but in her agitation had forgotten.

As she lifted the heavy gold ring, its shiny surface caught and reflected an arc of morning sunlight. Suddenly she saw in the flash an ardent young man, his blue eyes blazing as he pressed the ring into her hand. Should she ever need him, he vowed, she need only send this, and he would move heaven and earth to come to her.

Tears stung her eyes and a great lump filled her throat. He came to see her often now—too often. Calling during regular hours, dancing with her at various functions, he'd adopted a teasing, elder-brother manner.

She still could not encounter him without pain, but the ache was dulling. Perhaps, given time, she could learn to consider him just a dear and valued friend. In another fifty or sixty years.

After each meeting with Sinjin, she seemed impelled to seek out Nicholas. Somehow, her husband's touch soothed the ache and made her feel—safe. Safe from Sinjin, or herself, was a question she didn't wish to examine.

If only she dared throw her heart, as well as her energies, into being Nicholas's wife, she might bury forever her lingering grief over Sinjin.

'Twas too risky a solution. She sighed heavily. Nicholas would support her, come what may, that she knew. But he would never, as Sinjin had sworn to do, ride *ventre à terre* to her rescue, words of love on his lips.

A breeze stirred the curtains, bringing with it a whiff of fresh green grass. The crops would be up at Wellingford. She felt a wave of homesickness.

Perhaps, after his mother's ball, she'd ask Nicholas's leave to go home. With a tremor of joy, she put her hand on her abdomen. She was certain now that Nicholas's nightly visits were no longer strictly necessary.

A pang marred her happiness. Once she broke the news, Nicholas would probably be more than willing to send her into the country. She closed her eyes to the image of a gloating Chloe Ingram.

Enough moping, she told herself, and rang for Becky. She'd make up a packet and mail the ring back this very day. Nicholas should be down for breakfast soon, and she had a little surprise for him this morning.

Nicholas smiled at Sarah as he entered the breakfast room. Attired in a gown of pale yellow, she looked like sunshine itself.

"You're up early, sweeting," he said as he dropped a kiss on her forehead. "I thought you'd be still abed, so fatigued were you last night. Have you recovered?"

"Quite. I've been up an age, and as you can see, was too famished to wait. Do help yourself, Nicholas."

She stopped eating and seemed to be watching with unusual intensity as he served himself eggs, bacon and toast. "Mama says you've been a great—what the devil?"

From under the lid he'd just raised wafted a hot breath with the distinct odor of tidal swamp.

"'Tis the squid you asked for. I hope Cook prepared them the way you like."

To tell the truth, he'd forgotten all about the wager. He eased the covered dish open cautiously, releasing another cloud of foul-smelling air. In the warmed dish, a congealed eye stared up at him. He felt last night's brandy rising.

"Good Lord!" he uttered with revulsion. Quickly he slammed the lid shut, vaguely noting a footman snicker. The stuff was every bit as repulsive as Hal had predicted. "James, take that—creature away!"

"But Nicholas, I thought—" Her anxious eyes on his face, Sarah bit back her reply.

Despite the closed lid, another pungent draft reached his nose, and he nearly gagged. "*Now,* James!"

"Yes, my lord," the footman said with trembling lips. As he hefted the chafing dish, he looked into Nicholas's revolted face, and a laugh escaped him.

Sarah stiffened. A rosy flush bloomed on her cheeks.

Glendenning cleared his throat and frowned at the footman, who converted his mirth to an unconvincing cough.

"The kitchen, James," Glendenning intoned with a curt nod toward the door. "Tea, my lord?"

Nicholas angled a glance at Sarah, but she was staring toward the open doorway through which the footman was now hastily removing himself. He followed her gaze.

To his consternation, milling about in the hallway were half a dozen footmen, maids and even a stable boy. Hell and damnation, he cursed under his breath.

Glendenning strode over and slammed the door. Sarah focused her gaze on her plate.

From behind the closed door, Nicholas could hear a babble of raised voices and the rumble of laughter. Sarah's flush deepened to brick.

Glendenning brought the teapot. As he poured, some of

the liquid spurted over the china rim onto Nicholas's wrist. With an oath, Nicholas jerked his hand away.

"Forgive me, my lord," Glendenning said in frigid accents. He gave Nicholas a totally unrepentant look before the usual mask descended on his features.

Staring straight ahead, Sarah took a sip from her cup. Nicholas might have been able to convince himself she was unaffected by the incident, were it not for the vivid color that still painted her cheeks, her ears—even her neck.

Guilt washed over him. He opened his lips to apologize, but the thought of confessing, before the obviously disapproving Glendenning, a wager that appeared more illjudged and sophomoric by the minute was too daunting. He gulped tea instead, and scalded his tongue.

"That will be all, thank you, Glendenning," Sarah said. She took another precise sip.

The moment the butler closed the hall door, Sarah threw down her napkin. She was halfway to the French doors leading to the garden when Nicholas reached her.

"Sarah, I'm sorry!" he cried, catching her hand. "'Twas naught but a foolish wager. I'd told Hal you catered to my every whim, would even feed me squid for breakfast, did I but ask for it, and he couldn't believe—"

"Nor can I believe it. 'Tis true ours was not a love match, my lord, but never did I think to have you make a—a *May game* of me in front of the servants!"

Ripping her hand free, she sped to the door, wrenched it open and fled into the garden.

His mouth still open, Nicholas watched her go. After a moment, he slowly walked back and reseated himself. He sipped his tea. It was tepid now.

Feeling like the lowest beast in nature, he pushed his equally cold eggs around on his plate. He could, he supposed, ring for Glendenning to bring warm ones. Although, he thought with a gallows grin, he'd not be at all surprised should the dour butler report back, with suitable effusions of regret, that there were no more eggs to be had. He might even bring back the squid.

With a sigh, Nicholas went out to the garden. If he didn't find Sarah now, he'd probably not have another private moment with her until late evening. He didn't want to give her that long to brood over his boorish behavior.

Though ill-judged, at the time Hal proposed it the wager had seemed harmless enough. He hadn't considered the effort Sarah would have had to put forth to produce the blasted creatures, or envisioned so large and interested an audience gathered for their delivery. *In truth,* he told himself acidly, *you didn't think at all.*

As exasperated as he'd sometimes become with her these past few weeks, never would he wish to hurt or embarrass her. Without question he had just done both.

Calling himself names under his breath, he spotted Sarah on a bench facing away from him, and stopped short. From the set of her bent head and her shaking shoulders, he realized she was weeping.

"Hell and damnation," he muttered, feeling worse yet. Uncertain whether to apologize at once, or wait till she was calmer, he hesitated. Then he noticed a flicker of light.

She held something in one hand, something small and shiny that she was rubbing over and over like a talisman. He stepped closer—and saw the object she clutched so tightly was a man's gold signet ring.

Nicholas froze. The ring might be her father's, though he doubted it. 'Twas not his, certainly. He could imagine but one other owner.

Sarah hadn't heard his approach, for her posture didn't alter. As Nicholas silently backed toward the house, she sat weeping softly, her thumb rubbing Sandiford's ring.

Chapter Thirteen

Vacillating between outrage and chagrin, Nicholas repaired to the library. After a short glass of brandy and a lengthy bit of self-examination, he mastered the former.

Sarah must have had the signet a long time. Upon reflection, he dismissed his first angry suspicion that the captain had given it to her during their recent interview, as a pledge of future intent. As he had reason to know, she'd not had the ring on her person immediately after.

She should have returned it long since, but so intimate an item must be given back privately. She could hardly hand it over at a ball or in a crowded morning room.

Why had she been clutching Sandiford's ring? His lips twisted in self-mockery. After that humiliation in the breakfast room, even a boorish, insensitive fool like himself could understand she might wish for comfort.

And what could be more comforting than an object that reminded her of the gallant young man who—he gritted his teeth—*loved* her, who had no doubt pressed his token upon her with vows of undying affection? Unlike the husband who groused to Hal of her solicitude, made her the object of a vulgar bet and exposed her to the ridicule of the staff.

"Will your lordship require luncheon?" Glendenning interrupted.

"Will her ladyship be taking some?"

"Her ladyship has gone out."

Disappointed, but hardly surprised, he cast an eye at the butler. Disapproval positively radiated from him.

"Something simple might be prepared, though Cook did take to her bed when the s-squid," he choked out the word, "was sent back untouched. For the second time today, I must inform you, the first being after she vowed such a nasty foreign creature would never see the inside of her cooking pot. However, the mistress soothed her with a posset. And the boy who washed the pot, the maid who bought the—"

"Enough, Glendenning." Nicholas got the clear if tortuously delivered message that the inconvenience caused below stairs had been laid by the staff squarely at his door.

With the persistence of one who'd served his master since he was in short coats, Glendenning seemed determined that Nicholas not miss the point. "The mistress is held in the utmost respect and esteem by the entire staff."

Nicholas essayed a deprecating smile. "Which is to say, I should expect cold tea and burnt mutton?"

"Certainly not, my lord. One has standards. However—" he unbent at last "—'twas not well done, Master Nicky."

"No," Nicholas agreed with a sigh. "I fear I'm in the basket now."

"'Tis not my place to say so," Glendenning intoned and bowed himself out.

Formulating elaborate and heartfelt speeches of regret, Nicholas whiled away the hours until teatime. Every afternoon Sarah prepared his tea—and presented a blasted macaroon along with it. However, although his tea arrived hot as promised, Sarah did not return to share it.

For her to neglect performing that ritual, she must be even angrier than he feared. Munching his tasteless plain biscuits, Nicholas racked his brain for a gift lavish enough to convey his deep contrition. He was about to call for his curricle to go buy the largest diamond Rundell and Bridges possessed when a better idea occurred.

Sarah wore little jewelry—he suppressed a pang at that reminder of a certain signet ring—and showed no interest in useless gewgaws. Indeed, she'd stripped her allowance to send supplies to Wellingford. What better gift than to set up a fund she might use to restore her beloved estate? With luck, he could have the monies transferred and be back in time to catch Sarah alone before dinner.

Several hours later, Nicholas waited in the hallway for Sarah. She was "resting," Becky had informed him frostily when he returned from the bankers, and could not be disturbed. Since his only opportunity to apologize before the ball would be to waylay her before she came downstairs for dinner, he'd dressed hurriedly and now lurked about like a guilty schoolboy anxious to make amends for a stupid prank. Which, he sighed, was not far wrong.

At last Sarah emerged, a thin shawl of spangled gauze across her shoulders. Her simple gown of gold-frosted emerald silk clung to her curves and glittered as she moved, reflecting the light much more provocatively than the fine Stanhope emeralds at her neck and ears.

Tonight his family would present her to the ton as his bride. She looked magnificent, he thought with pride.

"Good evening, sweet Sarah."

"Nicholas!" she gasped. "You—startled me."

He let his appreciative gaze travel over her figure. "No one will have eyes for any other lady tonight."

To his surprise, she frowned. "The bodice is too low, just as I feared. I shall change immediately."

"No, the gown is lovely! Truly, Sarah." He caught her arm. "You've no need to change."

She stiffened at his touch and glanced up warily, as if she expected he might bite. "Are you sure?"

The open, trusting look he'd grown accustomed to had

vanished totally. He felt an almost physical ache. "You look stunning. I'll be the proudest man in London tonight."

Raising a skeptical eyebrow, she put her hand lightly, almost reluctantly on his arm. "Shall we go down, then?"

She took a step. Nicholas stood motionless, perforce halting her. "I came earlier to apologize, but Becky absolutely refused to let me in. I am sorry, Sarah, terribly sorry. I should never have played such a stupid, ill-judged trick. I expect you'd gone to a deal of trouble, and you have every right to be angry."

"I'm not angry," she replied, "not anymore. I suspect I've been…smothering you with my attentions. I don't have enough to keep me busy." She offered a small, polite smile. "I must confess, I did wish you'd chosen to bring the matter to my attention in a less, ah, dramatic manner."

Nicholas wished she'd rip up at him, call him a cad—she could scarce come up with a name he'd not already applied to himself. Anything but this distant wariness.

Had he only yesterday thought how nice 'twould be to distance himself from his oversolicitous wife? Well, Sarah had withdrawn from him, quite definitely. And he hated it.

As he fumbled for an apology abject enough to thaw the chilly caution in her eyes, his mother arrived. "How lovely you look, Sarah! Is she not beautiful, Nicky?"

"So I've just been telling her, Mama," he replied, trying to keep the frustration from his voice.

Setting the cap on his disgruntlement, Sarah turned to her mother-in-law with a smile of genuine warmth. "Not half so fine as you, Lady Englemere."

"Stuff and nonsense," his mother said, linking her arm with Sarah's. "Shall we go dazzle our guests?"

'Twas nothing for it but to offer an arm to each lady. Near fuming with frustration, Nicholas escorted them down.

Would the dratted ball never end? Nicholas thought as the night dragged on. As usual, he'd exchanged a bare handful of words with Sarah. After they'd been released from the receiving line, so assiduous had his mother been in taking Sarah round to chat with their many honored guests, he'd managed to nab her for only one dance. Since that had been the opening cotillion conducted under the attentive gaze of several hundred people, it had hardly offered him a chance for any private remark.

Perhaps he could steal her away now. He walked toward the head of the stairs where he'd glimpsed his mama greeting some late arrivals. The full figure and sinuous carriage of the lady now ascending those stairs caught his eye, and his heart nearly stopped.

Appropriately dressed in scarlet, the rubies he'd once given her flashing on her bosom, came Chloe Ingram. His horrified gaze expanded to include an all-too-familiar hussar on whose arm Chloe hung. What the devil did she mean coming here? Had Sandiford brought her?

Speechless with outrage, Nicholas stood frozen. He thawed quickly as his mother threw him a look of furious reproach. Mystified and seething, he hurried to her.

"So kind of you to include me, Lady Englemere," Chloe was saying. She turned to Nicholas, her eyes glowing. "My lord, I can't tell you how happy I was to be invited."

His mother looked at him accusingly. Wishing the floor would swallow him up, Nicholas prayed Sarah was in the refreshment room. While his mother murmured something polite to Chloe, Nicholas leaned to the captain.

"Did you bring her?" he said in a furious undertone.

"Me?" Sandiford lifted an eyebrow. "Certainly not. I came in while she was handing her invitation to the butler and she latched on my arm like a barnacle."

Chloe had an invitation, then. How in heaven had she gotten it? Never in this life would his mother have sent one. While he racked his brain, Chloe sent him a smoky, intimate glance, ending it with a pantomimed kiss.

Nicholas felt ill. There was no question what interpretation Chloe had applied to his bidding her, so she thought, to his wife's presentation ball. Save Sandiford, who'd just disclaimed with unfeigned disgust he'd had no hand in it, who could detest him—or Sarah—that much?

Even as he asked it, he knew the answer. How Findlay had gotten Weston to manage it, Nicholas had no idea, but this had to be his handiwork.

Never would Nicholas have believed himself capable of uttering the next words out of his mouth, but gritting his teeth, he managed it. "Would you watch Sarah for me while I get rid of—her?" he asked the captain under his breath.

His face contemptuous, the captain's chill blue eyes held Nicholas's impassioned green ones.

"I tell you, I had nothing to do with this!"

"Nothing?" The captain's glance traveled to the magnificent ruby necklace nestled between Chloe's breasts. "Oh, I daresay you had something to do with it. But for Sarah's sake, I'll do as you ask."

Nicholas didn't waste time arguing. "She may be in the refreshment room. Give me fifteen minutes."

Nodding, the captain took himself off. Nicholas groaned, thinking of Sally Jersey and her Almack patroness friends waltzing just beyond the open doorway. *Pray God I get her out of here before anyone else sees her.*

Dropping a fulsome compliment, he took his mistress's gloved hand off his mother's affronted sleeve and began walking her downstairs.

"Where are you taking me, Nicky?" she asked, her face still lit with triumph and pleasure. "Oh, you naughty thing. Not at your own ball, surely!"

"How did you come to be here, Chloe?"

"Why, I received an invitation, and knew immediately what you intended. How sweet of you to make so public a gesture, if a bit—indiscreet?'' She gave him an arch look.

They reached the bottom of the staircase. ''Summon Mrs. Ingram's carriage,'' Nicholas told Glendenning curtly.

Chloe's warmth cooled as she looked up at Nicholas's unsmiling face. ''Nicholas?''

''Chloe, I regret treating you with such brusqueness, but we're both the victims of a particularly vicious practical joke. You must realize the last thing my mother—or I— would do would be invite you to my wife's ball.''

Understanding dawned in the luminous dark eyes. ''I take it that my presence is, shall we say, *de trop?*''

Nicholas nodded grimly. ''I appreciate your understanding about this, Chloe.''

''Oh, certainly. You'll find I can be wonderfully *understanding*. My friends were so surprised when I got the card. Whatever shall I tell them?''

Nicholas shot a glance down. Some strong emotion stormed across her face, but the smile that followed it was sweet—altogether too sweet. ''I'll not forget this, Nicky.''

A rigidly disapproving Glendenning handed Nicholas her cloak. Before he could drape it about her, Chloe stayed his hand. ''Am I permitted to use the retiring room? Or must you have me ejected immediately?''

Nearly gnashing his teeth with impatience to spirit her away, Nicholas could hardly deny that request. He made himself smile. ''Down the hallway, to your left.''

An angry glitter in her eyes, she walked off. Chloe might be furious, but Nicholas had few thoughts to spare for that. 'Twould be nothing to the uproar in the ton should someone see her here. Nicholas paced as he waited, the loud ticking of the tall case clock in the entry sounding like a warning of approaching doom.

After what seemed an age, during which Nicholas kept throwing anxious glances from the front door to the stairway to the landing, Chloe finally reappeared. Strangely, her spirits seemed much revived.

"Thank you, Chloe," he said, relieved she'd not treated him to a full-scale scene in front of Glendenning and the attendant footmen. "I'll not forget your consideration."

She laughed. "Oh, I daresay you shall not."

Her humor fading, she wrenched her shoulder from under his hand. Glendenning already held the door open. Without further goodbye, she raised her chin and walked out.

Nicholas hastened up the stairs. He encountered the captain, minus Sarah, coming out of the refreshment room.

"I kept her as long as I could. Insisted then she must check the kitchens." He frowned. "She's worn to the nub, and ought to retire."

Despite his gratitude, Nicholas stiffened at the implied criticism. "Thank you, Captain, for your *concern.*"

Just then Sarah appeared. She did indeed look so pale Nicholas felt a wave of anxiety—followed immediately by panic. Had someone seen Chloe after all, and told her?

Forgetting the captain, he went to her. "Sweeting, you look tired. I daresay some guests will stay till dawn, but there's no need for you to do so. Shall I take you up?"

To his immense relief, he could detect nothing more alarming in the smile with which she greeted him than fatigue. "Should I not remain?"

"Mama will say whatever is necessary."

Sarah made no further protest. "I have been rather fatigued this hour and more," she admitted. "If 'twould be no discourtesy, I should like to go up."

"I'll escort you, then, and inform Mama when I return."

She nodded. "Good night, Sinjin," she called over his shoulder. "Thank you for coming to the ball."

"Good night, Sarah. Rest well." Sandiford bowed to her and, after a brief accusing look, to Nicholas. With a fervent prayer of thanks for letting him escape so disastrous a situation unscathed, Nicholas led her upstairs.

* * *

Becky had readied her for bed, tucked her up and snuffed the candle, but despite her very real fatigue Sarah lay sleepless against the pillows.

She would make preparations to leave for Wellingford tomorrow. She simply must get away.

Sarah stared into the fire's glowing embers. She was still humiliated and furious over the squid incident, deeply hurt that Nicholas would repay her honest efforts so shabbily. And the manner of it! After she had bared her soul to him, gathered up her courage to reveal how deeply gaming distressed her, he had gone right off and made her, his own wife, the object of a wager.

The very thought of it still made her so angry she could scarcely breathe. He had not understood—he would never understand the lack of responsibility, the reckless toying with disaster that gambling represented to her.

And yet he could also be so kind. So thoughtfully attentive and considerate, she'd been completely unprepared for casual cruelty. She'd deluded herself into believing she was being wary, when in truth she'd been much too trusting—in too many ways.

As she discovered this evening after visiting the kitchens. Having ensured all was in train for the midnight supper, she stopped at the ladies' retiring room—and literally bumped into Chloe Ingram.

Chapter Fourteen

For a moment she was too astonished to say a word. Oh, Mrs. Ingram had been all that was polite. She complimented Sarah's gown and expressed her appreciation at being invited. As if Sarah had included her.

Only Nicholas could have done so. The full import of that invitation was just now dawning on her weary mind. That Nicholas had bade his mistress be present could only mean he was continuing their liaison. More than that—he was virtually trumpeting that fact to the ton.

Perhaps someone was competing with him for the favors of the beauteous Mrs. Ingram. Whatever his purpose, the lady herself made her own intentions perfectly clear.

"Of course, I expected your ball to be lavish and your gown lovely," she said after her pretty compliments. "Nicky is ever generous." And she smiled sweetly, lowered her glance and patted the magnificent rubies at her breast.

Though the woman insinuated nothing she did not already know, Sarah had been cut to the quick by that deliberate reminder of her husband's regard for another. And furious.

With the regrettable impetuosity she had thought long since mastered, she shot back, "Generous indeed, Mrs.

Ingram. Only remember, when all you have of Nicholas are those rubies to recall him by, I shall have his son.''

She swept out of the room, regretting as soon as they were uttered words as uncharitable as Mrs. Ingram's gesture. And as true. She must quit London.

Wellingford's rolling meadows and tranquil woods beckoned to her. Yes, she'd go to Wellingford tomorrow.

Too restless to sleep, she jumped up and paced to her desk. She would start her packing lists immediately.

She was drawing out pen and paper when the door opened. Nicholas stepped in and halted abruptly.

''Sarah, what are you doing up? I thought you asleep long since. I was just about to retire myself.''

How could I go peacefully to sleep after all you've done today? she wanted to shout. Aghast she'd nearly cried the words aloud, she bit her tongue and thanked the dim light that hid her flushing cheeks.

''Now that my presentation's complete, your mama will be returning to Stanhope Hall. I thought to visit Wellingford. The prospect was so exciting, I couldn't sleep.''

''You'll want to check on the improvements you ordered, I expect. And see about that—what was it, rapeseed?''

''Yes, I will.'' His immediate acquiescence shouldn't have hurt, but it did. Fool, she told herself crossly. Had she expected him to urge her to linger? Once his officially presented *wife* left town, he could take back up with his officially presented *mistress*.

''I'm pleased you were thinking of Wellingford, for I have a surprise for you that concerns it.''

She must have looked alarmed, for Nicholas winced. ''Don't distress yourself, Sarah. I'm reasonably certain this surprise you shall like.''

He cleared his throat. ''After my inexcusable behavior today, I wanted to express my heartfelt regret for upsetting you. I considered jewelry, but then I decided a fund for Wellingford would please you more. So I've set up an initial account of five thousand pounds, in your name only. You may draw on it when you wish, as you wish.''

Sarah sat stunned. Then she recalled Mrs. Ingram's sly words, and a pain twisted in her heart.

"I hardly know what to say. 'Tis wondrous generous.'' She managed a slight smile. "The affront was hardly that great, my lord.''

"The affront cannot be measured, sweeting. You were only trying to please me, and I callously threw your efforts in your teeth. If that weren't bad enough, 'twas in the form of a wager, something you could not help but despise.''

The hard edge of her anger softened. Perhaps Nicholas did have some inkling of what his actions had meant to her.

"I know I can't buy your goodwill, Sarah, but I should earnestly like to have it.'' He took her hand and kissed it. "Can you forgive me? I promise you, I shall do my utmost never to treat you so shabbily again.''

Whether he understood fully or not, he did realize he'd hurt her—and how. He was offering a handsome and un-questionably sincere apology. She should accept it in like spirit.

What of Mrs. Ingram? her heart whispered. She stifled the thought. When she accepted Nicholas, she had ac-cepted Mrs. Ingram as well. 'Twould be dishonorable to go back on her bargain now, no matter how difficult she found the keeping of it. "Of course I forgive you.''

He searched her face so intently she had to look away, then sighed. "Your lips speak of forgiveness, but your eyes tell me no. I shall have to be at my most charming during our country sojourn if I hope to win back your regard.''

"Our? But you cannot mean to come with me!''

"Of course I shall come. As it happens, I have a minor holding not too distant from Wellingford. It's been under a cousin's management, and I've not checked on it in a great while. You can start on my lessons in estate management.''

Sarah was flabbergasted. Why would Nicholas wish to leave London, when he might take advantage of her absence to dally with Mrs. Ingram?

"You needn't escort me, Nicholas. I'll have Becky."

"Besides, you've told me so much of Wellingford, I'm quite anxious to see it."

Ah, he wished to discover if his money had been wisely spent. "The improvements I've ordered are necessary and well worth the expense. There's no need for you to inspect Wellingford personally."

"I'm sure you've done as you ought. I should enjoy seeing Wellingford, though, and visiting your family again."

He was being remarkably persistent, Sarah thought with exasperation. "I'm afraid the way I've described Wellingford—the way it lives in my imagining—and its current state have little in common. I'd rather show it to you after it has been restored. Besides, my stay might be rather extended, and you cannot wish to be gone long."

"But if you go, sweeting—" he lifted her hand to kiss her palm "—then of course I must be with you."

Ah, that. A bittersweet pain spiraled through her. Well, she could allay that concern. "You needn't trouble yourself," she said softly. "'Tis quite fitting that you stay in London whilst I repair to the country. Is that not where breeding wives are supposed to go?"

"Only wives who enjoy—" His teasing smile faded. "What did you say?"

"I said, breeding wives are supposed to—"

He seized her in a hug. "Sarah! Are you sure?"

She nodded, feeling suddenly shy. "Yes, I'm quite certain now. I hope you're pleased."

"Pleased? 'Tis wonderful news! Mama will be thrilled." His excitement ended abruptly. "But should you travel at such a time? Should you not remain and rest?"

Sarah laughed. "Nicholas, I'm breeding, not dying. 'Tis no reason I cannot travel or pursue any of my usual activities. Surely I will rest better in the country. So," she added soberly, "'tis no reason for you to accompany me."

Surely he understood her innuendo. Sarah held her breath, waiting for him to realize the truth of it, to cheerfully acquiesce and send her away.

"Sarah," he said quietly at last, "have I so offended you that you no longer wish my company?"

"No, Nicholas, 'tis not that at all! You prefer London. I'd not have you drag yourself away out of kindness and a sense of duty."

"'Tis not kindness or duty. Unless you truly find my escort repugnant, I wish to accompany you. So as not to burden the staff at Wellingford, we can stay at Stoneacres. Do say you'll let me come, Sarah."

"L-let you—!" She sputtered. "As if you needed my permission to visit your own estate. You truly wish to accompany me?" she asked, completely baffled.

Nicholas kissed her. "I truly do. But I've had to so coerce and cajole you into accepting my escort I'm certain you've not really forgiven me."

He was right—but she must make herself. "You're wrong, Nicholas," she said firmly. "I have forgiven you."

"Prove it, then," he murmured, and bent to trace his lips down the column of her neck.

"This isn't—necessary—any longer." She gasped, trying to stay coherent despite the flood of tingling warmth his kiss evoked. "You've already—done—your duty."

"Have I?" he whispered, his fingers at the laces of her nightrail. "Then let us take our pleasure."

A few days later they arrived at Stoneacres, the small estate Nicholas had inherited from his grandmother. True to his word, Nicholas accompanied her—not only accompanied her, but was at every stage so thoughtful and attentive that her remaining anger dissolved.

'Twas most difficult, she thought as Nicholas handed her carefully out of the carriage, to maintain a prudent distance from her handsome husband when he persisted in being so undeniably charming—and so irresistibly near.

Nicholas's cousin and manager, Hugh Baxter, along with the complete staff, came out to welcome them.

The neatness and comfort of the snug manor house impressed Sarah. Indeed, she was somewhat surprised to find the furnishings in the first style of elegance and the master's suite, which Mr. Baxter insisted on giving over to them, equipped with every modern convenience.

But upon closer inspection of that gentleman when they met again for tea, she was less surprised. Mr. Baxter was quite the dandy, she realized. His waistcoat of heavily embroidered gold silk, and the elaborate arrangement of his neckcloth and carefully pomaded locks, would have pleased the most meticulous Bond Street beau.

"Stoneacres looks to be most prosperous, sir."

Mr. Baxter shrugged. "I suppose. I'm not much interested in farming, myself, but my man Grimsby is a good agent. Most of my friends reside in London, and I bolt off to the metropolis as oft as I can."

Nicholas raised an eyebrow. "Do you, cousin? A wonder I've not chanced to meet you."

"Well, Nicky, I can hardly claim to move in such exalted circles as yours," Mr. Baxter replied with a boyish grin. "And I tend to favor—" he winked at Sarah "—more, ah, bachelor entertainments."

Sarah's smile thinned. Why did she feel his every word and gesture were calculated?

"Ah, here's the butler. Feeling you would both be fatigued, I took the liberty of ordering a simple meal. Briggs, take Lady Englemere's cup, man, and don't be so slow about it. My lord and lady?" He gestured toward the door.

If he meant to impress them with the alacrity with which he was obeyed, on Sarah his curtness had the opposite effect. He was beginning to strike her as an idle, self-centered man with little thought beyond his own comfort.

The hostile look she chanced to glimpse crossing Briggs's face underlined that opinion. To her surprise, though, his aggrieved glance encompassed Nicholas as well.

Not that the butler reinforced her suspicion by any word or action. Briggs's manner was deferential, as it should be toward his actual, if absentee, overlord, and his service impeccable. But after ten years of settling household disputes, Sarah's instincts were well honed, and the impression of discord lingered.

She shrugged. If there were problems at Stoneacres, doubtless Nicholas would discover and correct them during their stay. In the meantime, tomorrow morning they would go on to Wellingford. No disquiet could dampen her excitement at seeing again, very soon, her beloved home and family.

Nicholas continued to embellish his role of doting husband. Overruling her desire to ride, he ordered a light carriage for the journey, reminding her they'd need to carry more than saddlebags, and that she tired more quickly now.

Despite her resolve, she found her caution melting in the warmth of his solicitude. But as they approached Wellingford land, the joy of seeing familiar terrain displaced all other thoughts. Finally the carriage turned at the weathered gateposts and bowled down the long drive.

Sarah held her breath as the facade came into view. The sun shining upon the expanse of mullioned windows in the central stone block seemed to flash a welcome. The carriage halted at the entry, and before the footman could even lower the stairs, her sisters, along with most of the staff, poured out to meet them.

Meredyth herded everyone into the parlor, commanded Mrs. Cummings to bring tea, banished the dogs and directed her milling sisters to their places. After refreshments, Meredyth dismissed the children to the schoolroom, warning she'd inspect their lessons later.

"Shall you mind sharing Papa's chamber?" Meredyth darted a glance at Nicholas, her face flushed. "Mrs. Cummings says the linens in the mistress's chamber are past mending. Unless you'd like your old room with me, Sarah."

"Your papa's chamber will do nicely," Nicholas answered for them. "No disrespect, Miss Meredyth, but I much prefer Sarah share my room." He winked at Meredyth.

Blushing, she smiled back. "As you wish. I'll inform Mrs. Cummings. Make yourselves at home, of course, and if there is anything you need, please let me know."

Sarah's initial euphoria had dimmed. As logical as it was that Meredyth had assumed her duties with the staff and children, it still caused her a pang to be displaced. Her disquiet deepened as they proceeded to her mother's chamber.

Suddenly she saw Wellingford as Nicholas must: the paucity of servants, the closed-up rooms and threadbare hangings, the blank walls where once paintings hung.

Lady Emily lay propped against her pillows, eyes feverbright and startlingly blue in the pale oval of her face. It seemed to cost her great effort to raise the fine-boned hand for Nicholas's kiss, and her shoulders, when Sarah hugged her, were impossibly thin.

They stayed but a few moments, and even that taxed her. Leaving the sickroom, Sarah hastened down the hallway to a small landing. Through eyes blinded by tears she gazed out over the rose garden below.

"She has failed since the wedding," Nicholas observed.

"She is dying," Sarah said flatly. "The medicine she takes, though it costs dear, only d-dulls the pain." Her voice trembling, she said fiercely, "I would have married the devil himself to make her last days easy ones."

"I hope I'm not a devil," Nicholas said, drawing her into his arms. "But do promise me one thing, Sarah."

Trying to master the tears, she looked up.

"Anything that is needed at Wellingford—the governess your sister evidently hasn't yet recalled, medicine for your mama, gowns for your sisters, anything—you'll let me see to it? 'Tis not favors you ask, sweeting. Your family is mine now. I cannot profess to love them as you do, but I wish just as fervently that they be well cared for."

Over the lump in her throat, Sarah nodded. Then impulsively, she hugged him hard. London and Chloe Ingram be damned. Whatever the reason he came, Nicholas was with her now, and she was going to treasure every moment.

Several hours later, Nicholas accompanied Sarah on a drive. She seemed to glow with purpose, Nicholas thought, as she made knowledgeable comments about sprouting crops he could not even identify, and cast an expert eye on the condition of barns, fences and hedgerows. Each time they encountered a laborer about his task, she paused to compliment work and exchange greetings, never failing to ask by name after family and kin.

As the sun was setting, Sarah stopped the carriage atop a rise. Below them lay Wellingford Hall, its sparkling windows and burnished brick set like a jewel in verdant terraced gardens. A fine wood stretched to the horizon, and in the fields crops grew near well-kept cottages.

"How grand it will be, when Wellingford is restored." She turned shining eyes to him. "Which will occur all the sooner, thanks to you, Nicholas."

"You love this place, don't you?"

"Yes. Growing up, I always thought of it as mine. Papa treated me rather like a boy, taking me fishing and hunting, letting me tag along after the steward." Her smile faded. "Until Colton was born, anyway."

"His manner changed then?"

"It wasn't just Colton's birth." She frowned. "As I got

older, I...noticed things I'd not seen before. Fewer crops being planted, needed repairs delayed. And each time Papa made a London visit, some precious object—a Restoration wardrobe, a family portrait—would vanish.''

She shook her head, her face pensive. "I wasn't very wise at thirteen. After learning one of our best fields was to lie fallow, I took Papa to task for not being a good steward of the land and for gambling away our wealth.

"'Twas no more than I deserved when he snapped back at me." She sighed. "Managing Wellingford was not, and never would be, my concern, he said. Colton would have it all. Papa was willing the land I loved with every fiber of my being to a babe still squalling in the nursery."

She turned her gaze to the far distance. "Wellingford isn't entailed, and I had thought surely I would be given some part of it. I was—shocked." Her voice faded. "'Twas the second worst day of my life."

"What was the worst?" he asked, curious.

Sarah started, as if just realizing she'd made that admission aloud. She remained silent so long he thought she wouldn't answer. Then she whispered, "The day Sinjin told me we could never wed."

Before he could gather his rattled thoughts, she gave him a cryptic smile. "So you see, I seem to have a long history of loving what can never be mine."

The words left his lips before he could imagine whence they came. "I'm yours. Love me."

She looked at him searchingly. Then she took his hand and rested it on the slight swell of her abdomen. "I suppose, in a way, you are."

He stepped behind her and drew her close. With a sigh, she relaxed into him. Together they stood silently watching as the sun, trailing its gold and crimson cloak behind it, set before Wellingford.

Back at Stoneacres two days later, Sarah lingered over morning tea. Nicholas had ridden to consult with the local magistrate and would be gone several hours. Perhaps she'd take that time to review the Stoneacres books. On the drive back from Wellingford, Nicholas had teasingly reminded her he was ready to begin those lessons in estate management she'd promised him.

Seeking out Mr. Briggs, Sarah ascertained that Mr. Baxter was in the study. However, the butler added in a colorless voice, 'twas his master's unfailing custom to retire there after breakfast and nap under his London paper until luncheon.

A cautious peek inside the door confirmed Briggs's information. Her husband's cousin reclined against the gold-striped settee, his stockinged feet on a cushion, his snoring breath fluttering the edges of the newspaper perched on his lavishly embroidered waistcoat.

She hesitated, then continued on to the estate office. Everything at Stoneacres, including its ledgers, belonged to Nicholas anyway. She could in good conscience inspect them without Mr. Baxter's permission.

An hour's perusal left her troubled. According to the entries, the furnishings of the manor house had been refurbished three times in as many years, including the purchase of an expensive new cookstove. In addition, a hefty sum had been entered each season under unspecified "Estate Improvements."

Acting on instinct, she called for a gig and set off for a quick inspection of the closest farms.

She returned an hour later, her vague disquiet transformed to towering rage, and went directly to the kitchen. In a puzzled voice, Mrs. Briggs confirmed the serviceable but by no means modern cookstove was the same one she'd been using for "donnamany years."

Swiftly she proceeded to the estate office. After demanding Briggs turn over all the keys, she locked it. No one, she instructed the butler, particularly not the estate agent or its manager, was to enter that office until after Nicholas had inspected it.

"My husband is a fair and kind man," Sarah told Briggs as they awaited the footmen summoned to guard the office's door and window. "He will not tolerate the abuses Mr. Baxter permitted. He will put things right, I promise."

Briggs bowed, his stern face relaxing. "Indeed, I hope so, your ladyship. And may I say how powerful glad we are to have you at Stoneacres."

Once the footmen arrived, Sarah straightened her shoulders and headed for the study. She had a few words for the dandified Mr. Baxter.

Sarah entered and cleared her throat loudly. Mr. Baxter snorted awake, fumbled the journal from his face and sat up. "Ah, Lady Englemere. Luncheon, is it?"

Sarah looked at the costly waistcoat straining over his rounded stomach, the expensive lace trimming the lavish cravat that framed his plump cheeks, and felt a wave of revulsion. "Not quite, Mr. Baxter. But I have some food for thought for you."

He looked blank, then gave her a genial smile. "Ah, yes. Have you seen this morning's London journal? The most amusing criminal conduct case—"

"Mr. Baxter, the criminal behavior I wish to discuss has occurred much closer to Stoneacres. I understand the tenants have had their rents raised *three times* these last seven years."

Mr. Baxter nodded condescendingly. "Ah, I collect you've been conversing with the laborers. A rather worthless lot, I fear. Indeed, I'd hoped to raise taxes once more, but the wretches protested they couldn't pay another groat."

"Mr. Baxter, the people are starving."

"Lady Englemere, you must know how such low persons exaggerate. Surely you've seen much worse in London."

"This is not London, Mr. Baxter. This is one of my husband's estates, and you have the care of it. In my opinion, you have grossly abused my husband's trust, and so I shall tell him.''

Baxter was speechless for a moment, and then his eyes narrowed. ''What was it my friend Lord John Weston told me? That you consider yourself something of an agriculturist?'' His false-jovial smile turned nasty. ''Ah, yes—the 'Farmer Bride.' Let me inform you, your *ladyship*—'' he spat out the title with disdain ''—Nicky has, very properly, always considered farm management beneath him. As I am a gentleman, I must caution you—though your behavior toward me hardly deserves the courtesy—not to embarrass yourself bringing to Nicky's attention matters in which he has no interest. All he cares for, I assure you, is the money Stoneacres adds to his coffers.''

''And to yours? Tell me, Mr. Baxter, although the rental receipts trebled over the years, how is it that the amount forwarded to my husband's account has remained constant? Yes, I've inspected the ledgers, so pray do not insult my intelligence by telling me 'twas invested back in cookstoves or farms.''

For an instant, fury—and then fear—transformed his face. Quickly he mastered himself and uttered a strained laugh. ''I've always heard ladies who are increasing suffer absurd fancies. 'Tis true, I see.''

''The ledger entries are not fancy, Mr. Baxter.''

He opened his mouth, then closed it. One hand went to the lace at his throat, as if he were finding his neckcloth suddenly too tight. He straightened and curved his lips in a sneer. ''Lord John was right—you are sharp-tongued. Nicky must have wanted an heir badly to have married you, for he generally prefers his ladies beautiful and sweet—like his current love, Chloe Ingram. He invited her to your presentation ball, did he not?''

Despite herself, she winced. His nasty smile deepened. ''Oh, yes, Lord John sends me all the London news. Can you imagine how they laughed after you went up to bed and Nicky came back to dance with Chloe?''

She ignored the pain lancing through her. "We were speaking of Stoneacres and your management, Mr. Baxter."

His eyes gleamed and he leaned closer. "Take my advice, little lady. Nicky never tarries long in the country. Annoy him with matters like this, and when he returns to London he's like to leave you here—permanently."

Sarah forced herself to gaze at him calmly. "You waste your time making idle threats. You would do better to prepare an explanation—if you can—for Lord Englemere. Something that might prevent his laying criminal charges."

Baxter's eyes shifted uneasily, but he remained uncowed. "I am his cousin! Nicky would never serve me so." He took a rapid step toward the door.

And stopped short as Sarah held up a key. "The office is locked, Mr. Baxter, and the windows guarded. No one will touch those ledgers until after Nicholas sees them. I believe they will speak for themselves."

Rage mottled Mr. Baxter's already florid cheeks. Hissing a violent oath, he stepped closer and raised his hand. Then he caught himself, and instead of striking her, he raked her figure from head to toe with an insulting glance. "'Tis a good thing you're so ill-favored no other man would look at you. Else, with Nicky so bewitched by Mrs. Ingram, the ton might suspect you carry a bastard."

After the wretched poverty she'd seen and the taunts about Chloe, that slur against her honor was too much. Lost in rage, Sarah slapped Baxter's face.

Both of them stood shocked in the aftermath of the blow. Slowly Baxter raised a hand to his reddened cheek. "You'll regret that," he growled, and stalked from the room.

Chapter Fifteen

When Nicholas returned two hours later, Briggs delivered him a message to meet Sarah in the study without delay. Wondering what could have prompted such an unusual summons, Nicholas hastened to the room.

He entered to find Sarah pacing, looking pale but unhurt, and released the breath he hadn't realized he'd been holding. "What's the matter, sweeting? From the note Briggs gave me, I feared you'd suffered some harm."

Sarah faced him gravely. "I'm sorry to attack you thus before you've even had your tea, but something terrible has happened. Rather, has been happening, here at Stoneacres for the past seven years or more. Something that, I hope you'll agree, Nicholas, must stop today."

He took in her grim face and agitated manner. "Sit down, Sarah. Have some wine, and tell me what has distressed you."

"Oh, Nicholas, I hardly know how to begin! I went driving this morning, and the conditions I found on every farm I saw were appalling! Cottages falling apart, men, women, children in rags, and all of them thin to emaciation. It seems Mr. Baxter has, over the past few years, trebled the tenants' rents, leaving them in virtual penury."

"That cannot be correct," Nicholas objected. "I

checked before we left London, and the income from Stoneacres has remained constant.''

''The increase wasn't transferred to the Stanhope account. As I discovered when I checked them, the ledgers show all the additional sums entered under 'Estate Improvements.' Oh, 'twas cleverly done! Should you visit Stoneacres, you would see only the bathing facilities and the fashionable furnishings. The rest of the money—a considerable sum—was supposedly expended for repairs and consumables—seed, fodder and such. I imagine Mr. Baxter doubted you'd ever inspect the farms, and even should you do so, you couldn't expect to find 'consumables' still about.''

While Sarah stopped to sip her wine, Nicholas struggled to assimilate the implications of his cousin's bookkeeping.

''Aside from improvements at the manor, there have been no repairs at all that I can tell. Not even in Wellingford at its most destitute have I seen such squalor.'' She leaned over to seize his hands. ''Oh, Nicholas, people are starving, your people! Tenants who look to you for their livelihood and protection. Your own cousin has allowed them to be overworked, beaten—in your name! That he misused Stanhope funds is bad enough, but that I cannot forgive.''

Nicholas could only gape at her. The charges appeared incredible, yet Sarah was a sensible lady who knew much of farm management. If she said these things were true, she was undoubtedly correct.

''I must tell you what I've done,'' she continued, jumping up and beginning to pace. ''After inspecting several nearby farms, I had Briggs lock the estate office. Here is the key. Then I confronted your cousin, warning him you would shortly demand an accounting.''

She turned a pleading face to him. ''Cousin or no, you must discharge him, Nicholas! The way he has treated these people is shameful! And when I think how he's muddied your name with his callous deeds—oh, were I a man, I should run him through!''

Deeply troubled, Nicholas nevertheless had to smile at her fervor. He took her hand and kissed it. ''Thank you for you defending my honor, sweet champion.'' His smile faded. ''If what you describe is true, Hugh has disgraced me and betrayed my trust. I'd best see him at once.''

''Thank you for believing me, Nicholas.'' Her fierceness fading, she looked drained and weary. ''Before you go, there is something else I must disclose, for Mr. Baxter will seek to discredit me, and is bound to tell you.''

''Tell me what, sweeting?''

Avoiding his gaze, she commenced pacing again. ''I know 'twas wrong of me, and I regretted it in an instant, but he made some—rather distressing comments, and I…I lost my temper. I'm afraid I, ah, slapped his face.''

''I beg your pardon?''

She swallowed unhappily. ''I slapped him.''

Nicholas blew out a gusty breath. ''Are you telling me my dignified, gentle wife, whom I've never heard so much as raise her voice to a lazy housemaid, slapped my cousin?''

She nodded, shamefaced. ''I'm sorry, Nicholas.''

He studied her. ''Just what 'distressing comments' did Hugh make that caused you to so forget yourself?''

''Well—I told him I'd been through the books, and he realized at once what that meant. He tried to cozen me into thinking you wouldn't care how Stoneacres was managed, as long as the money came in, and that you'd be irritated with me if I tried to interfere.'' She gazed at her foot as she tapped it on the turkey carpet. ''When I refused to be cowed, he became quite enraged. At the last, he made an—insulting remark, and I—slapped him.''

A growing outrage at his cousin's perfidy put an edge to his voice. ''What remark, Sarah? I'm sorry to be so persistent, but if my cousin insulted you, I insist on knowing what he said. 'Tis a matter of honor.''

"A matter of honor," she repeated. "In truth, it was. Could we leave it at that?" She cast him a look of appeal.

She seemed so distressed, Nicholas nearly relented, but he felt strongly that his cousin could not be allowed to insult his wife with impunity. "No, Sarah. I'm sorry, but to deal with him properly, I must know."

She inspected the toe of her half boot. When at last she spoke, her voice was so soft he could scarcely hear her. "He said that, as all the world knows how—occupied— you are with your mistress, if I weren't so plain no other man would want me, the ton might believe I carry a bastard." Hearing his explosive intake of breath, she finished gruffly, "As if I would serve you such a trick."

White-hot anger burned all thought from his brain but the primitive desire to drag his cousin to the south lawn and demand immediate satisfaction.

After a moment, sanity returned. Much as the cur deserved so dire a reckoning, he wanted no public scandal. However, he vowed, his hands balling into fists, Hugh Baxter was about to suffer far more than a simple dismissal.

Nicholas gently raised her chin. "My dear, it grieves me exceedingly that a kinsman of mine could have so vilely insulted you. He will be dealt with."

"Deal with him about Stoneacres. The other doesn't matter."

"It matters to me." He touched her forehead lightly with his lips and went out.

On leaden feet, Sarah entered the sitting room adjoining their chamber. She sank into an overstuffed chair, faintly disgusted at having to use the same objects Nicholas's despicable cousin had touched.

She had done all she could. Though Nicholas might be more at home in a London drawing room than on a Hampshire farm, he was both intelligent and fair. The ledgers told the tale only too eloquently, and once he inspected them and the land, he would be as outraged as she.

Though she told herself they were uttered in pique, and came from Lord John, a most unreliable source, Baxter's words still lashed her. So all the ton had tittered at Nicholas tucking his wife away to dally with his mistress? She staggered at the rage and anguish that image brought.

Dismiss it, she told herself sternly. *What matter if the shallow sophisticates of the ton laugh?*

But that wasn't the real reason behind her pain, she forced herself to admit. 'Twas Chloe.

How complacent she'd become here in the country, secure in Nicholas's constant escort, lulled by his assiduous attentions. How easy it had been to put the lady out of mind. Baxter's ugly insult made her confront the fact that his woman—no, Nicholas's *mistress,* was still a reality.

Honor your bargain, she urged herself. *You told him he might go his own way. You told yourself it wouldn't matter. Live up to your agreement.*

But I don't want to! her heart cried. *'Twas a bad bargain, made in ignorance. I don't want to accept it now.*

Nicholas seemed truly content here with her. Though her experience in such matters was admittedly limited, she knew beyond doubt he enjoyed her as a woman. If she could find the courage to ask, perhaps he might be willing to give up Chloe—even once they returned to London.

Her spirits leapt at the thought. And immediately plunged. Why should Nicholas give up Chloe just because he also enjoyed his wife? Unfathomable as it was to her, the men of her class seemed quite able to keep both wife and mistress. Why should she expect Nicholas to be different?

'Twas only one reason compelling enough to induce him to dismiss his longtime paramour: he would have to be in love with his wife. She would have to fill his life so completely that he found taking another woman unthinkable.

An ache of sadness and regret washed through Sarah. That circumstance was the most unlikely of all.

She took a deep breath and squared her shoulders. No matter. She could stand whatever she must, including tolerating Mrs. Ingram. Why should she wish for the unreliable love of a gambler anyway?

Ignoring the raw spot that continued to bleed inside, Sarah rang for tea. Nicholas would probably report back to her after he'd talked with his cousin. She must regain her composure. If Mr. Baxter's brutal lesson finally taught her the value of maintaining a greater distance from her far-too-attractive husband, perhaps 'twas worth the pain.

His temper as raw as his bruised fists, Nicholas stormed into the small salon. After downing the meal and a mug of foaming home brew Mrs. Briggs had waiting for him, he felt calm enough to ask after his wife. The mistress was reading in the study, the housekeeper informed him.

Sarah looked like a little girl, curled up on the sofa by the fire, he thought with a smile. His amusement faded when she glanced up and he saw the wariness in her eyes. Nor did she make room for him beside her. His ire at his cousin reviving, he took the wing chair opposite.

"Hugh will depart first thing in the morning. After I examined the ledgers, we agreed it would be to our mutual benefit were he to seek employment in some other region of England. In fact, I highly recommended emigration."

He shook his head. "I can still hardly credit it. Hugh and I grew up together. Never would I have suspected he could have— Well, trusted cousin or no, I should have kept better watch. I intend to make amends to the tenants, insofar as I can. Will you ride with me?"

The grateful look she sent warmed him to his toes. "I should be honored."

He crossed to her and lifted her fingers for a kiss.

She stiffened, and as soon as politely possible, pulled at her hand. He held on, wincing slightly, and she noticed for the first time his scraped, oozing knuckles. "Nicholas," she said with a gasp. "You—"

Apparently surmising how he'd sustained the injury, she colored and looked away. "You shouldn't have."

"Shouldn't have punished a man who so vilely insulted my wife? Were he not my cousin I might well have shot him!"

"'Twas only pique, and fear over his future."

"Then I should have shot him for stupidity, to say such a thing to his employer's wife."

"I expect he realized that employment would shortly end. And I daresay he never imagined I would repeat it. Nor would I have, had you not forced me. I should like to forget it, and my own deplorable behavior, if you please."

She gently pulled her hand from his and rose. "You'll want some quiet after such a trying interview. Mrs. Briggs said you'd dined. I'll leave you to your port."

She was retreating again, just as she had after the squid incident. Well, he had no intention this time of letting her go. "Wait, Sarah."

She halted, her back to him.

"Sarah, come here."

She looked over at him, then at the door, every taut line of her body eloquent of a desire for flight. Her eyes implored release. Implacable, he held her gaze.

With slow, reluctant steps, she walked to him.

He took her limp hand and kissed it. "I only broke his nose, but I swear to you, Sarah, had I known his vicious comments would make you shy, I would have broken his neck."

She mumbled and tried to wiggle her fingers loose.

"I'm sorry he upset you. Surely you didn't heed his ridiculous words." She said nothing, and suddenly he realized she had indeed taken them to heart.

He remembered how, before their marriage, she'd promised not to *interfere* in his life. Remembered Hal telling him Lord John had accosted her about Chloe at Lady Jersey's ball—that she'd seen Chloe giving his arm an intimate squeeze.

Anger at his cousin warred with chagrin. "You did heed them, didn't you?" he asked incredulously.

She shrugged and shook her head.

Despite his discomfort in addressing the issue, he must put this to rest for good and all. Taking her chin, he gently forced her to look up. "You should *not* heed them, do you understand, Sarah? That—other matter—is settled. You're my wife, sweeting. No one can threaten your place."

"I know, Nicholas," she said softly.

But when he drew her into his arms, she remained wooden, neither inviting nor repulsing him.

Alarm shocked through him. Never before had she failed to respond. She'd been bludgeoned with Chloe's existence several times without offering a word of reproach. Had Baxter's nasty, wounding words been the final straw?

Surely he could still reach her, too intent upon doing so to ask why immediate reconciliation was so important.

He massaged her shoulders, willing her to relax and open to him. She sighed, leaned ever so slightly into his ministering fingers. But when he pulled her closer for an embrace, she held back.

An urgent need seized him to make her yield, to reaffirm the bond between them. Hands gripping her shoulders, he kissed her forehead, her eyelids, her cheeks. "Love me, Sarah," he breathed against her lips. "Love me."

At last she softened, opening her mouth and molding her body to his. Relief swamped in a tide of panic-sharpened hunger, he swept her up and carried her to the couch.

Sarah sat down to breakfast in the dining salon in solitary splendor. Though Nicholas had been gone only a few hours, she missed him already.

After Hugh's departure last week, he had asked her to start instructing him in estate management while they awaited a replacement. One day when the post brought him a parcel of papers from London, he teased her into the library and began explaining the complicated business of investing.

Much against her inclination, she was forced to admit that, risky as some ventures undoubtedly were, the business of choosing and balancing them fascinated. Their consultations, on both agriculture and finance, became a daily routine.

She sighed. Once again Nicholas was disarming her caution. But, she told herself hopefully, the longer he remained with her in the country, the better. She didn't know much about such arrangements, but perhaps after a time Mrs. Ingram would grow weary of waiting, and look for a more attentive protector?

It was thus with the greatest reluctance she'd reminded Nicholas of Mrs. Waterman's rout party. At this annual event, Hal's mama paraded before him her preferred candidates from the current Season's crop of marriageable misses for the position of daughter-in-law. Reminding Nicholas they had pledged Hal their support through this ordeal, Sarah convinced her husband to return alone while she stayed to tend Stoneacres.

He'd seemed genuinely reluctant to leave her, and agreed to go only after much persuasion.

She grinned at the memory of some of that persuasion. Would Nicholas linger in London? Her spirits sagged at that possibility. Firmly she put Chloe Ingram out of mind.

Then she felt it again—little fluttering pains, like tiny needles pricking her. Sarah grimaced and shifted her position on the chair. The odd, darting pains recurred as she ate, though, and a low ache started in her back. Perhaps, were she to lie down awhile, it would subside.

Reaching her chamber, she encountered Becky, but fobbed off the maid's concern by claiming she needed a nap. To her surprise, Sarah did manage to sleep. She woke to a sharper pain in her belly and a heavier ache at her back. And when she used the necessary, she saw blood.

On legs gone suddenly shaky, Sarah stumbled to the bellpull and back to bed. As she waited for Becky, a stronger pain gripped her. She breathed hard, fighting it and trying to stem a concern that was rapidly approaching panic.

Becky came so promptly Sarah suspected she must have been loitering in the sitting room. "'Twas a good nap, mistress. Are you feeling better?"

Sarah made herself smile. "Somewhat. I've a curious ache at my back, though, and…and I'm bleeding a little. I'm sure 'tis nothing, but I'd like to bring Dr. MacPherson from Wellingford. Just a precaution."

Becky strode to the bed and gripped Sarah's hands. "Don't fret yourself, Miss Sarah. You stay here with your feet up and we'll fetch that doctor." She paused. "I sent word to his lordship."

"Oh, Becky, you didn't!" Sarah protested. "'Tis but a trifle, and he particularly needs to be in London tonight!"

"That's as may be, but if there's even the smallest problem, the master would wish to be here, and well you know it. Anyway, 'tis done now."

"I suppose it cannot be undone, but I'm displeased nonetheless," Sarah grumbled. "If Lord Englemere speaks sharply to you, 'twill be only what you deserve."

"Yes, my lady," Becky replied, obviously discounting Sarah's every word. "I'll wrap you up and fetch some tea."

No longer sleepy, Sarah found the hours dragged as she lay staring over a book. The ache in her back continued, and the pains were sharper and more frequent. Finally she abandoned any attempt to read and stared out at the rain-darkened sky, straining her ears for sounds of the doctor's arrival. *Please God*— she closed her eyes to pray over and over —*please God, let no harm come to my babe.*

Just as night fell, she heard the welcome sound of the

doctor's hearty Scots voice. "What's this trouble ye be havin'?" the doctor boomed as he strode into the room.

Briefly Sarah told him. He frowned and shook his head. "Yer lady mother na had a bit o' problem carryin' her babes. Bleedin', ye say? I'd best have a look."

He finished his examination, his face sober. "I'll tell ye straight, lass. There's some that bleed, and carry the babe, and some who lose it. Ye must stay abed—no getting up for anything, hear? Stay abed, and we'll see."

Fear such as she had never known clutched Sarah. "Lose it?" she whispered. She seized the doctor's hand. "Surely you can do something."

The doctor's bluff face softened. "Dinna fash thyself, lass. I've known ye since ye were a wee bairn, and knew ye'd want the truth of it. 'Tis strong ye are, and likely all will be well. But there's naught to do but stay abed and keep yer mind easy. The rest is in God's hands."

Becky's summons reached Nicholas as he sat in his study fortifying Hal with brandy for the upcoming rout. Despite Hal's initial protests, he left at once. Becky was an older, experienced woman, not given to flights of fancy. If she thought the matter grave enough to recall him, 'twas likely to be serious indeed.

Within an hour he had strapped on a saddlebag and was guiding Valkyrie through the London traffic. Worry churned in his stomach. A barn-raising had been planned, and Sarah would doubtless have supervised. Had there been an accident? Becky's note provided no details. He pressed his horse harder.

When Nicholas calculated he'd reach Sarah before nightfall, he hadn't reckoned on the driving rain that began flailing him as soon as he left the environs of London, or on the pathetic condition of the hacks he was forced to hire after Valkyrie tired. It was past dark when at last, soaked through and jarred in every limb, he beheld the torches burning on the gatehouse at Stoneacres.

Never so glad in his life to surrender anything as he was to turn over the last sorry nag to a stable boy, he half fell from the saddle and stumbled up the front stairs. Briggs opened the door before he could knock.

"So glad you've come, Lord Englemere." The butler reached up to help him out of his sodden greatcoat. "The doctor's with her ladyship now."

"*No!*" Sarah's anguished cry ricocheted down the stairwell and lanced through him. For a moment after the echo faded, both men stood frozen, Briggs's hands clutching the collar of Nicholas's coat. Then Nicholas stripped off the dripping garment and took the stairs two at a time.

"No," Sarah repeated in a whisper. Even before the examination the doctor had just completed, she'd known the bleeding was heavier. The pains came often, and had intensified to wrenching spasms. Still, she refused to believe it. "There must be something you can do, Doctor—anything! I'll do anything to keep this babe!"

"Sarah, child, 'tis naught ye can do but accept. 'Tis young ye are, lass. There'll be other babes."

"You don't understand. My husband needs an heir. I owe it to him. I must carry this child!"

"Sure, and all men wish for sons, lass. But ye canna stop what's meant to be." He patted her hand, his eyes sorrowful. "Rest, now. 'Twill be over by morning, belike."

He turned to Becky, who stood by the bed. "Give her laudanum for the pain." He looked back at Sarah's rigid face and sighed. "Take some and rest, lass."

This isn't happening, Sarah told herself, locking her hands over her belly as if by so doing she could ward off the catastrophic process going on there. "No," she moaned.

Becky wiped her eyes with a corner of her apron. "I'll fetch you hot tea, Miss Sarah, and be back in a twink."

But when the door opened a few moments later, it

wasn't Becky with the tray. His wet hair plastered against his head, his sodden clothes steaming in the room's warmth, Nicholas paused on the threshold. ''Oh, Sarah.''

Sarah closed her eyes and turned her face to the wall.

Chapter Sixteen

She heard Nicholas shut the door, felt the mattress shift as he sat on the bed beside her. "The doctor just told me. I'm so sorry, Sarah."

She couldn't bear to face him. Struggling for control, she lay with her back to him, her eyes locked on the wallpaper. At last she managed to calm her breathing.

"I'm sorry, too, Nicholas," she told him, still facing the wall. "Dreadfully sorry. You didn't need a housekeeper, for your household runs like an oiled watch, or a friend, for you've many, or a lover, as—well, no matter. Only one thing did you need from me. And I have failed to provide even that."

"Don't, Sarah!" Nicholas cried. "Calm yourself, sweeting. Such things happen, the doctor said. You must dismiss such absurd fancies and rest."

She turned then. He looked distraught, she thought with numb detachment. As well he might. He'd bought a wife dear, and had no return yet for his investment. When he continued to gaze intently at her, she realized with a small shock he was genuinely worried.

With a supreme effort, she damped down the agony scouring her. "I shall be fine, Nicholas. I'm sorry you were dragged out of London to no purpose." She managed a weak smile. "You're dripping on the bedclothes."

Nicholas studied her. Seeming reassured, he smiled back. "Let me get food and dry clothes, and I'll return."

He stepped toward the door, then halted. "I wanted to come, Sarah—'twas no inconvenience. You should know, if anything happens, my place is with you." He wet his lips as if to say something further, then closed them. After a moment he said, "I'll be back shortly."

Sarah fixed her smile in place until the door shut. Then she fell against the pillows, and with a sigh that was half groan, half sob, turned her face back to the wall.

Finally dry in borrowed clothes, for the ones he'd packed in his saddlebag were scarcely better then those he'd arrived in, Nicholas warmed himself by the kitchen fire and hurriedly downed a plateful of food. As he drained the last sip of ale, Becky came in, her tearstained face anxious.

"Will you be going up to my mistress?"

"Directly, Becky." He put down the mug. "How is she?"

Becky's lips trembled and her hands twisted the ends of her apron. "The pains be stronger now. I tried to coax her to take the laudanum, but she'll have none of it. Powerful sorry I am about the child, your lordship."

"Thank you for caring for her. And for sending word. Did she read you a scold over that?"

"Aye, a bit. But I feared 'twas this from the first, and thought you'd want to be here." Her voice broke on a sob. "Oh, my poor lamb! She wanted this babe so much."

"I'll go up and see what I can do about the medicine."

When Nicholas entered, Sarah still lay facing the wall. Though she was motionless, he knew she wasn't sleeping.

She looked so small on that big bed. Seeing her still, her air of quiet competence vanished, Nicholas realized again how fragile she was. His heart cried out at her pain, and he wanted nothing so much as to comfort her.

He eased himself beside her on the bed, took one limp hand and chafed it. "Sarah, sweeting, how can I help?"

She turned to him slowly, infinite sadness in her shadowed eyes. "Nicholas," she murmured. "You must be exhausted. A miserable ride through the rain, only to learn of the l-loss of your child."

"'Tis you who concern me. What can I do?"

"Nothing." She took a ragged breath. "There's nothing anyone can do. Go to bed, Nicholas."

Her flat, emotionless voice moved him more than tears. He fumbled with the laudanum bottle. "Sarah, at least take some medicine. 'Twill ease—"

"Go, Nicholas," she repeated in a whisper. "I'll be better by morning." She pulled her hand from his and once more turned toward the wall.

"Sarah?" He cupped her shoulder, yearning to gather her into his arms. She held herself stiffly, resisting.

"Go get some rest, Nicholas." Her muffled voice was barely audible. "Please—for me?"

He sat immobile, stricken that she refused the comfort he wanted so badly to give. Finally, though the urge to embrace her almost consumed him, he forced himself to honor her all-too-plainly stated wishes.

"All right, Sarah, I'll go. Rest, sweeting." He kissed her averted head.

Settling for maintaining a sort of vigil in the adjoining room, he had Briggs place a cot by her door and, unutterably weary, dropped onto it. He was too distraught to be surprised at the ferocity of his need to hold and console her. Only by stern effort of will did he restrain himself from sleeping by her bed.

When next he thought at all, wan dawn light filled the sitting room. He jumped up and eased her door open.

Sarah lay quietly, and he could tell by the relaxed line of her body that she slept.

She looked peaceful. Would that serenity last when she woke? Stubborn, strong-willed, courageous—under her se-

rene demeanor she was all that, and more. But from the
first, she'd been openly passionate about one thing only—
giving him a son. Without doubt, she'd take this loss hard.

Stretching his cramped muscles, he went to the bellpull.
He'd get a shave, put on his own hopefully-dried-by-now
clothing and be ready to attend her when she woke.

"Get out! Get out and leave me alone!"

At his wife's shriek, Nicholas started so badly he cut
himself. Swiping at the shaving soap with a towel, he
threw down the razor and ran. "Mistress, you mustn't!"
He heard Becky's voice.

"I will ride this morning, I tell you! 'Tis a morning like
any other!" The sound of a chair overturning followed.

Nicholas charged through the open door and stopped
short. "What the devil?"

Becky stood by the bed, weeping. Propping herself on
her forearms, Sarah lay on the floor by the toppled chair.

As Nicholas entered, she looked over at him. "I will
r-ride," she repeated, but her voice faded and broke. Pressing clenched fists to her head, she began to weep.

"Leave us," he barked. Sobbing, Becky hurried out.

Gently Nicholas gathered Sarah in his arms and carried
her to the bed. Holding her tightly, he rested his cheek on
her tangled hair while she wept with deep, wrenching sobs
that cut to his heart. He held her till his arms and shoulders
ached, though that paltry ache couldn't begin to approach
his anguish at her misery. Finally, the sobs subsided, and
he eased her back a little.

Pulling up a corner of his half-tied cravat, he wiped her
tear-blotched face. "'Twill be all right, sweeting."

"W-will you h-hold me, j-just a little l-longer?"

He kissed her red, swollen eyes. "Of course."

She'd been limp in his arms before, but she clung to
him now, as if he were her sole support in a crumbling
world. Ignoring the protests of his already cramped limbs,
he hugged her close, murmuring incoherencies until at last

the tension left her and she slept. When her breathing was deep and regular, he gently laid her against the pillows.

Sarah sat over a tray several hours later with a dull sense of calm. *It's over,* she thought. *My precious babe.*

She had no more tears, for she'd cried them already—all over Nicholas, soaking his coat and ruining his cravat. *Ah, Nicholas,* she thought, sighing, *what a sorry wife I've been.*

She'd reached another equally bleak conclusion. In the solitude of her room after that bitter night, Sarah finally accepted the fact she'd been evading this month and more. Despite their unemotional bargain, despite her apprehensions about his gaming, she'd fallen in love with Nicholas.

That was why she could no longer view with detachment his liaison with Chloe Ingram. Why she missed him after a mere hour's absence, why her heart warmed and her whole being quickened when he so much as walked into the room.

Fool, fool, a thousand times fool, she told herself savagely. *How could you stupidly succumb to an emotion Nicholas doesn't want, an emotion that will make it impossible to remain the cool, detached wife he does want?*

The very idea of Nicholas in Mrs. Ingram's embrace was enough to curl her fingers into claws and tighten her chest with outrage. How could she encounter his mistress at a rout, at the opera, with even a modicum of distant courtesy, when all she wanted was to tear the woman's hair out? How could she politely send Nicholas off to his club, wondering every time he left if he were going to visit *her?* And if he should not return of an evening, how could she face him calmly over breakfast the next morning, Chloe's cloying scent on him, and not rant like a fishwife?

Sarah covered her face with her hands. Countless highborn wives managed to carry on in perfect charity with, or at least feigned indifference to, their husbands' other lives.

She had promised Nicholas she would do the same. But she couldn't—not now that she loved him.

If she'd carried the child, she might have managed. She could have channeled all the love she felt for the father into his son, absorbing herself so completely that she had little time to consider her husband's pursuits.

But now there was no babe. The idea that the arms that held her so gently while she sobbed out her grief might, in just a few hours' time, be holding Chloe Ingram, sent a lancing spear of rage and pain through her. How could she share her husband with that woman—any woman?

Would she really have to? her ever-hopeful heart asked. Had Nicholas not been passionately attentive, even after he learned she was breeding? Perhaps he was ready to dismiss Chloe. She could summon her courage, and ask.

Almost, she could believe he might pledge fidelity, if not love. But what if she were wrong? If she broke their agreement, demanded a change in the terms of their arrangement, Nicholas might be annoyed, even outraged.

She remembered his anger the night of the Sheffingdons' rout, and shuddered. She didn't want to live with coldness and distance the rest of her life. If she hadn't won his love, she dared not risk destroying their friendship.

He had bidden Chloe Ingram to her ball. All London saw the woman there, Mr. Baxter said. Kind gestures and passionate interludes could not argue away the only logical explanation for that very public display of favor.

I've settled it, Nicholas had told her. Yes, he'd settled it all right, clearly demonstrating he'd not relinquished his claim on the woman. *You're my wife, and no one can threaten your place.* He meant, of course, that he would protect and provide for his wife and children, regardless of where his attentions might wander.

What else had he said, standing there dripping on the carpet? *My place is with you.*

No ardent vow of affection, that. The statement he'd made mere hours ago would not support the faint hope that, during their country sojourn, she'd managed to capture his heart so completely he'd happily discard his mistress.

Which led to the bitterest truth of all. For if her husband had a duty to her, she owed him one as well: a son and heir. As soon as the doctor said 'twas permissible, she must try again. No matter how much her heart ached, she'd have to bid him come, listen to his love words and lie with him, knowing he might go straight from her bed to Chloe's.

Her whole bruised, heartsick being revolted. *I can't do it,* she thought, tears beginning to slide down her cheeks. *Maybe later. Next month. But not now.*

Send him back to London alone, the thought flashed into her head. *Get Dr. MacPherson to tell him I must recuperate here, and let Nicholas return without me.*

It shouldn't be too difficult—he'd never intended to remain in the country. The ploy could buy her at least a little time. Sarah set aside her tray to summon the doctor.

"Better now, are ye?" the doctor asked as he entered. "I'll be on my way, then. 'Tis nothing amiss with ye time canna heal, and I've sick ones to tend."

"I must speak with you about—healing, Doctor."

He gave her an inquiring look. Sarah took a deep breath. "Please, Doctor, will you h-help me," she said in a faltering tone, "convince my husband to return to London alone? Tell him I need peace and quiet to, ah, recover, and that it would be best for me to stay in the country. He'll be wanting to leave here immediately, and I cannot face London just yet."

"Aye, 'twould be good to avoid the fevers and congestion of the city, lass." The doctor nodded his head approvingly. "Ye should recover fully within a fortnight. Surely yer man would be willing to wait that long."

"I was thinking of a more extended stay, actually. A month or more. I'd not wish to tie him here that long."

The doctor gave her a shrewdly appraising glance. "'Tis

not uncommon to lose a first babe. In most cases, such women have no trouble after. Dinna fear to try again.''

"I know my duty, and I shall do it. But I'd like to…wait. Longer than a fortnight, at any rate.''

"Surely yer husband will understand that, too. Doubtless 'twill be difficult at first, but I think it best if ye return and get on with yer life.'' He patted her hand. "'Tis a comfort in such times to have yer man about.''

"But it isn't!'' The words burst out. Dr. MacPherson raised an eyebrow at her and waited.

She bit her lip, for the first time regretting the doctor knew her so well. He'd not press for an explanation, but if she wanted his help, she'd have to confess the whole.

Pride warred with desperation and lost. "Ours was a marriage of convenience,'' she began, "but over the course of it my—emotions have become rather strongly engaged.''

"And yer man's have not?''

"There's another woman,'' Sarah whispered.

"Ah.'' The doctor gave a sympathetic nod.

"Do not misunderstand—my husband is everything considerate.'' She swallowed and willed the tears away. "But I cannot go back to London now, knowing who— what I will find there. Not yet. Please, will you help me?''

"What is it ye wish me to do, lass?''

"Just tell him my health requires an extended convalescence in the country.''

"And if he wishes to remain?''

Nicholas might well think that his duty, so she'd already prepared her argument. "Could you not tell him I feel I've failed him—'tis true enough—and that his presence would be a constant reminder of that failure? Tell him I need some time alone to…recover my spirits.''

The doctor stayed silent so long she feared he would refuse. Finally he said, "To my thinking, if it's his affections ye wish to engage, ye'd do best to get with child again at the earliest opportunity.''

Sarah blanched. "Oh, but Doctor—"

"There, there, dinna fash thyself. I'm but a man, and lacking in sensibility, or so my wife is always telling me. I suppose, after what ye've suffered, if 'tis solitude ye wish, ye should have it. Mind, I'm not agreeing 'tis best."

Sarah gave him a tremulous smile. "No doubt you're right, and in a week or two I'll come to my senses and pack my trunks. Thank you for giving me the choice."

He nodded brusquely. "I'll talk with yer man, and be on my way. Keep thyself safe, lass."

Weary but relieved, Sarah leaned back against her pillows. She'd have a month, perhaps more. Surely in that time, she could reconcile herself to her duty.

Nicholas was finishing his repast when Dr. MacPherson entered the breakfast room.

"I've just checked yer lady wife. 'Tis my opinion she'll make a good recovery, given time. As she has no further need of me, I'll be going."

Nicholas rose to shake the doctor's hand. "Thank you for tending her."

"No need for thanks. I've a great regard for Miss Sarah. Everyone about Wellingford does." The doctor hesitated, frowning, and motioned Nicholas back in his chair. Seating himself, he said, "I must tell ye, she's taking this hard, just as I feared. I strongly recommend ye let her stay here, or at Wellingford. Keep her out of the noise and filth of London."

"Of course. Is there anything else?"

The doctor paused a long moment. "Yers was what they call a marriage of convenience, was it not?"

Nicholas cocked his head at the unexpected question. When he thought he understood the doctor's intent, he stiffened. "It was not a love match, if that's what you are asking. I assure you, however, I hold my wife in the greatest respect and esteem."

"Never inferred ye did not. However, in such cases, the

wife is bound to feel she has failed in her duty." Nicholas flinched and the doctor nodded. "Aye, I can see she's talked of it to ye. Some husbands, in such cases, can be quite brutal—" he held up a hand when Nicholas would interrupt "—not that I'm suggesting ye would. What I mean is, even when the husband is understanding, the wife often feels her failure strongly, as strongly as she feels grief for the child. The two feed on each other."

"What are you trying to say, Doctor?"

"That each time she sees ye, Lord Englemere, she's remembering her failure, and thinking again of the child she lost. Having ye here is, ye might say, a constant reproach. 'Twould be better, I think, were ye to leave without her."

"Leave her? But surely my place is here with her."

"Not if your presence will prolong her pain."

"Would it not be better to stay and divert her from that pain?"

"Divert Miss Sarah when her mind's set?" The doctor sighed. "Change the course of the Thames as easy, I'm thinking. Understand now, 'tis miracles she's used to making. Half a dozen times she's saved her family from the workhouse. Why, she was scarce sixteen the first time. Her poor papa, God rest his soul, tried to auction off some land the girls' grandmama had left them for dowries. A rare foiter it was, and whispered about the county what a shame for the lasses to be left penniless. But not for yer wife to stand by and do naught."

The doctor shook his head and laughed. "No, what must that halich do, but ride to the auction and tell the crowd did they buy the land, she went with it, for without dowry she was as good as ruined anyway!"

"Wait!" Nicholas had been listening impatiently, but a vivid memory shocked him alert. "This auction—did it take place seven years ago, near the village of Picton?"

"Aye, that would be the place."

"But I was there," Nicholas burst out. "The land

marches with a corner of Stoneacres, and my father had sent me with a sealed bid. I saw a girl ride up on a lathered horse…and talk the buyers out of bidding! That was Sarah?''

"Aye. Ye did not recognize her?"

"I never saw her up close." Nicholas gazed out the window, watching in his mind's eye as a tall girl in a faded cotton dress, hair hidden under a chip straw bonnet, climbed the stile. Bracing herself, she confronted the curious, gawking buyers like a warrior defending the ramparts.

"What a Trojan she was. I was too far away to hear every word, but she convinced them. When the auctioneer insisted on proceeding, not a single man bid. The caller was furious, and stormed over for my father's offer." Nicholas smiled. "I tore it to pieces in front of him. What a risk she took!"

"Aye. Right fearless she was—'twas the talk of the neighborhood, some holding as 'tweren't fitting for a well-bred lass to put herself forward so. Most, though, thought her resourceful, and uncommon brave."

"Yes. She's surely that."

"So ye see, my lord, having done the near-impossible, 'tis powerful hard for her to accept she's failed in this. 'Twill take time for her to forgive herself and go on."

"You truly think it better if I just abandon her here? I tell you, Doctor, that flies in the face of both duty and inclination."

"Let's just say 'twould make the lady easier in her mind. 'Tis not the body that worries me, 'tis her spirits."

Nicholas sighed heavily. Every instinct told him to stay, and he wanted desperately to help soothe the grief he'd seen in her eyes and felt in her anguished body. But if the doctor, who had known Sarah much longer than he, felt he should not remain…

Defeated, he said, "I suppose I must leave, then."

The doctor nodded. "Don't be fretting yerself, my lord.

Yer lady wife is resilient, in body and spirit. Give her but some time, and she'll come back, and I daresay present ye with a brace of sons ere long.''

"Sons I would have, but 'tis Sarah that concerns me now. Thank you for your advice, Doctor.''

As he was mounting the stairs, another memory recurred, and his hand clenched on the balustrade. He saw a second rider galloping up *ventre à terre* on a lathered horse...reining in at the fence rail...leaping from the saddle and pulling the girl down. From his gestures, and the murmurs of the dispersing crowd, Nicholas had surmised the newcomer was a brother giving the girl a thundering scold. Until she threw herself in the lad's arms and kissed him passionately. He'd chuckled, thinking the young lovers would soon be making use of that dowry.

He didn't chuckle now. After leading the girl apart, the young man came to thank him for destroying his bid. The handsome youth's skin was fairer, his hair a lighter ash. Still, Nicholas had no doubt the grateful suitor had been St. John Sandiford.

Surely the captain would visit his mother before returning to the army—and Sarah would be here, just a few hours' ride away. When he heard of her tragedy, would he ride *ventre à terre* to her, as he'd ridden to her rescue that day long ago? Would Sarah welcome his comfort?

Another image flashed in his head: Sarah sitting in his garden, weeping over a gold signet ring.

Chapter Seventeen

Nicholas sat at the desk in his London library, his eyes on a book but his thoughts back at Stoneacres. Three weeks after his return, he still felt uneasy and displaced.

Sarah had been so cool and distant when he went to see her after the doctor left, her face a blank mask, her manner that of the ice maiden they'd once joked about. He might have thought her angry with him for some unknown misdeed, had it not been for the stark agony in her eyes.

An agony that called to him to discard the doctor's advice and take her in his arms. To nurse her back to health, then to ride and joke and laugh with her, warm her in his bed, until the misery faded and she began to forget.

But when he took her hand, she drew back, as if anticipating a blow. Shocked, he merely stood there while she slowly pulled her fingers free.

She wouldn't look at him. Her voice as distant and impersonal as her manner, she stared at some point beyond him and said, politely as if to a stranger, that she was sorry to have been such a burden and she would try to make it up by tending Stoneacres until a new manager arrived. Of course, she had no desire to tie him to an invalid in the dull fastness of the country—he must return to London as planned. She wished him a safe journey. Pleading fatigue, she leaned back upon her bed.

He sat with her after dinner, but his one-sided conversation lagged and finally died out altogether. She lay silently, her eyes fixed straight ahead, and never once looked at him.

There was no need for words. Her rigid body and averted eyes said only too eloquently, "I don't want you here."

So the next morning he left. She was sitting, motionless and silent, a book on her lap, in the window seat that overlooked the drive when he came to say goodbye. She turned her face to take his kiss on her cheek instead of her lips. As he rode away, he saw her there still, silhouetted against the light of the opened window. She didn't wave.

Almost, he could have been angry with her, except the look of numb misery had intensified, rather than diminished with the passing hours. To his dismay, she was retreating ever further into some private world of grief.

Why could she not have accepted the comfort he wanted so badly to give? It was his loss, too. Surely she could not believe he would reproach her. And if, in the raw grip of grief, she couldn't yet bear the thought of conceiving another child who might expose her to similar pain, did she not imagine he could understand that, too? Did she think him so unfeeling he could not restrain himself until she was ready? Why must she reject him?

As Lydia had.

But then, 'twas not the same. Lydia left him for spending too little time with her. In her frantic search for frivolity, she had ever needed to be the center of attention. Sarah, so much stronger and more independent, chose to bear her burden of grief and pain alone. Or at least, without *his* help.

Would she let Sandiford mourn with her? As well he might, since until Sarah delivered sons the captain had forsworn any claim on her.

The captain's lands marched with Wellingford, not so very far from Stoneacres. Was he there even now, holding her weeping against that broad, blue-coated shoulder, as Nicholas had held her the morning after she lost the babe?

He slammed the book shut. *Stop it,* he told himself furiously. *You'll drive yourself mad.*

With a sigh, he jumped up and paced to the window. The dull gray fog swirling outside matched the restlessness within. When he'd first returned, still smarting from Sarah's cold dismissal, he'd contemplated seeking out Chloe. The briefest of reflections revealed he now found the idea of bedding Chloe—or indeed any other woman— distasteful.

He sat down straightaway to pen a cordial farewell note. Charging his secretary to deliver it personally, along with a handsome sum of cash, he dismissed Chloe from his life with no regrets.

Nicholas traced a raindrop's pattern along the window glass. He could look up Hal, or perhaps go work off his fit of the dismals at Jackson's. Invitations to an assortment of dinners, routs and musicales sat heaped on his correspondence tray, but he could muster no enthusiasm for any of them. Perhaps he would dine at his club.

Nicholas smiled grimly. In the inscrutable way servants have, the household had learned of his loss, and upon his return, Glendenning had expressed the sympathy of the entire staff.

Though the starchy butler would probably have choked before allowing any sign of emotion to cross his face in the presence of outsiders, when he saw his master had returned without the mistress, he unbent enough to express surprise, and then shock when he discovered Nicholas meant to leave Sarah in the country for some weeks. The butler's clear disapproval had speedily been conveyed throughout the household. He could dine at home without fearing the horrors of burnt roast and cold potatoes, but did Glendenning not pride himself on his standards, Nicholas half suspected such might be his fare.

'Twas bad enough, he thought sourly, to have one's wife

send one away, without then having to suffer one's household treating one like an insensitive boor.

No, his club didn't appeal. What he needed was Sarah. He'd given her almost a month of doctor-recommended solitude. Perhaps he should go to Stoneacres and fetch her.

The idea brought a rush of excitement, as quickly dashed. What would he do, should he arrive and find that look of cool reproach still on her face? A stabbing pain lanced through him at the thought. No, having been so definitely dismissed, he'd not return unbidden.

Then a happy idea broke through his despondency. Sarah seemed to find solace in the country—why should not he? Not at Stoneacres, if she didn't want him, but at the Hall. He could, he hoped, count on a warm welcome from his mother. More than that, Mama had lost two babes herself. Mayhap she would know what he could do to reach Sarah.

The idea touched some chill, aching spot in his heart and warmed it. Feeling better than he'd felt in three weeks, he decided to depart on the morrow.

"Nicky, darling, how wonderful to see you!" Emerging from his embrace, the dowager held him at arm's length, her lovely eyes scanning his face. "Where is Sarah? Is something wrong? I thought you said she was recovering."

"She is, as far as I know." He released her hands and paced past the tapestry frame to the morning room window.

His mother seated herself on the brocade sofa and patted the place beside her. "Come, Nicky, and tell me what is troubling you."

He laughed shortly and ran a hand through his hair, disordering the carefully brushed locks. "Is it so obvious? I expect it is to everyone. I'm afraid my care-for-nothing society image is in the process of being ruined."

She raised an eyebrow at the bitter edge in his tone and paused, as if uncertain how to continue. "Is it the loss of the child? As I wrote in my note, I was so sorry to hear of it.''

He acknowledged her sympathy with a nod. ''Partly, though it's difficult to grieve over what was scarce more than an idea. Sarah had been breeding for but a few months. No, it's Sarah herself who concerns me.''

She handed him a sherry and he took a sip, struggling for the right words. ''She's always handled everything with consummate composure. Even Findlay, and he's as nasty a business as I'd ever care to meet. I expected the baby's loss would disappoint her. I was disappointed myself. But she was much more than that—she was devastated.''

''Oh, Nicky,'' the dowager said, a catch in her voice. ''My son, no pain in life approaches the loss of a child!'' She patted his hand, remembered sorrow in her eyes. ''Sarah will grieve—'tis only natural. A mother must, whether she loses her child at two, or twenty, or before birth.''

'''Tis more than that.'' Nicholas paced to the fireplace and held out his hands to the flames. He dreaded broaching the rest of his dilemma, truly didn't know how to begin. His mother waited patiently. Sighing, he turned to her.

''Sarah's taken this ridiculous idea in her head that she failed me. That our marriage brought her every advantage, and she had but one boon to offer me—an heir. And she has failed to provide it.''

''Ah—'' his mother nodded ''—well, in simple terms, 'tis true. You married for an heir, and she to rescue her family. Not an uncommon bargain, but a bargain nonetheless. My marriage to your father was a love match, so I can't pretend to know how Sarah feels, but I think I can imagine.''

''When I reached Stoneacres that first night, she was lying alone in her chamber, her face to the wall. She wouldn't even look at me.'' Staring into the fire, he felt a pang of remembered anguish. ''She said I'd needed only

one thing from her, a son. She apologized for being such—
and these are her words—a 'sorry bargain' of a wife.

"Lord, Mama!" The words burst from him. "She was
in such pain, and I didn't know what to say! 'Quite, my
dear, but I hold you in respect and esteem'?" He kicked
savagely at a log on the grate, sending sparks flying. "Paltry, don't you think, in the face of her grief?"

"So you came back to London," his mother said softly.

"No! Did you think I just abandoned her for the diver-
sions of the city? Mayhap you do, since even my own
butler seems to believe that. Well, it's not true—rather the
opposite. She sent me away, Mama."

When his mother made no comment, he continued,
"She even got the doctor, an old stick of a Scotsman
who's known her practically all her life, to add his bit.
Insinuated I might chide her for failing in her duty, the
impertinent sawbones! Well, I set him straight. He seemed
to believe me, but said Sarah couldn't accept or forgive
herself, yet." He drew a ragged breath. "He said just looking at me shamed her. That I should give her time to
grieve, and heal."

"Poor child," the dowager murmured. "His advice
sounds sensible, Nicholas. She probably just needs time."

"But it's been nearly a month! How much longer can
she need?" He leaned his hands on the hearth, focusing
on his own signet ring winking in the firelight. "She's my
wife, Mama. If she's distressed, I should be with her."

"From what I know of Sarah, she'd not want you to
stay out of duty."

Nicholas smiled wryly. "You'll not let me off so easily,
will you? All right, I admit it. I miss her, Mama. True, the
household runs smoothly enough, but 'tis somehow…
different without her. And I don't mean only Glendenning's disapproval."

He looked back at the fire, his lips curving of their own
accord into a smile. "It's not just that she makes me comfortable, though she caters to my wishes far too much.

There's a kind of—serenity—about her, and yet, at the most unexpected moments, such fire as well. She's so easy to be with, almost like a man who knows when to speak and when to be silent. We are friends, as I'd hoped we would be.''

He drained the last of the sherry. ''The staff misses her, too. Not a day goes by that someone, from the butler to the lowliest tweeny, doesn't ask if I've had word of her return.'' He laughed shortly. ''Glendenning positively quivers with disapproval every time he greets me.''

''Why don't you go fetch her?''

Uncertainty, distress and resentment swirled in him as it had so often this past month. ''I don't know if she'd receive me,'' he admitted, and felt a pang at that avowal.

''I see.''

He looked back at her and was shocked to find a little smile on his mother's face, so inappropriate to the gravity of the moment that anger stirred. Then the smile vanished, and she said, ''Would you like me to visit her for you?''

''Would you?'' Irritation forgotten, Nicholas strode over and seized her hands. ''Would you go to Stoneacres? Her notes say she is recovering, but I cannot be easy about her. Would you check her for me and find out—well, you'll know how to go about it discreetly—if she's ready to come home?'' He kissed her fingertips and released them. ''Tell her I miss her,'' he added gruffly.

''Excellent,'' his mother said, rising in a swirl of skirts. She returned his sharp look with a guileless one. ''Excellent notion, I meant. I'll be happy to carry a note for you, that you might tell her yourself. And now, you must excuse me. It seems I have a journey to prepare for.''

Nicholas caught her up in a fierce hug. ''Thank you, Mama. I know you won't fail me.''

She touched his cheek with a finger and gave him a faintly amused smile. ''Certainly not, dear son. After all, what are mothers for?''

* * *

Three days later, when Sarah returned from riding to the village, Briggs informed her the Dowager Marchioness of Englemere had come to visit.

Surprised and curious, Sarah smoothed her windblown braids. She felt a stir of foreboding. What brought Nicholas's mother all the way to Stoneacres? Had something happened to Nicholas? A shock of fear pierced her. She whirled and ran down the hall.

"Lady Englemere," she said as she burst into the morning room. "What a delightful surprise! I'm sorry I was out when you arrived. Everything is well, I trust, with you, and—and Nicholas?"

"Sarah, dear. Yes, we're both fine." Her mother-in-law came over to envelop her in a hug. Enormously relieved, Sarah returned it warmly.

The dowager looked at her appraisingly. "Have you fully recovered? I was so sorry to hear about the babe."

Sarah swallowed the lump in her throat. Even now, it was impossible for her to talk about it. She nodded.

The dowager had been watching her face. Her lips trembled and her eyes brimmed over. "Oh, my dear," she murmured, and drew Sarah back into her arms.

I will not weep, Sarah told herself fiercely. *Weeping cannot change things, and I will not weep.*

Despite her best efforts, a few disobedient drops leaked out the corners of her eyes. "Sorry," she said gruffly, swiping at them with a trembling hand.

The dowager led Sarah to the sofa. "You needn't apologize, Sarah. I've lost three children, you know. A babe, a man, and one before b-birth." Her voice wobbled. "'Tis the most crushing blow life can deliver."

Sarah thought of the pain she felt, multiplied by three. Suddenly her grief seemed less overwhelming. "I'm sorry, I didn't know."

"Nicky didn't tell you? I suppose it didn't occur to him. Much as he may love his children, a man cannot know how it feels to carry a child under his heart. But men do grieve, you know. Nicky surely is.''

Sarah looked away. "I'm so sorry I—"

"You didn't fail him, Sarah, though I understand how you might think so. When I lost my first, I considered it the most monstrous injustice in the world. Any ignorant housemaid could carry a child—indeed, unmarried ones had a habit of doing so with alarming frequency. Yet for all my health and wealth and desire, I could not do that for the husband I adored.''

Sarah could sympathize only too well, but dared not say so. "It is difficult," she said finally.

"I know just how difficult. Time will dull the pain. But Sarah," she said gently, compassion in her eyes, "nothing will take it away. Not blaming yourself, or hiding away in the country. I don't wish to interfere, but I tell you from bitter experience, you must accept your loss and go on. God willing, you'll have other babes.''

Sarah could hardly tell Nicholas's mother that 'twas the idea of sharing her son in such intimate creation that prevented her doing just that. "I...I don't feel ready."

"Nicky is worried. And he misses you, Sarah.''

A dull ache squeezed Sarah's heart. "Did he send you?''

"Yes. Not that I haven't been concerned, but I wouldn't have intruded, had he not asked. He's suffering, perhaps more than you can guess. You see, he's taken this absurd notion you can't tolerate the sight of him.''

"I can't—" Sarah gasped. She felt a pang of guilt. "But 'tis ridiculous! 'Twas my fault, mine alone!''

"'Twas no one's fault, Sarah. But if you're not angry, will you not go back to him?''

You don't understand, she wanted to shout. *I can't go back and be the meek, disinterested wife he wants. The jealous, possessive shrew I've become he wouldn't want.*

She put a trembling hand to her cheek. "I can't," she whispered, rebel tears escaping again. "Not yet. He is dearer to me than you can imagine, and I would hate to cause him a moment's anxiety. You must tell him that!''

The dowager stared at her for a long moment. "Has Nicky ever talked about Lydia?''

"Lydia?'' Sarah asked, startled. "His late wife?''

The dowager nodded.

"No, ma'am. Clarissa told me that after she died in an accident he mourned her for years. Nicholas has never mentioned her and I—I didn't wish to pry. He must have loved her very much.''

Again the dowager sat silent. Finally, with a sigh, she began, "Nicky never speaks of her. Only his two closest friends know, and 'tis not my story to tell, but I think it important that you hear it.''

Mystified, Sarah watched the dowager rise and pace to the window, distress clear in her face. She turned back to Sarah. "Yes, Nicky mourned, but not just for the reasons you think. You see, when Lydia's carriage overturned, she was leaving Nicholas.''

"Leaving him?''

"Yes. She was unhappy in their marriage, apparently, and left a note saying she went to one who loved her more. He set out after her, and came upon the wrecked carriage.''

Incredulous, Sarah shook her head. "I cannot imagine any sane woman leaving Nicholas.''

That earned her a smile. "Nor can I, darling Sarah. But Lydia,'' she spat out the name with distaste, "apparently found some nameless soldier—Nicholas never learned who—more to her fancy.''

She strode from the window to grasp Sarah's hands. "Can you not see? The situation is scarcely the same, except that once again, someone he cares deeply about has turned him away. He's my son, Sarah, and I feel his pain.''

Agonized, Sarah gasped. "But I never meant...! How could he think...?''

"You couldn't have known. And Nicholas does understand, at least in his head, your need to grieve alone. It's been a month now. Perhaps 'tis unfair of me to ask, but if you truly care for him, could you not try to put aside some of that grief and go back to my son?''

Nicholas, rejected by the wife he loved. Nicholas, betrayed and abandoned. The enormity of it exceeded the bounds of comprehension. But anguish she could understand, and his pierced her to the core. ''Oh, N-Nicholas,'' she whispered, her voice breaking on a sob.

The dowager hugged her close, and when she released Sarah her own eyes were wet. ''Forgive me, I didn't mean to distress you further. I won't press. Consider returning with me, 'tis all I ask.''

She dabbed at her face with a lace handkerchief, started to put it in her reticule and stopped. ''I nearly forgot! I have a letter from him for you. And the latest London papers.''

She pulled the articles out of a large embroidered bag beside the reticule. ''I'll leave you in private to read them. Now I should like to rest before tea.''

Sarah remained in the study, still struggling to accept the dowager's incredible information. Then a shocking thought sent her flying to her feet.

Lydia had left Nicholas—for a soldier. Whatever must he have felt about her reunion with Sinjin?

Even a husband with no particular apprehensions would have been less than happy with the situation. She could not begin to imagine the dismay it must have caused a man whose wife had run off to a soldier.

He'd seemed stiff around Sinjin, but not more than she would expect of a husband dealing with his wife's former suitor. Other than that, never by word or deed had he displayed the anxiety or resentment he doubtless felt.

Gamester that he was, Nicholas must have accepted the risk inherent in remarriage as the cost of fulfilling his duty. But nothing she had endured in the past or feared for the future could compare to the gamble he had taken in trusting her to behave honorably about Sinjin.

He had shown rare courage and consideration. She owed him no less. Whether or not he would ever love her, despite the situation awaiting her in London, she must return.

Three days later Sarah saw her mother-in-law off to London. During the remainder of her short visit, the dowager did not once refer to the matter of Sarah accompanying her, nor did she show a single sign of reproach when Sarah confirmed she would stay on alone.

Just until the new estate manager, due the end of the week, settled into the job, Sarah had assured her. 'Twould give her at least ten more days to prepare herself.

Sarah wandered into the library and picked up the London paper, but her eyes wouldn't stay on the page. She'd kept her sorrow close in a sort of righteous anguish. Yet rare was the woman who saw more than half her babes grow to adulthood. Who was she to shut herself away, as if she alone had ever suffered such a loss?

Nor, selfishly wrapped up in her own misery, had she ever thoughtfully considered how Nicholas must feel. No, she'd discounted his grief as mere disappointment. Then, unable to stomach keeping the bargain she herself had made, she'd banished him, compounding one failure with another.

It shouldn't have taken the dowager's heartrending history to make her realize how her dismissal could wound her husband. Worse yet, in her selfish preoccupation, she'd ripped open the scars of betrayal. "Oh, Nicholas," she whispered, a tear sliding down her cheek, "never would I wish to deepen your pain."

Unquestionably she owed it to Nicholas, as well as to duty, to return to London. Somehow she would just have to tolerate Chloe Ingram.

Chloe, with her hand possessively on Nicholas's arm, smiling with satisfaction as she patted the magnificent rubies adorning her equally magnificent bosom. Sarah slammed her mind shut against the image.

Her restless fingers rustled the paper in her lap. With a sigh, she scanned it. One name seized her attention.

Sir James Findlay, the entry said, had the pleasure to announce his engagement to Miss Angela Buxley, daughter of Baron Buxley of Windfeld Manor, Kent.

Sarah sat up straight, running through her mind a catalog of the Season's debutantes. Then a face came to view, and consternation gripped her. She saw a pale, slender girl with long golden curls and a gentle, almost frightened expression that made her look younger than her years. A girl with a gamester father deep in debt.

Sarah closed the paper and looked down to the scar at her wrist. She smelled again the stench of hot candle wax and scorched flesh, felt the agonizing rasp of Findlay's tongue against the raw wound, heard him warning her to submit. She remembered with a sickening shock the vile practices he'd described to her on her wedding day.

At the time, she'd had only a hazy idea what he meant, but as a bride of several months her images of what Findlay's wife could expect were revoltingly clear.

'Tis none of your affair, part of her argued. *The girl has parents to protect her.* But Sir James could be charming when he wished—only see how he'd turned Lady Beaumont up sweet. And if the father were drowning in debt, and the girl had been pressed to do her duty, she might be too frightened to tell them what her suitor was like.

That Findlay had revealed something of his nature to Miss Buxley, Sarah had no doubt at all. He'd feed on the terror he could inspire in her.

A cold calm descended on Sarah. Ready or not, she must go to London the minute her bags were packed.

If her sense of obligation to Nicholas had nearly been enough to push her into returning immediately, this announcement made it imperative. She could not live with her conscience if she let Sir James marry such a vulnerable innocent without doing everything possible to prevent it.

Chapter Eighteen

In the late afternoon two days later, Sarah's traveling coach pulled up at Nicholas's London residence. The footman handed her out, and with a deep breath, she walked up the steps.

At her rap, Glendenning opened the massive door. His eyes lit and his austere face creased with the hint of a smile. "Lady Englemere! Come in out of the chill!"

He bustled her in and helped her out of the traveling pelisse. "Your message must have gone astray, for we didn't expect you. May I say, 'tis a pleasure to have you home."

"Thank you, Glendenning. I didn't send a message. My decision to travel was rather—sudden." She ignored a sniff from Becky, who passed by with her jewel case. The maid, until finally silenced by Sarah, had nattered on at length that, much as she approved Sarah's decision to return, the mistress should have sent for her husband's escort.

In truth, Sarah was so uncertain about Nicholas's reception she'd not dared send a note. What if he had grown so...comfortable with his London arrangements he preferred she remain in the country?

"What's all the commotion, Glend—Sarah!"

Nicholas stopped short and stared at her. Cursing herself

for a fool but unable to help it, Sarah stood there like a looby, drinking in every dearly remembered detail of her husband's handsome face.

The crisp dark hair she loved to curl her fingers in. The deep green of his eyes that sometimes glowed like molten emeralds. The sensuous lips that could make her thoughts dissolve into longing.

She forced herself to look away. Shocked he certainly was, but when that faded would he be pleased—or angry?

"Are you weary, my dear? Should you like to refresh yourself, or can you take tea with me?"

His voice sounded welcoming. Though her hair could stand brushing and she felt the dust of the road, she'd not had her fill of gazing at him. "I'm not tired, Nicholas."

"Tea in the morning room, then, Glendenning." Taking her arm, he led her in.

"When Mama left yesterday, she warned not to expect you for several weeks. You should have let me know you'd changed your mind, Sarah. I would have come to fetch you."

"You're not angry I returned?"

"Angry? No! I'm delighted!" He raised her hand and kissed it. "I've missed you, Sarah."

"Have you?"

"Very much indeed." At the quiet intensity of his voice, she could not help but look up. And met an equally intense gaze whose warmth was unmistakable. With a little cry, she went into his arms.

He murmured her name and held her fiercely, his cheek against her hair. So sweet was it to be in his embrace, she wasn't sure how long they stood thus, but after a time he moved her back an arm's length.

"Does this mean I'm forgiven?"

"Forgiven? For what?"

"Whatever sin I committed that made you banish me."

Guilt flushed through her. "Don't be nonsensical. I

didn't wish to tie you to an invalid's bed. I'm a terrible patient, I must confess. And you prefer London.''

"I'm not so sure. You were beginning to teach me a great appreciation for country matters, and studies, and—''

The pain cut so deep, she could scarcely breathe. "Don't, sweeting,'' he cried, consternation on his face.

She forced a wobbly smile. "I'm all right, truly. It's just that I d-did—'' she made herself say the words "—so want to give you a s-son.''

With infinite tenderness he kissed away the one tear that escaped the corner of her eye. "You will, Sarah. I'll take great pains to ensure it.'' And then he was kissing her forehead, her cheeks and finally her mouth.

Any thought of maintaining distance vanished. With all the hunger of love long denied, she kissed him back.

Sometime later she vaguely heard the sound of a throat being cleared. Nicholas pulled away, and blinking in bemusement, she saw Glendenning with a tea service, James bearing another tray beside him. Judging by the grin on the footman's face, they must have been there some time.

With a grimace that might have been annoyance, Nicholas guided Sarah to the sofa.

Glendenning followed with the tea. "Not knowing how long ago you'd had sustenance, your ladyship, Cook took the liberty of sending along more substantial refreshment.'' The butler gestured to the overladen tray James was depositing.

Sarah looked at the assortment in awe. Cold ham and roast beef, three kinds of cheese, fresh biscuits, jam, honey, scones, cherry tarts and an assortment of fruit met her astonished eyes. No macaroons, however.

"Cook must not believe I took nourishment the whole of my stay at Stoneacres!'' She smiled at Glendenning. "Tell her it looks delicious, and I thank her for her concern.''

"All the staff have been concerned, if I may be permitted to say so, your ladyship. Very happy we all are to have you safely back with us.''

Sarah felt a lump in her throat. ''Thank you, Glendenning. I'm very happy to be here.''

The butler and footman withdrew, leaving them to their feast. As they ate, Nicholas regaled her with what had been going on in society during her absence. He did not, she noted, mention Sir James Findlay's engagement.

When they'd finished their tea, he came to sit beside her on the sofa. ''Are you happy to be back, Sarah? I hope so. For I'm devilish happy to have you here.'' He took her hand and kissed it. ''I trust you've gotten over the absurd idea you failed me. Such things happen, as Mama surely told you. I still consider myself the most fortunate man in England to have married you.''

Joy, pain and a wild hope she tried hard to restrain surged through her. ''Thank you, Nicholas,'' she whispered.

''Sarah, I may be only a man, but I have some idea how difficult this has been for you.'' He cleared his throat. ''I want to assure you, I won't…ask anything of you until you're ready.''

Feeling unaccountably shy, she looked away. Though she'd not expected he would force himself on her, she was nonetheless touched. Over her days of packing and travel, however, she'd decided that it was foolish to deny herself any longer the pleasure and comfort of intimacy with him.

Fiercely she pushed aside the thought of Chloe Ingram. While Nicholas loved her, he was hers alone, and she'd been stupid to forgo that ecstasy simply because she could not have him exclusively. Besides, perhaps the doctor was right, and if there were another child…

But first, she must deal with Sir James Findlay.

Reluctantly breaking their warm intimacy, she asked, ''What entertainments are planned this evening? Would your hostess be offended to accommodate an extra guest?''

''Hardly, when that guest is my wife. But are you sure

you wish to go out? You've had a long journey, and so recently after—well, I don't want you tiring yourself.''

"I'm fully recovered, Nicholas. And after living in London, the country can get a bit dull.''

She told that plumper with barely a quiver. 'Twas true for some people, even if it was not her own opinion, she silently justified herself.

"Certainly we'll go out if you wish it, sweeting. Hal's coming to dine. We've cards for several functions, Lady Richardson's ball being the most important.''

Clare had once informed her nothing less than a deathbed illness would keep a member of society from this exclusive fete, whose invitation list was sometimes laughingly described as the membership roll of the haut ton.

Surely Findlay, who prided himself on his lineage, would be there—with his betrothed and her parents.

"I think I should like that, if you care to go. Clare's told me so much about it.''

"If we're to attend, you must rest before tonight.'' Nicholas kissed her hand one more time and retained it, as if reluctant to let go. "Hal arrives at eight. Shall I walk you up?''

Reveling in his touch, Sarah could not force herself to refuse. "Thank you, I should like that.''

Nicholas tucked her hand in his arm and went slowly up the stairs, as if he feared a more vigorous pace might overcome her. After escorting her to her sitting room, he rang for Becky. He glanced toward the door of the adjoining bedchamber, and his eyes took on a well remembered glow.

Sarah felt her pulses quicken, but Nicholas straightened. He took a deep breath, then made her a bow. "I'll leave you to Becky's care. Rest well, sweeting.''

Sarah watched him go with regret. Tempted as she was to give him some signal she was ready for the interlude his heated glance promised, she did need to rest. More important, she needed to plan.

Given his opinion of the man, Nicholas would doubtless want her to avoid the baronet. Sarah had thus decided to attempt resolving the matter of Findlay's marriage unassisted. As wedding plans were already in train, she must begin tonight.

Sarah found it easier than anticipated to get a private chat with Miss Buxley. Spying the young lady headed for the withdrawing room, she sped after her.

As they reached the corner, Sarah bumped into the girl. "Oh, how clumsy of me. I do beg your pardon!"

Miss Buxley turned to her a pale, blue-eyed face even younger than Sarah remembered. "'Twas nothing."

"Miss Buxley, is it not? I'm Lady Englemere," Sarah offered a hand and a friendly smile. "I've just returned to town. Let me congratulate you on your engagement."

Was it a trick of the light, or did the girl pale? "Thank you, Lady Englemere."

"You might know that before my marriage, Sir James was much in my company. I came to know him rather well."

The girl shot her a glance from under a heavy fringe of lashes. Sarah saw caution—and fear. "You did?"

"Yes. Forgive my bluntness, and any offense this might cause you, but do you wish to marry him?"

The girl's lips trembled and she looked away. "'Tis a good match, Mama says. He will make a handsome settlement."

"'Tis shockingly intrusive of me, but I was very nearly compelled to marry Sir James. I *know* him. And so I ask again—do *you* wish to marry him? Trust me, please!"

"No, I don't wish it!" the girl burst out, and clapped a hand over her mouth. She looked around wildly, as if afraid someone might overhear. "No," she repeated, "but what can I do?" Her face crumpled. "He—he frightens me!"

Silent sobs shook her slender shoulders. Sarah looked

at the childish face with its flaxen curls, the delicate frame, and knew whatever it required, she could not allow Findlay to get control of this innocent.

"I told Mama." Miss Buxley raised tear-spangled eyes. "She just said all brides suffer from nerves, and if I pleased Sir James, he would treat me well." The girl paused, mingled fear and loathing in her face. "But I don't want to do—what he said."

A bolt of pure rage tempered Sarah's concern. The despicable sadist. Could he not choose a more worthy adversary? This poor child wouldn't last a fortnight.

"They can't force you to marry him, you know. 'Twill be difficult, but simply tell your father you will not have him. Lovely as you are, you must have other suitors."

"But none so rich." The girl sighed unhappily. "And Sir James gave Papa a large sum of money when the betrothal was announced, he told me. So that I should not think to cry off." She twisted her handkerchief between her fingers.

"Tell your papa what Sir James said you must do."

"I could never!" Miss Buxley gasped, scarlet flushing her pale face. "I did *try* to tell him I could not like Sir James, Lady Englemere, but he only said I should be a good girl, and not bother him, and sent me off to Mama. I want to be a credit to Papa, but—but I can't please Sir James." She gave a helpless sob. "And they will not listen."

Frowning over the golden head, Sarah patted the girl soothingly. Clearly, she was too weak-willed to flatly refuse Findlay. Sarah would have to approach her parents.

"Don't despair, Miss Buxley." She handed over a fresh handkerchief. "I shall contrive something."

"Oh, Lady Englemere, if only you could!" Miss Buxley clasped her hand fervently. "Sir James mentioned you to me, you know." A puzzled look crossed her guileless face. "He said you owed him a debt, but I would repay it. I cannot imagine what he meant."

A chill ran through Sarah. The ton had followed Findlay's assiduous courtship of her, had doubtless snickered over her last-minute preference for Nicholas. A man of his pride could not forgive that.

That he might take out his rage on this child sickened her. Without doubt, she must prevent their marriage.

Being a marchioness had its advantages, Sarah thought ruefully. Miss Buxley's mama was only too happy to stroll with her on the terrace.

Lady Buxley's pleased look at being singled out faded rapidly, however, when after listening to a lengthy discourse about wedding plans, Sarah pressed her about her daughter's feelings toward her intended.

"Having spoken with Miss Buxley, I received the distinct impression she held Sir James in aversion."

"Surely you misunderstood, my lady," the mama protested. "Sir James has been everything courteous."

"She has never mentioned feeling ill at ease?"

Lady Buxley shifted uncomfortably. "Well, if she is a bit nervous, 'tis only normal. She's been well brought up, and is rather—uninformed about the duties of matrimony."

"Lady Buxley, I believe your daughter fears Sir James. And I must tell you, she does so with good reason. Do you not know his two previous wives died, under what can only charitably be called *mysterious* circumstances?"

Lady Buxley twitched her shawl. "I'm sure I don't listen to gossip, Lady Englemere. Nor, with all respect, can I see that this is any business of yours."

"Please, Lady Buxley, it may be improper of me to interfere, but I was once nearly engaged to Sir James. Having every expectation of marrying me, he revealed aspects of his character that, I implore you to believe, render him unfit to be the husband of a delicate young girl! I cannot claim to know your daughter well, but this I do know—if you care for her, do not force her to wed Sir James."

"But the trousseau is ordered and the preparations in train!" Lady Buxley twisted her hands. "And Sir James is so charming. Surely you are mistaken."

Sarah fixed a grim gaze on the lady. "I wish I were, Lady Buxley, but I promise you I am not. Sir James is a widower twice over. 'Tis her very life at stake."

Strong emotion flitted across the woman's face. Then she flung off Sarah's hand, as if by breaking that contact she could erase the disturbing picture Sarah had sketched.

"I appreciate your concern, Lady Englemere. But Angela's papa has conversed extensively with Sir James. He has his daughter's welfare at heart, I assure you, and if there were anything untoward in Sir James's character, he would have discovered it. Now, if you will excuse me."

With a nervous glance, as if she feared Sarah might compel her to remain, she hurried back across the terrace. Sarah ground her teeth.

The woman was uneasy over the match. But she obviously preferred to pass responsibility for it onto her husband. Sarah would have to seek out Baron Buxley.

Fortunately, as it had been nearly half an hour since she left the ballroom and her solicitous husband would soon be searching for her, she'd already concocted a plan for accosting that gentleman. And the card room was probably the last place Nicholas would think to look for her.

Sarah found Lord Buxley just as a hand of piquet broke up. Quickly drawing him into conversation, she praised his skill and begged he might engage her for a game.

Lord Buxley preened a little. "Be happy to take you on, your ladyship. I'll endeavor not to fleece you too badly." He laughed heartily at his own joke.

Sarah chatted of idle matters until the cards were played out, herself losing heavily, before broaching her subject. "I wished to speak with you about a different lamb, Lord Buxley. Your daughter Angela. She's to marry Sir James Findlay, I understand."

"Yes, a fine man. Excellent family."

"Lord Buxley, do you know of Sir James's past?"

The baron's genial glow dimmed. "I've heard some nonsense. Nothing to it. Have only to speak with the man to know that. True gentleman."

"My lord, much as I regret it, I must disagree. I was once nearly promised to Sir James, and I assure you those—rumors you heard are not exaggerated."

Lord Buxley looked annoyed. "See here, your ladyship, I've talked with the man, and I'm satisfied. I expect your husband is waiting for you." Nodding a dismissal, he rose.

Sarah grabbed his sleeve. "Sir James may be charming, but he is dangerous as well." At her last hope, she unbuttoned her glove to the wrist and held her arm out. "I displeased Sir James once, and he did this."

He glanced at her wrist and quickly away. "Sir James is a gentleman. Yes, and a generous one. I've no doubts about my daughter's safety and happiness, none whatsoever." He scowled at Sarah. "*She* will not displease him." He tugged at his sleeve.

Sarah did not release it. "And if he cannot be pleased? Do you care for her so little you will risk that?"

"This is ridiculous," the baron said in a furious undertone. "Of course I care for my daughter. I begin to think you deranged, my good woman."

Then his face lit. "Ah—just remembered. Lost a child a month ago, didn't you? Poor lady. You're still distressed, naturally. Such a thing's bound to upset a female." He patted her shoulder.

"Have your husband take you home to rest, that's the ticket. And don't worry, my gel's future is well in hand."

With a fatuous smile, such as the nervous bestow on lunatics, he pulled loose his sleeve and walked off.

Slowly Sarah refastened her glove, despair settling over her. So much for dissuading the Buxleys. They either could not, or would not listen.

She looked up to find Chloe Ingram's dark eyes on her.

The woman gave her a mock-sympathetic glance and smiled.

I have Nicholas, the smile said. *What do you have?*

It needed only that to cap off the evening. Her eyes brimming tears, she brushed past the woman, sped blindly down the hall and ran headlong into a tall, blue-coated figure.

Sinjin steadied her. "Sarah, whatever is wrong?"

"N-nothing."

"Was it Mrs. Ingram?" he persisted, his eyes searching her face. "I saw her at the doorway to the card room. Did that doxy say something to upset you?"

"Not at all. She merely smiled at me."

Sarah had never been a good liar. Sinjin took another look at her face, steered her into an adjacent room and handed her a handkerchief.

With admirable compassion, he looked away while she mopped her eyes. "Thank you, Sinjin. I'm better now."

"Are you better, Sarah? I was so sorry to hear about the child. I didn't dare write, but I grieved for you."

Sarah had recourse to his handkerchief again. After a moment, she got her emotions under a modicum of control.

"You should count yourself fortunate." She attempted a smile. "I've turned out to be a rather wretched wife."

"I could never think so."

"'Tis true, nonetheless. Thank you for assisting me, but I must get back."

"No, it wouldn't do for *Lady Englemere* to be found with Captain Sandiford," he said with bitter emphasis.

"Nicholas would not like it."

Sinjin looked at her searchingly. "'Tis more than that, isn't it, Sarah? I've felt the change for some time. You love Englemere, don't you?"

She didn't attempt to deny it. This was Sinjin, and he knew her too well. "Yes," she whispered.

He swore softly.

"Oh, Sinjin, you mustn't feel that diminishes the love I

had for you! Do you believe our hearts so poor and mean they can admit affection for one person only? You will always be dear to me, so dear that, regardless of my husband's views, I dare not trust myself alone with you."

She gave him a tremulous smile. "Can you truly say you would settle for the illicit affair that is the only relationship possible for us? I could not so dishonor the love we shared, and neither could you!"

"Could I not, Sarah darling?" For a fraught moment, she feared that, after her rash admission, he might pull her into his arms. But he merely stared at her, a gentle sadness slowly replacing the bitterness on his face.

"I leave London the end of the week," he said at last.

"To rejoin your regiment?"

"Yes. Who knows, after we've beaten Boney, I might stay on soldiering. There's little enough for me here."

"Your mama wouldn't like that."

He curled his lip. "No, Mama would doubtless give me an earful, were I to see her."

"You've not visited her yet? Oh, Sinjin!"

"I'll post down to Sandiford before I leave. I've that much sense of duty."

"Have compassion on her, Sinjin. In her own way, she loves you very much."

He gave her a twisted smile. "What a fortunate lad. Blessed with two ladies who love me 'in their own way.'"

He put a finger to her lips before she could protest. With a hungry gaze so powerful she could feel its heat, he whispered, "One last time I will say it—I'll love you till I die, Sarah Wellingford. If ever I can serve you, send for me."

She could not have spoken had she wished to. Once again, her eyes brimmed with tears.

"Easy, sweetheart. I'll not distress you further." He offered her the handkerchief. "Tell that handsome husband of yours he'd best make you happy, or he'll answer to me."

"Sarah, there you are—Sandiford!" Stopping short on

the threshold, Nicholas's anxious expression turned to surprise, then anger.

"Lady Englemere was distressed." The captain indicated the soggy handkerchief that Sarah had used to wipe her tears. "I escorted her here to compose herself."

Nicholas glared at Sandiford. How dare that blue-and-silver-braided popinjay secrete himself with Sarah! Nicholas had half a mind to call him out for his effrontery. And what had Sarah been thinking, to let him? What if Sally Jersey had walked in on them? "If my wife is *distressed,* I am fully capable of assisting her."

"Then why were you not nearby to *assist?*"

"Nicholas, Sinjin, please!" Sarah burst in. "You are both distressing me now."

"I'll take you home, Sarah. You look tired."

"I am, Nicholas. Perhaps I should not have come. Sinjin, thank you for the handkerchief."

"Keep it, Sarah. Should I not see you before week's end, goodbye. My lord." He bowed curtly and walked out.

Seething, Nicholas propelled Sarah from the room.

"Sinjin did assist me, Nicholas," Sarah said as he hurried her down the hall. "Someone reminded me of—of the child. He found me a private place to recover, and offered his own condolences, which he wanted to do, he said, before leaving London. He rejoins his regiment next week."

"Next week?" Nicholas couldn't stem an upsurge of gladness. He struggled to come up with some sincere expression of regret, and failed. "I'm sure his unit needs him," he offered finally. "He's a fine officer."

"Yes, he is. He's a fine man as well, Nicholas. I had hoped you two might be friends."

When pigs fly, thought Nicholas. "Here's the carriage. I feared going out tonight would be too much for you."

Sarah was quiet on the ride home, from fatigue—or distress—Nicholas could not tell. Was it the thought of her lover's departure that made her shoulders sag and brought that numb misery to her eyes? His anger revived.

He handed her out of the carriage and marched her upstairs. "I'm sure you'll wish to retire immediately."

Sarah looked at him wearily. "I'm sorry, Nicholas. I should have better control. People will comment about—about it. I can't be dissolving into tears every time someone offers me condolences, no matter how sweetly false."

Becky bustled in, clucking and fussing over Sarah, and Nicholas withdrew. She had not, he noted, apologized for the indiscretion of slipping off with Sandiford. His brow puckered, he walked moodily back to his own chamber.

He poured himself a brandy and flung into his chair. Then a phrase echoed: "and offered his own condolences."

The implications of the remark hit him like a blow. Sandiford hadn't visited her at Stoneacres. Relief and a savage joy flooded him.

Shame stemmed the flood of gladness as he recalled Sarah's wan, strained face. After swearing to himself upon her return that he would not—*he would not*—ever again let his jealous imagination fly away with him, at the very first test he once again succumbed. How could he be idiotic enough to doubt Sarah's distress when someone mentioned her lost child? Had he not himself witnessed over and over the depth of her grief?

Instead of jumping to inane conclusions regarding the captain, he should have offered her comfort, a warm shoulder and a sympathetic ear.

Regret stabbed at him. He would apologize at once, before she fell asleep.

Sarah reclined against the pillows, her braided hair under a frilly nightcap. The depth of the curtsy Becky gave him as she exited indicated the maid held him responsible for his wife's pale weariness.

Nicholas handed her a glass of wine. "'Twill help you sleep. I hoped an apology might help as well. I'm sorry for my brusqueness tonight."

"You've no need to apologize. Even though upset, I should have realized I must not allow Sinjin to assist me alone." She gave him a small smile. "He's been a friend so long, 'tis sometimes hard to remember the meaning—others might attach to his attentions. I shall do better, I promise. Now, is that not a familiar theme?"

"We shall both do better. But you look exhausted, sweeting. Perhaps we should remain at home a few days. I don't think you're recovered enough for the late nights one keeps in London."

"I'm not tired, really. 'Twas the incident that upset me, and the sooner I learn to deal with it, the better. I cannot spend the rest of my life hiding in Stanhope House."

Nicholas drained his glass and went over to the bed. "You mustn't push yourself. You do that, you know. Give yourself time, Sarah." He picked up the end of the long plait and stroked his fingers along its satiny length.

The slippery softness recalled the feel of her bare skin. During their marriage he'd become delightfully accustomed to sharing her bed nightly. He'd not done so in nearly five weeks, and at the thought of her silken body under the thin veiling of nightrail his heartbeat quickened and a tremor spiraled in his gut. Reach out his arm, and the little buttons could be undone, the fabric pushed back—

He realized he'd been reaching out in truth. Clenching the hand into a fist, he jammed it at his side. Sweat broke out on his forehead. If he meant to leave her untouched, he'd best remove himself with all speed.

Instead of her lips, he leaned to kiss the tip of her braid. "Sleep well, sweet Sarah," he said through a tight throat. He forced his reluctant legs toward the door.

"Nicholas."

He halted to look back at her.

"Are you still angry with me?"

"No, sweeting. I thought I'd told you that."

"Then, can you not—stay?"

Heat, like the blast from an opened oven, suffused him. He stilled, his pulse frantic, his ears roaring, and tried to keep his eyes from lingering on her lips, her breasts.

"I don't want to injure you, sweeting."

"I'm fully recovered, Nicholas. Stay, please?"

So much for good intentions. Before the plea left her lips, he reached the bed.

Smiling, Sarah put the last pin in her coil of braids. What a fool she'd been, hiding away at Stoneacres. Nicholas had been particularly tender, especially passionate last night, and she had no doubt as he loved her that his mind had room for no one else. If she could lure him to her nightly, when would he have time for Chloe?

And as he had at Stoneacres, he'd not left her after their joining, but gathered her close and slept in her bed. Surely there could be no more wonderful feeling under heaven than waking in the arms of the man you love.

Her euphoria dimmed as she headed for the breakfast room. Her attempt to dissuade the Buxleys had failed totally. Though she hated to risk breaking their lingering contentment, she must talk to Nicholas about Findlay.

His eyes lit when she entered and he rose to kiss her. "Fill your plate, sweeting. If you're like me, you must be famished." He gave her a naughty grin.

She couldn't help grinning back. She allowed herself to delay the discussion until they finished their meal and were pouring a last dish of tea. In what she hoped was a casual voice, she asked, "Did you see the notice of Sir James Findlay's engagement?"

Nicholas grimaced. "I did. And wondered about the taste—or intelligence—of his affianced bride."

"I doubt she had much choice about it. Do you not recall her, Nicholas—Miss Angela Buxley? Shy, slender, blue-eyed with golden curls? She's scarcely more than a child. And her father is a debt-ridden gamester."

Nicholas raised his eyes to hers, suddenly grave. "Appears to be a pattern, does there not?"

"Except the intended victim this time is much younger and more vulnerable than I. Oh, Nicholas, she's a delicate little thing, and she's terrified of him! I tried to talk with her, and then her parents last evening, tried to make them see what he is, but they wouldn't listen."

"You spoke frankly to the Buxleys?"

"Yes, and you may spare me the lecture that 'twas not my place to do so. I know Sir James as perhaps no other woman—still living, that is," she inserted grimly. "How can I let some poor innocent be delivered into his hands?"

"Sarah, I admire your courage and concern, but this truly isn't your problem. The girl *does* have a father. 'Tis his task to protect her."

"Not when the glitter of gambling money beckons," Sarah said bitterly. "I tried to reason with him, warn him—I even showed him my scar. But Findlay has him charmed—and well paid. Baron Buxley would hear nothing against him."

"Then you've done all you could. And proceeded much further than most would have been willing to go."

"But it isn't enough, Nicholas. I suddenly realized last night that, even had I succeeded in dissuading the Buxleys, Findlay would only seek another victim, until he found one gullible or unprotected enough."

She looked away from Nicholas's disapproving face. "Should I manage to blacken his reputation among the ton so thoroughly that none would countenance a union with him, it would still not be enough. He would merely target one poorer and more vulnerable still. Does not a maidservant or a shopkeeper's girl have just as much right to protection from such as he as the daughter of a baron?"

"I concede the point." Nicholas frowned. "But I fail to see what you can do about it."

Sarah took a deep breath. "Is not assault a crime punishable by law? And is this—'' she pointed to the scar at her wrist ''—not evidence of assault?''

Nicholas stared at her in horror. ''You cannot mean to bring him to the dock upon assault charges!''

Nicholas took her hand and kissed the scar fervently. ''My darling Sarah, I applaud your spirit and good intentions, but I could not permit you to expose yourself in a public courtroom in such a manner.''

'''Tis only my wrist, Nicholas.'' She smiled.

He wasn't amused. '''Tis a great deal more, and you know it,'' he snapped back. ''The mere thought of the vulgar display a trial would occasion—cartoons in the press shop windows, crowds in the courtroom—makes me shudder. The family would clamor for me to divorce you. No, you must not consider it.''

The urgency of the task and her desire to please him battled within her. Could she not convince him to help?

''When I spoke with Miss Buxley, she told me Sir James said I owed him a debt that she would repay. She had no idea what Findlay meant, but I do. Do you not see? As inconvenient, as scandalous as it may be, I am responsible. I cannot just turn away and forget.''

Nicholas looked grimmer than she'd ever seen him. ''How could you think to prove assault? The scar is old now, and there were no witnesses to the attack. Sarah, as your husband I absolutely forbid you to proceed in this matter.''

So searing had the experience been, she hadn't considered her scar might be worthless as evidence. Before she could ponder the implications, Nicholas pinned her with a gimlet glare. ''Don't even think of approaching Findlay himself, Miss Save-the-World! I swear, if you so much as look in his direction, I'll—I'll lock you in your room.''

Sarah stared. ''On bread and water?'' she asked dryly.

His severity softened into a grin. ''Bread and tea, perhaps. And—'' he winked at her ''—I would *visit* often.''

Then his face sobered. ''This worries me, sweeting. If

Sir James does harbor a grievance, we must be careful. I'll not underestimate his menace, for I should never forgive myself were something to happen to you. The other maidens of this world will have to find another champion. I will not bend on this, Sarah.''

He grasped her scarred wrist and rubbed it gently, frowning. ''We should take precautions. I'll escort you to any functions we attend, and if you wish to go out shopping, you must take the carriage and two extra footmen.''

She agreed without argument. Then, pleading the need to prepare for just such an expedition with Clarissa, she put down her cup and slipped from the room.

In the refuge of her chamber, Sarah mulled over Nicholas's words. She yearned to believe him, to abandon her dangerous enterprise. The warmth with which he'd treated her since her return, the ecstasy of their loving last night, made every fiber of her being protest proceeding in a mission that might forever destroy any hope of happiness together.

She could pursue this only over Nicholas's most adamant disapproval. Should she press a court action, 'twould likely mean all the vulgar scandal he'd predicted, and more. *I should have to divorce you,* he'd said.

Would he go that far? Dare she find out?

What other choice did she have? In her heart she knew her treatment of Sir James had, however unwittingly, added fuel to the fire of the demon that drove him. Because of her, did she not succeed in stopping him, innocent girls would suffer, and perhaps die.

If she had a duty to Nicholas, she owed her conscience an even greater one. She could not live with herself knowing she had allowed the maiming or death of blameless fellow creatures. She must go forward.

Then she recalled Nicholas's other objection. She carefully inspected her wrist.

The scar, thin, white and puckered, ran for scarcely an inch. As Nicholas had said, 'twould be difficult to judge its age. Findlay might well claim her charge was spite, that she carried the scar from some earlier mishap.

The implications of that realization frightened her to her bones. If she intended to stop Sir James, she would have to present fresh evidence.

She thought a long time before the plan came to her. Her turmoil settled into a cold, firm resolve. *Forgive me, Nicholas,* she said silently. *I love you, and I'm sorry. But I must do this.*

Chapter Nineteen

That night they attended Lady Cunningham's rout. As the Cunningham daughter was a friend of Miss Buxley and the party honored both girls, Sarah was certain Sir James would be present. How she would manage to slip away from Nicholas long enough to have a private word with Findlay concerned her, but it proved easier than she expected.

Nicholas's Aunt Amelia and the Odious Archibald chanced to be attending. When Archibald, ostensibly a suitor to the hand of Miss Cunningham, left his mama, Lady Stanhope latched on to Nicholas's arm and declared he must escort her to the refreshment room.

Sarah realized this was her best chance. As soon as Lady Stanhope steered Nicholas out of the ballroom, Sarah scanned the crowd.

She saw Sir James at the far side. It seemed he was watching her, for his eyes met hers and he nodded.

Findlay pulled Miss Buxley forward. From the pained look on the girl's face, he was holding her hand in a merciless grip. As he bent and kissed her fingertips, the girl's eyes widened. She tugged at her hand. When Sir James released her, she cradled her hand to her bosom and fled from the room.

Sir James watched her go. Then he raised his fingertips, touched them to his lips and waved to Sarah.

A rage greater than her loathing filled her. He'd staged that incident just for her, she was certain of it.

He was still gazing at her—doubtless awaiting her reaction. Clenching her teeth, she inclined her head toward the terrace. He smiled and shook his head.

Would he refuse to meet her? Somehow she must goad him to it. She looked toward the refreshment room where, had he truly been watching her, he would know Nicholas had gone. She turned back to stare at Findlay, and when he did nothing, raised an eyebrow scornfully. Then she made her way deliberately to the terrace.

Would he take the challenge? He had only to ignore her, and she could truly do nothing. Her heart pounded in double time as she waited on the darkened terrace, and despite the warmth of the evening, she shivered. Almost, she hoped he would not come, and she could return with a light heart to Nicholas—

"So, little dove, you seek a meeting. Tired already of your new husband? Or is it that he neglects you too often for one of—how shall I put it—superior charms?"

Sarah gathered her courage. "'Tis not of Nicholas I wished to speak, but of your betrothed. She's a child, Sir James. Hardly worthy of you."

"True. She has none of your spirit, and taming her will be a paltry business." He stepped closer. She forced herself to stand firm. "That slender little body is lovely, though, so frail and—delicate. And I do have a man's... appetites."

A door slammed, and Sir James looked back sharply. "Charming as this interlude is, I mustn't linger. So unreasonable of Englemere to restrict your movements, little dove, whilst feeling himself free to entertain Chloe. But alas, I have learned to respect his displeasure."

He bent his head until the light from the ballroom windows illuminated his face. The Grecian perfection of his nose, she saw with a shock, was marred by a crooked bump.

"Yes, your lord husband is rather close with his possessions. He counts even a dance an effrontery."

He ran a finger along the fracture, and suppressed rage roughened his voice. "I shall collect for this, never doubt." Falling back into his languid pose, he smiled at her. "From someone." He turned to walk away.

"I've not yet said what I wished," she called after him. "Perhaps if I call on you tomorrow?"

The baronet halted. With slow deliberation he turned back to her. "You would visit my home?"

She took a deep breath. "The proposition I wish to deliver is rather—private."

He stared at her, and she could almost see him weighing the risk of retribution from Nicholas against the prospect of having her once again in his power.

"But—if you fear Nicholas..." She shrugged. "'Tis nothing for it, then. Good evening, Sir—"

"I fear no man," he barked. He smoothed his cravat, frowning. She held her breath and waited. Just when she thought she must scream from suspense and frustration, his lips curved and that hot glow she had always found so disturbing began shimmering in his eyes.

"I don't suppose I could be held responsible for your visit," he said, half to himself. "Come if you wish, my lady. I shall be at home." He raked her body with a hot glance. "Perhaps you're deciding you made a mistake."

She watched him walk away. "Someone has," she whispered.

Too late now to question the wisdom or necessity of her plan. He'd taken the bait. Tomorrow she must spring an airtight trap.

Before that, though, she had one last night with Nicholas. Casting aside every restraint but love and need, she intended to make the most of it.

* * *

Sarah heard Nicholas approach her chamber door, and a shiver of anticipation tingled along her spine. He had come to her eagerly last night, and their loving had been joyous and passionate. Even so, ever mindful of her pledge, she had held back, responding rather than seeking a response.

This time there would be no holding back. If, after this night, she were fated to leave Nicholas, she would bear what she must. At least this once, though, she intended to touch and taste and love him with full abandon.

He closed the door and stepped into the candle-bright room. She would have preferred daylight, to see him more clearly, but the massed candelabra on the mantel and the bedside table would have to do.

Nicholas looked around in bemusement at the extravagant array of wax tapers. Then his glance reached her. His eyes widened, his breath caught and he stopped short.

Sarah reclined against the pillows, the coverlet at her ankles, clothed only in the shimmering fall of her hair. She'd fanned it loose, and like a pale ocean it flowed up over her breasts, down into the trough of her belly, breaking here and there over an elbow, a boulder of hipbone, before subsiding in a satin pool above her knees.

"I'm glad you've arrived," she said, her low voice loud in the charged silence. "I was getting chilled."

"L-let me warm you," he rasped. In two swift strides, shedding his dressing gown as he went, he reached the bed.

She let him kiss her, reveling in the taste of him, but when he reached to pull back her hair, she caught his wrists. "I want to look at *you,*" she whispered. "Let me."

With an inarticulate sound, he dropped his hands. His eyes focused on her, he let her guide him back against the pillows, adjust them behind him. Still half concealed, half revealed in her robe of tresses, she knelt beside him and simply looked.

His gaze followed hers as she studied his naked body

with a thoroughness she'd never before been able to indulge. That hollow at his throat looked made for kisses, she noted, and the little dimpled places beneath his collarbones. She wondered how the flat, rigid nipples would taste, whether the fine dark hair of his chest would tickle against her cheek, and felt a wicked delight that soon, she would find out. She drank in the sinewy curve of arm, the bony bend of wrist, the concave plane of abdomen.

Then she feasted her eyes lower, on the crinkly ruffle of curls, the tensed thighs from which his erection projected, a marvelous construction of taut length and smooth skin. Though she moved nothing but her eyes, his shaft leapt under her gaze.

"S-Sarah," he groaned. Perspiration had broken out on his forehead, his chest. He pushed to sit up.

She stopped him with her palm, gently insistent. "Stay, my lord. I'm not finished."

With a murmur, he subsided, but propped himself on his elbows to watch as her glance traveled lower still, to the plump sacks at the junction of his saddle-muscled thighs, the sharp angles of his kneecaps, the round of calf and bump of ankle, the toes splayed with tension.

"Do I turn over?" he asked.

Her secret places throbbed with heat and damp at the knowledge of what she would do. "No," she replied unsteadily. "I want to see you watching me."

She moved a fraction, and he tensed. Hands clenched on the bedclothes, he stared at her, the pulse beating visibly at his throat. In the candlelight, his moist skin glowed.

But she didn't touch him, not yet. She merely bent her face to his foot and exhaled over it, watching as her warm breath ruffled the tiny hairs of his toes. Securing her trailing hair behind her, she traveled slowly back up his body, blowing over his ankle, calf, knee, thigh.

Her whole body was pulsing, her nipples burning and tender, her passage drenched and ready, by the time she reached his rigid member. She had to stop, draw in a deep breath, before she could direct a long continuous flow of air over it.

Nicholas cried out, and her heart exulted with sensuous joy and lascivious power. Though his face contorted, his eyes squeezing tight and his shoulders writhing, she knew it was sweet torment and delicious agony that held him prisoned, prone before her.

"S-Sarah!" he begged, his voice strangled.

"Soon," she promised.

He opened glittering eyes to watch her, sucking in his belly at the soft erotic wind of her passage, hissing through clenched teeth as it crossed his nipples. He arched his neck back at its touch on his throat, thrust his head forward again to take the breath of her on his jaw, opened his mouth to feel it on his tongue.

And then she kissed him.

With a growl he grabbed her, slick against his chest, his mouth devouring. She kissed him back just as hungrily, but when he tried to roll her over, move her under him, she pushed him away. After a moment, his grip loosened.

He glanced at her, his eyes wild, unfocused. "Sarah, please! Now!" But when she sat back, he let her go.

She wanted more. She wanted him beyond control, transported out of mind and senses, lost totally in her and her loving of him.

"I want to touch you," she said. "Let me."

"Touch," he said hoarsely.

She bent and kissed him, not his mouth but the skin just beyond it. Holding his chin, she traced her lips along his brow, his jaw, nibbled at his earlobe, feeling him exhale hot against her face. She touched her tongue to the pulse at his throat, tasted the hard ridge of collarbone, the tickly curl of chest hair.

When her lips reached his nipples, he clenched her buttocks, kneaded them as she nipped her way across the taut skin of his belly.

She paused before his rigid shaft. "Sarah," he gasped, a plea.

Gently, sheathing her teeth, she took him in her mouth. His skin was velvet under her tongue, his taste heat and salt. Then he was moving, thrusting against her, his breathing frantic gulping pants, like a runner nearly spent. She adjusted to his rhythm, pulling him deep, sliding him free. A moment later he convulsed, crying out her name.

Her own heart doing a rapid tattoo, she released him. Murmuring, he pulled her to his chest, wrapped his arms about her and held her close. She felt his stampeding heartbeat steady, then slow.

A ferocious exaltation flooded her. Hers. This time, he was fully, completely hers.

Finally, with a low moan, he sat up. He gazed at her a moment, as if he couldn't quite believe what had just transpired, and drew one finger gently down her cheek. "Oh, Sarah, that was..." He shook his head. Then he slid his hand to her breast and grinned wolfishly. "My turn."

She pulled his fingers away. "Not just yet."

"More?" He gave her a theatrically exaggerated look of horror, but reclined readily back upon the pillows. "Lady, I am yours to command." He laughed, sounding bemused. "I begin to believe I'm enchanted, and you're a handmaiden sent straight from Aphrodite to drive me to madness."

"Believe it," she whispered.

She shook out her tangled hair and dried him with it, from his damp shoulders downward. By the time she reached his toes, his flaccid manhood had begun to stir. Wrapping a fistful of hair around her hand so the massed ends became a brush, she slowly dusted him with it, all along the length of his body, each plane and crevice, made him turn over so she could sweep his back and thighs and bottom.

She reveled in the muffled sounds she brought forth, in the way his buttocks puckered when she played the whisk of hair over them and down between his legs. When she turned him back over, he was fully ready.

But she again commanded him to stillness. Beginning at his toes, she slowly kissed her way up his lower body. She licked the balls of his feet, took his toes into her mouth and nibbled them. She tongued the soft soft skin below his ankle, the hollows beside his kneecaps, drawing from him deep, strangled groans.

When she reached his upper thighs, he was slick with sweat, his breathing once again a hoarse panting. He'd gone up on his elbows to watch her, expectant. But when her mouth moved from smooth muscled leg to suckle the pebbled sacks at the junction of his splayed thighs, he bent his head back and emitted a toneless, primitive wail that made her body surge with wetness and her heart exult.

Hers, hers, his body stretched and ready, and hers the power to bring him to such a pinnacle of anguished joy.

Grasping him, she took his sleek heated flesh deep in her mouth and carried him over the edge into ecstasy.

Afterward he lay limp. "Sarah," he sighed, a mere whisper of sound, and half raised a hand to her. Then his wrist fell back, his eyes flickered closed and he dozed.

The candles had burned down to thumb-sized wedges, dimming the light to a misty glow. Her heart filled with a piercing, bittersweet sadness, she lay beside him, rested her head on her crossed arms and watched him sleep.

She had given him every pleasure her love and imagination could devise. Forever and always, come what might, she would treasure those moments.

A short time later he awoke. He smiled at her and drew her atop him, molding her hips against him. "Now," he whispered, "you cannot say me nay."

Gladly she let him claim her. Following her lead, he stimulated, stroked and tasted every inch of her, bringing her over and over to the summit, drawing her back, and finally joining her in luxuriant fulfillment.

Near dawn, satiated, they at last pulled the damp sheets

up around them. Nicholas propped her against the pillows and gazed down at her, awe, tenderness and something else she dared not name in his face.

She waited, but after a moment he merely shook his head, as if at some great mystery. "Sarah," he said on a breath of wonder. "Sarah."

Nonetheless, after he gathered her against him, she fell asleep certain that whatever happened tomorrow, however far he might send her on a journey through courts and divorce and shame, he, too, would never forget this night.

Smiling in bemusement, Nicholas sat at his desk the next morning reviewing with relish every delightful, astonishing detail of his night with Sarah.

Such a blend of well-bred restraint and unbridled passion, he marveled. Over breakfast, as he poured tea, she sat cool as an untouched virgin. When he made an oblique reference to their near-sleepless night, she blushed.

In memory he traced his fingers the length of her satiny skin from collarbone to ankle. He could hardly wait till this evening. He was aroused already.

A knock sounded and Sarah entered. He beamed at her. Tremulously she smiled back and crossed to the desk.

"I've some commissions to complete, dull household matters, else I'd ask your escort. I'm meeting the factor to inspect the quarter's dry-goods supplies."

"I'm to be abandoned for meal, flour and coffee?" He sighed in mock outrage. "Will you be back for tea?"

"I'm not certain. Probably not."

Taking her hand, he drew her to him for a lingering kiss. "Can I not tempt you away from your duty?"

She gave him an odd smile. "So easily, I must depart forthwith." She stepped back as if to leave, then halted.

Placing her fingers on his temples, she gently traced his face from cheekbone to chin, as if he were an object infinitely dear. Her face glowed with such tenderness, such soul-searing warmth, that his breathing suspended.

"Goodbye, Nicholas," she whispered.

Nicholas sat motionless. He'd never seen such a look on her face before. A dancing spark of excitement licked up his veins. Could Sarah love him?

Hal seemed to think so. As they sat over port after dinner two nights ago, Hal had announced in his usual enigmatic fashion, "Dotes on you."

"Dotes?" he said, at sea.

"Sarah," Hal replied patiently. "All April-and-May with 'er. Eyes follow you around the room, watches you when you don't know she's lookin'." He made a sweeping hand gesture, as if closing an argument. "Macaroons."

"You mean," Nicholas said, as he pieced it together, "you think Sarah *loves* me?"

"See it in her eyes. Dotes on you."

Dare he believe it? He replayed every detail of that glowing look and came up with no words short of "love" to describe it. And last night—surely she must entertain the warmest of feelings to behave as she had.

Exhilaration flooded him. He'd never thought to want that emotion from her, but he found himself delighted.

Glancing down, he discovered Sarah's glove on the desk, where she'd evidently forgotten it. He lifted the soft leather and inhaled.

The scent was chamois and lavender, its touch silky soft. Like Sarah.

He couldn't remember what task had brought him to the library. Whatever it was, he was no longer interested in it. Or anything else. He should have gone with Sarah.

He was acting like a besotted bridegroom, he thought with a chuckle. Then much-belated illumination finally cracked him over the head like a cricket bat.

Could it be he loved Sarah as well?

The shocking idea froze him to his chair. After Lydia, he hadn't thought it possible he could love another woman—the hurt and distrust went too deep. His feelings for Sarah had built imperceptibly, layer upon layer, from a base of admiration and friendship. But upon assessing the depth of his concern for her, the strength of his desire to be with and protect her, and his unslakable passion, no other word seemed adequate.

Still marveling, he grasped the idea cautiously, like a precious goblet too fragile for handling. Could Nicholas Stanhope, wary, world-weary Marquess of Englemere, truly have fallen in love with his own wife?

My, how the ton would laugh. He didn't give a damn.

Already impatient for Sarah's return, he wandered into the hall, paused at the cheval glass to check his cravat. His face sported an idiotic grin. How many hours until tea?

Sarah checked the watch in her reticule. Delivering the package to Sinjin's batman had taken little time, but she'd had to purchase gloves before meeting the factor. That merchant would have thought it strikingly singular for the marchioness to arrive gloveless, and she hadn't dared risk returning to Stanhope House—and encountering Nicholas.

She couldn't have endured another goodbye. Would she ever see him again? Her heart seared with longing, she ordered the carriage to proceed to Portman Square.

Almost, her courage failed her. She made herself envision Angela Buxley's face and the nameless faces of all the innocents who would suffer if she did not act.

The carriage slowed to a stop. Her heartbeat already speeding, her fingers clammy in her new gloves, she climbed down and dismissed the carriage. When Martin, the footman Nicholas had detailed to protect her, protested the master instructed she wasn't to go anywhere without him, she replied at her most imperious that she was calling on a friend, and another friend would see her home.

Before mounting the stairs, she handed him a folded note. He should deliver it to Nicholas, but not until after tea, she instructed.

She must do this—and she would. She climbed the stairs and rapped firmly.

A thin man with a scarred face bowed her in without comment. Over the sudden thundering of her heart, Sarah heard the neigh of horses and the clatter of wheels as the Stanhope carriage drove away. Then the door closed behind her.

Leading her up a graceful cantilevered stairway to a reception room, the gaunt butler intoned in a colorless voice that he would inform his master of her arrival.

Knowing she was now enclosed with Sir James sent a shiver up her spine. This room, like its master, was on the surface perfectly appointed and polished. Were she to press it, she wondered a little hysterically, would she find rot under the satinwood inlay, mold beneath the brocade sofa?

Would Sinjin come? *Portman Square No. 13, Four of the clock. Do not fail me. Sarah,* she'd written. And inserted the note in his signet ring.

Now she must provoke Sir James. Could she control his violence once she unleashed it? Having no wish to become a martyr for the sake of conscience, she could only hope so. And pray that Sinjin would be on time.

"Well, well. So you did come."

Sir James stood in the doorway, impeccable in a black coat over buff breeches and a cream figured waistcoat. "Some wine, Manners," he called over his shoulder as he entered. "Surely, on such an auspicious occasion, you will take a glass with me, my dear."

Sarah had chosen a wing chair near the fireplace. Sir James approached it, smiling faintly. "Shall we observe the amenities, or do you wish to proceed immediately to this proposal you hinted at?"

"Let us begin. It is simply, as I said last night, that I cannot permit you to marry Miss Buxley."

"Having robbed me of a more fitting bride, you can hardly object if I seek matrimony with another. Have a few months of dull propriety with Englemere made you recognize your error? How sad 'tis too late."

He sighed. "Regret cannot alter my need to marry. So

pleasingly permanent an arrangement. Despite any—disagreements—a wife cannot go running off.''

''Or lay testimony against you?''

''Precisely. Such a discerning wit you have, little dove. 'Tis one of the things I've always admired.'' He smiled that slow, mocking smile she detested and walked toward her. The hair on the back of her neck bristled.

He reached for her, then checked his hand as the door opened to admit the butler with wine and glasses on a tray.

''On the side table, if you please. That will be all, Manners. Please note, we don't wish to be disturbed.''

Sir James poured wine and handed her a glass. She accepted it, willing her fingers not to tremble.

''A toast to you, my dear. Quite brave of you to come with nary a maid to lend you countenance. Why did you, I wonder? Has your toplofty husband washed his hands of you, now that you've lost the brat?''

Sarah gritted her teeth, fighting the pain any mention of her loss still caused her. She took a sip of wine.

Sir James sighed in mock sympathy. ''I warned he wanted you only for breeding, did I not? Of course, I've taken some pains to accelerate his disgust—my 'Farmer Bride.' ''

She stared in shock. Findlay had schemed with Weston to discredit her? ''You—''

''Ah, yes.'' He waved a negligent hand. ''A trifle, perhaps, but one misstep does build upon another. Though you quite cleverly avoided several of the traps Weston set. Did you not realize I would never passively accept Englemere's theft of you?''

He touched a finger to her chin. She made herself pull back slowly, without flinching. Findlay laughed softly.

''We are well matched. Have I not always said so? Your dull but exacting husband cannot appreciate, as I do, your many qualities. Your wit and courage. That irrepressible urge to do good. 'Twas why you came today, was it not, little dove? To flutter your pretty wings and lead me away from Miss Buxley?

"And so," he said triumphantly, his blue eyes chilling, "does my ultimate plan succeed. I had hoped choosing the very young, very innocent Miss Buxley would bring you back to me. Not, had that purpose failed, that she hasn't merits of her own. Such a lovely bud about to unfurl."

He paused, a distinctly lascivious look coming into his eyes. Sarah felt sickened.

"Not of your caliber, of course. However, marriage doesn't preclude additional, quite satisfactory arrangements, does it, my dear? One need only ask your assiduous captain. How fortunate he returns to Spain."

Before Sarah could think or move, Sir James closed the distance between them. "We are fated to be together, don't you feel it, little dove? You bear my mark." He seized her arm and stripped down her glove. "Ah, yes, there it is."

His smile faded. "And I bear yours." He touched his fingers to the crooked bridge of his nose. "What retribution should I exact, I wonder, for this?"

Sarah ignored the impulse to appease him. "I had nothing to do with that."

"Did you not? True, that lummox Waterman perpetrated the outrage, but you cannot deny you were the cause."

He stepped back, making an elaborate show of studying her. Sarah forced herself to meet his gaze squarely. He wanted her to be afraid—he thrived on it. She would not allow him the pleasure.

"I doubt you do anything," she said evenly, pleased at how coolly disdainful her voice sounded.

He laughed, a nasty sound. "My dear, are you that careless of your reputation? I have but to detain you while I call a few friends. How long do you think it would take before the news galloped round the ton that Lady Englemere paid an unescorted call to my bachelor dwelling? Your very proper husband might well divorce you."

"He'd be more apt to shoot you."

"On what grounds? Manners, and your own coachman, would attest you came here willingly. Besides, do you really think Englemere would exert himself over a wife who not only failed to provide an heir, but has already embroiled herself in several tawdry little scandals?"

He tightened his grip. "Of course, you may be right. I take a risk. But 'tis what makes it interesting."

Although she strained away, he raised her wrist and kissed the scar. "A divorce might be convenient. I could install you here. And Miss Buxley, of course. What has Englemere taught you, I wonder?" He jerked her nearer and looked in her eyes. "Would you enjoy a *ménage à trois?* I shall likely have to tie her down. Such a little thing, 'twill be bloody. Shall you want to watch?"

"You are disgusting."

He smiled as if she'd paid him a pretty compliment. "Shall I call in those friends—or let you go? Even do I release you, I must extract payment. What would be fitting, do you think?"

He forced her arm up and ran her bare hand down his damaged nose. "Not your own sweet nose. No, we need something that would be our little secret. One slender finger, perhaps?" Holding her rigid, he waited for her reaction. For her fear.

She laughed, albeit shakily. "You wouldn't dare."

"Wouldn't I? My servants are both well paid and... deaf, when it suits me."

"I am Nicholas's wife. Injure me, and he'll kill you."

He nodded, as if she'd just scored a point at whist. "Perhaps. Something more subtle, then."

Suddenly light glowed in his eyes. "Why not enjoy what was stolen from me? And what better mark, than to plant a tow-haired bastard to be Englemere's heir?"

Hauling her against him, he trapped her in his arms. "Now, this," he groaned, rubbing the hardness in his breeches against her, "I can truly enjoy."

For an instant, Sarah panicked. She forced herself not

to struggle. To be raped had been no part in her plan, but if she resisted, he would quickly overpower her. *Think,* she told herself furiously.

Making herself move slowly, she strained away from him. Immediately he tightened his hold. Still pressing him away, she uttered a low, passionate moan.

Findlay stilled and gave a triumphant laugh. "Yes, moan for me, little dove." Noticing the opening she'd made, he slid a hand down to fondle her breast. His breathing erratic, with his other hand he fumbled at the buttons of her gown, shifting his body back a few precious inches.

It was enough. Bracing herself, Sarah slammed her knee up against the bulge in his breeches.

He broke away with a howl and doubled over. Sarah retreated toward the fireplace, heart hammering, every instinct screaming at her to flee.

She glanced at the clock. Three-fifty. Whatever Findlay did next, she prayed she'd survive it. And that Sinjin would not be late.

Slowly Sir James straightened. In his expression, nothing of humor or lust remained. "You little bitch," he whispered, his eyes blazing. Then he smiled, and from his waistcoat pocket extracted a small knife. Flicking the blade open, he advanced on her.

Chapter Twenty

Still grinning, Nicholas loped up the stairs of Stanhope House. Too restless to work until Sarah's return, he'd borne Hal off to Jackson's. He'd astonished master and disciples alike by allowing an untried fledgling to land a glove on him, and then laughing over his lapse.

Jackson reproved him for lack of concentration. Hal looked at him strangely. He smiled genially back.

Now it was teatime, and although Sarah had said she would probably not return, he'd come back just in case.

Glendenning brought tea and ushered in a footman.

"Mistress says I was supposed ter give ya this, but ya weren't to read of it till after tea."

Nicholas took the note. From its paper wafted the faint scent of lavender he always associated with Sarah. He inhaled deeply. "You left Lady Englemere somewhere?"

"Aye, master. Said as how she was avisitin' a friend in Portman Square, and would be brung home by anudder."

"Portman Square?" he repeated, trying to recall who of their acquaintance lived there. Probably some old dowager in precarious health Sarah was paying a duty call on.

"Thank you, Martin," he said, and propped the note on the tea tray.

What was Sarah proposing? Another little tryst, dare he

hope? He tapped the scented envelope. She said to wait until tea. Surely he had that much patience.

As he stroked and gentled her tonight, would she murmur out her love? In the aftermath of passion, should he confess first? Despite the newly discovered fervor of his emotions, he was still hesitant about voicing them. Awkward as a green boy in the first throes of infatuation, he thought with a chuckle.

"Sweet Sarah, I love you," he whispered experimentally. But then, 'twas nothing urgent about saying it—they had years and years, the rest of their lives. The idea of being in love, of Sarah loving him in return, was still so novel he felt a sense of awe and joy at the thought of it.

Probably he was letting his imagination run riot, and the note was merely a reminder of which function they were to attend tonight, or a message from the factor.

But with Sarah, he couldn't be sure. Only think of his reception last night. Biting into a macaroon, he leaned back against the chair, reliving once more his entrance into his wife's bedchamber.

Some niggling sense of unease clouded that arousing vision. Then the memory surfaced.

Did the job right. Broke his nose for sure. Bled all over m'carriage when I carted him back to Portman Square.

For a moment, he froze. Then Nicholas grabbed the note and ripped it open.

My dearest Nicholas, You have forbidden me to interfere in the matter of Sir James Findlay's marriage. After much reflection I must conclude I have a duty to my conscience that transcends even that which I owe you.

I beg you will understand, dearest husband, that I cannot turn away and allow the death or molestation of young innocents, knowing it is within my power to halt it. Thus, I must gather the evidence that will prevent Sir James—

His heart stopped and a bolt of sheer terror shocked his body. Turning so abruptly he knocked over his chair, he yanked on the bellpull and dashed from the room.

He nearly ran down Glendenning in the hallway. "Send Martin to the mews, and have Valkyrie saddled immediately!" he shouted as took the stairs two at a time. Careening into his chamber, he kicked off his tasseled Hessians, pulled on his riding boots and raced for the stairs.

Please, God, he prayed to the pounding cadence of his footsteps. *Please, God, don't let him hurt her.*

He sped past the astonished Glendenning and out to the stables. Spying Martin leading Valkyrie, he shouted, "Which house on Portman Square?"

The footman broke into a trot, bringing the horse to meet him. "Number thirteen, master."

"Have John Coachman send the carriage. Hurry."

Grabbing the reins of the snorting, sidling horse, he jumped into the saddle, applied both spurs and whip and galloped off.

Carts pulled aside and pedestrians scattered as the stallion thundered down the street. Images jumped out at him from the blur of faces. Lydia, lying broken beside her broken carriage. Edmund, his eyes staring sightlessly from a face white as river foam.

He clutched the reins, scoured by anguish. *Please, God, this time don't let me be too late.*

Then he remembered the colt in the stall at Tattersall's. Bitter gall rose in his throat. Applying the whip again, he bent low over Valkyrie's back.

Portman Square appeared quiet as he brought his lathered horse to a plunging halt. He leapt from the saddle, ran up the steps and put his shoulder to the door. To his surprise, it opened easily. He shoved it to the wall and raced into the marble entryway.

From the top of the staircase, he could hear grunts, the crash of crockery and the clash of steel on steel.

"Sarah! Sarah, where are you?"

He'd leapt up two steps when Findlay, sword in hand, backed onto the landing, hard-pressed by Sandiford.

The captain lunged, Findlay countered. As the force of the check rang out against the stone floors and wall, Findlay shoved the captain back and ran for the stairs.

Perhaps seeing Nicholas startled him, or mayhap his boot caught on the carpet. Whatever the reason, he seemed to check at the top of the stairs, then fell headlong.

Nicholas stepped aside. Findlay reached out as he tumbled past, frantically clawing at Nicholas's boot. He continued to bounce and slide until he reached the bottom.

With a sharp crack, Findlay's head hit the marble floor. He emitted a long, low groan and lay still.

Swiftly the captain sheathed his sword. "I'll finish this." He jerked his thumb toward Findlay. "Look to your wife. First chamber on the left."

Nicholas scrambled up the stairs. "I've a carriage coming," he called back. "Will you watch for it?"

At the captain's nod, he turned and ran down the hallway. "Sarah! Sar—oh, my God."

Facedown and motionless, one hand outstretched, his wife lay on the floor before the fireplace.

In two bounds he reached her. "Sarah," he whispered, his heart racing as he picked up the hand to check her pulse.

He recoiled, for her arm lay in a crimson pool. With each faint pulse, a spurt of warm blood gushed from her wrist to stain his gloves and drip onto the floor.

Gasping in his panic, he clawed at the knots in his cravat, finally tearing it free. He doubled the cloth and bound it tightly around her wrist.

Holding her hand to the floor, he pushed his whole weight against the pulse point. Not until the tips of her fingers turned bluish did he dare decrease his force.

It appeared the bleeding had slowed. Clamping a hand over her wrist to maintain the pressure, he rolled her over, intending to lift her into his arms.

Her head lolled back, and as he reached down to support it, he saw the bodice of her gown had been sliced to ribbons. A crisscross maze of small cuts covered her chest.

With a trembling finger he pushed aside the ruined material. The cuts all appeared shallow, and though the skin still oozed, none bled actively. She lay limp and lifeless, but a faint pulse throbbed at her throat.

His chest tight in an agony of rage and pain, Nicholas carried her to the sofa. He sat, one hand still clamped about her slashed wrist, and cradled her against him.

She had not submitted tamely, he noted as he tried to wrap himself around her chilled body. The room was a chaos of broken knickknacks and overturned chairs. With each puff of breeze from the open doorway, downy feathers wafted from a jagged gash in the sofa cover.

His fingers numbing, he shifted her bandaged wrist. 'Twas cut at the same place as the burn scar, he realized.

How could you think to prove assault? His impatient words burned in his ears.

He should have known she would not abandon so important an enterprise. He should have known, and helped her, instead of goading her to this deadly confrontation.

"Forgive me, Sarah," he whispered. "Forgive me, forgive me." Laying his face against her braids, he wept.

Through a silent eternity punctuated only by the steady ticking of the mantel clock, Nicholas waited.

Finally he heard boot steps echoing down the hall. Sandiford strode in. His swift glance took in Sarah's unconscious figure, and his jaw clenched. "Can you carry her?"

Nicholas nodded.

From behind an overturned chair, Sandiford produced a military cape. "I have no idea where her pelisse might be. Seems the servants bolted. Best wrap her in this."

Nicholas covered Sarah and lifted her gently. Sandiford frowned. "You're a pretty ghastly sight yourself."

Nicholas looked down. A ragged tatter of neckcloth hung from his collar, dark stains spread from his lapels down his stiffened shirtfront, and the cuffs of his jacket were soaked a blackish red.

Sandiford tucked the long ends of the cloak up over Nicholas's shoulders, masking the damage. "Let's go."

Within moments they had her in the carriage. The captain had primed the coachman, for he stood with his whip at the ready and gave them no more than a glance.

Once the carriage rolled forward, Nicholas looked over to Sandiford. "I owe you a debt I can never repay."

The captain waved away his gratitude. "I would do anything for Sarah," he said simply.

"What happened back at—" A black rage fired in him, and he couldn't choke out the name.

"I'm afraid I don't know much. My batman found me about teatime with a package from Sarah. It contained my signet, wrapped in a note demanding I meet her in Portman Square at four of the clock."

He held out the ring. "I'd given this to Sarah three years ago, telling her if she ever needed me, she had only to send it. Naturally, I came at once. But Findlay had already—" Sandiford's voice broke, and he swallowed hard "—already cut her when I arrived. Why she went there, or why Findlay attacked her, I have no idea."

Guilt and bitter regret scalded Nicholas. "She knew him well. When she learned he meant to wed a very young girl, she felt she must at all cost prevent it. He had—hurt Sarah before."

"He what?" Sandiford exploded.

"Just before their engagement was to be announced, Sarah displeased him in some way, and he burned her wrist. She carries the scar still. 'Twas one of the reasons I married her." Nicholas laughed without humor. "To protect her. What a bloody botch I've made of that."

"'Tis not the first time she's flung herself into peril, doing what she felt she must," Sandiford soothed. "You've known Sarah only a few months. You couldn't have dreamed she would be so foolhardy."

"But I should have guessed," Nicholas cried. "She told me of her anxiety. I knew what Findlay was capable of and wanted Sarah nowhere near him. So when she suggested she bring charges against him, I, arrogant fool that I am, flatly forbade it. I even said, God help me, that her scar was too old to serve as e-evidence."

He gritted his teeth, too anguished to speak. After a moment he whispered, "I didn't think...I never suspected—" He closed his eyes and bent his cheek to her head.

Sandiford said nothing, but the sting of his own reproach was goad enough. A few moments later they reached Stanhope House. Sandiford assisted him out, then distracted Glendenning while Nicholas carried Sarah up. He was helping Nicholas lay her on the bed when Becky rushed in.

She halted, her face paling. "Oh, my lady!"

Sandiford caught her arm. "Steady, Becky. Remember when she was ten, and fell out of that apple tree I dared her to climb? Looked a sight then, too, I remember."

"Master S-Sinjin?" Becky clutched the captain's arm. She took a deep breath and straightened. "I'm all right now. Let me get her out of that h-horrible gown. You'd best step outside, young master."

"May I call tomorrow?" he asked Nicholas humbly.

"Of course."

Sandiford nodded. He stepped toward the door, but then, as if drawn by an irresistible force, walked instead to the bed. The expression on his face as he gazed down at Sarah left no doubt of the depth of his emotion. With a half apologetic, half defiant glance at Nicholas, he bent to brush a wisp of pale gold hair from her forehead. "Wake soon, dear Sarah," he said huskily, and strode out.

Nicholas helped Becky ease Sarah out of the ruined gown. By the time she had bathed away the crusted patches of blood and bundled Sarah into a soft flannel nightrail, Becky was weeping silently. "My poor, sweet lady."

Nicholas collapsed in a chair. Already the day felt years long, and night had not yet fallen.

In the predawn stillness, Nicholas sat on a chair by Sarah's bed. During the long, interminable evening he had had his physician check Sarah.

Keep her warm and get fluid into her if you can, the doctor had advised, adding she would likely not regain consciousness for some time. Then, if she hadn't lost too much blood and if wound fever didn't set in… Tonight would probably tell, he concluded soberly. Leaving a powder to administer in case of fever, the physician promised to return in the morning.

Some time ago, Becky had brought him supper. Knowing he needed food to maintain his strength, he'd eaten mechanically, the meal like dust and ashes in his mouth. While Becky dozed in the sitting room, he sipped brandy-fortified coffee, able only to wait—and think.

Sandiford's reassuring words could not ease his guilt. Sarah had spoken to him of this, concern eloquent in her voice. Instead of bending every effort to assist her, he'd played the dictatorial husband.

So naturally, when in peril she sent to Sandiford. A wise choice, was it not? Unlike him, the captain had neither argued nor questioned, but come at once.

An equally dismal thought struck him. She must have returned from Stoneacres to confront Findlay—not because she missed her fool of a husband.

With a heavy sigh, he looked down at her note and read it once more to the end.

I hope it is within your power to forgive. If not, I will understand, thank you for the happiness you have brought me and pray fervently that a merciful Providence may in future bless you with a wife more worthy than I.

She had believed his threat to divorce her, apparently. Would she welcome it, and fly back to Sandiford, the man who trusted and supported her? Nicholas had no doubt the captain would be delighted to receive her, and would care naught for the ruin divorce would bring her reputation, and his.

For perhaps a second, Nicholas entertained the idea of standing nobly aside—and then angrily rejected it. She had pledged herself to him, and he would hold her to it. Damn it, he loved her!

After Lydia, he had built such a wall of suspicion and distrust around his heart he'd not believed any woman could broach it. Yet, somehow Sarah had.

Given his past, he might never be able to trust her completely. But he also knew beyond any doubt that, even were the obnoxious captain to reside next door, a permanent thorn in his side, keeping Sarah's warmth and passion in his arms and his bed and his life would be worth every risk.

Surely she cared for him a little. The tenderness in her face when she bade him goodbye—was it just this morning?—the way she touched him, loved him that rapturous night, must mean she cherished some warm emotion.

He would woo her passionately until he won back her respect and earned her affection. Until she no longer regretted the loss of her former love. He'd begin, he vowed, the moment she woke.

Feeling more hopeful than he had since tearing open the note twelve hours ago, he leaned over to stroke her cheek. Hot, dry skin scalded his hand.

Panic drying his tongue, Nicholas stumbled to the door and called for Becky.

While the maid ran for water and cloths, Nicholas mixed the powder the doctor left and carried it to Sarah. Raising her by the shoulders, he shook her gently, then with more vigor, to no avail. He could not rouse her.

For several hours, he and Becky dipped, wrung out and applied the cold cloths to her face, chest and arms. Becky had the fortuitous thought of tearing a strip from one of them, soaking it in medicine water, and trickling it in her mouth. From time to time she swallowed and they managed to get at least a fraction of the drug in her.

As his hands worked feverishly, his mind confronted the reality Sarah might die. Wretched as he'd felt before, the agony of that idea made his previous anxiety pale.

Disconnected images of her flitted through his fear-fogged mind: how she tilted her head and looked at him inquiringly…her charming gurgle of a laugh, and the golden lights that danced in her eyes…her head nestled on his shoulder as, after loving, she drifted asleep.

He thought of her independence, her stubborn pride, her insistence on driving herself to fulfill what she saw as her duty. He thought what a desert his life would be without her.

Most of all, he had never in his life regretted anything more than not having told her he loved her.

Finally, pale dawn light peeped through the curtains. Sarah's fever seemed lower, though she lay unconscious still. Nicholas's body ached in every limb and his hands were numb from wringing out cloths.

Becky glanced at him and must have read the weariness in his face. "Master, will you not lie down? I've slept some, but you've not had a wink all night. You must rest. The mistress will be needing you when she wakes."

In truth, Nicholas wasn't sure he could force himself to continue much longer. Funny little lights were dancing before his eyes, his head felt as if it might float to the ceiling, and his ears buzzed. But the thought of leaving her terrified him.

"All right, Becky, I'll sleep. Here, by her bed." He

dragged a wing chair over. ''Wake me at once if—if anything happens.''

Wrapping up in a blanket, Nicholas leaned his head on the chair's padded arm. Despite his anxiety and grief, he was asleep in a moment.

Slowly Sarah rose to consciousness to discover her chest afire, her wrist throbbing and her parched mouth filled with a bitter taste. Wanting nothing so much as a drink of water, she reached toward a glass.

Her hand fell back, startling her. She realized she was in her bed at Stanhope House, and terribly weak.

Oddly, Nicholas slept in a chair beside her. His shirt wrinkled and cravatless, his hair untidy, he rested his unshaven face on one hand. Dark circles, black against the pallor of his skin, shadowed his eyes.

Concern jolted her awake. And then she remembered.

Findlay had come after her with a knife, his lips curled back in a snarl as he called her names she didn't even recognize. Though she dodged his first furious lunge, inevitably, he caught her.

Trapping her against the fireplace, he pinned her arms behind her. Still mouthing obscenities, he methodically slashed her bodice, making the cuts shallow so that some rent only cloth, some pierced skin. Finally, growling this time he'd make his mark indelible, he forced her wrist up and sliced open the scar.

Faint with pain and terror, she heard Sinjin roar her name, saw him burst in, sword drawn. Findlay shoved her aside and grabbed his own sword from above the mantel.

She seemed to remember a clash of steel before a cold faintness stripped her fingers from their hold on the fire screen and she fell into darkness.

Had Sinjin brought her home? She felt a rush of gratitude. Dear Sinjin, who had come without question, and without question saved her life. Thank Providence he would be out of the country so the horrific scandal sure to follow this escapade would not touch him.

It would tarnish Nicholas. No wonder he looked ill! Probably he was waiting for her to wake so he could tell her where he meant to send her during the court case. Where she might stay while a divorce bill went forward.

Was this the last time she would see him? Despite the fire in her body and the ache in her heart, she cherished this one, lingering chance to gaze at him.

Through her despair a tinge of humor emerged. Never had she seen her impeccable husband look so unkempt.

He stirred, groaned and opened his eyes. Sarah noted how bloodshot they were, how pale and drawn was his face. Her alarm revived.

"N-Nicholas," she croaked. "Are you all right?"

He jolted upright. "Sarah? Oh my God, Sarah!"

He stumbled to the bed and touched her forehead with trembling fingers. "The fever's nearly gone, praise heaven!"

"Are you ill? You look dreadful."

Nicholas seized her uninjured hand and kissed it fervently. "If I do, 'tis all your fault. What a scare you've given me! But you must be thirsty."

He caught up the bedside glass and held it to her lips. She drank it down without stopping.

"Thank you, Nicholas. I tried to reach it, but I seem to be amazingly weak."

"'Tis not surprising after what you've been through."

Cold reality snuffed the joy of seeing him. "I'm so sorry, Nicholas, I—"

"No, Sarah, 'tis I who am sorry! When I read you intended to confront that madman, I was never so frightened in my life. You sweet, courageous fool."

"I had to, Nicholas. I tried to think of another way, but nothing less would stop him." She sighed unhappily. "The scandal will be dreadful, I'm afraid."

"No one knows you went to Findlay's. I gave out to

the servants that the activities of London proved too much, and you collapsed at a friend's. 'Twill be no scandal.''

Sarah took a deep breath and regretted it as hot prickles blazed across her chest. "I must go forward with this, Nicholas." Bittersweet longing and regret filled her. "I expect you will divorce me, and I don't blame you. I've been a shockingly poor bargain of a wife."

"Don't say that," Nicholas cried. "I know when you needed me most, I failed you. But I promise to do better. I don't want a divorce, and I won't let you marry him."

"Findlay?" Sarah shuddered. "I wouldn't consider it."

"Sarah, Findlay is dead. That's why there will be no scandal. You don't need to testify."

"Dead?" Shocked, she sagged back against the pillows. "Did Sinjin—?"

"No. They were dueling on the landing. Findlay tried to break for the stairs, and fell." Nicholas made a noise that sounded like a growl. "More's the pity! I should have taken great pleasure in driving a blade through his heart."

"Bless Sinjin," Sarah murmured.

"Sarah, I know how you feel about him, how you've always felt, and I know he cares for you. But we took vows. I want to honor them. This time, won't you let me stay and nurse you? Can we not begin again?"

A wild, impossible hope soared through her. "Do you mean, after all the trouble I've caused, you still want me?" Her heart commenced to beat at double time, and she dared not look at him as she awaited his response.

"More than ever."

Her glance shot up. Nicholas was smiling, his sincerity unquestionable. Exultation robbed her of breath.

Then her conscience prodded. "Before you decide, Nicholas, I must confess I can no longer keep our bargain. You see—" she twisted the coverlet between nervous fingers "—I'm sorry, but I'm afraid I've fallen in love with you."

To her surprise, Nicholas grinned and eased himself on

the bed. "Have you, now? The prospect sounds delightful."

"But you don't understand," she wailed. "You've seen how—impassioned I become about those I care for—my family, the tenants at Stoneacres. I shall be demanding and possessive." Her courage nearly failed her, but she forced herself to make it plain. "What I mean is, I—I can no longer tolerate your mistress."

"What mistress?"

She gave him an aggrieved glance. "Nicholas, do not trouble to deny your understanding. I saw her there, at my presentation ball."

His grin vanished. "You saw—! No, 'tis impossible!"

"Then her twin sister accosted me in the ladies' withdrawing room—wearing a necklace of robin's-egg rubies. Besides, from what Mr. Baxter said, several hundred other guests saw her dancing with you as well."

"He told you that? No wonder you were so angry! Believe me, my darling, 'tis a lie. First, I never bade her to your ball. I've not been able to prove it, but I suspect Findlay had Weston forge an invitation, just to foment trouble. Second, I hustled her away before she ever reached the ballroom."

Before her disbelieving brain could comprehend the full impact of that, he seized her hand. "I swear to you, I've not seen Mrs. Ingram except at social functions since I asked for your hand. I love you, sweet Sarah. I want no woman but you."

She stared, her mouth falling open. Could she have heard him aright? He loved her? Her heart swelled.

He grinned again. "You could kiss me," he suggested.

She leaned eagerly toward him—and remembered the last, worst part of her confession. *Must* she tell him? Yes, her conscience insisted.

"There's one other matter." She felt her face flush. "I must warn you I may sometimes f-forget myself." He looked at her blankly. "As I did our last night."

Nicholas sighed. "Our last night was wonderful."

"Now, Nicholas, you told me most plainly you didn't want a spirited, passionate wife!"

"Not want—?" Nicholas shook his head violently. "I never said anything so cloth-headed!"

"You most certainly did!"

"I must have been foxed." An arrested look crossed his face. "You mean every night of our marriage might have been like the last, had I not made that bacon-brained remark?"

"Perhaps not *every* night. You did teach me—things."

Nicholas cupped her face in his hands. "So did you teach me. That I wanted no other—I dismissed Chloe weeks ago! That in spite of the past I could love beyond doubt. Yes, let us forge a new bargain."

He slipped off the bed and went down on one knee. "Will you take a chance on loving me, my one and only darling? I promise a return you will never regret."

Gambler's words still. Sarah gazed at the earnest entreaty of his eyes. Could she really commit herself, heart and soul, to this unrepentant gamester?

Had she not already made that decision? "My dear husband," Sarah said as she urged him back on the bed, "that's the one gamble I'm prepared to take."

* * * * *

Marrying the Major
by
Joanna Maitland

Joanna Maitland was born and educated in Scotland though she has spent most of her adult life in England or abroad. She has been a systems analyst, an accountant, a civil servant, and director of a charity. Now that her two children have left home, she and her husband have moved from Hampshire to the Welsh Marches, where she is revelling in the more rugged country and the wealth of medieval locations. When she is not writing or climbing through ruined castles, she devotes her time to trying to tame her new house and garden, both of which are determined to resist any suggestion of order.

Readers are invited to visit Joanna's website at www.joannamaitland.com

For Jenny

Prologue

1805

Emma Fitzwilliam settled herself high in the
branches of her favourite oak, glancing only a little
ruefully at yet another tear in her cotton pinafore. She
was not usually so clumsy. She would be well scolded
for that when she returned to the house, but her pun-
ishment would be much worse if they discovered she
still climbed trees. Her old governess was still trying
vainly to make a lady of her. And Papa—dearest
Papa—had lately said one or two things to suggest he
was less than totally happy with the way she behaved.

Dearest Papa. For him, if he asked, she would *try*
to become a lady, but it would be terribly difficult—
and terribly boring. Ladies had to walk sedately instead of romping around the estate, they were never
allowed out without an escort, they certainly could
not go swimming in the lake, or fishing, or climbing
trees—and they weren't even supposed to laugh out
loud. Emma frowned at that last thought. Gentlemen

were allowed to laugh—and frequently did—but ladies were supposed to smile demurely or, at most, give a melodious tinkle to signify amusement. It wasn't fair. Nor would it be fair to make her spend all her time at ladylike pursuits. Emma could play and sing pretty well, and even set a neat stitch, but she could not imagine doing so *all* the time, with only slow, boring walks for exercise, accompanied by a stony-faced groom. Ugh.

She wriggled about until she could reach into her pocket for her book and her apple. Then she settled down to read, munching blissfully. This was one of the pleasures of *not* being a lady—and she would not give it up.

'Young Lord Hardinge and his friend have called to see Miss Emma, sir,' intoned the butler gravely from the study doorway, 'but…no one is quite sure where she is. Shall I—?'

'Show them both in here, Godfrey,' said Sir Edward Fitzwilliam, rising from his deep wing-chair with a welcoming smile already on his cheery features. 'No doubt my daughter will appear soon enough. She seems to have some kind of sixth sense about welcome visitors—and unwelcome ones, too.' He laughed at his own wit, wondering, none the less, how it was that his mischievous daughter was never to be found except when it suited her. For Richard Hardinge, who was like a big brother to her, she probably would appear. She had been trailing him for years, after all, and Richard had never once rejected her, no matter how demanding she had become. Soon, it would all have to stop. Emma was fast maturing into a young lady—and young ladies did not cavort around the estate with male friends, no matter how trustworthy they might be, nor how indulgent her father. No—soon it would be necessary to find a proper female companion for his only daughter, to give her the polish that a young lady required, the polish that her dear mama would have provided if only she had lived.

Sir Edward sighed slightly at the sad memory, but assumed a polite smile when the door opened again to admit his two guests. The young men were remarkably alike, both tall and dark-haired, with open features and merry eyes. They seemed to have been laughing at some shared joke.

Richard Hardinge bowed politely to his host. 'I collect we have lost her again, sir,' he said with an ironic shake of the head. 'And Hugo was so anxious to make his farewells in due form, too.' Richard grinned at Hugo, who seemed to be unmoved by his friend's sly jibe.

'I suggest you both sit down,' said Sir Edward placidly, nodding in the direction of the old-fashioned sofa on the opposite side of the huge fireplace. 'She will appear, sooner or later.' He turned to Hugo Stratton. 'But I'm sorry to learn that you are leaving, my boy. I had understood from Lady Hardinge that you were to remain at Harding for a month or so yet.'

'That was so, sir,' said Hugo. 'Lady Hardinge was kind enough to invite me to stay for the summer—until my commission came through. The thing is...well, sir, the fact is that my regiment is ordered

to Deal next week—the rumour is that we are preparing for embarkation for north Germany—and unless I join them now, I'll have to wait for months,
besides missing the chance of a crack at Boney.' His
grey eyes were shining with enthusiasm as he spoke.
'I really do have to go, you see, sir. I'm leaving for
home this afternoon.'

Sir Edward nodded sagely. He had seen enough of
Hugo Stratton these past few weeks to recognise the
makings of a good officer in him, in spite of his
youth. 'I understand your haste, my boy. I was much
the same at your age. In the circumstances, it's good
of you to make the time to call on Emma. You must
have a host of more important things on your mind.'

Hugo was still young enough to be able to blush.
He stammered a little. 'After all your kind hospitality,
sir, it is…the least I could do.'

'Think nothing of it,' said Sir Edward, 'nothing at
all.' He rose and paced to the window, pulling back
the heavy velvet curtains to gaze out on the deserted
terrace and the sweeping lawns beyond. 'Drat the
girl,' he said quietly to himself, 'where on earth is
she?' He turned back to his guests, smiling apologetically. 'I can understand that time is pressing for you,
so I will not attempt to detain you. Since Emma has
not condescended to put in an appearance, she will
have to make do with second-hand farewells. I will
tell her you called, and why. Perhaps now she'll learn
not to disappear quite so often.'

Hugo and Richard had risen politely with their
host. Hugo took a step forward. 'I still have half an
hour, sir. May we not go and look for Miss Emma?

She's bound to be in the garden somewhere—and Richard probably knows where to look. He should, after running tame round your estate for so many years.' This time, it was Hugo's turn to grin at his friend's discomfiture.

Sir Edward smiled indulgently at them. 'Very well, if you wish. But do not, on any account, allow that little minx's pranks to delay you beyond your time.'

The two young men were already making their way into the garden. Watching them, Sir Edward gave a weary shake of his head, 'Heaven help me. Whatever shall I do with such a hoyden?'

Emma was so deeply immersed in the fantastic adventures of the heroine of her novel that it took several minutes before the voices penetrated her concentration. Goodness—they were standing almost directly beneath her. She offered a quick prayer that they would not look up and sat as if frozen.

'Well, she's clearly not here,' said one voice with just a thread of irritation in it.

Emma immediately recognised Richard's voice—and the annoyance. They had been fast friends almost since she was in leading strings but, of late, he was a little less indulgent than before. Her father said that Richard was now too grown-up to bother with a grubby little hoyden, that once he finished university he would have no time at all for Emma. But Richard wouldn't do that, would he?

Emma opened her mouth to call down to Richard, but thought better of it. Someone else was with him...

'When she doesn't want to be found,' said the second voice, 'she seems to disappear into thin air. I'd have expected you to go straight to her hiding-place, Richard. After all the time you've spent on this estate, you should know every nook and cranny.'

Emma smiled slightly at the second voice. It was Richard's friend Hugo Stratton, and he sounded more amused than annoyed. Hugo was not like Richard— except a little in looks, perhaps. Hugo did not treat Emma like a grubby little sister, to be teased and provoked. Hugo treated her almost like a lady.

Almost, she repeated to herself. For Hugo Stratton had a wicked sense of humour. He was quite capable of behaving like a perfect gentleman while secretly laughing at everyone around him. Only the decided glint in his eye betrayed his unholy glee—and Emma had quickly learned to look for that, before anything else.

But now, from her vantage point, all she could make out was the top of his head.

The tree shook suddenly, as if some giant had leaned heavily against it. It was only the wind, but Emma clutched at her book, loose in her lap, to prevent it from falling. She was too late to retrieve the apple core, though, which rolled down through the branches. Mercifully, it stopped, caught on a tiny twig a few feet below Emma's perch.

'I thought I did know all Emma's hiding-places,' said Richard's voice thoughtfully, 'but clearly not. The little brat has obviously been keeping something from me. And if we don't find her soon, she won't have a chance to see you before you go—and then she'll be fizzing mad.'

'Why should she be?' Hugo sounded puzzled. 'She hardly knows me.'

'With Emma, that's not the point. She may be only thirteen, but she believes she has a divine right to know everything about everyone round here—and to put in her two penn'orth. If you leave without saying goodbye, she'll ring a peal over me for ignoring her.'

'But she's only a child—'

'Only sometimes, Hugo. Sometimes, she sounds exactly like a Society lady. It's uncanny—especially since she still looks like a child, all dirt and scratches and tangles.'

'Maybe she's growing up,' said Hugo quietly.

'Now, that *would* be a pity,' replied Richard. 'We've had such fun together. She's a great sport, you know. Never complains about cuts and bruises, or getting wet and muddy when we go fishing. I can't imagine her as a young lady, all prim and proper and simpering—and clean!' He laughed aloud at that.

Emma did not pause to wonder why Hugo was leaving, for she was almost overcome by righteous anger at Richard's words. She was not *always* a grubby urchin as he seemed to believe and—

And then her eyes became riveted on the apple core. The tree was moving again, almost as if it were responding to Richard's laughter. The apple core had become half-dislodged and it was starting to slip...

She held her breath. For a long moment, there was silence.

'I wish I were going with you, Hugo,' said Richard, sounding suddenly very serious. 'But with m'father the way he is...'

'I know.' Hugo sounded sympathetic. 'But even if Lord Hardinge were not ailing, you still wouldn't be permitted to go, you know. There are times when I'm really glad I'm only a younger son. And this is one of them. My mother's brother has told me what great fun he had when he first joined the regiment. The older officers played all sorts of tricks on him of course—it's a bit like school, in that sense—but he had such adventures…'

'Yes, I know. You told me, remember?' Richard was more than a little envious of his friend's good fortune. Emma could hear it in his voice. As an only son, he would never be allowed to join the army.

'Where on earth can she be?' said Richard with a sudden burst of fury. 'You go and look in the orchard, Hugo. I'll search down by the river, but that's it. If we don't find her in the next ten minutes, we'll have to go. You can't afford to be late.' He thumped the tree in exasperation. 'Blast the brat. Why can she never behave?'

The apple core jumped just a fraction, hung suspended in mid-air for what seemed like seconds, and then disappeared down through the leaves.

Emma swallowed a gasp. Then, with a tiny shrug of her shoulders, she leaned towards the gap in the branches. She might as well give in gracefully. They were bound to find her now.

But Richard had gone, striding angrily across the lawn in the direction of the river.

Down below her, a sudden shout of laughter was quickly stifled. Hugo's voice, rippling with amusement, said quite clearly, 'Now, that *is* strange. My education must have been sadly at fault. I'd have sworn that this was an oak tree, but it's obviously an apple. Unless this is an oak-apple… Yes, that must be it. And the teeth-marks must have been made by a…a squirrel, I suppose. Very large squirrels they have on this estate. Next time, I'll bring my gun…'

Emma could have sworn she saw a flash of white teeth through the leaves. The next moment, Hugo was sprinting across the grass to the orchard, without once looking back.

She stuffed her book into her pocket and began to climb down, automatically finding the well-known footholds. Little brat, was she? Never clean? Well, she would show Richard Hardinge.

She raced across the lawn to the side door, raging inwardly all the while. With Nurse's help, she would be clean and ladylike in a trice—well, ten minutes, at most. She would appear as a prim, proper—and demure—young lady. She'd show him…*them*.

No. That wasn't fair. Hugo Stratton had not called her a grimy brat. Hugo had known perfectly well where she was, but he had just laughed—and flashed that wonderful smile…

Chapter One

1816

Emma Fitzwilliam slowed her chestnut mare to a relatively sedate trot just before she came in sight of the lodge gates. It was bad enough that she had ridden out without her groom. No need to make matters worse by galloping into the Harding estate like a mannerless hoyden.

She patted her blonde hair into place. Time to assume the role of the perfect lady—the role that she had long since learnt to don as easily as a pair of fine silk stockings.

Emma was longing to see Richard and his wife again. It was only a few months since the Earl and Countess Hardinge had left England for the Continent but, to Emma, it seemed like years. Surprisingly, given that Richard had been her childhood friend, it was his wife, nicknamed Jamie, whom Emma had really missed. The two women had become as close as sisters since Jamie's marriage. Letters had been exchanged, naturally, but that always meant delay; communications with France remained, at best, uncertain, even though the war had been over for nearly a year and Napoleon was now safely installed on St Helena.

There was nothing like a long, comfortable coze— and that was precisely why Emma had come.

She urged her mare to slightly greater speed.

As she rounded the corner of the house, Emma saw a little group of figures sitting on the lawn under the ancestral oak. She started towards them, but then paused, for Jamie was not there. Two men were sitting on a rug with a very small child, much hampered by his petticoats. Goodness, how Dickon had grown. Emma barely recognised her little godson. He must be nigh on a year old by now.

Dickon's anxious nursemaid was hovering as close as she dared, watching lest the clumsy males should mishandle her charge. Not much chance of that in Richard's case, Emma thought, for he doted on Dickon and spent much more time with his little son than most fathers did. The other gentleman, however, seemed not to have noticed the child. He was half-turned away, apparently gazing into the middle distance.

Emma screwed up her eyes against the glare to get a good view of the second man. She did not know him, she was sure, though she could see little more than his profile. He was dark, like Richard, but his lined face looked older and much more serious— rather austere, in fact, in Emma's opinion. She hoped, secretly, that she would not have to meet him. It would spoil the happiness of her day to meet a man who preached at her.

At that moment, little Dickon started to toddle towards the newcomer, holding out his arms and grinning toothily. His inarticulate squeals of joy at his own prowess carried across the lawn. The nursemaid started forward, arms outstretched to catch her darling before he fell. Richard—apparently unconcerned—smiled benignly. Dickon took two more steps, rocking unsteadily from one side to the other. His precarious balance was obviously beginning to desert him; his infectious grin was turning into the quivering lip that promised a wail of disappointment.

And then the stranger turned back towards the child, bending forward to catch him and lift him high in the air. In a matter of moments, Dickon was convulsed in shrieks of delighted laughter.

When, at last, the man moved to return the child to his father, Emma caught sight of his profile once more.

She could scarce believe what she saw. Why, he was almost like a different person. Playing with Richard's child had transformed the unknown from a harsh, forbidding man into someone much younger, someone whose face was alight with laughter and a flashing smile…and all because of one tiny child.

Emma suddenly felt as if she were eavesdropping on the visitor's innermost thoughts. Instinctively, she urged her mare towards the house.

The door opened well before she reached it. The butler stood waiting for her, his normally impassive countenance wreathed in smiles for the young lady who had been running around the Harding estate almost since she had learned to walk. 'Good day to you, Miss Emma. Her ladyship will be delighted to learn that you have called, I am sure. If you will just step into the blue saloon—'

'Oh, I don't think her ladyship would have us bother with such formality, do you, Digby?' Emma bestowed a dazzling smile on the butler. 'I'm sure I don't need to be announced.' Laying her whip and gloves on the hall table and lifting the generous skirts of her blue velvet habit with both hands, Emma started to run lightly up the stairs. 'I assume Lady Hardinge is in her sitting room?'

'Why, yes, ma'am,' the butler called up to the disappearing figure, 'but her ladyship is—'

Emma was not paying attention. She was much too keen to see her dearest friend again.

She knocked quickly and entered the Countess's sitting room without waiting for an invitation.

Lady Hardinge was seated on the low chaise longue by the bay window, looking out across the lawn towards the oak tree. 'Emma!' she cried delightedly. She started to rise from her place, leaning heavily on the back to push herself up. After a second or two, she abandoned the effort and sank back into the cushions. 'Forgive me, Emma. It is rather difficult to rise from this seat. You see—'

Emma flew across the room to embrace her friend. They hugged for a long time. Eventually, Emma stood back and said, in a voice of concern, 'Are you unwell, Jamie, that you cannot...?' Her words trailed into nothing as her eyes came to rest on Jamie's middle.

'Oh. I see,' she said, a little uncertainly, mentally calculating the months since she had last seen her friend. 'You did not tell me you were increasing before you left.' Emma regretted the words as soon as they were spoken. They sounded like an accusation.

'No,' agreed Jamie with a somewhat tired smile. 'I didn't—' she reached for Emma's hand '—because I wasn't.'

Emma looked at Jamie in disbelief. Surely she was at least six months gone?

'The midwife in Brussels said it was twins,' Jamie explained, 'and, judging by how tired I feel—never mind the size of me—I think she must be right.'

'Twins?' Emma sat down quickly on the footstool by the chaise longue. 'But—'

Jamie patted Emma's hand reassuringly. 'I know it sounds rather frightening, but I've had time to get used to it now. And it's not my first, remember…'

Emma forced herself to return her friend's smile. 'Congratulations, Jamie. I should have said so at once, but I was so…you looked so…'

Jamie laughed. 'Richard was at a loss for words, too, when I told him. I don't think I've ever seen him look so…so stricken. I told him there was nothing to worry about. I'm as strong as a horse. And I say the same to you, Emma. Don't worry. Please.'

Emma squeezed Jamie's hand. 'I promise I'll try not to. When is it…when are they due?'

'Ah, now, that is more difficult. In the autumn, I think, but the midwife said twins are always early, often by several weeks. So, I don't really know. Probably not before October.'

Emma's eyes opened wide. Jamie had sounded almost nonchalant. 'I see,' Emma said non-committally. To be honest, she was not sure she really wanted to see at all. Marriage was bound to involve babies, of course, but it was such a dangerous business, besides being plaguey uncomfortable in the months before. Only a very special man would make it worth the pain and risk, in Emma's view. Jamie and Richard were a special case—they adored each other. But to marry a man one did not love…

Emma suddenly realised she had heard not a word of what her friend was saying. She shook her head to clear her thoughts. 'Forgive me, Jamie,' she said. 'I was wool-gathering. What were you saying?'

Jamie looked indulgently at her friend. 'I was telling you about our trip. There is so much devastation, Emma, you would be horrified to see it. Houses and villages in ruins, people in rags and starving. And everywhere, mutilated men begging for a crust. We helped where we could but… Honestly, Emma, I wept sometimes at what I saw. Oh, I know we had to defeat that tyrant, but the cost was so much more than any of us could have imagined.'

Emma nodded. 'Yes,' she said seriously. 'The beggars are in England now, too, and it seems that very few of us are grateful for their sacrifice. Papa said he saw several of them being driven out of town only last week. He has taken one of them on as a stable hand, but he was unable to do much for the others, unfortunately. The money he gave them will not last all that long.'

Jamie was silent for a space, thinking. 'Your father

is a good man,' she said at last. 'He cares for the
weak.' She looked up suddenly, her eyes alight. 'We,
too, have an extra hand in the stables now, a man to
whom we owe a debt we can never repay. He helped
save the life of Richard's dearest friend. Richard was
sure he was dead on the battlefield. I never told you—
for Richard asked me not to speak of it—but we went
to Brussels in hopes of finding the grave. Instead, we
found… Well, suffice it to say that Richard is over
the moon at what has happened. He says that just
finding Hugo alive is more than he had dared to hope
for. Against that, it matters not a whit that—'

'Hugo? Hugo Stratton?' cried Emma, jumping up
from her stool and knocking it over in her haste to
reach the door.

'Why, yes,' replied Jamie, puzzled. 'You don't
know him, do you? He's down in the garden with
Richard and Dickon, but— Emma, wait!' Jamie was
again trying to lever her ungainly bulk out of the
chaise longue. By the time she had regained her feet,
Emma was gone.

Emma raced across the lawn, berating herself at
every step. How could she have failed to recognise
Hugo Stratton, the man whose wickedly smiling face
had haunted her girlish dreams for months on end?
The identity of the stranger had burst upon Emma like
an exploding star the moment Jamie had mentioned
his name…

The little group was still sitting under the oak tree.
Emma smiled to herself, deliberately slowing her pace
to a more ladylike walk. How apt that they should

meet again under an oak, even if not the same one. Emma had climbed Richard's oak, too, many and many a time when they were children. She knew it almost as well as she knew her own.

And much better than she knew Hugo Stratton.

What on earth was she going to say to him?

Emma gulped. Would he recognise her? She was a fine lady now, nothing like the grubby little brat he had generously allowed to tease him. She had been a mere child when Hugo left to join the army. To be honest, there was absolutely no reason why he should remember her at all, especially after all he had been through. And yet...

As Emma neared the little group, she saw that Dickon was now sound asleep in his father's arms. Richard looked proud and happy—and just a mite self-satisfied, too. Hugo was talking quietly to Richard, his back towards Emma. It seemed that neither was aware of her approach.

She hesitated. Then, noticing the enquiring look thrown at her by the nursemaid, she lifted her head a notch and marched across the lawn, arms swinging, skirts trailing unheeded on the warm grass.

'Why, Richard...' she began.

Richard, Earl Hardinge, rose to his feet in a single athletic movement, the child in his arms cradled snugly all the while. He smiled broadly, nodding sideways towards the nursemaid to come and relieve him of his son. He did not speak until he had carefully transferred his burden to her waiting arms. Even then, he still whispered.

'Emma. How wonderful to see you so soon. I had planned to call tomorrow...'

Richard's words were cut off as Emma threw her arms round his neck and kissed him heartily on the cheek. 'I could not wait to see you both...no, all three of you.' As Emma spoke, she became conscious that she had not included Hugo in that number—and that Hugo had not risen to meet her. Intrigued, she turned around.

Hugo was struggling to stand up, pushing an ebony cane into the soft turf in an effort to gain a purchase for his weak legs. His head was still bent, but Emma could see from the heightened colour on his neck how much the effort was costing him. How awful for him. He had been gravely wounded, clearly—Richard had thought him dead—and he was still not fully recovered. The explanation was simple enough—and obvious now she stopped to think about it. Probably it would be best to pretend that nothing was amiss.

Emma fixed her friendliest smile on her lips and waited for Hugo to regain his balance. When, at last, he seemed to have overcome his weakness, she began, cheerily, 'You may not remember me, Hugo, but I certainly remember the last time we met. I owe you a debt of gratitude for not betraying my presence to a certain mutual friend of ours—' she turned back to grin conspiratorially at Richard '—a friend who fails to understand the significance of apple cores.'

'I remember you very well indeed, Miss Fitzwilliam, and I was happy to be of service.'

His tone was flat and formal. And his use of her full name struck Emma almost like a blow. She whirled back round to look at this man who was so quick to reject the easy friendship she was offering.

Emma could not suppress an audible gasp. If only she had been prepared…

Hugo Stratton was nothing like the memory she had treasured. Gone was the handsome, eager young man who had smiled up into her favourite oak tree. Under his obviously new civilian clothes, this Hugo Stratton was thin and pinched, so weak that he could not stand upright without the help of a stick. The profile she had seen earlier was lined, right enough—but the lines were clearly lines of pain, not of joy or laughter. And, on the left profile that had been hidden from her, a thin purple scar ran from forehead to chin, bisecting his eyebrow and his cheek and continuing down below his collar. Heaven alone knew what damage lay below.

He stared her out. And he did not smile.

Emma swallowed hard and bowed her head politely, desperately trying to disguise the horror she instinctively felt. It was a full thirty seconds before she felt able to say, 'How do you do, Mr Stratton?'

Chapter Two

'I am so glad you have met Major Stratton again, Emma, since he will be staying with us for a time—while he recovers his strength.' Jamie was sitting on a high spoon-back chair in the first-floor drawing room, dispensing tea from a fluted silver pot and looking hopefully at her inarticulate guests.

Richard carried a cup to Emma with an encouraging smile. But Emma still could not bring herself to speak again. Out on the lawn, she had wished for the ground to open and swallow her up. Now her feet were resting on a priceless Aubusson carpet, but the feeling was the same. She stared at the delicate pattern, willing it to slide back beneath her chair.

The strained silence continued while Richard ferried tea to his friend, who was seated rather awkwardly on the sofa with his cane propped up beside him. His left leg did not seem to bend very well at the knee.

'Hugo—' began Richard.

'Major Stratton—' said Jamie at the same moment. Richard and Jamie broke off and grinned at each other, quite unabashed. Richard made a very grand bow, indicating that his wife should go first.

'Ignore him, both of you,' Jamie said. 'He's play-acting. Fancies himself to be dressed in a wasp-waisted satin coat and buckled shoes with red heels, making a leg like the veriest macaroni.'

Richard contrived to look pained. 'Nothing of the sort, wife,' he said. 'I was merely conceding the prec-edence that you have so often informed me is your due.'

His face was such a mixture of innocence and mis-chief that Emma found herself laughing along with Jamie.

But Hugo did not join in, Emma noticed. He seemed to have withdrawn into himself. And his tea sat untouched by his hand.

Emma decided then that it was up to her to make the attempt to draw him out. After all, her total want of manners had been the cause of severe embarrass-ment to Hugo. She must stop thinking about how badly *she* felt. Hugo's position was surely far, far worse.

'I am sure you will make excellent progress here, Major Stratton,' Emma said, trying to infuse her voice with as much warmth as she could. 'I know at first hand what attentive hosts Richard and Jamie can be. And the estate is a delight in summer.'

Hugo turned his head to look directly at Emma. There seemed to be a challenge in that look. It seemed, somehow, familiar. Now that she was begin-ning to see beyond his terrible scars, she could at last recognise something of the young man she had re-

membered so vividly. His hair was still glossy and
dark, his eyes still gleamed like polished steel, and
his generous mouth still looked as if it might smile
at any moment. But it did not. And his eyes remained
hard as they swept over Emma's figure. Emma detected not the slightest sign of approval of what he
saw. Probably he favoured taller women...or bru-
nettes.

'I am sure you are right, Miss Fitzwilliam,' replied
Hugo at last, 'especially about Lady Hardinge's hospitality, for which I am most grateful. As to the estate,
I shall do my best, but as I am unable to ride or to
walk very far, I doubt I shall see all that much of it.'

Emma was suddenly quite sure that Hugo was relishing her discomfiture. Embarrassment vanished, to
be replaced by an unwonted surge of anger. How
dared he? He obviously thought his wounds gave him
licence to behave outrageously. Well—she would
show him.

Emma smiled dangerously. 'I am sure that, with
time and Lady Hardinge's care, you will soon regain
your strength, Major. I pray it may be so. And, in the
meantime, you may fish and shoot to your heart's
content, may you not?'

'No.' He dropped his gaze so that Emma could no
longer see the expression in his eyes. 'I'm afraid not,
Miss Fitzwilliam. My left arm is much too weak for
either.'

'But I saw you throwing Dickon up in the air—'
Emma blurted out the words without stopping to
think. How tactless she was suddenly becoming.

'Dickon is not exactly a heavyweight, you know,'

Hugo explained patiently. 'And besides, my good arm took most of the strain.'

Emma looked away. She could think of nothing to say to cover yet another appalling *faux pas*. She ought to apologise—but that would probably just make matters worse. What on earth had happened to the Emma who was held up to débutantes as a pattern-card of feminine grace and good manners? Emma cringed inwardly. Somehow, Hugo Stratton was making her forget all the lessons she had ever learned about how to be a lady in polite Society.

The chiming of the long-case clock in the hall broke the renewed silence.

'Good gracious,' said Emma, 'how late it is. I must go.' She rose quickly from her seat. 'I'm afraid I was so excited about seeing you all, that I failed to tell anyone where I was going. Papa will be worrying by now. I only hope he hasn't sent out a search party.' With an apologetic smile, she started for the door. 'Oh, pray, do not get up,' she said hastily, as both Jamie and Hugo struggled to rise. 'I know my way very well.'

Richard was only just in time to open the door for her.

By the time Richard returned from escorting Emma to the stables, Hugo was alone in the drawing room, leaning against the folded wooden shutter for support as he gazed out across the park.

'Miss Fitzwilliam has an excellent seat,' Hugo said as Richard joined him at the long window.

'Mmm,' agreed Richard. 'Almost as good as Jamie's. Where is my wife, by the way?'

'Lady Hardinge went upstairs to rest. She was rather tired by all the excitement, she said.' Hugo could not drag his eyes from Emma's retreating figure. The urchin had become a real beauty. Her manners were not exactly faultless, but her behaviour was certainly a remarkable improvement on the impossible child he remembered. Besides, she had been doing her best to conceal how repulsive she found him— which could not have been easy. He should not judge her.

Richard put a hand on his friend's shoulder. 'What say we adjourn to the library, Hugo? It's more comfortable down there, and there's some decent madeira.'

Hugo half-turned from the window. Emma was just passing out of sight into the trees. 'I'd rather not, if you don't mind,' he said softly, with a note of apology in his voice. 'It will soon be time to go upstairs to change for dinner, and—'

'And your host has the manners of a boor to wish to condemn you to incessant stair-climbing. I'm sorry I was so thoughtless, Hugo.' He crossed to the bell-pull. 'I'll have the madeira brought up here.'

Hugo looked at his friend and smiled warmly. He owed Richard so very much—and Lady Hardinge, too. Who else would have taken in the wreck of a man that he had become?

'How long is it since you last saw Emma?' said Richard, dropping on to the sofa and stretching out his long legs.

Hugo limped slowly across the room to join his friend, noting that Richard now knew better than to make any attempt to help him. 'More than ten years.' He lowered himself awkwardly on to the spoon-back chair that Lady Hardinge had vacated, grateful for its relatively high seat. 'In fact, it was the day I left Harding to join my regiment. I could never forget that. I was so excited—so certain of adventure, and glory, and...' Hugo's words trailed off into heavy silence.

Nothing more was said until the butler had received his orders and returned with the tray of refreshments.

Pouring out the madeira, Richard showed a renewed determination to be cheerful. 'So, what do you think of Emma now? You have to admit, she's changed.'

Hugo nodded. 'She didn't have the look of a beauty then, certainly.'

Richard laughed. 'How could you tell, under all that dirt?'

Hugo raised an eyebrow. 'Your memory is at fault, old friend. By the time we actually saw her that day, she was really quite clean. And remarkably well behaved, considering she'd been skulking up trees.'

'Had she?' Richard drank his madeira thoughtfully. 'You may be right about that day. I'm afraid I don't actually remember it very well at all. Emma's been around for so long that all my early memories of her tend to merge. She was always there, always ready for anything, and always dirty. Until her father took her in hand and insisted she learn to be a lady. By the time of her come-out, she was totally transformed. A blonde beauty—with faultless manners for every occasion. I was quite sorry, in a way. I was very fond of her mischievous spirit. I miss it.'

Hugo said nothing. Richard spoke as if Emma had been moulded into a completely different person, a sort of beautiful automaton. What made him think that Emma's mischievous spirit had been extinguished? Surely, having known her so long, he could see that Emma was still the same person under her conventional façade? Wasn't it obvious?

'In one way, though, she is still the same girl,' Richard continued after a moment. 'Can't tell you how many offers she's had, but she's refused them all. She's already mistress of her own household, of course, and a considerable heiress to boot, so she can afford to be choosy—though I fancy Sir Edward is beginning to worry that he'll never see his grand-children. He still dotes on her. And she knows exactly how to wind him round her little finger—just as she does with almost every man she meets. She may have perfect manners—but I warn you that she's highly accomplished at getting her own way.'

'Sir Edward may have hoped that *you* would offer for his daughter,' said Hugo. 'After all—'

'I did think of it at one time,' interrupted Richard, looking slightly embarrassed. 'But then I met Jamie...'

Hugo nodded. Marriage to Emma Fitzwilliam would have been a business arrangement, a marriage of convenience, whereas Richard's marriage to Jamie was a union of two souls. Hugo took a deep breath and closed his eyes in sudden pain. He envied Richard his happiness. There was no point in denying that, not to himself. Once, he too might have hoped to marry for love—but now he would never marry at all. Love—and children—were not for him. No woman would have a disfigured cripple—especially one whose honour was as scarred as his body. The best he could hope for would be a comfortable home and kindly servants to wait on him. At least he had wealth enough to secure that, and his own independence. He would make a life for himself, somehow, however much the world might shun him. He would learn to survive alone.

Emma was sure Hugo was watching her from the house, but she refused to turn in her saddle or to increase her pace. He would not be allowed to see how much their meeting had unnerved her.

'Just a few yards more, Juno,' she said, stroking her mare's glossy neck, 'and we'll be hidden by the trees. Then we'll take the shortcut home across the fields. I think we could both do with a good gallop.'

The chestnut's ears twitched in response, as if she understood.

Emma continued to stroke the mare's neck absently, allowing the horse to make her own way along the familiar route from Harding to Longacres. There was something niggling in the back of Emma's mind, a fleeting memory about Hugo Stratton, but she could not catch it. Like a soap bubble in the bath, it floated out of reach every time she tried to grab for it.

'Oh, fiddlesticks,' groaned Emma, deliberately swallowing the curse that had risen automatically to her lips. 'I've let him see enough bad manners for one day. I'd better practise being a lady for the rest of it. Once I reach home, at least...' She dug her heel into Juno's flank. 'Come on then, Juno,' she urged. 'Let's show them what you can do.'

The chestnut flew across the grass as though the devil were at her heels. By the time they reached the stable yard, Juno was in a lather—and Emma was gasping for breath. But at least they had lost no more time.

'Where on earth have you been, Miss Emma?' cried the grizzled old groom, dashing out of the stables to grab Juno's bridle. 'Your father's worrying fit to burst. He—'

Emma slid from the saddle and stopped the old man's tirade with an apologetic smile and a touch on his arm. 'One of the keepers told me Lord Hardinge was back from London—so I called in at the house. It was on my way—more or less,' she added, hoping she was not blushing. 'But I stayed too long. Is Papa very worried?'

'Well—he hasn't started scouring the woods yet, Miss Emma, though I dare say he might have done, in another hour or so. If only you wouldn't ride out alone, Miss Emma...'

Emma grinned. 'Look after Juno for me, please,' she said. 'I'd better present myself for inspection, to prove I'm all in one piece.' Looping the tail of her habit over her arm, Emma hurried up to the house and her father's study.

'Emma!' he cried, the moment she appeared in the doorway.

Emma could hear the note of concern in his voice.

Oh, dear. First, she had upset Hugo, and now her father.

She ran to him, wrapped her arms tightly round his neck and kissed his cheek. 'Forgive me, Papa, for being so thoughtless. I went to visit Richard and…and I'm afraid I lost track of time. I'm sorry you were worried.'

Her father cleared his throat rather loudly. 'Emma, if you would only take a groom with you, I'd have no cause to worry. Why don't you—?'

Emma fixed her wide blue gaze on her father's face. 'Oh, Papa, must I? Don't you think I can ride well enough to be trusted out on my own?'

'It's not that—and you know it,' he responded gruffly, removing each of her arms in turn. 'The very best of riders can be caught out. That includes you, Emma.'

He was right. Even Juno had been spooked on occasion by a strange noise or a sudden movement.

Emma kissed her father a second time. 'I'll try to be good, Papa, I promise,' she said. His answering smile told her she had won him round yet again. He was easily satisfied.

'Well,' he said, settling himself back in his favourite chair, 'tell me about Richard. Is he well? And little Dickon? Did you see Lady Hardinge, too? I dare swear she is worn out, after all that travelling.'

'They are all very well, Papa. And Dickon has grown so much that you will not recognise him. He is starting to walk, too. Jamie is…' Emma hesitated. 'Jamie is…increasing again. The midwife says it will be twins.' Her words all came out in a rush.

'Twins?' echoed Sir Edward. 'Oh, my... Oh, dear...'

Emma could see that he was thinking back to the loss of his own wife, when Emma was born. Emma sat down beside him and patted his hand. 'Don't worry, Papa. Jamie says she's as strong as a horse. And it's not as if it's her first...' Emma's voice tailed off once more. What a stupid thing to say, reminding her father that first babies—like Emma—were by far the most dangerous. What was the matter with her today? Her brain seemed to be scrambled.

'You'll never guess who is staying at Harding, Papa.' Emma changed the subject with exaggerated cheerfulness.

Sir Edward smiled a little wanly. 'Tell me,' he said.

'Hugo Stratton. *Major* Hugo Stratton. Do you remember him?'

Sir Edward nodded. 'Yes, I do. A Major, eh? Well, I'm not at all surprised. I thought he had the makings of a good officer, even then. Let me see—how many years is it since he joined the colours? Eight?'

'Nearly eleven, Papa,' said Emma.

'Really? Strange that he hasn't made Colonel, then,' said Sir Edward, half to himself. 'Though he'd have to compete with all those fellows buying their promotions, I suppose. There aren't that many field promotions, even in wartime. And a majority is still something to be proud of.'

'Papa, I don't understand. What is wrong with being a Major?'

'Nothing, my dear, nothing. I'm sure Major Stratton has had a distinguished career. He's sold out now, I suppose?'

'I...I don't know, Papa. He...he has been badly wounded. I'm not sure how, or when. He walks with a limp and has to use a cane. And he...his face is horribly scarred, Papa.' Her father's shock was evident. 'Oh, I'm sure it will look better in time but, at the moment...'

Suddenly, Emma's eyes filled with tears. 'Oh, Papa, I've done such a dreadful thing. I didn't know, you see. And when I saw Hugo, I got such a shock that I...I embarrassed him terribly, staring at his scars. I couldn't tear my eyes away. And Hugo was insulted. He could hardly bring himself to speak to me. Oh, Papa, I'm so ashamed. What shall I do?'

Sir Edward patted her shoulder consolingly. 'You must apologise,' he said quietly.

'I tried to, but I couldn't get the words out, not when he was staring me out with those hard grey eyes of his. And now, it's too late to say anything. That would only make matters worse.'

He offered her his handkerchief. 'You may be right, my dear.' He paused to pull at his ear lobe, as he always did when he was worrying about something. 'Well, if you cannot tell him you are sorry, you must show him, go out of your way to help him to...to come to terms with his injuries. Can you do that, do you think?'

Emma nodded dumbly and wiped her eyes, feeling more ashamed than ever. She never lost control. She had always prided herself on that. And she *never* allowed herself to cry—especially not in front of her papa. He liked her to be gay, and cheerful, and…and strong-minded. As she would be again.

Even with Major Hugo Stratton.

Chapter Three

'No. I could not accept.'

Jamie cast an imploring look towards her husband.
She had clearly exhausted her own arguments and
was desperate for him to intervene.

'Hugo, please reconsider,' Richard said seriously.
'The Fitzwilliams are our oldest friends. They will be
very hurt if you refuse.'

'I have absolutely no intention of providing a raree-
show for Miss Fitzwilliam and her dinner guests,
Richard. Acceptance is out of the question. Now, if
you will excuse me…' Hugo limped towards the door.
'My apologies to you, ma'am,' he said as he opened
it, 'if my refusal creates difficulties for you with your
friends. But my mind is made up. I will not attend.'
He closed the door quietly behind him.

'Oh, dear.' Jamie's shoulders had slumped. 'How
will we ever persuade him to return to Society if he
will not attend even a small dinner amongst friends?'

Richard shook his head sadly. He hated to see his
wife so upset. 'I don't know, my love. I really don't.
I'd ask Emma to talk to him—but, after yesterday's

encounter, he seems to wish to avoid her completely.'
He started to pace. 'I had better ride over to Longacres to warn Emma, though, before she receives
Hugo's note. If she learns of his refusal by letter, we
really will be in the suds.'

'Tell her how hard we tried, Richard,' said Jamie,
a little wearily.

'I will—but she will know that without my telling
her. Remember, she knows *you*.' Richard bent to
place a gentle, lingering kiss on his wife's lips. 'Don't
worry, my love. Even if we can't resolve this now, it
will soon blow over. And Hugo is bound to become
less sensitive—eventually.'

That thought remained with Richard throughout his
ride across his own estate to Sir Edward's. Hugo was
as stubborn as a mule—and stiff-necked besides, as
well as proud, touchy, exasperating... Richard could
have continued with his list for some time, but he did
not. Hugo was a good man, and a good friend, who
had suffered a great deal during his years as a soldier.
With time, his testiness would mellow—probably.

'Richard!'

Emma was almost upon him before Richard realised that she was there. Damn! He hadn't yet worked
out how he was going to explain to her about Hugo's
refusal.

Emma was too full of her own laudable aims to
notice that there was anything amiss with Richard.
'You weren't coming to visit me, were you, Richard?'
she asked brightly. 'No need, for I am before you.
And since I have already covered a much greater dis-

tance than you, it would be ungentlemanly in you to expect me to retrace my steps—' she smiled like the cheeky child she had once been '—would it not?'

Richard's answering smile was a little forced, Emma thought. Perhaps he had been coming to remonstrate with her in private about her unacceptable treatment of Hugo. He had cause, but she would not permit any man to lecture her. 'To tell you the truth, Richard,' began Emma, more seriously now, and determined to make a clean breast of her failings, 'I was hoping for a chance to talk to Hugo, to apologise for my behaviour yesterday—' that was not quite true, she realised '—or, at least, to try to show him that I mean us to be friends again. It was just that I...I was unprepared for the change in him. I—'

'Jamie did try to warn you, Emma.' Emma recognised Richard's 'big brother' voice. 'If you hadn't rushed out so quickly—'

'I know. And I'm sorry, Richard. Truly.' Emma tried to look contrite, but she knew she was not making a very good fist of it. She was going to make amends. Surely that was enough? 'However, once Hugo has been introduced to all his old friends, he will have no more cause for concern. I shall visit all the guests before the dinner party to warn them so that—'

'Hugo refuses to attend, Emma.'

'No! He wouldn't! He—'

'He's adamant, Emma. That's what I was coming to tell you.' Richard was looking away suddenly, unable to meet Emma's eye. 'He...he thinks you invited him in order to use him as a sort of...' He cleared his throat rather too noisily. 'He hates to be stared at,' he finished at last.

Emma was shocked, then disbelieving, then angry when the import of Richard's words sank in. She urged her mare into a trot. 'So that's what he thinks of me,' she said hotly. 'Well, let's see if he has the gall to say so to my face. How dare he assume—?'

'Emma.' Richard caught up with her and laid a hand on her arm. 'Emma, calm down. Please. If you fly up into the boughs with Hugo, he'll probably pack his bags and leave. And considering the trouble we had in persuading him to come here in the first place—' Richard broke off suddenly. From the look on his face, Emma fancied her friend had said more than he intended.

Emma slowed Juno to a gentle walk, forcing Richard to do the same. 'Richard,' she said earnestly, 'I don't really understand what is going on. I know I behaved unpardonably yesterday; and I do want to set matters right. That was why I persuaded Papa to hold a little dinner party for Hugo. I thought he… Well, no matter what I thought. Obviously, I was wrong. From what you say, it seems as if it's more than just… Oh, I know the scars are dreadful, but surely they will fade?'

Richard hesitated for several moments. 'Hugo has changed a great deal, Emma. It's more than just his wounds, I think, but he will not speak of his experiences, even to me, his oldest friend. Jamie had the devil's own job persuading him to come to Harding at all. He was set to bury himself on a rundown manor miles from anywhere.'

'Oh.' Emma did not know what to say. Nothing in her upbringing had prepared her to deal with a man like Hugo Stratton.

'Perhaps it would be best if you didn't come to Harding for a day or two, Emma. Give Hugo time to come down from his high horse.'

'Of course, I...' As she spoke the words politeness demanded, Emma knew instinctively that they were wrong. 'No,' she said flatly. 'I shan't give him time to persuade himself that I am a heartless trophy-hunter. I was *not* planning to put him on display, as he seems to think, and I intend to make him admit as much.' She shook her head in frustration. 'Devil take the man,' she said fiercely. 'Can't he see that I'm trying to help him?'

Emma's resolution had all but deserted her by the time she finally caught sight of Hugo among the trees. He had walked much further from the house than she had expected. Judging from his painfully slow pace, it must have taken a very long time to come this far.

Emma swung the tail of her claret-coloured velvet habit over her arm and hurried down the woodland path to intercept him. She knew she was looking her best in her new habit and jaunty little hat, and she was determined not to make a mull of this second meeting.

'Major Stratton.' She smiled encouragingly at Hugo's tense figure. He had stopped at the sight of her. She stepped forward to meet him, holding out her gloved hand. 'Good morning to you,' she said, refusing to be daunted by his hard gaze and willing her hand not to shake.

Eventually, Hugo transferred his cane to his left hand and quickly shook Emma's hand. 'Good morning, ma'am,' he replied.

Emma could detect no trace of warmth in his deep voice, nor any hint that he wished to prolong their encounter. But she would not cry off now. 'I see that I was wrong to take you at your word yesterday, sir,' she began in as light-hearted a tone as she could muster.

He threw her a sharp glance from beneath frowning brows before busying himself once more with his walking cane.

'You told me you could not walk very far, did you not? But I find you a considerable distance from the house. I collect you have been bamming me, sir.' She looked straight at him then, letting him see the smiling challenge in her eyes.

He returned her gaze frankly for what seemed an age, but she could read nothing of his thoughts.

'Even cripples may improve, ma'am,' he said quite softly. 'The more I walk, the more I shall be able to walk. Would you have me lie down and moulder away?'

'No, certainly not. How could you think it?'

The tiniest smile crossed Hugo's lips as she spoke.

Emma's temper snapped like the dry twigs beneath her boots. 'Oh, you are quite impossible, Hugo Stratton, all thin skin and stiff-necked pride. You imagine that everyone is relishing your misfortunes or repelled by your scars. You believe that I invited you to my father's house in order to provide cheap entertainment for my other guests. You think—' She shook her head so sharply that the long red feather on her hat whipped at her cheek. 'Whatever you think, you are wrong,' she continued quietly as he made to speak. 'When I was a child, you were my friend. I wanted us to continue to be friends—so much so that, as soon as I realised who was sitting with Richard and Dickon, I dashed out to meet you without listening to what Jamie was trying to tell me. So—yes—I was shocked when I saw you. And I...I wish to apologise for my rudeness. I hope you will forgive me.'

Was there a slight softening in Hugo's stern features? Emma ventured a small smile. 'I hope we can still be friends.'

Hugo sighed softly. 'I am no longer the boy you knew, Miss Fitzwilliam,' he said at last.

'No,' replied Emma, 'but I do not believe that it changes matters.'

Hugo raised his good eyebrow. 'Indeed?'

There was something about that quirked eyebrow... Years before, it had always been accompanied by a gleam of hidden laughter...

'Major Stratton—' Emma stared at Hugo through narrowed eyes '—I declare you are laughing at me.'

Clearly, she must be wrong, for there was not the slightest trace of amusement in his face as he took a menacing step towards her. Emma retreated automatically, but the heel of her riding boot caught on her trailing hem, throwing her off balance.

A strong right arm saved her. In that same moment,

Emma heard Hugo's cane clatter against the granite rocks alongside the path.

Emma found she was gasping for breath, like a winded fighter. The arm supporting her felt immensely strong, much too strong for Hugo's emaciated frame. It felt warm, too, and somehow gentle. How strange that—

'Are you all right, ma'am?'

Hugo's question brought Emma back to earth. At last, that cold, hard edge had gone from his voice.

Emma used her free hand to pull her trailing skirt from under her heel. The skin of her other arm was beginning to heat within Hugo's sustaining grasp. The glowing warmth was like nothing she had ever experienced before.

'Miss Fitzwilliam?'

Emma blushed rosily. What was she thinking of? 'Thank you, Major,' she said. 'Your prompt action prevented me from becoming an undignified heap on this path. I am most grateful.' She smiled up at him through her lashes, forcing herself to maintain the expression even when he withdrew his hand from her arm. 'If you will permit me to say so, sir, you are much stronger than you look,' she added saucily.

Hugo grinned briefly and, Emma fancied, somewhat ruefully. 'Needs must when the devil drives, ma'am,' he said. 'With only one good arm, I could not have lifted you from the ground, you know. So I had no choice but to stop you while I still could.'

Emma stared at him in frank amazement. Was he actually laughing at himself? This time she could not be mistaken, surely?

She stooped quickly to retrieve his cane—and to hide her whirling thoughts from his penetrating eyes. She could not begin to understand him. Her childhood friend was still there—somewhere—but, overlaid on the young Hugo there was the oddest chameleon of a man...

'Your cane, Major.' Straight-faced, she handed it to him.

'Thank you, ma'am,' he said politely. There was a moment or two of awkward silence between them. Then Hugo surprised her yet again by saying, 'I was about to return to the house, as it happens. If it would not be too tedious for you, I would welcome your company for a space.'

Emma nodded in astonished agreement. What had come over him? He sounded—

'I am only sorry,' Hugo continued in the same polite tones, 'that I cannot offer you my arm.' He flourished his cane with his right hand as he spoke.

Emma smiled to herself but said nothing. For twenty minutes, they walked slowly along the path in companionable silence. The pine needles and the previous season's dry leaves crunched beneath their feet. A faint scent of crushed pine rose up around them. A woodpecker was drumming in the distance.

By the time Emma had worked out what she needed to say, they had reached the edge of the wood. From there, the long path led straight up to the stables and the house. They were now in full view of anyone watching from the windows.

Emma stopped under the last oak tree, waiting for Hugo to turn back to her. She smiled at him in wide-eyed innocence, hoping for even the slightest hint of a response. With most men, she knew exactly what reaction to expect, but Hugo was totally unpredictable.

At last, his gaze seemed to soften the merest fraction.

'Major,' she said gently, 'I do hope you will accept our dinner invitation.' He started to frown, but she hurried on. 'It is to be a very small affair, you know, just ourselves and the Hardinges...and a few old friends. You remember the Rector and Mrs Greenwood, I'm sure, and Mrs Halliday? I know they would all like to meet you again.' She dropped her gaze and let her voice sink a little more. 'I promise you that all of them are much better-mannered than I. You will not be embarrassed.'

Emma could feel the heat of a flush on her face and neck. She did not dare to raise her eyes.

'How can I possibly refuse?' said Hugo quietly.

Emma looked up at last to see that he was limping slowly back to the house. She had won.

But she had guaranteed Hugo would not be embarrassed in her house. Could she ensure that her promise was kept?

Chapter Four

Hugo lay back on his pillows and gazed out through the open bed-curtains at the first faint glimmerings of the dawn. Years of living in the Peninsula had taught him to love the huge expanse of the night sky and the unchanging patterns of the stars. He would never again permit drawn curtains to shut them out—or to shut him in.

Gingerly, he raised his injured left arm so that he could clasp his hands behind his head. That simple movement, never before achieved, gave him profound satisfaction. Yes, he was making progress—a little progress.

He focused on the day ahead—and on the evening. He was a fool to have accepted her invitation. It would mean nothing but embarrassment for him; and the usual expressions of pity and horror at his injuries. But she had been so apologetic about their disastrous first meeting. And, for just a single moment, she had made him feel like a whole man again.

Hugo groaned aloud. It would not do to remember Emma too clearly. Her figure-hugging riding habit

would have fired any man's blood; and that long
feather had reached down from her saucy little hat,
caressing the soft bloom of her cheek like a lover's
hand. He had known that she was working her wiles
on him—but, even as he recognised how artfully she
was using her huge blue eyes, he had found himself
unable to resist them.

The hoyden child had become a siren woman.

Hugo closed his eyes once more, trying to shut out
Emma's persistent image. It would not do for him to
think too kindly of her. She was a spoilt, flirtatious
little minx—in some respects she had not changed
one jot—and she obviously enjoyed making a May
game of every man she met. How many offers had
she rejected out of hand? Richard had not said precisely, but there had certainly been quite a number.
And, in spite of such behaviour, she was still the toast
of London Society, with every eligible male dangling
after her.

Hugo's weak arm was now very stiff. He straightened it with difficulty, and some pain, which reminded him that he, at least, was far from eligible.

Hugo leant back in his chair, his right hand playing
idly with his glass of port. So far, at least, the Longacres dinner party had passed off much better than he
had dared to hope. None of the guests had stared; and
no one had embarrassed him in any way, not even by
offering to help him on the stairs. Clearly, Emma had
been as good as her word. Hugo felt himself warming
to her even more. She might be a little spoilt—just a
very little, he had now decided—but she could be

thoughtful, and kind. She was upstairs now with the ladies, where she would be dispensing coffee with that radiant smile of hers, and ensuring that every one of her guests felt she had been singled out for special attention.

Exactly as he had felt, when he arrived with the Hardinges.

Naturally, Emma's first priority had been Lady Hardinge, but she had welcomed Hugo with gentle words, and with warmth in her eyes and in the clasp of her hand. He had had leisure, then, to admire her from a distance while she settled Lady Hardinge into a comfortable chair in the saloon, putting extra cushions in the small of her back. It was no wonder that Emma had become the toast of London Society, he had concluded; her radiant golden beauty would have ensured her success, even if she had been penniless. Tonight, she was glowing in a simple gown of cream silk, with a posy of forget-me-nots at her bosom, their clear blue serving only to point up the intense colour of Emma's eyes. Hugo found himself envying the man who would win her.

'Don't you agree, Hugo?'

Richard was speaking. But what had he said? Hugo raised his glass and sipped, savouring the rich sweetness for a moment. Then he smiled a little ruefully. 'Forgive me, Richard. I was miles away. What did you say?'

Richard shook his head. 'I never had you down for a dreamer, Hugo—except about adventures, of course.'

'That was a long time ago, I fear,' Hugo responded

neutrally. These last few days, Richard had begun to make oblique references to their shared past and to Hugo's years of soldiering. It was necessary, Hugo knew, and he was grateful to Richard for his tact.

'As it happens,' Richard continued with barely a pause, 'we were talking of the Derby. Sir Edward's Golden Star is being heavily backed at Tatt's. Is that not so, sir?' He turned to his host at the head of the table.

Sir Edward paused in the act of refilling his own glass. 'I'm afraid so,' he smiled. 'Odds are terrible. I wouldn't hazard your blunt on him now, Major, even if he is the favourite. There's no such thing as a certain winner for the Derby, as I know to my cost. You'd get better odds on one of the others. Try Grafton's nag. After all, his horse won last year. Can't remember what this one's called…something foreign, I fancy.'

'Alien,' put in the Rector from further down the table. Beyond him, young Mr Mountjoy nodded eagerly.

Hugo suppressed a chuckle at the thought of such precise knowledge coming from a gentleman in clerical bands. The Reverend Greenwood had been an avid man of the turf in his youth and made no secret of his continuing interest, even though he had long ago ceased to place bets himself. 'Thank you, sir,' said Hugo. 'And is he worth a wager, in your opinion?'

'Possibly,' said the Rector doubtfully, 'though I prefer Nectar myself. But if Golden Star is on form, he'll show them all a clean pair of heels, you mark

my words. I suppose Alien might be good for a place,
though.'

'Thank you, sir,' said Hugo again. 'I think I'll save
my blunt for better odds.'

'You're probably very wise, Major,' said Sir Edward, nodding. 'But I hope you'll join our party to
Epsom, none the less. It promises to be a very jolly
affair. Richard is coming, are you not, Richard?'

Richard looked suddenly somewhat disconcerted.
'Well, sir,' he began, 'I'm not exactly certain. I…
Jamie's condition…'

Sir Edward reddened visibly and cleared his throat.
'Beg pardon, Richard,' he said gruffly. 'I'm afraid
I—' He rose abruptly from his chair, without draining
his glass. 'I fear we are neglecting the ladies. Shall
we adjourn to the drawing room, gentlemen?'

Hugo allowed all his companions to move out
ahead of him, so that he would be the last to mount
the stairs.

Emma was deep in conversation with Mr Mountjoy
when Hugo gained the drawing room. As house-
guests of the Rector, the young man and his sister had
had to be invited, even though they were not close
friends of the Fitzwilliams. Hugo could see that the
brother appeared to be much taken with Emma—for,
although he was conversing with animation, his eyes
held the slightly dazed look that tended to afflict very
young men on first meeting a ravishing beauty. Hugo
himself had been the same—a lifetime ago.

Miss Mountjoy rose from the pianoforte and
crossed the room to join her brother. 'Oh, Miss Fitz-

william,' she began impulsively, 'this is such a lovely room—just made for dancing. Might we not make up a set? It would be such fun.'

For a moment, Emma seemed to be at a loss for words. Hugo thought he could see the beginnings of a flush on her neck.

Mr Mountjoy beamed at his sister's suggestion. 'Why, that would be wholly delightful,' he said. 'I should be honoured if you would consent to partner me, ma'am.'

Emma's flush was mounting. Hugo wondered how she would respond to her young guests' highly improper proposal without embarrassing them. Lady Hardinge could not dance, given her condition. The Rector's wife and Mrs Halliday would probably view such an impromptu affair with stern misgivings. That left only Miss Mountjoy herself—and Emma.

'Well…' began Emma doubtfully.

Lady Hardinge intervened. 'I'm afraid I am not able to dance myself,' she said with a mischievous twinkle in her eye, 'but I would gladly play for those who can.'

That settled it, for no one would gainsay the Countess. Hugo saw that Emma was both relieved and sorry. However, she said nothing more on the question, merely turning her attention to ensuring the servants set about rolling back the Turkey carpet.

Hugo tried to avoid Miss Mountjoy's hopeful glances. In spite of her youth—and his disfigurement—she had clearly marked him down as the only bachelor in the room. She was pretty enough, but incredibly gauche—seemingly she did not begin to grasp that country dances were quite beyond Hugo's capabilities at present.

Richard came again to the rescue. 'My wife may have excused herself from dancing,' he said brightly, 'but that is no reason why I should deny myself the pleasure. Will you honour me, Miss Mountjoy?'

The sudden glow on the girl's features suggested that she had never before been led into the dance by a peer of the realm.

Two couples looking somewhat sparse, Sir Edward offered his hand to his old friend, Mrs Halliday. Then Lady Hardinge struck up the opening chord and, in no time, the set was forming and re-forming.

Hugo crossed to the instrument to offer to turn for her ladyship.

As he bent forward, she said softly, 'I hope you will forgive me, Major—but Miss Mountjoy does not really know how to go on. She is so very young...' Her voice trailed off.

'So young that you stepped in to save her blushes—as Richard saved mine,' said Hugo warmly. 'You are, both of you, most thoughtful, ma'am. Miss Mountjoy may be too unschooled in the ways of the world to collect what was done for her, but I certainly am not. Thank you.'

'Major Stratton—now you attempt to put *me* to the blush,' said Lady Hardinge with mock severity, 'besides distracting me from my task. Emma will upbraid me roundly if I fail to keep time.'

Hugo smiled down at her, even though she was looking at her music rather than at him. Her playing was expert—not a note out of place. He was lucky to have such friends.

At the end of the set, Miss Mountjoy came rushing back to the pair at the pianoforte. 'Oh, Lady Hardinge, that was such fun. Thank you so much. You played quite beautifully.'

Her brother appeared at her elbow, echoing her thanks. 'Could you be persuaded to just one more set, ma'am?' he continued. 'This is terrifically good sport.'

Lady Hardinge nodded and began to leaf through the music on the instrument.

Mr Mountjoy was clearly remembering his manners, at last. 'But I must not monopolise our hostess,' he said, looking towards Emma and then back to Hugo. 'If you wish to stand up with one of the ladies, sir, I should gladly take over your duty here.'

Hugo swallowed the biting snub that rose temptingly to his lips. The young puppy meant well enough. And his sister was still looking hopeful, unfortunately. 'Thank you, but no,' Hugo said. 'I do not dance this evening.'

Mr Mountjoy bowed and withdrew, looking relieved.

Lady Hardinge, having selected her music, was about to begin to play once more. 'Major,' she said in an undertone, 'I really do not need a page-turner, you know.'

Hugo laughed quietly. 'Thank you, ma'am. I shall take that as my *congé*,' he said. With a polite bow, he made his way to the door as quickly as he could without drawing attention to his departure. He would go down to the terrace, just for a quarter of an hour or so, to smoke a cigar in private. All the ladies were occupied. He would not be missed.

Emma was not best pleased to be dancing a second set with Mr Mountjoy. She told herself it was because a hostess should not allow herself to be monopolised by a single guest—but out of the corner of her eye, she found she was watching Hugo's every move. She felt very proud of him—even though she knew she had no right to be, for she was nothing to him, not even a friend. She had feared he would snub silly Miss Mountjoy—or her equally silly brother—but he had shown remarkable restraint. Probably he had been used to dealing with rash young subalterns during his army days and knew just how thin-skinned they could be.

Noticing Hugo slip out of the room, Emma remembered that he, too, was thin-skinned. It was not surprising that he wanted to escape from the Mountjoys and the dancing. Emma wondered, while she mechanically executed the steps of the figure, whether Hugo had liked to dance before his injury. All the more distressing for him, if it were so. Poor Hugo.

No, not 'poor Hugo'. She was beginning to feel sorry for him—as he was feeling sorry for himself. But it was wrong to encourage him to withdraw even further into his shell. No matter how dreadful his injuries, he should not hide from the world. No true friend would permit him to do so. It was already obvious that he was making some progress; he climbed the stairs much more easily than before. Surely he

could learn to ride again—and to drive and to shoot—
if he were but prepared to make the effort? Emma
resolved to enlist Richard's help in making Hugo face
up to the future. Between them they could help Hugo
to become more like the man he had been. Why—he
might even be able to dance again, one day.

At that moment, Emma thought she heard the
sound of the front door being opened. Hugo could not
be leaving, surely? He would not be so impolite. And
besides, he could not leave without Jamie and Richard. No. Someone else must have called.

Emma gratefully excused herself to Mr Mountjoy
and hurried out on to the landing to see what was
happening. Looking over the balusters, she saw that
a complete stranger had been admitted. A tall dark
man was lounging carelessly against the delicate spin-
dle-legged table in the hallway and lazily twirling an
ivory-handled quizzing glass. On his face was an expression of acute boredom.

But he was, without doubt, the most beautiful specimen of manhood that Emma had ever beheld.

Emma stood transfixed on the landing, unable to
tear her eyes away from the gentleman's finely chis-
elled features. Then, from the vicinity of her father's
study, she heard Hugo's voice exclaim in surprise,
'Kit! What on earth are you doing here?'

The newcomer raised a mocking eyebrow, but did
not move an inch from where he stood. 'Why, waiting
for someone to relieve me of my coat,' he replied in
an affected drawl. 'What else did you think I might
be doing, brother?'

Chapter Five

Emma was still standing as if frozen when her father—probably alerted by her hurried departure from the dance—appeared at her side. He took one look into the hallway below and rushed down the stairs as fast as his bulk and his tight satin breeches would allow.

Sir Edward strode across to the newcomer, hand outstretched. 'Welcome, my boy, welcome,' he boomed, clapping the new arrival on the shoulder. 'What brings you here at this hour? Something important, I'll be bound.' Without giving anyone a chance to reply, Sir Edward turned in the direction of the servants' door. 'Godfrey! Where the devil are you, man? Do you not know we have guests?'

The butler materialised almost immediately on the landing behind Emma and glided down the staircase with no appearance of haste or of concern. He bowed politely to the visitor. 'May I take your coat, sir?'

Emma watched in trancelike immobility as the newcomer allowed himself to be relieved of his caped driving coat and curly-brimmed beaver. He had smiled at Sir Edward's greeting, but the expression of lazy disdain had returned to his handsome face a moment later. It seemed he was too bored to speak—or even to look around him.

Sir Edward did not appear to have noticed anything amiss. 'I am sure you'd like a private word with your brother,' he said, gesturing vaguely in the direction of Hugo who was standing motionless in the shadow of the gallery, leaning on his cane. 'But I hope you will join us upstairs when you're done. We are entertaining a few friends—quite informally, you understand—and the young people are dancing. My Emma would—' He broke off, looking round suddenly. The butler had disappeared as quietly as he had come. 'Where on earth is she?' he said in a burst of irritation.

From her vantage point above them, Emma stirred at last. 'I am here, Papa,' she said, trying vainly to tear her eyes from Hugo's incredible brother.

Three heads turned. Three pairs of eyes looked up at her. The brothers were remarkably alike, even though they did not have the same degree of beauty. Nor did they share the same colouring, Emma noted absently. The younger man's hair was lighter—dark brown, highlighted with glints of red, like finest rosewood. His clear blue eyes were skimming over the female figure above him, making a rapid assessment of her face and form. Emma felt herself beginning to flush under his all too obvious scrutiny. His faintly lifted eyebrow and curling lip did nothing to reduce her embarrassment. She was behaving like a chit just out of the schoolroom, both thunderstruck and tongue-tied at the sight of a handsome male face.

She tossed her head in annoyance. The spell broke. This young man was too well aware of his effect on hapless females, Emma concluded with sudden insight. Let others fall at his elegantly shod feet. She most certainly would not.

Lifting the hem of her cream silk gown with one hand, she laid the other on the polished banister rail and moved serenely down the staircase into the hallway. She knew the newcomer's eyes would fix on that tantalising glimpse of a shapely ankle. And she made a play of dropping her skirts and straightening them demurely before she looked at him. Women, too, could use the tricks of flirtation, she reckoned. She doubted that young Stratton could be more adept than she at the arts of allure.

A movement behind her reminded Emma that they were not alone. There was the click of a cane on the chequered marble before Hugo's voice said politely, 'Miss Fitzwilliam, you will allow me to present my youngest brother, Christopher—usually known as Kit.'

Kit took a small step forward so that he could take Emma's hand. For a moment, she thought he was going to kiss it—that would have been totally in character, she decided uncharitably—but he did not. He simply bowed gracefully and relinquished her hand. There was nothing to cavil at in his company manners. He would be the perfect gentleman—were it not for that calculating look in his eye.

'Your servant, Miss Fitzwilliam,' Kit said.

Emma dropped the tiniest curtsy, but did not bow
her head by as much as an inch. 'I am delighted to
welcome any relative of Major Stratton's,' she said
with a polite smile. 'You already know my father, I
take it?'

'Indeed, I do,' replied Kit. 'We have had—'

'Belong to the same clubs, m'dear,' broke in Sir
Edward quickly. 'Had one or two encounters over the
card table. Young Stratton here seems to have the
devil's own luck—playing against me, at least.' Sir
Edward laughed good-naturedly. He loved to gamble,
Emma knew. And he could afford to lose. But what
of Kit Stratton? Could he?

'Where are you staying, Kit? You can't mean to
drive on again tonight.' Hugo was smiling indulgently
at his younger brother.

Kit smiled back with genuine warmth. 'Don't
worry, brother. I shan't be importuning the Hardinges.
Arranged to rack up at the White Hart. Got to make
an early start in the morning. Things to do, you
know.'

The corner of Hugo's mouth quirked in sudden
irony but he said only, 'I see. London calls, no doubt.
And the urgent business that brings you here in the
middle of the night?'

Emma made to move back towards the stairs. She
had no desire to eavesdrop on Hugo's family affairs.
Her father was obviously of a similar mind, opening
the door of his study so that the two guests might
converse in private.

Kit still did not move an inch. 'Oh, it's nothing so
drastic, Hugo. John asked me to let you know that

they're off travelling again—Scotland, this time, I think he said—so the house at Stratton Magna will be shut up for a few months. He didn't want you arriving to find you'd been abandoned. Knows you find travelling difficult.' Kit cast a surreptitious glance at Hugo's weak leg and then quickly looked away.

'Good of him,' Hugo said curtly. 'But he could as easily have written, you know. A crippled leg doesn't affect my ability to read.'

Kit grinned like a naughty schoolboy. 'Oh, very well. If you must know, I offered to come. Wanted to see for myself how you were. Should have known you'd be just as cantankerous as ever.'

Hugo cast his eyes up to the heavens for a second and then turned to Sir Edward. 'It is not surprising if I am, sir. John and I have tried every avenue we could think of over the last few years, but nothing can tame this scapegrace brother of ours. Gambling, drinking—' He stopped abruptly. Such matters should not be mentioned in front of young unmarried ladies.

Emma broke the taut silence by saying politely, 'Will you come and meet our other guests, Mr Stratton? There will be refreshments upstairs, too—if you can spare the time, of course.'

Hugo stifled a laugh. 'I'm sure he can, ma'am, no matter how early his call to London. He never did seem to need much sleep.'

Kit cast a quelling look at his brother, but it produced no response at all, Emma noticed. Hugo was really very good indeed at dealing with provoking young men.

Emma re-entered the drawing room a little behind

Kit and her father. She knew that Hugo would hate her to watch his slow progress on the stairs. And yet, she lingered by the door. She was not needed immediately. Her father would make the necessary introductions.

A soft gasp, quickly swallowed, made her turn back to the drawing room. Miss Mountjoy's eyes were as round as guineas as she gazed at the new arrival. Her mouth hung partly open. Emma suppressed a desire to take the girl by the shoulders and shake her. No wonder Kit Stratton had such a disdainful view of womankind if this was the reaction he had learned to expect.

Emma did not wait to witness the introductions. It was all too embarrassing. She moved instead to meet Hugo who had just regained the landing.

'Your brother has certainly made an impression,' she said somewhat tartly.

'It is to be expected,' said Hugo in a flat voice. 'Kit has the happy knack of being welcomed wherever he goes.'

Emma thought Hugo was about to say something more, but he did not. She wondered what was hidden behind his apparently simple words. He had called his brother a 'scapegrace', after all. Was there something to be ashamed of about this beautiful—and undoubtedly somewhat arrogant—young man? She would have to find that out for herself. Of a certainty, Hugo would not tell her.

'I was just about to order the supper brought in, Major. I am sure your brother would welcome some refreshments after his travels. And you, too, perhaps?'

'You are most kind, ma'am,' replied Hugo, stopping in the doorway. Emma, too, paused to survey the scene. Jamie was seated at the instrument once more, choosing her music. Kit Stratton was leading a blushing Miss Mountjoy on to the floor. Emma was relieved to see that Mr Mountjoy was partnering the Rector's wife. If the young man had been forward enough to ask Emma to dance a third time, she would have been forced to snub him. That would have given her no pleasure at all.

The Rector came to claim Emma and lead her into the set. Her father looked on, smiling benignly. He liked nothing better than to see his guests enjoying themselves—even if it was a little improper for them to be dancing in this way.

Hugo crossed to the pianoforte once more. 'May I turn for you, Lady Hardinge?' he asked quietly.

'If you wish,' she replied. 'Your brother's arrival was unexpected, I collect? I hope he has not brought bad news?'

'Have no fears on that score, ma'am. It's only Kit's insatiable curiosity. He always has to know everything about John and me. A problem of being so much younger, I think. He always wanted to do whatever we could do, and long before he was old enough. He's a born rebel, I'm afraid. He was sent down from Oxford because of it. And, of course, he was much indulged, being the child of my parents' old age— besides having the face of an angel.'

Hugo smiled wryly, fearing for a moment that he might have said too much. But the Hardinges, of all people, were to be trusted. He bent to turn the page of music and received a brief nod of thanks. 'I would not have you think unkindly of Kit, ma'am,' he continued earnestly. 'He is a little wild, I admit, but he has a good heart under that splendid exterior. It is only a pity that the ladies cannot see beyond the handsome face.' And that he trades on it with so little compunction, Hugo added to himself. In spite of Kit's comparative youth, he had left a string of broken hearts behind him—never mind the discarded mistresses. Every one of them had thought she would reform him. And every one had failed.

Hugo raised his eyes to watch the dancing. Miss Mountjoy was gazing up at Kit as if she had never beheld anything so beautiful. Hugo shuddered inwardly. Yet another impressionable female...

Emma, now...Emma was clearly made of sterner stuff. Hugo assessed her carefully. Her attention was firmly focused on her conversation with her partner. She was sparing not a single glance for Kit. And earlier, in the entrance hall, she had seemed to have the measure of him. Perhaps...

At that moment, the dance brought Emma round to face Hugo and she looked directly at him. She smiled, fleetingly, before turning back to her partner.

Entranced, Hugo watched her retreating back move down the set. He could see that Kit was watching her closely, too. But Emma was studiously ignoring Kit Stratton. Excellent tactics on her part.

Kit had broken altogether too many hearts, in Hugo's opinion. It would do him the world of good to fall in love a little, especially if his love were not returned in equal measure. Hugo had little experience of Society ladies—he had spent too many years with the army—yet it seemed to him that Emma was just the kind of woman to give Kit the lesson he needed…if she once decided to take any notice of him at all. But why should she?

Hugo allowed himself a little smile. It would not be so surprising, surely, in the down-to-earth world of *ton* matches? Emma, as an heiress, was in need of a husband. Kit was a very attractive man—and better husband material than many a suitor. He might be a scapegrace… No, that was not quite true. Hugo had to admit to himself that, at twenty-two, Kit was already a fair way to becoming an out-and-out rake—though without as much wealth as he would have wished to fund his spendthrift habits. A good marriage might be the making of him. And what woman could resist the challenge of reforming a rake?

Hugo turned back to the music, feeling suddenly guilty. How quickly his mind had moved from love to marriage. It was not his place to arrange Emma's future, even to help tame his incorrigible brother. Kit was still very young, younger than Emma. Flirtation might provide a useful lesson—but marriage would be a disaster. He should not interfere. Let the young people make their own decisions.

A sudden burst of laughter from Kit drew everyone's attention. Most of the dancers were soon laughing heartily, too. Miss Mountjoy looked a trifle embarrassed though she, too, joined in eventually. Emma, however, was looking daggers at Kit.

In that instant, Hugo realised that Emma was aeons

older than his frivolous young brother. They would never suit—not for a moment.

A wicked thought arose unbidden. Poor Kit—her wealth would at least have kept him out of the sponging house.

Chapter Six

'You sent for me, Papa?' Emma shut the study door quietly behind her.

Her father rose from his favourite chair, smiling determinedly. He carried a letter in his hand. 'Emma, my dear, how well you look this morning,' he said, admiring the picture she made in her simple sprig-muslin gown. 'No after-effects from last night's entertaining?'

Emma returned his smile. 'No, indeed, Papa. It was most enjoyable. And I am used to dance till dawn when I am in London, you know. Country parties—even our own—are much tamer affairs.'

He pulled at his ear lobe. 'Ah…that was what I wanted to talk to you about, m'dear. Your Aunt Augusta has written.' He waved his letter in Emma's direction. 'She thinks you should return to London. Says you are missing too much of the Season. That, at your age, you—'

Emma was relieved to learn that the letter contained nothing worse. Her father's widowed sister was a busybody of the first order. Having no children of her own, she did her best to arrange Emma's life instead. 'Forgive me for interrupting you, Papa, but I'll wager I can quote my aunt's letter word for word. At my age,' she began, mimicking Mrs Warenne's very proper voice, 'I am like to be left on the shelf if I do not bestir myself to attend every single rout party. New gentleman are constantly appearing in town and it is *so* important to make an impression on them at the very *first* opportunity.' She looked up at her father's face through her long dark lashes. His hand had left his ear and he was trying not to laugh. 'Do I have it right, Papa?'

'Yes—well, it is much along those lines, I admit. But—' he was suddenly serious once more '—Emma, your aunt is only being sensible. You are twenty-three years old and still unmarried.' He must have detected hurt in Emma's eyes, for he hastened to say, 'Oh, I was more than happy to send all those fortune hunters to the rightabout. Not one of them valued you as he ought. But… My dear, I am concerned about your future. I am not as young as I was, you know, and when I am gone, you will be alone here.'

Emma's eyes widened as she took in the import of his words. He shook his head a fraction to forestall the protest that had sprung to her lips. 'I would so much like to see you happily settled, Emma. As would your aunt. And, however much you love the country, my dear, even you have to admit that it is not exactly awash with potential suitors.' He looked sadly down at her, counting off the names on the fingers of his left hand. 'Richard is married. Kit Stratton is a reckless young ne'er-do-well with much too fine a face. And Mountjoy is barely out of leading strings. Apart from the old widowers—who are not for you, I sincerely hope—no other eligible man has put in an appearance in this neighbourhood for years. So... much as you may prefer the country, m'dear, I'm afraid it has to be London.'

Emma was silent for several heartbeats. Then, in a very small voice, quite unlike her usual confident tones, she ventured, 'You did not include Major Stratton in your list, Papa.'

Her father's eyes widened in surprise. 'No, of course I did not,' he said brusquely. 'The Major may be a very fine man. A hero, too, perhaps, I dare say. But he is not...' He put a heavy hand on his daughter's arm and warned sharply, 'Emma, he is scarred and crippled. He may not even be a whole man.' He reddened slightly as he realised what he had said in front of his unmarried daughter, but he was clearly too angry and too concerned to stop. 'He is no fit husband for you, Emma—nor for any other young lady. You must not give him another thought. Indeed, I doubt he is marriageable at all. It is a pity, I admit, but there is nothing to be done.'

Emma was staring at her slippers, trying to make sense of the tumbling, whirling thoughts that her father's words had provoked. She wanted to re-establish her easy friendship with Hugo Stratton, that was all. She had never thought of him as a husband. At least...when she was a child...but those were only a child's romantic daydreams and long ago forgotten. Besides, the man who had returned from the wars was nothing like the fantasy she had fashioned in the schoolroom. Nothing like. With a flash of insight, Emma now saw that Hugo believed himself to be unfit for marriage. He would never propose to any woman of his own free will.

She swallowed hard. Her father must be right. He had her best interests at heart, as always.

She was about to say that she would do as he asked, when another picture of Hugo rose in her mind, a picture so vivid that he might have been before her—Hugo's laughing eyes as they had once been. Could they not be so again? There had been a moment during that walk in the wood at Harding when he had been so close to his former self... Must he remain a bitter recluse just because he had been wounded in the service of his country? It seemed so very unfair.

'Emma?' Her father was now beginning to sound more impatient than angry.

Emma smiled sweetly up at him, waiting until the last remnants of his anger had melted away. 'No doubt Aunt Augusta is right, Papa. London in the Season is the place for suitors—and fortune hunters, too, alas. I will go back and join the throng. Will that content you, Papa?'

'Aye,' he smiled. 'You were ever a sensible lass, Emma. You know it is for the best.' He sounded relieved.

Emma's smile dimmed. 'Oh, Papa—but what about the Derby? You said you planned to go. But if I am in London with Aunt Augusta... Surely you would not deny me the chance to see Golden Star run? You always said you named him for me.' Her face was set in a picture of childlike innocence as she gazed hopefully up at him.

He plucked at his ear. 'Well…' he said, looking again at the letter in his hand. 'I suppose it might be possible to make up a party, if your aunt agreed. I'd have to take a house nearby, of course. Too far to go otherwise. Might be a goodish notion, though,' he mused abstractedly. 'We could all see the race then. And your Aunt Augusta could ensure that a few eligible young people were invited to join us at the same time.'

Emma groaned inwardly at the thought of a houseful of young ladies, all carefully schooled by their matchmaking mamas, and Aunt Augusta's choice of eligible gentlemen. But, at least, it would be a change from the interminable London round. After so many full Seasons, that was beginning to pall.

Her papa seemed to have convinced himself. 'Yes,' he said, 'I'll write to your aunt today. And I may tell her that you will be returning to London immediately, Emma?' His raised eyebrows demanded a precise answer.

'In a day or two, Papa,' Emma said. 'I should like to spend a little time with Jamie before I go.' Her eyes lit up with sudden mischief. 'If I try really hard, I might even persuade her to join your Surrey house party, Papa. Would that not be delightful? It was so clever of you to think of it.'

Papa—who had a very soft spot for the lovely Countess—agreed that his daughter might remain in the country for a few days more, in hopes of adding the Hardinges to his guest list.

Emma kissed his cheek. 'Thank you, Papa,' she
beamed. 'I had better ride over to Harding at once to
begin to work on her, do you not think? And, before
you mention it, I *will* take a groom. I am resolved to
prevent you from worrying about me any more.'

Sir Edward sighed contentedly and patted her arm.
'Thank you, m'dear. You are a good girl.'

Emma left the room before he could remember that
any visit to Harding must provide yet another opportunity to meet the unmarriageable Major.

'Good morning, Miss Emma.' The butler beamed
at her. 'You will be pleased to know that my lord has
driven over to the Dower House to visit his lady
mother.'

Emma's spirits lifted at the news. The Dowager
Countess had been almost like a mother to Emma for
as long as she could remember. Emma resolved to
ride on to the Dower House as soon as she left Jamie.
It would be a happy duty to welcome Richard's
mother back home.

'That is splendid news, Digby,' Emma said. 'I will
go to pay my respects to her ladyship this very day.'
She picked up her trailing skirts, turning to make for
the stairs and Jamie's sitting room.

Behind her, Digby coughed discreetly. 'I believe
her ladyship is in the conservatory, Miss Emma.'

'Oh.' Emma turned quickly on her heel. 'Yes, of
course. It is such a lovely spot when the sun is shining. Don't trouble to announce me, Digby. I know
my way very well.'

Emma walked briskly along the corridor to the conservatory at the end of the house, where Richard had created a luxurious oasis for his wife's enjoyment. Jamie's green fingers had ensured that all kinds of exotic plants now flourished there. And it had given her an opportunity to indulge her passion for gardening in even the most inclement winter weather. Emma knew her friend would probably be surrounded by cuttings and compost. Even heavily pregnant, Jamie was rarely to be found simply enjoying the delights of her private paradise.

The door opened silently on well-oiled hinges. The warm, moist air settled around Emma like a fine velvet cloak and the sweet scent of newly turned soil filled her nostrils. She breathed deeply, savouring the moment. For Emma, this place was a peaceful haven, a refuge from all the artifice of Society life.

The conservatory seemed to be empty. Jamie's workbench was strewn with soil and potting implements, but she was nowhere to be seen. Emma was just turning to leave when she heard a muffled noise. It sounded like a groan.

Someone was there. And something was wrong.

Emma pushed her way through the lush greenery to the far side of the conservatory. Jamie was there, sure enough, sitting awkwardly on the edge of a small wooden bench.

But Jamie was not alone. Hugo Stratton loomed over her, his hands clasping her face and his eyes gazing down into hers. As Emma watched in shocked astonishment, Hugo lowered his head to Jamie's.

Emma whirled and fled from the scene, unwilling to believe the evidence of her own eyes. How could he? Jamie was the wife of his best friend…and pregnant, besides. It was wicked. It was dishonourable.

And Jamie…Jamie had not seemed to be resisting Hugo's advances…

Emma choked back a sob. Her heart was beating as rapidly as if she had fled from a charging bull. Her knees seemed to have turned to water. She had to lean her forehead and breast against the cool paintwork of the corridor to stop her legs from buckling beneath her.

Jamie—and Hugo!

It was indecent.

It was utterly beyond her comprehension.

'Emma?'

Jamie had appeared in the conservatory doorway. Her cheeks looked remarkably flushed, and she was holding a handkerchief to her eye as if she had been crying.

Perhaps she had not welcomed Hugo's kisses after all?

'I thought I heard someone in the conservatory… Why—are you quite well, Emma? You look as if you are about to faint.'

Emma shook her head dumbly. Her throat was so dry that she could not utter a sound. She forced her lips into a somewhat shaky smile.

'Go and sit down in the conservatory, my dear, and I will send some water to you immediately.' Jamie sounded concerned now. 'Forgive me for not staying with you, but I must get Annie to help me bathe my eye. I stupidly allowed some soil dust to get into it. Major Stratton assured me he had removed every speck, but the desire to rub and rub is overwhelming. If I cannot do something about it, I swear I shall scream.' With an apologetic smile, Jamie hurried away to find her faithful abigail, Annie Smithers.

Emma took a deep breath and swallowed hard. It had all been perfectly innocent.

Or had it?

Emma forced her legs to carry her calmly back to the conservatory. However much she wished to avoid setting eyes on Hugo Stratton, she had no choice. The servants would certainly expect to find her there. And there was no knowing what the Major—or Jamie— would read into her actions if she left without a word.

She must behave as if she had seen nothing at all. A short, polite conversation was what the situation required...followed by a speedy retreat.

Emma had her fingers on the handle of the door when the butler arrived, carrying a carafe of water and a glass on a tray. 'Thank you, Digby,' Emma said, smiling. 'I am much better now, but I would welcome a glass of water and a moment of quiet repose. Perhaps you had better announce me after all. But have Juno brought round in ten minutes, if you please. I cannot stay longer.'

Hugo looked up in surprise when Emma was announced. For once, he had been sitting in a comfortable chair, Emma noticed, but the lower seat made it a struggle to rise, especially as he seemed to be without his cane. The exertion was apparent in his face. If there was guilt there, too, Emma was unable to discern it. She remained standing just inside the door to give him time to collect himself before moving forward to offer her hand. Behind her, the butler quietly withdrew. Emma heard the soft click as the glass-panelled door closed at her back. In any other room, the door would have been left ajar, as convention demanded. Here, their actions could still be observed—yet Emma felt trapped by that tiny sound.

'Good morning to you, Major,' she said in her most cheerful voice. 'I hope I find you well after last night's exertions.'

Hugo bowed, frowning slightly as if he were looking for a hidden—and offensive—meaning behind her words. Emma forced herself to remain polite and in control, though inwardly she bristled. How dare he? *She* had done nothing wrong.

'Your brother will have left for London by now, I collect?' she continued rapidly. 'What a pity he could not stay to be presented to Richard's mother. I am sure Lady Hardinge would have been charmed to make his acquaintance.' Emma stopped short. Why on earth was she gabbling so? She had been so determined to remain calm.

Hugo was looking searchingly at her. She hoped he could not read the suspicions behind her polite façade.

'No doubt,' Hugo replied quietly. 'Kit was ever a charmer.'

Emma's heightened senses were fully alert to every nuance in his voice. If he betrayed himself by so much as a breath, she would know it. But his voice was laced with irony; and she fancied she detected a hint of something deeper, too. It could not be envy, surely? It was true that the contrast between the brothers was now very great, but—

'May I say that you look blooming this morning, ma'am?' Hugo's words interrupted Emma's train of thought. 'Obviously you thrive on company. It was a splendid party. I am sure all your guests enjoyed the entertainment.'

Emma was not deceived. He was obviously determined to put her on the defensive in this encounter by making clear that he disapproved of the dancing—which she knew she should not have permitted at such a gathering. She threw him a challenging look. 'A good host,' she said rather tightly, 'will always have the wishes of his guests at the forefront of his mind. And if those desires should prove to be somewhat…less than conventional, a good host will ensure that nothing occurs to embarrass his guests.'

Emma saw—with a silent crow of triumph—that Major Stratton was trying to suppress the faintest glimmer of a smile. He tilted his head a little to one side as if to examine her better from that angle, though it might have been to hide that unwilling twitch of the lips. 'And you, ma'am, are most certainly a very good host.' His quiet words sounded almost sincere, but there was a gleam of something unfathomable in his grey eyes that warned her not to believe him. He would always find a way to turn her barbs back on her. Besides, he was clearly a practised deceiver.

Emma dropped a tiny curtsy. She must get away from him. 'Thank you, sir,' she said, taking refuge in convention once more. 'You are most kind. But, if you will excuse me, I must be on my way to the Dower House. My horse is at the door.'

Hugo bowed a trifle stiffly. 'I hope you find the Dowager well after her travels. I know Richard is delighted that his mother is returned. He is very much concerned about his wife's health.'

Emma looked up sharply. For the first time, Hugo had said something to reveal his inner thoughts. He appeared to be worried for Richard—and glad that the Dowager had returned to share her son's burden. It made no sense at all. She found herself replying more sharply than she had intended. 'Jamie will not permit herself to be cosseted, Major, even by Richard and his mother. You would understand that, if you knew her history. She is—'

'I do know,' he said softly.

Oh, dear. Jamie and Hugo must be even closer than she had imagined. Not many people were entrusted with the secret of how Jamie had disguised herself as a garden boy to escape from her stepmother's machinations—and how Richard had married her out of hand when he discovered who she really was. Oh, poor, poor Richard.

'Lady Hardinge told me herself,' Hugo said. 'I think,' he continued pensively, 'that she did so to show me that she, too, had episodes in her past that were best not discussed in polite Society. I admire her a very great deal.'

'That—if I may say so, sir—was perfectly obvious.' Emma's angry outburst echoed in the sudden stillness. She closed her eyes in despair and bit down hard on her lower lip, but she knew it was too late.

How could she have allowed herself to say such a thing?

She turned to leave. She did not dare to look at him.

'A moment, ma'am.' Hugo's voice was as hard as granite and as cold as ice.

Emma stopped but did not turn.

'What—precisely—was the meaning of that last remark?'

She could feel his warm breath on the back of her neck. He had moved to stand mere inches behind her. The threat in his voice was unmistakable. She had two choices—retreat…or attack.

Emma took a single step forward, putting just a little distance between them, and then spun around to face him. Her finger pointed accusingly. 'I should have thought the meaning was obvious, Major,' she said, pouring out all her pent-up fury. 'It means that I saw you kissing Richard's wife. Do you dare to deny it? You are a guest in his house, and you—'

Hugo's face had blanched under his tan. The thin line of his scar stood out starkly, drawing Emma's unwilling gaze. Articulating every venomous word as if he were a judge handing down a sentence of death, he said, 'I am a guest in Richard's house and a man of honour, Miss Fitzwilliam.'

Emma stood motionless, staring at him with bitter contempt. She could not trust herself to speak.

'Your accusation is writ plainly on your face, ma'am. You believe I would be Lady Hardinge's lover, do you not?'

The silence seemed to stretch endlessly between them.

At last, Hugo broke it. 'You do not have the first idea of love, if you could so mistake my actions,' he said grimly. 'I fear your education is sadly lacking.' He took a step forward to close the space between them and seized Emma roughly by the shoulders, his fingers biting into her flesh as if the barrier of her habit did not exist. 'I'll show you what lovers do,' he said, lowering his mouth to hers.

Emma could not move. She could not think. She could only feel. Hugo's hard, bruising kiss was full of anger, frustration and—Emma somehow understood—dawning desire. For what seemed an eternity, he continued to punish her with his mouth, holding her body prisoner between his hands. Anger appeared to have given them unexpected strength.

At last, the grip of his weakened hand relaxed. The pressure of his mouth on hers seemed somehow gentler, too. His fingers began to stroke slowly over the fine velvet of her sleeve. Emma was sure Hugo's touch was burning through to her naked skin, just as his lips had put their brand on her mouth. No man had ever kissed her with any kind of passion. Fury had caused this, to be sure, not love—and yet Hugo's kiss was wildly exciting. Emma's heart was racing and every inch of her body seemed to be glowing so hot it would melt at any second. It was glorious to be so alive. Emma willingly yielded to the temptations of pure feeling.

When Emma moved her head the tiniest fraction—not to pull away, but to enjoy this wonderful sensation to the full—Hugo reacted instantly to forestall any possible escape. He clamped his right hand to the back of her head, his fingers splayed across her silky hair to hold her steady for his continuing kiss. He started to explore the pleasures of her mouth with his lips and tongue, testing and teasing, while his left hand caressed her arm with never a pause.

Emma was close to fainting from the pleasure of it. She no longer cared who—or where—she was.

Until the loud rattle of the door handle announced that they were no longer alone...

Chapter Seven

Dear God, what had she done?

Emma dared not turn to see who was at the conservatory door. She knew that one glimpse of her flushed face and bruised lips would betray her. It mattered not that she was now alone, or that the lush greenery had probably concealed their embrace from anyone looking in from the corridor. Her behaviour had been scandalous. A lightskirt from Covent Garden would have known better.

It seemed a very long time before the door was opened. And the handle rattled much more than usual. Emma had time to take several deep breaths, and to pray that her flush might be fading.

'Miss Emma.'

Emma was perversely glad to be discovered by the butler who had known her all her life. Jamie would have understood her plight, but what Emma needed at this moment was absolute discretion—not sympathetic questions.

'Miss Emma, her ladyship is in her sitting room upstairs. She asked if you would join her there, instead of riding over to the Dower House. She expects that his lordship will bring his lady mother back with him.'

'Thank you, Digby, I—'

'I shall tell her ladyship that you are still feeling a little faint, shall I? And that you will join her presently?'

'Thank you, Digby. Yes, I shall. Presently.' Keeping her back to him, Emma busied herself with examining a curiously shaped leaf, hoping that she appeared totally engrossed. Her sudden interest in plants might also excuse her rather strained tone of voice…and hide her shaking hands.

She closed her eyes, breathing deeply. Digby was still standing behind her, waiting. Drat the man. Why would he not go? She dare not turn round.

At last he said, sounding remarkably like her father, 'I shall convey your message to her ladyship. Shall I have your mare taken round to the stable, too?'

Emma almost laughed at being so easily caught. Everyone knew that her first concern was always for her horses, yet she had completely forgotten that her beloved mare was standing at the door. Digby, at least, would not be deceived. And she would not act the coward before him any more. She turned slowly, saying, as calmly as she could, 'Thank you, Digby. You think of everything.'

Digby was studying the pattern on the tiled floor. And he managed to make his exit without once looking into her face.

Emma sank into the low chair that Hugo Stratton had vacated. It all seemed like hours ago. She covered her face with her hands. Her cheeks still felt burning hot…though not nearly as hot as the rest of her body. Hugo's passionate kisses had set her every fibre aglow in a way she had not thought possible. *This* must be why the matchmaking mamas took such care to chaperon their maiden daughters on every occasion…and why the gentlemen were always so eager to tempt the ladies into a shady alcove or a secluded bower. If mere kisses made a woman melt as she had done, what was there still to be discovered in the love between a man and a woman? Surely nothing could be more thrilling than the feelings she had just experienced in Hugo's arms? And yet…

Hugo forced himself to move through the pain. It was the least he deserved. He had told her he was a man of honour. What kind of man of honour would take advantage of an innocent and helpless young woman as he had just done? Never mind that his honour was smirched even before he set eyes on her.

Guilt overpowered him, like water bursting through a dam. Soon it was overflowing.

Why had he done it? Had he absolutely no self-control?

After a pause, his re-awakened conscience supplied the answer. No. These days he had precious little self-control—and none at all where Emma Fitzwilliam was concerned. He had desired her from that first moment, when she stood staring at his scars, her back ramrod straight in her tight riding habit and her eyes like saucers as she took in the horror he presented. He had wished himself anywhere but there—exposed—in the middle of the sweeping lawns of an English country house. The bloody battlefield would have been preferable to the horror and disgust he had seen in Emma's eyes.

Or so it had seemed.

Hugo paused in his headlong flight from the conservatory. His only thought had been to protect Emma's reputation. She must not be found alone with him, and certainly not in his arms. His desire to protect her must have given a strength to his limbs that he did not know he possessed, for he was now a good hundred yards from the house. Somehow, he had pushed his way out through the plants and halfway across the garden without even his cane to aid him.

A further sharp pain in his left leg reminded him of the weakness that was trying to dominate his every waking hour. This time he refused to acknowledge it. If concern for Emma's reputation could bring him this far, then sheer stubborn determination would enable him to become a whole man again. He might never aspire to Emma Fitzwilliam, scarred and dishonoured as he was, but he would not permit her to pity him. Anything but that.

And yet…and yet, it was not pity that had made her respond to him as she had. She had resisted at first, to be sure, but that was hardly surprising, given the violence of his attack on her. Hot-blooded fury had governed him at the thought that she believed him capable of such perfidy…but it had taken mere seconds for his anger to evaporate. The touch of her soft lips had been his undoing. He had wanted to hold her, to caress her, to kiss her until they were both mindless

with passion. Heaven alone knew what he would have
done if they had not been interrupted for, somehow,
he knew that—on this occasion at least—she would
in no wise have been able to resist him. He should
feel nothing but shame.

Hugo struck out for the woods, willing his legs to
obey him. He had behaved like the worst sort of
lecher, the kind of man he had always despised. He
would walk until he could walk no more—and until
long after Emma Fitzwilliam had returned to the
safety of her father's house.

'Oh, dear,' Jamie said. 'It is a splendid idea, Emma,
but—'

'But sadly impractical,' put in the Dowager briskly,
patting Emma's hand fondly to soften her words. 'We
cannot just abandon Major Stratton, Emma. It would
be the height of bad manners—especially as the Major's brother has shut up the family house. Where
would the poor man go?'

Emma bit back the highly improper response that
rose to her lips. She was torn between anger and guilt,
but neither must be permitted to show. 'He may join
the party too, ma'am,' she said quickly, trying to
sound her normal light-hearted self. 'I am sure a
change of air would speed his recovery. Why, he
could even take the waters at Epsom. They are said
to work wonders, I believe.'

'If you can stomach the foul taste.' Richard's voice
emerged from the depths of a chair by the fire.

Everyone laughed. The last vestiges of Emma's
tension dissolved. She would reflect on what had hap-

pened—and those intensely strange feelings—later, when she was quite alone.

'I suppose we might succeed in persuading him,' added Richard thoughtfully. 'He was ever one for the turf in his early years. Horse mad. Second only to being army mad, of course. But it will depend on you, my love,' he said, looking at his wife with some concern. 'Do you feel able to contemplate such a trip? The doctor said you needed to take care—'

'The doctor would have me spend the whole of the summer in bed, not moving so much as a finger,' Jamie said with more than a touch of asperity. 'I am not such a poor creature, Richard. I refuse to be treated like an invalid. I am not ill. Besides, I have never been to the Derby. I am sure I should like it extremely.' She turned to Emma. 'You, too, Emma.'

Emma looked at Jamie in surprise. Her friend sounded…different. But the mischief in Jamie's eyes gave her away. She was plotting. If she had her way, the Derby excursion was settled—and Major Hugo Stratton would have no choice in the matter, either. Jamie smiled at Emma in silent understanding. She clearly believed she was forwarding Emma's own plans.

But Emma could not begin to know what she wanted where the maddening Major was concerned. Not here. Not yet. She had to get away from Harding.

'Mama, you will join Emma's party, too, will you not?' Jamie continued bluntly. The Dowager looked a little taken aback, but laughed when Jamie added, 'We cannot allow the Major the slightest hope that he has anywhere else to go, you know. It must be the Derby for us all.'

'I am so glad that is settled,' Emma said, ruthlessly suppressing the wayward emotions that threatened to overpower her. She rose from her place on the sofa beside the Dowager. 'Papa will be so pleased. And now I must go home to finish my preparations. I am returning to London first thing tomorrow.' She did not attempt to hide a little grimace of distaste. 'The Season is—apparently—bereft without me.'

Richard laughed heartily. 'I am sure it is, Emma. All those poor young men…'

Emma allowed herself to give vent to something very close to a snort. 'Poor, indeed,' she said vehemently, preparing to launch into a tirade against the fortune hunters who plagued her at every turn.

'Now, Emma,' said the Dowager gently, 'you really must not blame them. It is not, after all, of their own choosing that they are younger sons, or penniless. What choice do they have? An heiress—especially one as lovely as you—must seem to them like manna from heaven. You should have pity on them.'

'Oh, I do, ma'am, I do,' replied Emma. 'Except when I am constrained to be in their company.'

Richard and Jamie dissolved into laughter. The Dowager, too, smiled broadly. 'Emma,' she said after a moment, 'you are become quite incorrigible. You will allow me to say it is a very good thing that the world at large is not aware of it. What would Mrs Warenne say if she heard you?'

Emma tried to adopt a prim and proper expression. She failed. 'My Aunt Augusta has endless patience with me, ma'am. She presents me with one eligible gentleman after another and is never deterred if they do not come up to scratch or—worse—if I refuse them. And she tries so hard to shield me from un-desirables, too.' Emma threw a conspiratorial glance at Jamie. 'Sometimes, I wish she would not,' she added with a flashing smile, 'for at least a few of the rakes are most entertaining. Why is it, Richard, that respectable gentlemen are always so very boring?'

Richard strode across the room to take Emma by the arm. 'I think I must escort you out, madam, before you become even more outrageous. Boring, am I, in-deed?'

Emma smiled her farewells to the ladies, shook her-self free of Richard's restraining hand, and dropped him an impudent curtsy. 'You are mistaken, my lord,' she said demurely, making for the open door. 'I should never have dreamt of calling *you*... "respectable".' With a final saucy toss of her head, she whipped through the door, leaving Richard trans-fixed in the middle of the room and his ladies des-perately trying to conceal their mirth.

'Emma...' began Richard menacingly, but he was too late. She closed the door firmly and ran lightly down the stairs, savouring her triumph.

Success, thanks to Jamie. It was quite wonderful— and consolation for the fact that she was bound to return to London and to the stuffy confines of the Season. Now, at least, she had the house party to look forward to. All the Hardinges would be there—and Major Hugo Stratton.

Emma swallowed hard, forcing her mind to concentrate on practical matters. Her father would not be overly pleased that the Major would be one of the party, but she was sure she could soon bring him round to the idea, especially as there was nowhere else for Hugo to go. No. Papa was a kind man. In the end, he would welcome Major Stratton, along with all the potential husbands that Aunt Augusta would marshal for Emma's approval.

Emma offered up a little prayer that Aunt Augusta's young men would not *all* be respectable and boring. There was nothing more difficult than refusing the suit of a respectable man, especially one who was conscious of his own worth. She had called Hugo Stratton thin-skinned, but that was surely preferable to the elephant hide of some of the pompous windbags who had pursued her, unable to accept that they might have any shortcomings in the eyes of an eligible young lady. At least Hugo had the grace to laugh at some of his own failings...

Chapter Eight

'And I am delighted to say that no one has declined.' Mrs Warenne was in full flow, at the same time dispensing tea to her brother and to Emma. The trio had already made themselves at home in the long, rambling Surrey mansion that Sir Edward had rented. None of the guests would arrive before the morrow and so Emma and her aunt would have plenty of time to organise all the final details for their large party. 'Even Major Stratton's brother has accepted,' Aunt Augusta said with satisfaction.

Emma's hand shook slightly as she took her cup. Kit Stratton one of their house party? She would never have believed that Society matrons would allow their daughters to stay in a house in such company, but, evidently, they had accepted. They would have been reassured by the presence of Aunt Augusta and the Dowager, but still… Perhaps Kit's reputation was not as black as Hugo had painted?

Aunt Augusta's flow continued without pause. 'I thought he would be company for his brother, Emma, since the Major cannot get about as well as the younger men. And Mr Stratton is a charming young man, quite charming. All my friends positively dote on him. He has been invited everywhere since his arrival in London.'

No doubt, Emma thought sourly. What was it that Hugo had said? That Kit had the happy knack of being welcomed everywhere. Yes, that was it. Why, then, did she feel not the least desire to welcome him herself? She could not be sure, but she suspected that she had glimpsed an aspect of his character that he was normally at pains to conceal. The man she had observed from the upstairs landing in her father's house was much too conscious of the perfect image he presented and of the charm he could exude at will. He knew how to manipulate—and he would do it for his own ends, she was sure.

She would be very wary of Kit Stratton.

'Good grief, who on earth is that incredible female?'

All the eyes in the Fitzwilliam barouche followed Kit Stratton's gaze to rest on the elderly lady in the opulent but old-fashioned open carriage. She was dressed in the height of fashion from more than thirty years earlier—powder and patches, a huge feathered hat, and a striped brocade gown over elbow panniers. Richard, sitting calmly beside his wife, laughed softly. 'Oh, don't you know, Kit? That's the Dowager Lady Luce. I thought you, of all people, would know her, considering how much you frequent the gaming tables these days. She—' A discreet cough from Jamie stopped him in mid-sentence.

'Lady Luce was a great beauty in her youth, I believe, Mr Stratton,' said Jamie calmly. 'I understand that she disapproves of modern fashions and modern manners—hence her refusal to adopt either of them. Have you met her son, the present Earl?'

Emma smiled to herself at Jamie's skill in changing the subject to avoid further mention of Kit's disreputable habits. The Dowager Countess Luce was renowned for her passion for gaming. She tended to win—or lose—extremely heavily and was known to be the despair of her son who, as often as not, found himself paying her enormous debts. Kit would certainly not have forgotten any encounter with Lady Luce. Given half a chance, she would win the shirt from his back. And what would Kit Stratton do then?

Jamie's polite conversation continued while Emma's attention wandered. But, after several minutes of inactivity alongside Sir Edward's barouche, Kit's black stallion was beginning to become restive. It was clearly unused to being in such a noisy and unpredictable crowd. Emma decided, uncharitably, that the stallion was a poor choice of mount for such an excursion. Horse and rider might make an admirable picture—especially in the eyes of impressionable young ladies—but the horse was much too highly strung for Epsom. Yet, in spite of herself, Emma found herself admiring Kit's skill, for he controlled the powerful beast without apparent effort.

Emma wondered whether Hugo would soon be riding alongside his brother. He had certainly made remarkable progress during Emma's weeks in London. He had now totally abandoned his cane—and his scars were much less noticeable than before. He had agreed to join the Derby outing with no hesitation at all.

Kit's sidling horse caught Emma's eye once more. She looked away deliberately. It chafed her to remain confined to the barouche, even in company with the Hardinges, but no lady could appear at the Derby on horseback. Convention demanded that, if a lady attended at all, she should sit demurely in her carriage accompanied by her chaperon. Unless the lady was old, and from a rich family, like Lady Luce. Such a woman could do exactly as she pleased. Emma smiled inwardly at the thought. If she remained single, she would—probably—become just as eccentric and demanding as Lady Luce. She might even take up gaming, too. After all, she would be rich enough to afford it...

'Emma?'

'I beg your pardon, Jamie. I'm afraid I was miles away.'

'Your father is returning. Over there.' Jamie pointed across the milling crowd. Sir Edward was struggling to force his way through. 'He looks as if he has lost a guinea and found sixpence.'

'Oh, dear,' Emma said. Her father looked ruffled, and irritated. That did not bode well for Golden Star. Perhaps their horse was injured?

'Is something wrong, Papa?' she said when he reached their carriage at last, puffing a little from his exertions.

'Not exactly,' he said. 'York's here, with his cronies, to see his horse run. He's invited us to join his party. Fellow owners together, he says.'

Emma knew that her father must be in two minds about this invitation. It was a great honour, of course, but Papa thoroughly disapproved of the Duke of York's scandalous and profligate mode of life. Like his brother, the Prince Regent, the Duke had ever an eye to a pretty woman. And, knowing the risks his only daughter could run in such company, Papa would certainly have no desire for any royal eye to rest too long upon Emma.

'I'm sure you will understand, ma'am,' Sir Edward said to Jamie, with a slightly hesitant smile, 'that His Royal Highness was most insistent. The royal party has a marquee near the winning post.'

'What about our other guests, Papa?' Emma was looking round anxiously to see what had become of the other carriages. She could not, as joint hostess, simply abandon her guests, no matter how illustrious the summons. And Aunt Augusta, in the second carriage with Major Stratton and two of the other ladies, was nowhere to be seen.

'I have sent the grooms to find them,' he said. 'I am sure they will appear in due course, if they can make their way through this crush. I did explain to the Duke how we were placed, but he just laughed and said they were all welcome—if they could actually reach his party. He must know that they will never get through the crowd at all if they do not start immediately—as we must. I fear we shall have to leave the barouche here, Lady Hardinge,' he added apologetically. 'Do you feel able to reach York's party on foot?'

Jamie shook her head. 'I do not think I should like to try it with this huge throng of people, sir,' she said. 'Even a royal invitation may be declined by a lady in my...interesting condition. Richard shall make my excuses.' She glanced up at her husband through her dark lashes and then quickly looked away.

Emma knew that Jamie was perfectly capable of making her way across the turf—but had not the least desire for the Duke of York's company. They both knew exactly how difficult it was to avoid the lecherous looks and touching hands of the Regent and his brothers. It was a pity that Emma herself had no excuse to offer.

Richard gave his wife a speaking look. 'As you command, my love,' he said. 'And I am sure that His Royal Highness will allow me to return to your side as soon as I have done so.' Richard jumped lightly down from the carriage and turned to offer his hand to Emma. 'Kit, will you remain here with Jamie until I return? It should not take me many minutes to do the pretty to our revered commander-in-chief.'

Rising from her deep curtsy, Emma listened with admiration to Richard's skilful handling of the Duke of York. Richard made it sound as if Jamie had been most eager to wait on His Royal Highness, and had had to be restrained for her own safety.

'Of course, Hardinge, of course,' replied the Duke genially. 'You had better return to her at once, too.

Can't leave her unattended in a place like this. Have to look after the little woman, eh?'

Richard bowed politely. Emma knew that he was delighted to have won his point so easily, but there was not the slightest sign of triumph on his handsome features. Emma schooled her own into an expression of concern. 'Take care of her, Richard,' she said. He bowed again, and left them. Emma could have sworn that he winked.

The Duke turned back to Emma. 'Delighted you could join us, ma'am. And you, too, Sir Edward,' he added, nodding affably at Emma's father. 'You will both have a much better view from here. And with your colt so heavily fancied, you will want to be in at the death, so to speak.' He laughed at his own wit. His entourage joined in politely.

Emma smiled up at him. 'Yes, indeed. But what of your own horse, sir? Might he not win?'

The Duke turned to one of the officers who accompanied him. 'What are the latest odds on Prince Leopold, Forster?'

'Pretty long, sir,' replied Colonel Forster, stepping forward to join the little group. At first glance, he appeared to be a handsome brown-haired man in his middle forties but, on closer inspection, his face showed the signs of dissipation common among the royal set. 'At least twenty to one, when I last checked. No one is backing him, it appears—apart from yourself, of course, sir.'

Emma found the Colonel's manner more than a little obsequious. And she did not like the way he looked at her. Small wonder, perhaps, given that he was one of the Duke's cronies.

'A lot of the money is chasing Sir Edward's Golden Star,' the Colonel continued. 'At this rate, he'll be the hot favourite by the time they go to post.'

The Duke sighed. 'Lucky dog,' he said enviously. 'Nothing like winning the Derby, Sir Edward. Nothing at all.' He turned to offer his arm to Emma. 'On the turf, at least,' he added with a knowing smile as Emma placed her fingers lightly on his sleeve. 'Shall we stroll down to the rail, ma'am? You will have a better view from there.' He placed his free hand over her gloved fingers and squeezed.

Emma had no choice but to agree—and to resist the urge to pull her hand away.

The crowd fell back respectfully as the royal party moved out. Emma was surprised to see Kit Stratton on foot, struggling to push his way through to them. He must have left his stallion by the carriage. Perhaps he had realised, at last, that such a beast was singularly ill-suited to Epsom on Derby day.

'Sir,' said Sir Edward formally, 'may I present Christopher Stratton, youngest son of the late Sir William Stratton, of Stratton Magna?'

The Duke acknowledged Kit's elegant bow with a nonchalant wave of his hand. 'Knew your father, my boy,' he said.

Kit bowed again. 'Sir, Lord Hardinge has charged me to say that he doubts that any other members of Sir Edward's party will be able to join you here. The carriages are hemmed in by the crowd and the risks of trying to bring the ladies across on foot are now too great, with all the world and his wife trying to get nearer the winning post. Lord Hardinge asked me to present his apologies, sir.'

'Of course, of course,' said the Duke. 'Not to be thought of. Can't take any risks with the ladies.'

Emma thought she detected disappointment in his face but he said nothing more. Recognising that she would now be the only lady present, she resigned herself to being the focus of his attentions until the start of the race, at least. With luck, he would be so intent on watching his horse that he would forget she was there.

Colonel Forster had stationed himself immediately behind the Duke. 'Unusual name, Stratton,' he said musingly, as if to himself, but loud enough to ensure he was heard. 'Had problems with an officer of that name a few years ago, in the Peninsula. Heard he was killed at Waterloo.' He turned to Kit, who was standing a few paces away, alongside Emma's Papa. 'Any relation to Captain Stratton of the 95th?'

Kit coloured slightly and drew himself up extremely straight. He was almost a head taller than the Colonel. Looking down at the older man with obvious distaste, Kit said, 'My second brother, *Major* Hugo Stratton, acquitted himself with great courage on the field at Waterloo, sir, where he was severely wounded. I collect that you yourself were serving in London by then?'

The scathing sarcasm in Kit's voice was unmistakable. His easy charm had completely vanished. Emma was astonished that he should behave in such a manner before royalty—especially the commander-in-chief—and profoundly grateful that Major Stratton himself was escorting Aunt Augusta and was therefore nowhere near the Duke's marquee. There was clearly something very wrong between Colonel Forster and the Stratton brothers.

A sudden commotion by the rail distracted them. A small weatherbeaten man in riding dress was desperately trying to push his way through. At the sight of the Duke's well-known figure, he stopped in his tracks, clearly uncertain as to what he should do.

The Duke of York was well versed in all matters of the turf. He might not have had dealings with Sir Edward Fitzwilliam's trainer, but he knew perfectly well who he was—and that only trouble would have led him to leave his runner at this stage of such a race. 'Chifney, ain't it?' he said, beckoning the man forward. 'Come through, man, come through. You need to speak to Sir Edward, I collect.'

Mr Chifney removed his hat and bowed very low. Emma could see that the back of his neck had gone deep red.

'Your Royal Highness…' Mr Chifney stopped, clearly unsure of how to proceed.

The Duke smiled at Mr Chifney's anxious face. 'Never mind the protocol, man,' he said genially. 'Your errand is obviously urgent, so spit it out. Don't keep Sir Edward on tenterhooks.'

'Thank you, sir,' said Sir Edward quickly. 'What's happened, Chifney? Is something wrong with Golden Star?'

Mr Chifney's reddened features paled. 'Your Royal

Highness…sir…' He cleared his throat. 'Golden Star is dead lame, sir.' The words came out in a rush.

'What?' exclaimed Sir Edward. Then, remembering where he was, he added, 'I beg your pardon, sir, but the horse was in top form when I saw him barely an hour ago. I don't see how he can be lame now.'

The Duke looked concerned. 'I sympathise, Sir Edward. Especially as he was like to be the favourite. Perhaps your man will explain how it happened?'

Mr Chifney looked more than a little guilty. 'Of course, Your Royal Highness,' he said before lapsing into silence once more.

'Well?' said the Duke testily.

Mr Chifney looked stricken. 'He…Golden Star… he was kicked by…by one of the other horses. He's dead lame, Your Highness.'

'You told us that before,' said the Duke. 'I am sure that Sir Edward will want to know how it is that such an accident came about. I dare say that someone has been negligent in the care of him.'

Mr Chifney tried to shake his head.

'And which of the other runners was responsible for this injury?' continued the Duke without a pause. 'Must be a bad-tempered brute, that's all I can say.'

Mr Chifney seemed to shrink in his clothes. 'It was…it was Prince Leopold, Your Royal Highness,' he whispered. 'Mr Lake's horse.'

The Duke reddened angrily. 'You mean *my* horse,' he barked. 'You, of all people, know perfectly well that Lake is my master of horse and has entered Prince Leopold on my behalf. And now you tell me that *my* horse has lamed the favourite. Good God!'

Sir Edward intervened, placing his own bulk between the Duke and the miserable trainer. 'I am sure it must have been an accident, sir. We all know how unpredictable these highly strung thoroughbreds can be, especially on a race day. With your permission, I will go and see Golden Star's injury for myself. With proper care, there will be no lasting damage, I am sure.' Sir Edward bowed in response to the Duke's curt nod and made his way to the rail.

Emma saw that a relieved Mr Chifney was backing his way out of the royal presence, bowing so low that his nose was almost touching his knees. Beads of sweat were dripping from the poor man's forehead. With his vision restricted, Mr Chifney almost collided with Kit Stratton, who had retreated to the edge of the group, as far as possible from the Duke and Colonel Forster. Kit's whole body still seemed to be quivering with rage.

Deliberately drawing the Duke's attention back to herself, she said, in the voice of a bewildered innocent, 'Oh, dear. Poor Golden Star. And I had put almost all my pin money on him, too. May I prevail upon you to advise me, sir, on what I should do now?'

The Duke patted her hand consolingly, though he still looked more than a little irritated. 'Well,' he began, 'the favourite is like to be Nectar now, I fancy. He did win the Two Thousand Guineas, after all. One of these gentlemen would be delighted to place your money for you, I am sure.'

Several of the gentlemen made to offer their services, but Colonel Forster was before them all. He immediately took a pace forward and bowed. Emma thought he leered at her, the moment his face was hidden from his royal master.

Emma produced a girlish giggle. 'Oh, no,' she cried blithely. 'I have had enough of favourites. Since your outsider has made such a point of asserting himself, sir—' she looked up at the Duke through her dark lashes, willing the last of his temper to disappear '—I shall put my money on him. Prince Leopold it shall be!'

Chapter Nine

The Duke was clearly finding it difficult to contain his excitement. His hand was squeezing Emma's fingers so tightly that she almost cried out in pain. 'Sir...my hand...' she began, but it had no effect at all. His attention was all on his horse.

'By God, ma'am,' he said vehemently, 'I do believe he could win.' Under his breath, he was muttering encouragement to his horse, but Emma could not make out any of the words. At least the Duke had enough consideration for the presence of a lady to moderate his language just a trifle, she thought waspishly. The moment he relaxed his grip a fraction, she gently eased her hand away, grateful that he seemed to notice nothing.

But then she, too, was caught up in the excitement of the last few furlongs. Though the favourite, Nectar, had led from the start, two other runners were starting to overhaul him in the home straight—and one of them was the Duke's outsider. For more than a furlong, the three horses battled it out. There was nothing to choose between them.

'Come on, Prince Leopold,' Emma breathed, balling her fingers into fists in her excitement. Beside her, the Duke seemed like to burst out of his tight-fitting uniform. His neck was becoming almost purple.

Half a furlong from home, the third horse started to fall back a little, but Nectar and Prince Leopold were neck and neck.

'Use your whip, man,' muttered the Duke testily.

It was as if the jockey had heard his royal master, for he applied his whip with even more vigour than before. Prince Leopold increased his pace a fraction and started to pull away from his rival.

'Nectar must be finished now,' the Duke grunted through clenched teeth. 'Never should have led from the off.'

Fifty yards to go. Twenty...

A great shout went up from the crowd. Prince Leopold had reached the winning post half a length ahead of the favourite. The royal outsider had won the Derby.

The Duke of York's beaming smile encompassed everyone around him. 'Dashed good show, what?' he said. 'Never would have thought he'd show such a turn of speed.' The Duke's entourage crowded round to congratulate him. Emma's father joined in, too, though his disappointment was evident on his face. Someone called for three cheers, which rang out lustily. In the crush, Emma felt sure that a hand brushed across her breast. She whipped round to find Colonel Forster at her side, with a knowing look in his eye. She shuddered in disgust.

Unfortunately for Emma, the Duke had no intention

of letting her go immediately. He soon had her hand back on his arm. 'Well, ma'am,' he said, patting her fingers even more forcefully than before, 'I congratulate you on your choice of runner. Splendid judgement, if you will allow me to say so. Much better than all these frippery fellows here. You will have made quite a tidy sum from today's business, I'll warrant. Good odds, eh?'

At the Duke's elbow, Colonel Forster nodded. 'Twenty to one, sir. Shall I collect Miss Fitzwilliam's winnings?'

'Do,' replied the Duke. 'I'm sure Miss Fitzwilliam would be grateful. You will find us all with the winner when you return.'

'Thank you, Colonel,' Emma said. 'You are most kind.' For a while, at least, Emma would be spared the sight of him leering at her, or worse. As soon as she had received her winnings, she could try to make her escape. Kit Stratton was surely broad-shouldered enough to clear a path through the crowd for Emma and her father. And Emma would welcome any opportunity to probe the reasons for that outburst against Colonel Forster. She was even beginning to feel some softening in her feelings towards Kit. He had, she decided, shown admirable readiness to defend his brother.

Glancing quickly at the young man, she saw that his fury had abated only a little. His face was now a picture of anger overlaid with chagrin. Emma decided that it would be wise to remove him from the vicinity of Colonel Forster, lest their quarrel flare up once more. The Duke had not noticed the earlier altercation—or so it had seemed. But any repetition could only spell danger for Kit—and perhaps for Hugo, too.

The Duke patted Emma's hand and invited her to accompany him to the winner's enclosure. She responded graciously—what choice did she have?—but her quick mind was already trying to think of acceptable ways for the Fitzwilliam party to make their excuses. Since the Duke had never before had a Derby winner, the celebrations were likely to become very rowdy, very soon. Emma had no wish to be a spectator of drunken revels, even royal ones.

'Well!' the Countess said gaily. 'Whoever would have thought it? Clearly all you betting men underestimated the Duke's colt.'

'Mmm,' her husband agreed ruefully. 'His Royal Highness will be celebrating for a se'ennight, I dare say. I shall take care to keep out of his way. I put my blunt on the favourite—and look where it got me. What about you, Hugo?'

Hugo, now sitting opposite the Hardinges, raised a knowing eyebrow. He had willingly accepted Lady Hardinge's invitation to join them in the barouche, since the Hardinges were considerably more congenial than the company in the other carriage. Mrs Warenne's non-stop chatter was more than a little trying. And the two young ladies in her charge simpered unbearably, even with him. They would certainly be much more at home with the dashing blade who had so readily taken his place. 'I am heartily sorry for Sir Edward. I might have backed his horse, too, but after Golden Star was scratched, I decided the game was

not worth the candle. So…I still have my guineas in
my pocket. Unlike you, Richard, it would seem,' he
added with a twitch of the lips.

'Hugo—'

'Major, I congratulate you,' said the Countess.
'Perhaps I might prevail on you to give my husband
lessons in self-restraint? He—'

Richard grinned and laid a gentle hand on his
wife's arm. 'Look,' he said, pointing, 'Kit has finally
escaped from the royal clutches. And now that the
crowd is thinning out a little, he should be able to
reach us without having the coat ripped from his back
in the process.'

Hugo followed Richard's pointing finger. Kit was
shouldering his way through the good-humoured
crowd, his unusual height ensuring that his progress
was easily followed. Behind him, in the space Kit had
cleared, came Emma and her father. Even at a distance, Hugo could see that Emma was a little flushed.
And her father looked decidedly irritated. Hugo was
not altogether surprised. Sir Edward had every right
to be cross at losing his fancied runner. And, no
doubt, the royal Duke had been up to his usual tricks.
Emma would do much better to keep away from such
a man, however much it might increase her consequence to be seen in his company.

As the little trio made its way slowly towards the
Fitzwilliam barouche, Emma took Kit's arm, forsak-
ing her father's. Moments later, the pair were conversing with real animation. Hugo was mightily surprised. Although Kit was a good fellow at heart,
Emma seemed to have taken against him, from the

moment they met. Hugo had been at a loss to account for it, since Kit usually had all the ladies almost falling at his feet. But then, Emma was not just any lady...

Hugo climbed awkwardly down from his place in the barouche so that Emma and her father would be able to rejoin the Hardinges. Now that the main event of the day was concluded, the whole Fitzwilliam party would wish to return to the house to enjoy a relaxing dinner. If some of the young men had their way, there would be many tales of wagers won and lost over the port tonight, and much commiseration with Sir Edward over his appalling luck. He was a genial host and would indulge them—for a while—but, even in his disappointment, he would not forget his duties to the ladies of the party. The gentlemen would be delivered to the drawing room in reasonable time, and not too much the worse for wear.

Emma was laughing gently when she reached the barouche. She looked, Hugo decided, absolutely radiant. Her earlier flush—had it been anger?—had subsided into most becoming colour and her golden hair was glinting under an elegant confection of silk and feathers. Most of all, her beautiful eyes were sparkling with mischievous good humour. For the first time in his life, Hugo found himself envying his brother. Kit seemed to have added Emma's name to his long list of conquests.

Kit was forced to relinquish Emma's hand when they reached the barouche, for Hugo had ensured he was standing ready to hand her up. Touching her might bring him pain, but he was drawn to her as to no woman he had ever known. He smiled down into her beautiful face. 'Allow me, ma'am,' he said quietly, trying to ensure that he sounded as normal as possible. He might still be haunted by that outrageous kiss and by the feel of her in his arms, but he was determined that she would never know. He prayed that she might have put it from her mind.

Hugo was perversely glad that Emma's gloved hand barely touched his as she stepped up into the barouche. She was as light as a piece of thistledown, he decided, though nothing like as fragile. There was nothing fragile about a lady who could ride her high-couraged horses for hour upon hour without the least sign of fatigue.

Behind him, Kit murmured softly, 'Prettily done indeed. Couldn't have done it better m'self.' Hugo could hear the smile in Kit's voice, but it vanished suddenly as he added, 'A word in your ear, brother...'

Taking her seat once more, Emma covered her burning fingers with her free hand. She could not tell whether she was trying to conceal her shaking or to preserve the warmth that had suddenly pervaded her fingers. Good God, she had barely touched him. If she could have done so without giving offence, she would have sprung up into the barouche without any assistance at all. But he was standing there, clearly waiting for her, and he had looked so...so...

She was at a loss for words. There had been something in his face...but she could not describe it, even to herself—and she certainly did not begin to understand it.

Sir Edward's voice broke into Emma's ravelled thoughts. He was telling Richard about his horse. 'The Duke was bent on making amends for the injury to Golden Star, though it was quite unnecessary. The accident was no one's fault. Prince Leopold is a thoroughly bad-tempered brute, but he won fair and square. I doubt my colt would have had the beating of him, even on his best form.'

Richard nodded absently; something seemed to have distracted him. 'What on earth can Kit have said to Hugo?' Richard nodded in the direction of the two brothers, who had moved out of earshot. 'He's got a face like thunder all of a sudden. He doesn't usually allow young Kit to get under his skin.'

Emma knew that an explanation was due, however awkward it might prove, but she was saved by her father's intervention. 'I doubt that young Kit is the cause, Richard. There's something havey-cavey going on with one of York's hangers-on, a Colonel Forster. Do you know him?' When Richard shook his head, Sir Edward continued, 'Forster made some very disparaging remarks about Major Stratton's time in the Peninsula and Kit naturally took umbrage. Seemed to me that Forster was baiting him deliberately. Don't know if the Duke heard what was said, but if Forster was repeating rumours from Horse Guards, the commander-in-chief is bound to know. Very awkward. Very.' He smiled lovingly at Emma. 'I was glad Emma extricated us so quickly from that little gathering. It could have become quite ugly, especially as the Duke was on the point of breaking out the champagne.'

Richard frowned. At his side, Jamie too wore a worried look. Emma reached out a hand to her. 'Pray, do not be concerned, Jamie. It seemed to me that Colonel Forster was simply trying to make mischief. And I'm certain that His Royal Highness ignored what was said.' Emma was trying to sound more optimistic than she felt. She had failed to glean any information from Kit after they left the royal party. He had been charming, and entertaining…but he would not be drawn on anything to do with his brother.

Jamie gave voice to Emma's thoughts. 'There is something of a mystery here,' she said after a moment, 'but I, for one, refuse to believe anything against Major Stratton. From what I learned in Brussels, he acquitted himself most honourably on the field at Waterloo. And I know him to be a very fine man. Colonel Forster sounds to be exactly the kind of man whom I would not wish to know.'

At dinner a few hours later, Emma was surprised to find that Aunt Augusta had seated her between Kit Stratton and the Honourable James Frobisher, a singularly dull young gentleman who had nothing but aristocratic lineage to recommend him. Emma, a practised hostess, was equally polite and friendly to them both. Watching her while she listened to Mr Frobisher's self-important discourse, no one would have known that she was longing for the moment when she could, with propriety, turn back to Kit. He, at least, was prepared to converse about something other than himself, his prowess on the hunting field, and his family's numberless acres.

Kit had certainly set out to be entertaining. He had also decided, Emma was sure, that the conversation would be steered well away from any discussion of his enigmatic older brother. Faced with Kit's resolution, Emma yielded with good grace, allowing the light-hearted conversation to range as widely as he wished. Since Hugo was seated at the far end of the table, and on the same side, Emma could not judge whether the other guests were succeeding in drawing him out. But she would be able to find that out from her father—later.

'And so we had no choice but to pretend that the handkerchief belonged to his mother,' said Kit, concluding a slightly racy but very amusing anecdote.

Emma laughed, as did all those within earshot. Kit was certainly an entertaining raconteur. She could not help but notice the envious glances cast her way by several of the young ladies present. For appearances' sake, Aunt Augusta had had to invite a number of débutantes to the house-party, as well as potential suitors. It was rather too obvious for Emma's peace of mind that Aunt Augusta's choice had fallen on young ladies who would be cast into the shade by her niece. Two of them were pretty enough, but too silly for words. The other two were really rather plain. And none of them—of course—was as great an heiress as Emma. No wonder they were looking daggers at her. Not only had they been excluded from an invitation to wait on a royal Duke, but the handsomest gentleman in the room was now focusing all his attention on Emma.

Miss Mayhew, who was not only plain but also ill-educated, in Emma's opinion, was making sheep's eyes across the table at Kit Stratton. Emma was glad to see that Kit was pretending not to notice, at least for the moment. His company manners were exactly as they should be. When the party was eventually reunited in the drawing room, however, Miss Mayhew was bound to resume her gauche assault. Although Kit would surely continue to bear it with good grace, it would be most embarrassing for the other guests. Emma resolved to have a word with her aunt. Although Miss Mayhew's mother had insisted on accompanying her daughter to the house-party, she had done nothing at all to restrain her daughter's unbecoming behaviour. It must fall to the senior hostess to drop a word in the girl's ear.

When Mrs Warenne rose to signal the ladies' departure, Mr Frobisher almost knocked over his own chair in his rush to help Emma from hers. His fingers brushed against her bare shoulder—intentionally, Emma was sure. She felt nothing. Mr Frobisher was neither attractive nor repellent. He simply left her totally unmoved…whereas the slightest touch of Hugo Stratton's fingers made her skin prickle and heat, even through several layers of clothing. She tried to remember whether it had been so before that incredible kiss. For the life of her, she could not say. All her encounters with the Major seemed to have merged, somehow; she was no longer sure what she had felt when they first met again. Perhaps that was because they had not touched until that fateful day in Jamie's conservatory? No…that could not be right. They must have shaken hands a score of times. It was a conundrum, to be sure, and Emma knew that it would require cool detachment to puzzle it out.

But, whenever Major Hugo Stratton was concerned, Emma's cool detachment seemed to fly out of the window.

Chapter Ten

'Perhaps you would favour us with some music, Miss Mayhew?' Emma was resolved to be kind to the girl, especially as she was likely to receive a sharp dressing-down from Aunt Augusta, some time later in the evening. 'You have such a sweet singing voice, you know. Some of the gentlemen have remarked upon it, most particularly.' Emma's generous compliment had the advantage of being true.

Miss Mayhew simpered and blushed a little, before making her way to the instrument. She must know that she would appear at her best if she was in the middle of a song when the gentlemen returned to the drawing room. And if she were in any doubt, one look at her smiling, nodding mother, comfortably ensconced on the sofa alongside the Dowager Countess, would have settled the matter.

Miss Mayhew had barely started her song when the door opened to admit the gentlemen. Emma was at first surprised to see that Major Stratton arrived along with the others, but a moment's reflection explained matters. This house, unlike her father's or Richard's, had all its public rooms on the ground floor, and only bedrooms on the floor above. It might have been expressly designed to accommodate a man who had difficulty climbing stairs. It was even possible to reach the garden directly from the drawing room, via a stone terrace that ran the length of the room. Emma had not yet taken time to explore the gardens, but Jamie had assured her that they were splendid, laid out in the old style with high hedges and secret nooks and crannies, all brimful of beautiful plants.

Emma looked longingly at the French windows. The room was already uncomfortably hot—and the arrival of eight gentlemen would certainly make it even hotter. A few moments in the cool evening air would be delightful…but, as joint hostess, she must not be seduced away from her duties to her guests.

Emma's father was looking quite pleased with himself. Good food and wine had helped him forget his disappointment. Taking his sister to one side, so that only Emma and Jamie could hear, he whispered, 'Here they all are, m'dear. Told you I wouldn't let them linger in the dining room. Now, what about a few tables for cards?'

Aunt Augusta gave him a withering look. 'There's no point in bringing them back early if you're going to allow them to be tied to card tables for the rest of the evening. Really, Edward, you should know better.' Her voice had risen enough to start attracting attention, but she simply turned her back on the other guests and said, in a voice that was almost a whisper, 'The young men must *circulate*, Edward, else what is the point of bringing them here in the first place?'

Emma looked at Jamie and then looked quickly away. It would not do for either of them to laugh. Emma forced herself to give all her attention to Miss Mayhew's performance on the pianoforte.

The song ended. Under cover of the polite applause, Jamie said quietly to Emma's aunt, 'I can quite understand that Sir Edward would welcome a rubber of whist, ma'am. Richard's mama is a fine player, you know. Perhaps Richard and I might make up the four?'

Aunt Augusta was surprised. 'Well, if you are sure, ma'am,' she said, hesitating a little. 'I suppose there is something to be said for indulging my brother's desire for cards—provided the table is set up in some other room. It would not do to distract the young men. It's difficult enough as it is…' She bustled off to collect the Dowager.

Emma's papa was beaming at Jamie. 'By Jove, ma'am, you think of everything.' Jamie merely smiled and led the way out to the library where the little card party would not be disturbed.

Aunt Augusta brought up the rear, fussing as usual. Emma was forcibly reminded of a sheepdog snapping at the heels of its flock. Aunt Augusta was quite determined that all the young male guests should have an opportunity of setting out their stalls before her niece, though Emma was very sure that none of them would suit. She looked around the room. One of the gentlemen would be at her side in just a moment, of that she was quite certain. Please, Lord, let it not be that boring—

'Mr Frobisher.' Emma smiled gamely at her erstwhile dinner partner who had come to station himself between her and the other guests. There was no escape.

'Delightful music, ma'am,' said Mr Frobisher. 'I hope you will favour us with a song or two in the course of the evening.'

Emma nodded politely. If Mr Frobisher was determined to monopolise her, the evening was set to become duller by the minute.

Hugo retreated as far as possible from the instrument the moment Miss Mayhew rose from it. None of the other three débutantes had any musical talent at all, and it pained him to be forced to listen to them. There was a darkish corner at the far end of the long room, by the French windows. From there, he would be able to watch all the younger men circling round Emma like vultures. And, if watching became too much of an ordeal, he would slip out on to the terrace and into the blessed solitude of the garden.

Hugo saw that Kit was being his usual charming self. While the males were buzzing round Emma, the females were using every trick in the book to attract Kit's attention. All except Emma. She was concentrating her full attention on the appalling Frobisher. He had been fawning over the poor girl all night, and now—

Hugo's senses were suddenly on the alert. Frobisher, presumably unable to hold his wine, was starting to paw Emma in a most unseemly fashion.

Before Hugo could get his stiff limbs into motion, his younger brother had taken charge. 'I think you've

had your share of our hostess's company, Frobisher,'
he said lightly. 'Time to give the other fellows a
chance, eh?' He offered his arm. 'Tempt you to a turn
about the room, Miss Fitzwilliam? It is a little hot—
especially in this stuffy corner.'

Hugo found himself smiling a little ruefully. Kit
was really very, very good. Frobisher was looking
stunned. Had he understood the import of Kit's
words? Probably not—especially if his brain was fud-
dled with wine.

Emma and Kit made an exceptionally handsome
couple promenading round the huge drawing room.
And all Emma's earlier hostility to Kit seemed to
have disappeared. It was more than mere gratitude for
having saved her from Frobisher, Hugo concluded.
The pair were laughing together now as if they had
been fast friends for years...perhaps more than
friends. Trust Kit to succeed with the most desirable
woman in the room. He certainly seemed much taken
with Emma. It would not be merely her beauty, for
Kit had had more than his fair share of Society beauties in his short career on the town. No, Emma was
a match for Kit in all sorts of ways. Above all, she
equalled Kit in independence of spirit. She cast all the
other ladies into the shade.

When all the guests had performed, the lot fell to
Emma. Hugo fancied she was trying to resist her
aunt's persuasions, but her protest could not last long.
Mrs Warenne was like the hot wind blowing up from
Africa—a wise soldier soon learned that there was no
alternative but to let it have its way.

Leaning back against the wall in his obscure corner, Hugo let Emma's music fill his mind. It was the first time he had ever heard her sing—and it was beautiful. Her singing voice was lower than he had expected, and full of honeyed warmth. She sang her simple Italian ballad with real feeling, almost caressing each word, as if she herself were that abandoned Italian girl mourning the loss of her love.

The enthusiastic applause was interrupted by the arrival of the tea tray. There would be no encore from Emma, who immediately set herself to pouring refreshments for her guests. Frobisher was among the first to present himself to her and seemed inclined to linger at her side. Watching, Hugo found his hands balling into fists.

'Will you inform the party in the library that tea is being served, please, Godfrey?' Emma said. As usual, her first concern was the comfort of her guests.

'The table has already broken up, Miss Emma,' replied the butler. 'The Countess and the Dowager Countess send their apologies. They wished to retire without intruding on the other guests. Lord Hardinge and Sir Edward have repaired to the billiard room.'

Hugo could see that Emma was disappointed at being deserted by her father. He was not therefore surprised to hear her encouraging Frobisher to join the billiard party. She must be heartily sick of the man after this evening's unsavoury performance. Unfortunately for Emma, Frobisher did not seem inclined to take the hint.

Kit intervened once again. Taking Frobisher firmly by the arm, he said, 'Splendid idea, ma'am. Know Frobisher is the very devil with the cue.' He took

Frobisher's cup and handed it to Emma, who was looking warmly up at Kit. 'You're not afraid of a challenge from me, are you, Frobisher?' Kit continued. The sarcasm in his voice was unmistakable.

Hugo almost felt sorry for Frobisher. The man had no chance at all against Kit's stronger will. With a few carefully chosen words, Kit had taken charge and propelled Frobisher out of the room. Emma would, undoubtedly, be very grateful. Not that it showed for even a second though, for no sooner had the door closed behind the pair than Emma was busying herself in organising further entertainment for her guests. In a moment, she would notice that Hugo was missing from the main party, and then...

Hugo slid his hand behind the curtain to undo the window latch so that he could slip out into the garden. He did not want Emma's solicitude. She would not look up at him as she had looked at his magnificent brother. For tonight, at least, he would rather she did not look at him at all.

Emma took a deep breath and stepped out on to the terrace, allowing the heavy drapes to fall back into place behind her. She needed just a few moments of solitude and cool air to clear her head, and then she would return to her guests. No one would notice her departure, surely? The party in the drawing room was now totally involved in a childish game of lottery tickets, the young ladies squealing with pleasure every time they won. Even Mrs Mayhew had been persuaded to play, though in rather more restrained fashion. And the billiard room group was bound to be deeply absorbed in their game. She supposed Major Stratton must have gone to join them, too. One moment he was leaning nonchalantly against the far wall, clearly unmoved by Emma's singing, the next he had disappeared. No doubt he preferred the excitement of billiards to the tame entertainments on offer in the drawing room.

His indifference hurt. Emma had to admit that to herself. Knowing he was listening, she had poured all her unvoiced longings into that song, immersing herself in the character of the heartbroken peasant girl. She felt those longings still, as if some part of that character were also her own. Strange, for she had never loved and lost. She had never even loved.

The grey stone balustrading was pleasantly cool under Emma's hands. It felt calming, somehow. Emma took a deep breath of the scented night air. She tried to distinguish the various perfumes, but could not. Jamie, with her vast knowledge of plants, would have known them at once, but she had retired to bed. If Emma wanted to find the source of the elusive fragrances assailing her senses, she would have to go into the garden and seek them out. Why not? It would take but a few moments. The heady perfumes were incredibly seductive, making her whole body feel as if she were relaxing into a warm, soothing bath, yet heightening all her senses at the same time. A most extraordinary combination.

Intrigued, Emma wandered from avenue to avenue, more than half-dreaming now. The scents were becoming stronger at every step, almost intoxicating. At the corner of a secret garden, she paused, wondering.

Yes, here! She closed her eyes and executed a lazy pirouette, relishing the feel of fine silken petticoats as her skirts billowed and then settled back against her limbs. It was as if velvet gloves had stroked her bare skin. Velvet gloves worn on gentle hands…

Emma paused to inhale yet more of the voluptuous perfume in the tiny garden. This strange place was meant to be seen by moonlight. Its white trumpet flowers shimmered mysteriously on long stems that were almost invisible. In the centre, a tall arch was dripping with pale roses. At the far end of the path, framed by the arch, was a marble statue of some ancient pagan goddess, beautiful and commanding. The venerable yew hedge, dark and brooding, stood sentry against any intrusion into her hidden grotto. Was this the secret garden of the fairy tales, appearing only once in a lifetime and then only to those in love?

For she *was* in love…in love with Hugo Stratton. It was as if she had always known it.

She picked a stem of the magical white flowers, inhaling deeply of their ravishing scent. For an instant, she felt as if she were hovering somewhere above the ground, looking down at her own body meandering among the flowers. And then she floated softly back to earth.

She reached up to pull down a branch of roses, awed by their pristine perfection. Were they white—or perhaps pale pink? It was of no moment. In the silvery moonlight, they were unbelievably beautiful. She stroked a soft petal, marvelling at its velvet bloom, like a baby's soft cheek.

If Hugo were here—and if he loved her in return—

he would pluck these roses and offer them to her as a token. He would tell her that the roses would fade and die, but that his love would last for ever. He would take her in his arms and...

The moon went behind a cloud. Emma sank down on to the old stone seat and closed her eyes. She could still see the magic garden in her mind. She knew she was dreaming, but she was unable to break the powerful spell that seemed to have wound itself around her. It was so enticing... She would let it carry her away...for just a little while. She put her hand on the cool stone, stroking languidly, wondering what it would be like to stroke a man's taut body, to feel his skin under her fingers—

A strong hand covered hers. She opened wide, unseeing eyes. In barely a heartbeat, she was pulled gently to her feet and into powerful arms. She knew that Hugo had answered her unspoken summons and come to claim her. And now he was going to kiss her, to reawaken those wonderful feelings that had been haunting her, it seemed, for ever.

Shafts of pain were stabbing through Hugo's body, but he could not close his eyes against the sight. The woman he loved was melting into the arms of his rake of a brother! By God, Kit had excelled himself this time! One day the pair were almost at outs, the next they were kissing like some latter-day Romeo and Juliet. Well, Kit Stratton was no Romeo, faithful unto death. Don Juan, more like. She would find that out soon enough. And it would be a fitting reward.

Hugo allowed his fury to overpower him, obscuring

the pain. He looked round, vainly, for an escape route
from his dark corner. There was only one entrance to
this tiny garden. He would be seen. He closed his eyes
deliberately then, dwelling on the picture they made,
trying to fuel his anger yet more. Not only had she
come to an assignation with his brother, she had even
arranged matters so that he was forced to provide an
audience for her wanton conduct. Damn her! She
was—

The stillness was rent by a woman's scream.

'Mr Stratton! Miss Fitzwilliam!' The high-pitched
outrage came from a slight figure in white muslin who
stood, transfixed, between the dark hedges flanking
the entrance to the secret garden. 'Oh, how could
you?' The figure turned and fled in the direction of
the house.

Kit and Emma had sprung apart at the sound, but
there would now be no hiding their guilt at being so
discovered. For a second, Hugo felt intense pleasure
at the thought of their fate, especially when he detected a hint of self-satisfaction on his brother's in-
sufferably handsome face. They would be well
served, the pair of them.

But the look on Emma's face banished all trace of
malice from his mind.

She was stricken. She was looking at Kit Stratton
as if she had never laid eyes on him before.

She took several steps back from him, like someone retreating from a horrifying apparition. Her hands
had gone to her flaming cheeks. Her eyes were wide,
fearful, and very dark in the strange half-light.

'Mr Stratton!' Her voice was a low, intense whisper, throbbing with suppressed emotion. 'Oh, how could you?' she said, echoing that earlier heartfelt cry. 'I thought…I thought I was… Oh, dear God, what made you follow me here?' She turned from him to lean her forehead against the rose arch. Her shoulders were shaking.

Kit made to comfort her but she thrust him away. 'Stay away from me,' she hissed, turning back to face him like a spitting snake. 'How dare you touch me? Would you do me even more harm? You have ruined me. Let that be enough for you.'

Kit stood motionless, undecided. Guilt was beginning to show on his features now—at last—but overlaid with a degree of confusion. 'Miss Fitzwilliam, I—'

Emma cut him short. 'There is nothing you can say to me now. Please leave.' As he still hesitated, she drew herself up to her full height, in the proud posture of the garden's marble patroness, and cried, 'For God's sake, go!'

Kit swallowed hard, bowed with considerably less than his usual elegance, and quit the field, totally vanquished.

Emma stood motionless until his figure was completely hidden from view. Then she crumpled, sobbing, on to the cold stone bench.

Chapter Eleven

It was suddenly very cold. Emma wrapped her arms around her bare shoulders, trying to stop the shivering that had taken control of her body. Tears were still running down her cheeks, though much more slowly now. She made no attempt to brush them away. She berated herself with the thought that, if someone should come to find her, she would present the proper picture of abject misery, entirely as expected for a lady whose reputation had been ruined.

How had it happened? And with Kit Stratton, of all people?

Emma did not know. It was something to do with the silence of the moonlit night, the hypnotic scent of the flowers in the magic garden…and her own folly in allowing herself to dream of Hugo Stratton. The arms that had enfolded her had been Hugo's. She had looked up into Hugo's grey eyes, warm with love. And Hugo had kissed her…

But it had not been Hugo—none of it. Surrounded by childish fantasies of her own weaving, she had persuaded herself that she was melting into Hugo's arms, but no amount of dreaming could turn Kit's kiss into Hugo's. Kit's was a practised, seductive kiss. But it was empty, none the less. And then that benighted child had appeared among the yews, screeching like a demented harpy, before Emma had had time to tear herself away from the wrong brother. She could never face either of them again.

'Miss Fitzwilliam. Emma. May I do something for you? Some water, perhaps?'

Hugo Stratton was standing before her, like some dread apparition come to haunt her. Where had he appeared from? Surely no one had come through the gap in the hedge? Dear God! He must have been there all the time. He must have seen—

Emma's tears stopped abruptly, overtaken by a surge of scorching anger that threatened to deprive her of speech. Blazing with fury, she stared up at her tormentor. How dared he look pityingly on her plight, when he was responsible for it? For all of it. Not only had he beguiled her heart, he had sat by, savouring her downfall, as she took the fateful step that would ruin her life. Hugo Stratton was utterly hateful.

'How dare you address me, sir, when you have behaved in such a dishonourable manner? You are not worthy of the rank you bear. And as for your brother...' Emma shook her head in disgust. She could find no words terrible enough to describe Kit Stratton. 'You will have the goodness to leave this place, Major Stratton.' With those cold words, bitterly spoken, Emma turned her back on Hugo Stratton and every vestige of love she had ever felt for him.

* * *

'Emma! Emma, where are you?'

It was Aunt Augusta's voice. Emma rose a little shakily to her feet and swallowed hard. She had hoped for more time. At least her tears had long since dried. No one—not even Aunt Augusta—should see how weak she had been.

'Emma, child, you are frozen.' Aunt Augusta tenderly placed a warm shawl round Emma's shoulders and then pulled her niece into a quick hug. She had never done such a thing before.

'That woman...' she began, with venom, 'that woman has absolutely no breeding. And as for her daughter...'

Emma put her hand on her aunt's arm. 'Tell me what happened, dear Aunt. I must know what they are saying of me before I return to the house.'

'Yes, of course. Yes, indeed.' Aunt Augusta looked flustered, and more than a little embarrassed. It took her some time to marshal her words. 'Miss Mayhew came running back into the drawing room and promptly had a fit of the vapours. As far as anyone could make out, she had come upon you and Mr Stratton alone in the garden, and had seen that he was behaving in a...a libertine fashion—and that you were doing nothing to deter him. Oh, I did my best to throw cold water on her story. After all, she is barely out of the schoolroom. How could she know what she saw? And, in any case, what was she doing alone in the garden at that time of night?

'Unfortunately, everyone in the room had already put the worst possible complexion on her hysterical outburst before I could say a word. If only the Dowager had been there...' Aunt Augusta sighed. 'There was only myself—and Mrs Mayhew, who immediately took it upon herself to pronounce you—' She stopped abruptly.

Even in the half-light in the garden, Emma could see that her aunt was mortified by this part of her tale. 'What did she say of me, Aunt?' she said quietly.

'Her words do not matter. And I would not repeat them. But... My dear, she took great delight in saying that you were ruined. And that her daughter, and the other three young ladies, would leave first thing in the morning, lest they be corrupted by further contact with the Fitzwilliam household.'

It was even worse than Emma had feared. Within twenty-four hours, the story would be repeated all over London. No member of Society would even acknowledge her in future. She was indeed ruined. And it could all be laid at Hugo Stratton's door. Hateful, hateful man.

Only one thing could make matters worse. 'Is Papa very angry?' Emma said in a small voice.

'Yes. I doubt even you can sway him this time, Emma. It matters not what you did—only what the world will say of you. Your father feels it very much. He is in the library.' Aunt Augusta took a deep breath. 'And Mr Stratton is with him there.'

'Mr Stratton? Mr Kit Stratton?' At her aunt's nod, Emma turned quickly away in an attempt to conceal the horror that must be written on her face. If Kit had been summoned to the library, it could mean only that her father was demanding he marry her to save her reputation. Kit would never agree, surely? Would he not laugh it off as just another of his many indiscretions? *His* reputation would not really be damaged by the tale. He would probably continue to be received by the *ton* as if nothing had happened.

But what if he did agree? What if her father presented Kit Stratton to her as a future husband? What would she do? She did not love him. She could not begin to trust him. He would be unfaithful, she was certain. He would take her dowry to fund his gambling. And, once forced into an unwelcome marriage, there was not the slightest reason why he should show her even a modicum of kindness.

Such a future would be bleak indeed. But could she endure the alternative?

Hugo was standing by his bedroom window, fully dressed and staring out at the night sky, when Kit finally made his appearance.

Hugo cast a quick look round at his loose fish of a brother and then went back to gazing out at the stars. Kit's reflection was all too clear—he looked like a man who had had a very bad night at the gaming tables, or with the bottle, or both.

Kit threw himself down into a chair by the empty grate and sank his chin on to his chest. After several moments, he broke the heavy silence. 'Nothing to say to me, then, brother?'

Hugo shook his head. 'I am sure Sir Edward has said all that needs to be said.' He had his temper well in hand, he was almost sure, but it would be best if he said as little as possible. Emma had been a fool—and Kit even more so. Kit must never find out what

Hugo had seen—or how he felt about Emma Fitz-william. That knowledge could only make matters even worse.

Kit jumped to his feet again and started to pace. 'You are right there, brother,' he said angrily. 'Oh, how very right. Sir Edward laid all my iniquities be-fore me in the starkest possible terms. How I had taken advantage of an innocent young lady when I was a guest in her father's house. How I had ruined her before the world. And precisely what he thought of my morals.' He laughed harshly. 'I will not bother you with a recital of that, Hugo. Your imagination can furnish all the necessary details, I am sure. How-ever—' He laughed again.

Hugo shuddered. The devil himself might be in his brother at that moment. He sounded half-mad.

'However,' Kit continued with heavy sarcasm, 'the abject state of my morals does not prevent my being a fit husband for his only daughter—and the sooner the better. The announcement of our impending nup-tials will be sent to the *Gazette* in the morning. I was only surprised that he didn't roust out the stables to send a messenger on the spot.'

Hugo still said nothing. He could not. He half-turned from the window, but could not bring himself to look his brother in the face. Kit was going to marry Emma! And Kit did not love her in the least. He would make her the worst possible husband. Having been forced into marriage, he could well come to hate his wife, and blame her for what had happened to him. The best she could hope for would be indiffer-ence…but Hugo did not expect that of Kit. Not at twenty-two, when he had thought he had years of single self-indulgence in front of him. No, Emma's marriage to Kit could well become a life-long penance.

Kit stopped pacing and stared into the grate for a while. Keeping his back to Hugo, he said, 'You're very quiet, brother. I'm surprised you don't want to know how it came to this pass.'

'Mmm?' Hugo hoped he sounded encouraging. It was the best he could do.

Still without turning round, Kit said in a flat, rather puzzled voice, 'I had gone out into the garden for a smoke. Billiards was downright boring in any case, with Frobisher prosing on all the time. Saw Miss Fitz-william—Emma now, I suppose—going into one of the gardens. She... You won't have noticed, Hugo, but this place is full of strange little gardens surrounded by high hedges. Absolutely perfect for a spot of love-making.' Kit gave a snort of anger...or perhaps it was disgust. Hugo could not be sure. He forced himself to remain silent.

'Shouldn't have followed her, I know that now, but I was intrigued. Couldn't believe such a pattern-card of respectability would dream of making an assignation with one of the guests. But she must have done—'

Hugo clenched his jaw to stop the cry of 'liar' that rose to his lips. He had seen her with his own eyes. She had been revelling in the beauty of the garden, nothing more. She would never have consented to the kind of clandestine meeting that Kit had in mind.

'She must have done,' Kit said again. 'She was sitting alone in that garden, I admit, but her face was such a picture of desire… God knows she's beautiful, but when her face is lit up with passion, she's…she's the most perfect woman I've ever seen.' There was something approaching awe in his voice. 'Whoever she was waiting for, he's a lucky man to inspire such devotion.'

Kit swung round suddenly to face the window. Hugo was grateful that his own face was still in shadow. Kit's face, dimly reflected in the window pane, was a picture of torment, but Hugo was pretty sure that his own would be worse. The vision of Emma in the grip of passion…

Kit laughed, a hollow, hate-filled laugh. 'I should say, rather, that he is *not* a lucky man. For he will not have her now, whoever he is. And if I ever find him out, I'll kill him with my bare hands. *He* is the cause of all this! She thought *I* was her lover…and the moment I touched her, she pretty well threw herself into my arms!'

That was nothing like the scene Hugo had witnessed. He had seen something a great deal more like seduction on Kit's part. Emma had not—

Hugo took a deep breath and tried to bring his rational mind into play. He must try to see things from Kit's point of view, or they would probably come to blows. On the other hand…

He looked towards his brother. 'Really?' he said.

Kit had the grace to look a little shamefaced. 'Well…perhaps not exactly. The truth is, I don't know what happened. One moment I was standing over her, and the next she was in my arms and I was kissing her. I couldn't help it, Hugo.' He sounded positively bewildered now. 'I didn't intend it to happen. On my oath, I didn't.

'And then that poisonous little Mayhew toad appeared, screeching like the devil himself had her by the tail. Must have seen me go into the garden and followed me.' At Hugo's start of surprise, he said venomously, 'She's been trailing after me like a puppy ever since we arrived. God, I wish I'd kicked her away when I had the chance, but you and John had me too well trained. "Young ladies just out of the schoolroom have to be treated gently," you said. "They may appear gauche and stupid, but if they are treated with kindness, they will learn," you said.'

'Kit—'

'I'm sorry, Hugo. That was unfair.' He ran his hands through his hair which was already considerably dishevelled. 'I've made my own bed, and I must lie on it. God, what a coil! I never dreamed I'd be leg-shackled like this!'

Hugo found that he was beginning to feel sorry for Kit, in spite of what he had done to Emma. Brotherly feeling must have something to do with it, but still…very strange.

'If only she'd refuse me,' Kit said despairingly, 'but she won't. Her father will see to that. He's even insisting on a special licence. God, what a coil!'

'You said that before,' said Hugo, not quite managing to conceal his still-simmering anger. 'I take it the announcement will be made in the morning?'

'Yes,' said Kit, 'before the Mayhew party leaves. Sir Edward intends to warn Mrs Mayhew against spreading malicious rumours…since his daughter's engagement is on the point of being announced. He'll take satisfaction in telling her that, I'm sure.'

'True,' said Hugo quietly, 'but he can derive precious little satisfaction from any other aspect of this affair.'

'I have already apologised to him,' Kit replied with dignity, 'and I will apologise to Emma, too, as soon as I have the chance. I will do my best to make her a good husband, I promise you that.'

'I think you should make that promise to Emma, rather than to me. Have you spoken to her?'

'No, not yet. I will, though…soon. Tomorrow, I suppose. Oh, if only Sir Edward were not intent on having us riveted so quickly. We could be engaged, all right and tight, and then, in a few months, when all the gossip had been forgotten, Emma could announce that she had decided we would not suit. And then we should both be free.'

Kit's words took Hugo by surprise for a moment. Kit was right, of course. In his aimless ramblings, he had lit on the only solution to save Emma from a disastrous marriage. But someone would need to persuade Sir Edward…and Emma herself.

Hugo took a step into the middle of the room and looked squarely at his brother. 'If you wish it, Kit, I will put your suggestion to Sir Edward…now.'

'Hugo—' A glimmer of hope flared and then faded from Kit's eyes. 'No, it would never work. The old man is too furious to listen to you or anyone else. He's made up his mind to a wedding next week.'

Hugo took a deep breath. 'If Sir Edward is as determined as you say, then only one person can move him. I will put your plan to Emma herself.'

Chapter Twelve

Emma reached up impatiently to rip back the bed-curtain and let in the early morning light. She had had very little sleep, and she knew she must look hagged. The new day had changed nothing. She was still betrothed to Kit Stratton! She lay back on her pillows and stared up at the bed-canopy. God, what a coil!

She tried not to remember that hideous interview with Papa, though she knew it would be engraven on her memory until the day she died. She had never seen him so fearfully angry, or so distant. He seemed to be immune to all thought of what his decisions were doing to his only daughter. It was almost as if he had ceased to love her. Not only was she to marry Kit Stratton, but Papa was adamant that the marriage would take place within the week. Emma had not been permitted to protest. In that totally one-sided interview, she had not even been permitted to speak. Papa had become a man she no longer knew, a man who could wrap her up like an unwanted parcel and despatch her without further thought.

Emma felt bereft and hollow inside. For all her life,

the bond with her papa had been so close, so loving—but one instant of madness had ripped it all away. An inner voice whispered that Papa had never stopped loving her, never would stop loving her, that, in his shock and disappointment at his daughter's wanton behaviour, he had allowed his justifiable fury to chase away every softer emotion. Perhaps, if she went to him today, he might relent a little, postpone the wedding? But then, what would be the point? If she was to be forcibly married off to Kit Stratton, 'twere well it were done quickly. It would be better for her to have less time to brood over the prospect of being a wife—wife to an irredeemable rake.

Emma turned her thoughts to the ordeal she was about to face. For all that Mrs Mayhew had announced her intention of leaving first thing in the morning, Emma knew that she would be in the house until ten o'clock at least, for Mrs Mayhew, besides being a poisonous gossip, was also a very late riser. She would take breakfast in her room, Emma supposed, but she would then muster her little coterie of débutantes and ensure she departed in style.

Emma knew that she must not hide away. That would only give the dreadful woman even more food for gossip. No, Emma must appear and act the part of the gracious hostess saying farewell to her honoured guests. Her papa would be bound to announce her engagement at the first opportunity and he would ensure that Mrs Mayhew was left in no doubt about the match. The woman might gossip as much as she liked—afterwards. The festering boil would have been lanced. Emma had a sudden picture of herself standing in the hallway to bid farewell to the guests and receiving their hypocritical congratulations without betraying, by so much as the flicker of an eyelid, the turbulent emotions underneath. She could do it. She must.

She pulled the bell. She must not remain in bed any longer. Now would be an excellent opportunity to warn the Dowager, and Jamie too, of what had happened. She threw a wrapper over her lawn nightdress and made for the door, but hesitated when her hand touched the cool brass handle. What was she going to say to the Dowager? She would find out the bones of the affair soon enough. The servants' quarters must be fairly buzzing with it by now.

Emma shook her head despairingly. No, she must not see either the Dowager or Jamie before the Mayhew party left. She was braced for her father's anger and the disdain of the other guests. She was determined that she would maintain her dignity in front of them. But the Dowager, who had known her from a child, was like to enfold her like a mother with a tumbled child, to soothe, and pet, and surround with sympathetic love. If that happened, all Emma's hardwon armour would crack and crumble. And with Jamie, it might be even worse. Emma must not see either of them.

Emma had barely given a thought to the two gentlemen at the heart of her troubles. Kit, by all accounts, had behaved most honourably in his interview with Papa. He had not sought to excuse his behaviour or to avoid its consequences—or so Papa had said. And Hugo? Hugo must know that he was about to become her brother-in-law. It was almost amusing, given that he had spent so much effort of late in trying to avoid her. That would become much more difficult when she was his sister. But he must detest her even more now, after the insults she had heaped upon him in the garden. She had impugned his honour. Was it only a few hours ago? It felt like years. It felt like part of her distant past, a past that was enshrouded in misty dreams and fading fast.

Hugo must certainly hate her. He would meet her with cold politeness and bitter feelings in his heart. There was nothing she could say to him. Apology was quite impossible, since she must avoid all future mention of that encounter in the garden. Her wicked words would lie between them like a great black chasm. It was better so, she decided hopelessly. It would give him reason to avoid his brother's company in the future. The less they were thrown together, the easier it would be for her to suppress her feelings. She would become the perfect picture of a perfect wife, no matter how Kit behaved towards her and no matter how much she might weep inside. She had learned, once, to become the perfect débutante and now, when that façade had slipped so tragically, she must learn another role—this time, for life.

Emma's abigail came in to deliver her mistress's morning chocolate. She took one look at Emma's face and clamped her thin lips together. Normally, Sawyer was full of merry gossip about the doings of the household but, today, she clearly knew better.

Sitting on the edge of the bed, Emma sipped her chocolate pensively. The maid was laying out a dark

blue cambric gown. 'No, Sawyer,' said Emma, 'not
the dark blue. It is much too sombre for such a joyous
occasion. Let it be something bright and sunny—the
jonquil.' Sawyer gave her a very strange sideways
look but obediently fetched the jonquil muslin gown
and held it up to her mistress. 'Yes, that will do very
well,' Emma said. 'Now I must hurry. I know that
Mrs Mayhew and her party are to leave early and it
would be most remiss in a hostess to fail to bid them
farewell. Make haste with my hair, Sawyer.'

Sawyer did as she was bid, but in unaccustomed
silence until she was putting the last few pins into
Emma's golden curls. 'Miss Emma—' Sawyer
stopped. She looked uncomfortable. 'Miss Emma...
Major Stratton asked me to give you a message. He
begs for the favour of an urgent interview with you.
He said he would be waiting in the library.'

'*Major* Stratton?' said Emma, horrified. 'Surely
you mean *Mr* Stratton?'

'No, Miss Emma, no. 'Twas the Major himself. Mr
Stratton is still abed—at least, his valet has not been
summoned. The Major, now, was up and about uncommon early. He called for his shaving water almost
before the range was lit. Had the kitchen staff in quite
a panic. And then, he went out walking in the
grounds. Must have been out there for hours. He has
only just come in.'

'I see.' For a second, Emma did not know what to
say. She would have accepted a summons from Kit
who, in a few days, would be her lawful husband and
entitled to command her obedience.

But Hugo? What could Hugo want at this hour?

'An urgent word', he had said. Perhaps he planned to berate her for entrapping his brother and insulting himself? Well, let him try. Let him try. Emma was no shrinking miss to be taken to task by Major Stratton like some erring ensign under his command. Not she. She would give just as good as she got. And if Major Stratton uttered one word out of line, she would tell him precisely what she thought of him and of his rake of a brother.

It was only then that Emma admitted to herself that she had already decided to face Hugo—and Hugo's wrath. There were many charges to be brought against Emma Fitzwilliam, but lack of courage would not figure among them.

Emma gave a tiny curtsy as she entered the library, leaving the door ajar in her wake. Major Stratton was standing with his back against the desk, idly gazing out of the window, but as soon as she appeared, he straightened. He strode to the door with surprising agility and closed it very deliberately.

'How dare you, sir?' she cried angrily, looking pointedly towards the door. 'You know it is improper for us to be alone together in this way. Or do you perhaps think that, since one Stratton brother has already compromised me, the other can continue the process, with my good will?'

Hugo said nothing, although she thought a shadow of guilt passed across his face. He simply moved back to the door and opened it a trifle. Without looking directly at Emma, he said, 'Will that content you, ma'am?' His voice was low and cold, almost sinister in its total lack of feeling.

Emma wondered what was to come. By losing her temper, she had given him the advantage of her—and she had promised herself she would not yield to him in any way. She moved towards the window, to be as far as possible from Hugo Stratton's looming figure.

Hugo made no attempt to approach her. He went back to stand by the desk at the far side of the room. 'Now that the door is open, ma'am, it would be best if we moderated our voices.'

This time, Emma refused to rise to the bait. Nor did she turn towards him. She simply nodded towards the windows and the garden beyond. Let him interpret her signal as he would.

The silence lengthened. Emma began to think she would scream if he did not speak. At last, driven to the point of exasperation, she said, 'There is something you wished to say to me, I believe, Major? I beg you will do so without delay, for I have many duties to attend to this morning. Most of my guests are leaving, you know.'

Her words seemed to provide the spur he needed. 'Yes, I do know that Mrs Mayhew and her party are leaving,' he said quietly. 'And I know, too, the reason for it. I am heartily sorry for the trouble my brother has brought upon you.'

Emma only just managed to conceal a start of surprise. She had not expected an apology, especially from the man she had so grievously insulted.

'And I know that the insult was made worse—for you—by the fact that I myself was witness to what happened,' Hugo continued. 'Believe me, Miss Fitzwilliam, I would liefer have been anywhere but there. As it was…' His words petered out. 'As it is,' he began again, 'I am sorry, and I know that it is you who will bear the brunt of Society's censure.'

Emma was puzzled now. It seemed that Hugo Stratton had asked for this interview simply to apologise on behalf of himself and his brother. Surely that was for Kit to do? Kit—the man she would soon marry. She had not expected any understanding from Hugo Stratton. His sympathy was becoming more uncomfortable by the minute. She really ought to leave. 'Major—' she began.

'Miss Fitzwilliam,' he said quickly, 'forgive me, but I beg you will allow me to lay a proposal before you.' He waited for her brief nod and then said, 'Pardon me if I cause you pain. I must be blunt. I know you do not love my brother, nor he you. But Kit—for all his shortcomings—is a man of honour. He has promised your father that he will marry you. And he has promised *me* that he will make you a good husband. None the less, I know it is something that neither of you can really want.

'I believe there may be a solution. Let the betrothal be announced, by all means. That is surely the way to silence the gossip and to ensure that your reputation remains unsullied. But let the wedding be fixed for some months ahead…in the autumn, say, or even at Christmas. There would be nothing surprising in that. By then, this unhappy incident would be forgotten and you, Miss Fitzwilliam, could discover—as a

result of your better acquaintance with my brother—
that you do not suit. You—'

'Thank you, Major,' Emma said bitterly, whirling
round to face him and giving him no chance to continue with his extraordinary proposal. 'And of course
there is absolutely *no* likelihood that the gossip will
resurface after I have jilted your brother. None at all.
It will be just as before—Emma Fitzwilliam with her
pristine reputation.' Emma's hands were shaking. She
gripped them together in an effort to moderate the
signs of her fury. She did not dare to look him in the
eye. He believed he was offering the solution to all
her problems. If he uttered one more word on the
subject, she would probably explode. But she must
not give him the satisfaction of seeing her lose even
more of her self-control. 'Thank you, but I have no
desire to be branded a jilt as well as a wanton. You
have little understanding of the ways of Society if you
think that your plan would succeed in saving my reputation. It would save your brother, certainly. But it
would ruin me.'

He made to protest but Emma would not permit
him to speak. 'Oh, I acquit you of the charge of du-
plicity in this. You have been too long abroad, I believe, to appreciate just how malicious London gossips can be. It will not do. After last night's episode,
I *must* marry. And it seems to me that the sooner it
is done, the safer I shall be. Your brother acted—shall
we say—unwisely? The penalty, I fear, is a life sentence.'

Hugo began to pace up and down before the desk.
There was almost no trace of a limp. His recovery

was clearly proceeding apace. Lucky Major Stratton, Emma concluded acidly.

'Will you not reconsider, ma'am?' Hugo said at last. He sounded weary. By now, he must be regretting that he had ever asked for this interview.

'How can I?' Emma burst out. 'In the circumstances, I *must* marry and your brother is the only available candidate. There is no choice for either of us.'

Hugo's face had twisted into something that was half-smile, half-grimace. That enigmatic look infuriated Emma beyond anything she could have imagined. It was so easy for men. They took the pleasure and the women endured the pain.

She glared at Hugo. 'There is *one* option, Major,' she said in a clipped, scornful voice. 'If you wish to save your brother, you could always offer *yourself* in his place.' There. That should put an end to this ludicrous interview, once and for all. He could have nothing more to say to her now.

Hugo's tortured smile became even more marked. An odd light flickered in his eyes for a brief moment. He raised his chin and—for the first time—looked directly into her eyes. Slowly, he closed the distance between them and extended his hand.

'If that is what it takes, Miss Fitzwilliam, I do most willingly ask you to accept of my hand in marriage.'

Chapter Thirteen

'No!' Emma's despairing cry seemed to be torn from her. Hugo felt it like a sword slash. Did she really hate him so much? Or was it that the thought of him repelled her?

He held her wide-eyed gaze until embarrassment overcame her and she looked away. In a voice that was so low as to be barely audible, she said, 'You mock me, sir. That is not the act of a gentleman.'

Hugo took a deep breath and sighed it out again. He had not withdrawn his outstretched hand. 'I have never been more serious in my life, ma'am,' he said softly. 'I beg you to believe that—even if you are not now minded to accept my proposal. I do truly desire to make you my wife.'

Emma raised her eyes to his once more. Astonishment was written in her gaze but not—Hugo was sure—any trace of hatred or revulsion. Perhaps she might yet be won over, if he could but find the means…for this was surely the right solution. It had come to him even as he spoke the words. Wounded and scarred though he was, he, Hugo, would make a better husband for Emma than Kit could ever be. Kit was too young and much too devoted to his own pleasures to care for Emma's bruised spirit. But Hugo understood what it was to be shunned by Society. And if the solution to Emma's dilemma should also bring Hugo a prize that he had believed beyond his reach...well, he would not refuse it.

He took a step towards Emma, clasping her hands strongly in both of his own. Her fingers shook, but she did not pull away. Her gaze seemed to be fixed on his cravat.

He chafed her hands gently, trying to warm her. 'Trust me, Emma,' he said in a low voice, willing her to look up at him. 'I am older—and, I believe, wiser—than Kit. *My* offer is made of my own free will, not under any duress. I have not Kit's looks, but I promise you I am well able to support a wife...and I do not often frequent the gaming tables, either.' He found himself smiling a little when he referred to Kit's obvious defects. She must not be allowed to think he was a strait-laced martinet who would blight her life. 'Emma, look at me.' He waited until she did so and then continued, trying to emphasise the importance of his words by the sustained pressure of his hands, 'I am convinced we could learn to deal very comfortably together. Will you at least consider my proposal?'

She took a deep breath. 'What time is it, sir?' she said crisply.

'I beg your pardon, ma'am?'

The tiniest hint of a smile twisted one side of her mouth. 'I asked you what time it was, sir. My father will wish to announce my betrothal as soon as the guests appear this morning. It would be…unfortunate if he were to name the wrong brother.'

Hugo took a gasp of air and held it, staring down into her clear blue eyes. Then he let the air out slowly and gently, making no sound in the sudden silence that surrounded them. 'You accept?' he asked bluntly, and then immediately wished the stark words unsaid. Emma needed gentler handling than this.

'I accept, Major,' she said, with remarkable self-possession. 'And I would urge you to inform my father of our agreement at the earliest opportunity. It would not do for me to have two fiancés in the same morning.'

To cover his astonishment, Hugo raised Emma's hand to his lips. His kiss was just as chaste as a duenna would have wished. Now was certainly not the time for passion.

'You have made me a very happy man, my dear,' he said. 'And, mindful of your wise words, I shall go at once to your father. I only hope that he is as open to the power of my arguments as you have been.'

Emma smiled then, but it was not the smile of a happy woman. There was an edge of brittle pain there…and her eyes were troubled once more. 'You may tell Papa that, if he continues to insist that I marry your brother, he will have the pleasure of watching me jilt him at the altar.'

'But I do not understand, Emma,' said Jamie. The whole affair was thoroughly perplexing. 'It was Kit

that you met in the garden and it is Kit that you are
to marry...or so Richard told me.'

Emma shook her head, smiling brightly. 'Richard
has misled you, Jamie. Husbands do, I believe.'

Jamie still felt bewildered.

'It is true that I was in the garden last night and
that Kit was there, too,' Emma said. 'But I promise
you there was no assignation. Kit is very handsome,
I admit, but not the sort of man who... Oh dear—'
Emma bit her lip, but she was smiling still 'I must
learn not to cast aspersions on my future brother-in-
law. What *would* the Major say?'

Jamie was forced to laugh. 'Emma, you wretch!
You do it deliberately, I declare, to keep me in suspense. Shame on you!'

This time, Emma laughed aloud, though, to Jamie's
ears, it sounded a little more high-pitched than normal. 'Oh, I am sorry, Jamie. I will try to do better, I
promise. It was just... Well—as I said, I was in the
garden. That silly little Mayhew chit had been pur-
suing Kit all evening. She even followed him into the
garden and so, unfortunately, she saw Kit kissing me.
She then announced to all the world that Kit and I
were lovers, and behaving in the most licentious fashion, to boot. There was uproar, naturally, especially
as neither you nor your mama was there to curb Mrs
Mayhew's malicious tongue. Not unnaturally, Papa
was furious and insisted that Kit marry me, giving
neither of us any choice in the matter. Papa was determined that we be married within the week...to stop
the scandalmongering, you understand.'

Jamie nodded. 'But—'

Emma's smile broadened. 'And then the Major intervened. He said that Kit and I should not suit—which is perfectly true—and that I had better marry him instead. So I said I would. There. Now you have it all.'

Jamie shook her head in exasperation at this bald narrative. It was so unlike Emma. She had always shared her thoughts and feelings with Jamie. 'Emma, you know very well that you have told me nothing, nothing at all. Why was Kit kissing you in the garden, if there was no assignation? Why did Major Stratton offer to take his place? Do not pretend that he sacrifices himself out of brotherly love and duty, for that makes no sense at all. And why on earth did *you* decide to accept him? That is the greatest puzzle of all and I beg you will explain it to me. Kit is a better prospect, surely? He is young and handsome, whereas the Major is—'

Emma laid a hand on Jamie's arm. 'Hugo is the man I will marry, Jamie. I will not go back on my word.'

Jamie was not prepared to give in so easily. 'And what does he think of what passed between you and his brother in the garden? That might not bode well for your future together. Husbands do not take kindly to other men making free with their wives, you know…or even to the thought that they might do so.'

'He knows exactly what happened. He has no reason to be jealous of Kit. Believe me, Jamie, there will be no trouble over that, at least.'

'At least?'

Emma coloured a little, but she did not attempt to

cover up her obvious slip. She rose from her seat, looking down at Jamie with eyes totally devoid of expression. 'Wish us happy, Jamie,' she said simply.

'I do, Emma. I do, most sincerely.'

Emma nodded politely and made for the door, excusing herself on the grounds of her duties to her other guests.

Jamie was far from satisfied, but there was nothing more to be gleaned from questioning Emma. She was taking refuge in her best company manners and treating Jamie like the merest acquaintance. It was all very strange.

Jamie hurried away to find her husband. He must, surely, be back from his morning ride by now?

Richard was in his dressing room, changing out of his riding clothes. He took one look at his wife's face and dismissed his valet.

'Richard,' she began, 'I do not understand what is going on. Last night Emma was to marry Kit. Today Emma tells me she will marry Major Stratton. Oh, I know that he is a fine man, but he is so much older than Emma...and dreadfully wounded, besides. He—'

Richard grinned wickedly. 'Hugo is younger than me, I'll have you know, *madame*, so that cock won't fight. Is that the best you can do?'

Jamie was not to be diverted. 'And what of Kit? How does he feel about being summarily rejected in favour of his older brother? Surely he feels the insult keenly?'

'Kit? I must tell you, my love, that Kit feels the insult so keenly that he has already left for Epsom.

Now that he is no longer an engaged man, he will not be forced to miss the Oaks. Had you forgotten the race was today? Kit had not, I can tell you. He plans to put all his blunt on the second favourite—and then go back to London to gamble away his winnings.'

'Oh, Richard, how can you?' Jamie tried to keep from smiling back at him. It was very difficult when he looked down at her in just that way. 'But is this true?' she said at last.

He nodded. 'Kit would have made an appalling husband for Emma...for any woman, in my opinion. He's not half the man that Hugo is. Hugo understands people. Kit thinks only of himself...and his extremely expensive pleasures. He's far too handsome for his own good, too. Give him a few more years on the town, and he might improve, I dare say, but only if he discovers that women will not always fall at his feet. A good dose of rejection would be the best possible medicine for Kit. Whereas Hugo has had trials a-plenty...'

He caught Jamie to him and started to nuzzle her neck. 'My love, I believe that this match will be better than any of us imagine. They will be good for each other. As we were, remember?' He began to kiss her greedily.

Jamie smiled into his kiss and wound her arms about his neck. There was nothing more to be said.

Emma was exhausted by the time she tumbled into bed. It was all her own doing, too, so she had no cause for complaint. She had kept herself busy all day, often to no purpose at all. So why could she not sleep?

She decided to focus on practical things—the journey home to Longacres, the arrangements for the ceremony, reorganising the apartments in the house so that Hugo could have a study separate from her father's. Surely she had enough control over her own thoughts to stop her unruly emotions from intruding? She had spent all day playing the part of the happy young woman celebrating her engagement. Why was it that the mask always cracked, the moment she was alone?

From a child, she had always had whatever she wanted. She had decided she wanted Hugo...and now she was to have him. Why, then, was she—?

She forced herself to abandon that train of thought. The ceremony...that was better. Richard had kindly offered the use of his private chapel. In the circumstances, it was preferable to the parish church where all the villagers would come to gawp. A special licence would be needed, of course, but Richard had plans for that, too. He had joked that he was certainly up to snuff, having done the same for his own marriage. On this occasion, however, some delay was inevitable. He and Hugo could post up to London on the morrow, but would have to cool their heels during the Sabbath. All being well, they would return to Harding by Monday evening. And Richard's chaplain would then perform the ceremony on Tuesday.

In four days, she would be Hugo Stratton's wife.

Why on earth had he done it? It could not be due to any degree of feeling for Emma herself, for—apart from that one, furious kiss—he had never shown her anything more than common politeness. Could it be that his kiss meant—? Emma stopped that fanciful thought before it was fully formed. He must have done it to save his brother, she decided firmly. Kit still had all his life before him. And Kit had all the advantages of looks and charm. He might make a brilliant match, one day.

But would any man sacrifice himself to save his brother?

Perhaps it was her money that had proved the deciding factor? How demeaning to think that Hugo was no different from all the money-grabbing fortune hunters who had pursued her over the years. But surely, he would have started courting her before, if that had been his aim? He had never courted her at all, though there had been opportunities at Harding…

Perhaps he had not courted her because of his wounds, believing she would never accept a disfigured husband…whereas now she had a stark choice between one of the Stratton brothers and disgrace. Had he seized on his only real chance of securing a fortune?

No, it could not be so. Hugo was neither devious, nor base. He was Richard's oldest friend…and Richard vouched for his integrity. Emma knew that Hugo was an honourable man. She had always known. He had asked her to trust him and she had found that she did, instinctively.

Besides, Hugo had wealth of his own. He had made that clear. So…his reasons must have been quite unselfish, after all. He was marrying Emma to save his brother. And what kind of basis for marriage was that?

That was a question Emma did not want to explore. She concentrated, instead, on solving the problem of her hot, sticky pillow. She sat up, turned it and smoothed it out before lying down again. That was better...cooler.

And she must coolly decide how she was going to behave. Hugo had been scrupulously polite, but distant, since the moment he proposed. Why had he not kissed her then? He had desired her once...and she had given him the right. She had been yearning for the touch of his lips, but he had behaved as distantly as if they had just been introduced—distant, and cold. And, since then, he had avoided being alone with her or discussing anything beyond the merest commonplace. She found she was relieved that he had to go to London for the licence—she would not see him again until the wedding—for his presence still tended to make her thoughts tumble and her limbs heat, even though he hardly ever touched her. During the whole day—the day when they had become betrothed—he had twice kissed her hand and that was all. The second time, he had simply bade her a cool goodnight— no mention of what would happen when they met again, no concern about her well-being in the meantime, nothing. He must be regretting his sacrifice already.

It really did not matter if he did, Emma concluded brutally. Nothing could now be altered, for either of them. Only the future mattered, and there, she would have control. In fact, her life would change very little and she was glad of it. She would continue to be mistress of her father's household, where her husband would also live. She would minister to the needs of two gentlemen instead of one. Hugo would learn about running the estate that would one day be his, while Emma would make sure that he recovered fully from his injuries. He was much too thin, for a start. She would order nourishing food for him so that he would fill out once more. And she would ensure he learned to ride and shoot again. His scars would fade but, until he regained those vital skills, he would be unable to fulfil the proper role of a country gentleman. It might take Emma a little time, but eventually Major and Mrs Stratton would take their rightful place in Society.

As soon as she arrived home tomorrow, she would set about the question of her makeshift trousseau. With the addition of some lace, her newest evening gown could be turned into a more than adequate wedding dress... It was fortunate she had chosen white silk... She would need flowers, too...

As she finally drifted into sleep, an unbidden thought floated through her mind. When Hugo had thought she would marry Kit, he had made Kit promise to be a good husband to her. How very strange...

Chapter Fourteen

'Emma, my dear child, you look ravishing.' Aunt Augusta was tweaking Emma's bridal skirts for at least the twentieth time. If only she would not fuss so much...

'Oh, look, your hem is ruffled.' Aunt Augusta knelt quickly to smooth the offending wrinkle. She seemed to take a remarkably long time over such a minor blemish. Then, in a strained and surprisingly quiet voice, she said, 'Emma, was there anything you wished to know? About...about being a wife.' She was still looking at Emma's skirt but she hurried on, 'If your mother had been here, it would have fallen to her, of course, but...' She took a deep breath. 'It is up to me to ensure you are prepared for what is to come.'

How ominous that sounded. Was there something that she should be concerned about? Emma racked her brains. She had worked so hard over these last few days—and slept so badly—that she could not think clearly any more. What could she have forgotten? And why should Aunt Augusta wait until now to remind her?

Emma reverted to the calm politeness that she had relied on since the day of Hugo's proposal. 'I am always very grateful for your advice, Aunt.'

Mrs Warenne looked up sharply, frowning. Then she rose and walked over to the window where she stood for several moments, gazing out. She cleared her throat more than once before she spoke. And she did not look at Emma.

'My dear…my dear, you are young…and innocent. Marriage is… There are aspects to marriage which you may not… Oh, dear, this is all so difficult. If only your mother were here.'

She coughed again. 'Emma, your duties to your husband will include a degree of…of closeness. It can be…a little upsetting for a new bride, but you must simply accept it. You will soon become accustomed. We all do. And it is necessary, in any case, if you are to have children. You want children, naturally. All women want children. They will be the focus of your life.' Aunt Augusta had begun to sound a little more like her usual self. 'And a husband's attentions do lessen later, especially when his wife is…especially when he has other distractions.' Aunt Augusta cleared her throat yet again. She turned at last, though she still did not seek to meet Emma's eye. 'Forgive me, Emma, but I am afraid we do not know how badly your husband was wounded.'

Emma was by now totally bemused. What was her aunt talking about? Nothing made any sense at all.

Her aunt hurried on. 'When you retire to your

chamber, you will find it best to greet your husband in the dark, my dear. Make sure the shutters and the bed-curtains are closed so that you do not have to look upon his wounds. And if, by any chance, his injuries have impaired his ability to…perform his duties, the darkness will hide his…his embarrassment. Major Stratton is a true gentleman, my dear, and will understand that you are too shy to receive him in the light. Do not be afraid to ask. I am sure he will grant you that one request.'

Emma nodded dumbly. Darkness. Yes. She would try to remember. Darkness was important.

Aunt Augusta seemed relieved. 'Good. That is done. I have prepared you as I am sure your dear mother would have wished. And now—look at the time. We must hurry. The carriages will be at the door. A bride must be late, but not so late that her groom wonders whether she will appear at all.'

Emma took her seat in the carriage beside her father's comforting bulk. He squeezed her hand once, but said nothing. Emma was grateful. It was so peaceful now that her aunt had finally gone ahead to join the little congregation at Richard's chapel. Aunt Augusta had done nothing but talk since the moment she arrived in Emma's chamber to help her dress, besides fussing over the silliest details. Emma was too pale— should she not wear rouge? Emma's posy of flowers was too small—it was not too late to send for more. Emma's veil would look better if she wore it with an aigret…or at least a circlet. Although Emma had dumbly acquiesced to every suggestion, it had not helped to stem Aunt Augusta's flow. Emma's head had begun to ache well before she was fully dressed. And from then on, it had become worse and worse.

She promised herself that everything would soon be over. She would simply concentrate on taking one step at a time. That way, she would be able to remain in control, for she was determined to appear resolute. She must thank the servants who had come to see her off. She must remember to hold her head up as she arrived at the chapel. She must not allow her knees to shake as she walked up the aisle. She must—

One step at a time. Concentrate on the carriage journey first. Smile farewell to the servants. Above all things, smile, always smile.

The drive to Harding seemed to be shorter than usual. Emma could not remember passing through the lodge gates. Had she smiled to the lodge-keeper? She supposed she must have done.

Papa—dear, dear Papa—held her hand firmly as he helped her down and led her to the door of the chapel. Jamie was there, apparently waiting for Emma. Should she not be inside? Ah, no, Jamie had offered to act as matron of honour. Someone had to be there at the altar to receive Emma's flowers.

Jamie straightened Emma's lace veil. 'You look lovely, Emma,' she said.

Papa patted Emma's hand. 'If you are ready, my dear child?'

Emma straightened her back. One step at a time. Walk slowly down the aisle. Keep your head up. Smile. Always smile.

'I am ready, Papa.'

They walked together through the doorway and started down the aisle, Jamie following a little way behind.

One step at a time. Keep your eyes on the altar. Smile.

After the sunshine outside, it was difficult to see clearly. The chapel was almost empty—a few hazy figures on the left, the white robes of the chaplain in the centre and, on the right, two tall dark men, standing shoulder to shoulder, waiting. Why was there no music to break this awful silence? The only sound seemed to be Emma's own footsteps.

One step at a time. Smile.

'Dearly beloved, we are gathered here...'

The familiar words were soothing, almost soporific. It would be over soon.

One step at a time. Her hand must not shake when it was given to Hugo.

'Who giveth this woman...'

One step at a time. Her vows must be strongly spoken.

'Do you, Emma Frances, take this man...?'

One step at a time. Smile.

'I now pronounce you man and wife. You may kiss the bride.'

Smile.

Hugo looked down at her. Her husband, now. What was he thinking? Should he not be smiling, too?

He lifted her hand to his lips. Then he bent to place a soft kiss on her cheek. Nothing more.

Smile.

Hugo turned, offering Emma his arm. Now they must walk back down the aisle, together.

One step at a time.

The sunshine beyond the open doorway was blindingly bright. Everything inside the chapel became dim in contrast. Emma walked slowly towards the light. Out there was her new life.

Dear God, what had she done? She was married. And to a man she barely knew. Had she really spoken those vows? She must have done.

For days, she had been wandering through a dream, a dream she had willingly created for herself. But this was no dream. She was walking out into the light of day on the arm of her husband.

She lifted her chin and focused her eyes on the bright light ahead of her. She was moving into a different world, now. She must live with the choice she had made.

Hugo Stratton was her husband. He had the right to command her obedience…in everything. He owned her, and everything about her, as surely as he owned the shirt on his back. She, whose slightest wish had always been granted, must bow to the whims of the dark, silent man at her side.

Hugo placed his hand over hers as they reached the door.

Emma did not need to look at him to understand the meaning of that casual gesture. It was a sign of possession.

'Jamie, what on earth has happened to Emma?' The Dowager had taken Jamie aside as soon as they returned to the main house. She sounded very concerned. 'She looked as if she were on a tumbrel, being taken to the guillotine. And what possessed her to wear rouge? It makes her look like a cheap painted doll.'

Jamie was just as concerned as Richard's mama. 'It was her aunt's doing, I am sure. As matron of honour, I should have been there to help her dress, but Mrs Warenne insisted on taking my place. She could see that I cannot bend, or kneel...at least, not very well. But now I wish I had not agreed. I am convinced Emma has the headache. And it is small wonder. The woman never stops fussing.'

'I will do my best to keep her away from Emma for the rest of the day,' said the Dowager firmly. 'Thank heavens we insisted on having the wedding breakfast here. At Longacres, she would have been impossible. Meanwhile, you must look to Emma herself. Help her to—' She stopped very suddenly. Then she looked down at the floor. 'Oh, dear. It occurs to me that... Jamie, Emma has no mother to prepare her. I wonder if her aunt...' She did not continue. Jamie could see that she was blushing.

'Whatever the problem, I promise I will help her, Mama,' Jamie said solemnly. 'You may rely on me.' In an attempt to relieve the Dowager's obvious embarrassment, she added, 'Provided, of course, that I can rely on *you* to deal with the impossible aunt.'

The Dowager's lip curled in scorn. 'In that, my dear daughter, you may certainly rely on me.' She moved purposefully towards Emma's aunt, who had just entered the room on her brother's arm.

Good. The gabblemongering aunt would now create no more trouble. But as for Emma... Jamie
frowned, scanning the room. Emma was standing between Hugo and Richard. All three appeared to be
conversing amicably enough, but the patches of red
on Emma's cheeks had begun to look like fever spots.
At this rate, she would collapse before the day was
half over.

Emma would have to sit through the wedding
breakfast, but with such a small gathering—even with
the chaplain, they were only eight—it could be kept
quite informal. Jamie should be able to ensure that it
did not last too long for Emma's comfort. She had
given orders for a suite of rooms to be prepared in
the guest wing, since there had been no time for Hugo
to make honeymoon arrangements. Hugo had been
quite apologetic about that, when he and Richard had
finally arrived back from London, dog-tired, but he
had accepted with good grace when Richard invited
them both to remain at Harding for a few days. In a
house as large as this, their privacy could be guaranteed.

The problem, Jamie realised, would be the interminable evening. Somehow she must create an opportunity to speak to Emma alone without arousing
the suspicions of her father or her aunt—and, before
that, she must work out exactly what she was going
to say...

Jamie glanced back towards Emma once more.
Good grief, she looked as if she were about to faint.
She must be rescued—now—before ever the wedding

breakfast began. There was no time for finesse. It must be a frontal attack.

In spite of her awkward bulk, Jamie reached Emma's side in a few quick strides and began to steer her away from her husband. 'Major Stratton,' she said archly, 'I do declare you have much to learn about the duties of a husband. Your poor wife is worn out with all the preparations and much in need of a little respite. You will allow me to take her upstairs for a few minutes?'

Hugo made to bow his agreement, but Jamie did not wait. She was halfway to the door when she heard her husband's laughing voice say, 'I suppose it's a little late to warn you against managing females, Hugo.'

'May we have a private word, Richard?' Hugo drew his best man away from the other guests in the drawing room. 'I ought to tell you that I've received word today from Lake Manor. Apparently the house will be ready to receive us by the end of the week, so we shall not be trespassing on your hospitality for more than a few days. I must say I'm amazed that everything has been done so quickly. The steward must have excelled himself.'

'I can understand your desire to have Emma to yourself, but are you sure the house will be habitable? I thought you said no one had lived in it since your mother died?'

'That's true, but John has been very good. He installed an excellent steward while I was abroad and visited occasionally to ensure that no essential repairs were neglected. He paid for some of them, too. I couldn't have wished for a better brother, you know.'

A slight smile quirked a corner of Richard's mouth but he said nothing. Hugo could read that smile—Richard was thinking about the unpredictable Kit, and wondering why Hugo's two brothers had so little in common.

'The land will need a great deal of work, admittedly,' Hugo continued, remembering the report he had received that very day, 'but I am glad of that. I know I have much to learn about estate management—I was not brought up to it as you were—and I would much rather do that well away from my father-in-law's watchful eye. Oh, don't mistake me, I have nothing but admiration for the way Sir Edward runs Longacres. In fact, that's the problem. There would be nothing for me to do here, nothing to change. I need to make my own mistakes, I think.'

'Knowing you, I doubt there will be many,' Richard said with a short laugh.

'You may laugh, but it's one of the most important things I learned in the army. You only do things wrong once.'

'What does Emma say about moving so far away from her father? They have always been very close, you know.'

'I haven't told her yet.' Hugo frowned at the sight of Richard's raised eyebrow. 'You know as well as I do that there has been no opportunity to speak to her about that, or anything else. However, I am sure she will be pleased to be away from the gossips for a while…and, with a new household to manage, and a whole new set of tenants, she won't have time to worry about what Society thinks of us. I'm sure it's for the best.'

'You won't be going to London?'

'Not while Kit's there. Not this year, at least. It could be awkward for Emma.'

Richard nodded. 'But won't Emma be bored? Lake Manor is pretty remote.'

Hugo was sure that remoteness was one of the main advantages of the small estate he had inherited from his mother. There would be no gossip…and precious little social intercourse at all. They would have time to become accustomed to marriage. And one day, there might even be a child, a sturdy little fellow like Richard's Dickon…

Richard cleared his throat rather too obviously.

Hugo hauled himself back to the present. 'I am not planning to keep my wife in isolation, you know,' he said. 'We shall come here often, to visit her father. And you, too, of course.'

'I'm glad to hear it,' Richard said with a wry smile. 'Otherwise Jamie would never forgive either of us. Still, at least you'll both be here tomorrow for Dickon's birthday. Jamie is planning a party on the lawn and Emma, as godmother, will have an important role to play…especially as neither of Dickon's godfathers will be making an appearance. Perhaps you'd like to deputise for them?'

Hugo bowed, smiling. 'I should be honoured.' Richard was much to be envied, having been blessed with a son so early in his marriage. In the wider Stratton family, there were many childless couples. Hugo's elder brother had no children at all, which was a source of much sadness to them all. Hugo fervently hoped that he was not destined for the same fate.

He glanced out at the sky. 'Lady Hardinge's wishes may be thwarted by the weather, though. I rather think we're about to have a storm.'

As he spoke, thunder rumbled ominously in the distance. The sky had become dark and threatening in the space of a very few minutes, but the air was still hot and sultry, even with the windows open. Emma's father and aunt would be bound to leave early if the weather did not improve. That would be a pity. And Dickon's birthday tomorrow might well be spoilt, too.

It occurred to Hugo that he should mention the fact that he and little Dickon shared a birthday—but, after a moment's thought, he decided against. After all these years apart, Richard had clearly forgotten the date. He would be mortally embarrassed to be reminded of it now. Hugo would say nothing. Today had been his day—and Emma's. Tomorrow should be for the child alone.

He would not allow himself to think about the night between.

Chapter Fifteen

Emma straightened the sheet yet again, tucking it under her body as far as it would go. It was really too hot for so many covers, especially with the bed-curtains drawn and the shutters closed, but, even in the dark, she felt a need to cover up the lacy night-gown that Aunt Augusta had insisted she wear. Emma was not sure what kind of a woman would wear such a confection but it was certainly not a garment for a lady.

Another rumble of thunder shook the house. It seemed to have been going on for hours, yet still it did not rain.

Emma had given up trying to fathom out her aunt's advice. First Aunt Augusta had told her to say she was shy, and then she had given her a nightgown that was fit only for a...

He would be here soon. How was she to put Aunt Augusta's advice into words? What was she going to say to him? All the words she tested sounded stilted, or stupid, even to her own ears. What's more, she did not even know how to address him. He had called her by her given name at least twice now, but he had never invited her to do the same.

Her restless fingers twitched at the sheet. It seemed to be sticking to her skin. If only the storm would break.

He would never believe her shy if she used his given name. Better to avoid any name at all. It was important to receive him in the dark, she remembered that, but she could not remember why. Aunt Augusta had said something about Hugo's wounds, but Jamie had made no mention of those. In fact, Jamie's advice had made even less sense that Aunt Augusta's. Jamie had said that love between husband and wife could be wonderful. She had said a great many other things, too, but Emma had understood none of them. She had felt too ill and too tired to try. And by the time the tisane had finally cleared her throbbing headache, she had been back among the wedding party, playing the part of the happy bride.

He would be here soon.

Hugo leant back against the oak and drew deeply on his half-smoked cigar. Its tiny glow seemed much brighter than usual. The thunder had passed over at last, but it had left darkness behind. Pity that it had not rained, to break the oppressive heat.

He pulled out his watch but could not see the hands. It must be very late by now. There were almost no lights to be seen in the house—and none at all in the guest wing. Emma must be there, in the dark, waiting.

Emma Stratton. His wife.

His wife had behaved like an automaton throughout her wedding day. She had looked like a painted doll. And she had acted like one—stiff limbs, wide eyes, fixed smile. The woman he had kissed in the chapel had been as cold as marble...and she had looked at him in horror. If she found him so repellent, why had she agreed to this marriage in the first place?

His simplest attempts at reassurance had been rebuffed. She had bristled with hostility at the slightest touch of his hand.

Hugo swore roundly at the oak above him, using words that the meanest of his soldiers might have used. It solved nothing. His wife had married him because she had no choice. His wife despised him. Had she not told him so?

He had done everything he could think of to make this day less of an ordeal for her, but not even Richard had succeeded in making her laugh...and he had certainly tried. The wedding breakfast had been a trial for them all. Emma had been polite—so polite that he had wanted to slap her. It had been a blessing when her father and her aunt had left. They had blamed the approaching storm, but Hugo had not believed them. Even the Dowager had seemed relieved to say her farewells.

And now Emma would have retired. She might even be in bed by now, waiting for him to come to her. Would she welcome him? He doubted it very much. She had no feelings of love, or even liking, for her new husband, as far as he could tell. And if she truly detested him, she would be as unyielding as the oak at his back.

Dear God, this was no way to think about his wife. He ought to be able to make her first experience of love a pleasure...but he was not sure that he knew how to begin. Emma was a lady, and a virgin besides. And Hugo had experience of neither. There had been plenty of women willing to become the mistress of a handsome young British officer, but not one of them had been a lady...and they had been anything but innocent. When he had first arrived in the Peninsula, still young but far from green, the dark-eyed Spanish women had been happy to teach him everything they knew about the arts of love. They had taught him to give pleasure as well as take it, and shown him that physical love could bring unbounded joy to man and woman alike.

But that had been aeons ago.

That was long before those last hectic weeks with Wellington's army, before Waterloo, before the noise and the stench and the gore...before all those hours that he had lain on the battlefield, soaked in his own blood and unable to move, staring up at the smoke-streaked sky. That was long before those months of lying on a filthy bed, trying to remember who he was and wondering if he would survive to see the next sunrise.

He had been forced to be celibate for a long, long time. Tonight he would find out whether it was too long. That knowledge could not be put off any longer.

Hugo threw away the remains of his cigar. He watched it arc through the darkness and disappear into the night, and then he strode back to the house and up the side stairs to the guest wing.

As instructed, his valet was nowhere to be seen, but everything was ready. His blue silk dressing-gown lay across the chair by the empty grate. Beside it, on a small table, was a decanter of brandy and a single glass.

Hugo pulled off his cravat and poured brandy into his glass. Then he thought better of it. He could not go to her reeking of strong drink. He owed her that, at least.

He methodically removed the rest of his clothing and donned his dressing gown. He would not take a candle. Its light, so close to his scarred face, would horrify her even more. He would trust to the light from the night sky.

Quietly, he opened the door to Emma's room. It was pitch dark. The shutters were closed and locked. And the curtains were drawn tight round the huge bed.

It was as hot as Hades, and as dark as a tomb.

At the sound of the opening door, Emma plucked convulsively at the damp sheet, trying to ensure that every last vestige of the nightgown was hidden. She still did not know what she would say to him.

In a moment he would slip between the bed-curtains and—

The crash of opening shutters echoed like thunder through the room. Hugo was pulling them back with incredible force...as if he hated them. And he was throwing open the windows too.

Emma felt the merest breath of cooler air through the tightly drawn bed-curtains. It was still dark, but she could sense the lightening beyond. She drew the sheet more tightly around her body, trying to make herself as small as possible.

Hugo's footsteps were not loud, but she knew he was standing beyond the curtain, between the bed and the open window. She saw two strong hands appear through the dark velvet. Then, in a single powerful gesture, the curtains were thrown open. Silhouetted against the dim light from the window was Hugo's tall figure, its arms still raised, forcing the curtains apart.

Without a thought, she shrank away from him. She could not prevent herself. His outline looked so huge, so dark, so menacing. If he wanted to humiliate her, to provide the final proof of his ownership, he could not have chosen a better way than this.

His hands dropped to his sides. Still she could not see his face. She closed her eyes, tightly.

'Emma?'

Keeping her eyes closed against the light, she said, 'I am sorry about the shutters. I...I thought that, in the dark, it would be easier to...easier for...' She could not go on. The words would not come.

She did not move. She could feel that he was looking down at her, thinking. For a long time, he did not move. She could not even hear him breathe.

At last she heard a tiny rustle of silk and then the edge of the sheet was lifted. The cool air touched her body. She shivered. It felt as if a hand had hovered a hair's breadth over her naked skin. Then the bed dipped as he lay down beside her and drew the sheet back over them both. Now, she could feel the waves of heat from his body reaching out to encircle her like a comforting arm. She opened her eyes in surprise. She could see now, just a little. Hugo was watching her, but his expression was unreadable.

He reached out a hand to touch her cheek. 'Emma—'

Dear God, he was naked! She closed her eyes in panic at the realisation. What on earth was going to happen now?

The scrape of curtain rings provided her answer. She opened her eyes to find that Hugo had closed the bed-curtains once more, offering her the gift of blessed darkness.

She screwed up her eyes again, not to shut out the light—for that was gone—but to stop the tears that threatened. She had not expected kindness, not from this man who had been so cold and forbidding. But she would not allow herself to weep. No matter what this night might bring, she would not weep.

Hugo lay awake, staring up at the canopy. Beside him, his wife was asleep at last, curled up like a child, with her back towards him. Had she wept? He did not know—and, in the dark, he could not see her face.

Surreptitiously, he pulled open the curtain on his side of the bed. The cooler air was sweet and refreshing but he did not dare to move. He might wake her if he rose. And then she would see the naked body that repelled her.

Was it always to be like this? He had always hated making love in the dark. He wanted to make her respond to him, to see her face come alight with passion, to run his fingers over her silky skin and watch it glow...

But none of that had happened. Even in the darkness she craved, she had not yielded to him. She had not even said his name. This was not the soft responsive woman he had kissed in the conservatory. This was still the woman in the chapel, who received his kisses as if she were made of cold white marble. Nor was she the dreamer, beautiful as the flowers around her, who had sat in the garden looking as if she longed to melt into a lover's arms. Here, in the dark, he had felt the tension of her skin and the tightening of her muscles wherever he touched her. She was capable of responding—he knew she was—but he must have frightened her into silence and revulsion with the strength of his own passions and the sight of his shattered body.

If only he had been more careful, gone more slowly...

It was too late. It was done...and badly done. Would she ever learn to forgive him? For the first time in his life, he cursed all those years with the army, fighting for his country while other men learned how to move among the *ton* and to woo and win Society ladies. He had promised they could be comfortable together, but there was nothing comfortable about this. He did not know how to make love to a lady, even when she was his wife. His overwhelming physical desire—the desire he feared he had lost— had driven him to lose control as he had never done before. With other women—before—he had been sometimes passionate, sometimes playful, but always in control. With Emma...

It must be the effect of being celibate for so long, surely? Next time, he would not let his passions overcome his reason. Next time, he would be caressing, loving—

He was not sure that he could.

The sight of Emma lying there had roused him to a height of desire he had not imagined. He must not let it happen again, not like that. And there was only one way to prevent it. They must not share a bed again until they were safely installed at Lake Manor and had learned to be more...comfortable together. As he had promised.

He looked back at her sleeping form. Her breathing was slow now, and measured. He could leave without disturbing her.

Very gently, he eased himself from the bed and closed the curtains around her. Then he retrieved his robe and made his way back to his own room and his decanter of brandy.

When his wife woke up to the light of day, she would at least be spared the sight of her husband, naked, beside her.

Chapter Sixteen

Emma awoke feeling cold. The windows must have been open all night. For several moments, she lay staring at the bed-curtains, trying to muster the courage to turn and look her husband in the face.

It could no longer be avoided. She took a deep breath and rolled on to her back.

She was alone in the huge bed. No wonder she had felt cold. She should have realised that Hugo's comforting warmth was gone from her side.

And she was naked!

She felt herself blushing as she remembered. Hugo had had no patience with the filmy silk and lace. He would have no barriers between them, he had said. In no time at all, the nightgown had been thrown to the floor.

And then...

And then Hugo had made her his wife. This time, he *had* kissed her, fiercely and possessively. It had been frightening at first—a little—but the fear had passed as soon as her body had begun to heat. This time, there had been no risk of their being disturbed.

She had felt free to glory in the way he made her feel, hoping that, if she lay completely still, the sensations he created would go on for ever.

But they had not. One moment he was almost devouring her with his drugging kisses, murmuring her name as if it were the only word he knew; the next he had taken her body under his own and... She remembered only the streak of pain and the sudden weight of his body on hers. Everything else was hazy—except that he was soon gone from her, silent, rolling on to his back and closing his eyes. He had not touched her again.

Emma understood none of it. First, those amazing feelings, as if something magical were about to happen, and then—nothing. It could not be right. Not like this. Jamie had said it could be wonderful. Was this what she meant? Surely not. Emma had felt as tense as a coiled spring—which was far from wonderful—and then she had felt...bereft.

Perhaps Jamie would explain, now that Emma was truly a wife?

Perhaps she would, if only Emma could find the courage to ask. She felt herself blushing even more. She could not possibly talk of this night, not to any-one.

Emma pulled the sheet round her body and reached out through the curtains for her nightgown. She would be mortified if her abigail found her naked. And what if Hugo came in? She hastily donned the robe. She was not sure whether a husband would think it necessary to knock.

She had so much to learn about being a wife, much

more than she had ever imagined. She could run a household, or host a dinner for royalty, without the slightest qualm. It was as easy as riding a horse. But she did not know what to say to her husband when they were alone, or whether she might touch him, or how to show him that she loved him.

For she did. In spite of everything, she did.

She had been stunned by Hugo's cold reaction to her acceptance of his proposal. It was as if he had slapped her. It seemed that he would not forgive her those wounding insults, that he was offering to marry a woman he despised, only because he wanted to save his younger brother. But by then it was too late—her words could not be unsaid. She had spent four whole days trying to shut out the thought of what she had done by accepting him, and the prospect of spending the rest of her life with such a calculating, cold-blooded man.

But there was nothing cold-blooded about the man who came to her bed. He might despise her—though she was no longer sure of that—but he was certainly not cold-blooded. His passionate kisses, the way his hands skimmed her body, learning its contours in the darkness, the anguish in his voice as he spoke her name, over and over... He had lit a flame in her, *certes*, but he, too, had been burning.

Throwing back the bed-curtains, she rose and donned a heavy silk wrapper. Its concealing folds helped restore much of her normal strength of mind. Today was her godson's birthday and she must make ready to face the world.

She had been a fool these last four days, allowing

her fears to rule her. There was no need. She was Hugo's wife and she could make him proud of her.

An unbidden thought arose. Perhaps one day he might even value her enough to care for her, a little? Perhaps then she would not feel so desolate?

She must try. She would prove to him that she was the perfect wife. Such a woman would care for her husband and look to his slightest needs without being asked. A husband would never have cause to find fault with such a paragon of wifely virtues. It could not be so difficult, surely?

Emma straightened her back and lifted her chin. It would be a role, like all the others she had played in her life. She would play it to perfection.

'You made all these arrangements without saying a word to me?' Emma's voice had not risen appreciably, but she was white with fury.

Hugo took his wife by the arm and steered her away from the rest of the guests on the lawn. Little Dickon was the centre of everyone's attention, chortling happily as he played with his new toys and was petted by first one, then another, of the admiring adults. No one would notice their departure.

When they were hidden by the broad trunk of the ancestral oak, Hugo loosed his hold on her arm. She stared at him, accusingly, rubbing her flesh as if it were bruised.

'There is no need for all this outrage, Emma,' he said, frowning. As a soldier, he had prided himself on his coolness in the face of provocation, but today he was having great difficulty in keeping a rein on his temper. She had no right to challenge him, especially in public.

'How dare—'

'I am your husband,' Hugo said as calmly as he could. 'Such decisions are mine to make. We leave for Lake Manor on Friday, and that is where we shall live, for the rest of this year, at least.' At the sight of the sudden hurt in her eyes, he tried to soften his tone. 'Trust me, Emma, it is for the best.'

It took her a long time to reply. Hugo thought she was weighing her words.

'What about my father?'

Hugo was tempted to remind her of her wedding vows, to forsake all others and cleave only to him, but that would have been too cruel. He ought to have prepared her for being uprooted from her home. He put his hand on her arm, gently this time. 'Your father knows precisely what I plan, Emma. And he is in full agreement. He knows we have to make our own life together, my dear. Living in your father's house is no way to do that.'

'You discussed all this with my father?' she said. She sounded shocked. She threw him a swift, angry glare and then fixed her gaze on the grass beneath her feet.

Hugo was not prepared to argue the point. 'Of course. He naturally wished to know how I planned to support his daughter and the kind of life I could offer her. He was relieved to learn that a man of means, rather than a fortune hunter, was about to become his son-in-law.'

Emma said nothing. She still did not look at him.

'And now, I think we should return to Dickon's party, do not you? It is the child's day and we should not spoil it with petty quarrels. Come, Emma.' He held out his hand.

For a moment she did not move. Then she nodded. 'You are right. A godmother must be gay on her godson's birthday.' Ignoring his outstretched hand, she walked out from behind the oak and rejoined the group around the child.

Hugo gritted his teeth and followed. She had started talking to the Rector as if nothing had happened. And she was laughing.

Emma watched Hugo out of the corner of her eye. She still wanted to hit him, though she had managed to restrain herself…just. That would have been a public humiliation for them both.

He was unfair. He was a tyrant. He was forcing her to live on his run-down estate, miles from anywhere, so that he could have her all to himself, so that she would be cut off from her father and her friends and all the places she had known since childhood. And she had no choice but to go with him. No one—not even her father—would take her part against her lawful husband.

She had been wrong about marriage. She had been wrong about Hugo. She could not begin to be the quiet, conformable wife she had pictured in her mind. She was not sure how she had ever thought to love a man who treated her with so little consideration.

She watched her husband throw little Dickon high into the air, catching him easily when he tumbled,

squealing, back to earth. Hugo had regained his physical strength much faster than she would have thought
possible. He would have no need of her ministrations.
He was self-sufficient to an extent that was almost
frightening.

Emma began to feel hollow inside. How many
more of her ambitions would be brought to naught by
this man she had married? Did he need her at all?
How naïve she had been, earlier, to think that she
could turn herself into the perfect submissive wife.
Hugo might welcome it—judging by his attitude today, he took her submission for granted—but Emma
had learned she was incapable of it.

Hugo and Dickon were down on the grass now,
playing with a pair of wooden horses. But Dickon
clearly wanted a real live horse—so Hugo obligingly
went down on all fours and allowed the child to ride
on his back. Emma watched, suddenly envious. Her
husband was more understanding of the needs of
Richard's child than he was of his wife's.

Richard came at last to retrieve his son, ignoring
Dickon's protests. Hugo yielded with good grace, but
there was something in his face that Emma recognised, even though it was gone in a moment. She had
seen that expression before, the very first time she had
seen Hugo on the lawn with Dickon. In a flash of
insight, she understood the hunger behind that look.
Hugo loved children. And Hugo had been convinced
he would never have a family of his own. Did he
think so still?

Emma could not continue to watch from a distance.
She was beginning to realise that her husband was a

very complex man. It was too easy to brand him a tyrant, on the grounds of a few sharp words. And, in truth, she had given him little choice by challenging him as she had. Having made his decision to take her to Lake Manor, he could not be expected to change it—in public—at the first sign of opposition from his wife.

She must try again…not to be submissive and unquestioning, for that would be beyond her, but to understand him better. Hugo might be more difficult than the other men she knew, but there must be a way to reach him. She had always been able to bend every other man to her will.

She would begin by apologising for her outburst. That would surely disarm him.

Emma made her way to her husband's side, but her good intentions were frustrated by the arrival of Richard's butler, in search of Hugo. 'May I have a word, sir?' Digby said quietly. That was all Emma heard. The rest of the butler's words were for Hugo alone.

Hugo raised an eyebrow but said nothing. Then, with a slight shrug of his shoulders, he followed the butler across the lawn to the house.

'Kit! What the devil—?' Kit was the last person Hugo had expected to see in Richard's bookroom. Digby had told him only that a gentleman was come, on urgent business.

Kit looked more embarrassed than Hugo had ever seen him. 'I'm sorry, Hugo,' he said. 'Believe me, I would never have intruded on your honeymoon if I'd had any choice. Emma…Mrs Stratton doesn't know I'm here, does she?'

'No. Digby was very discreet. But what on earth possessed you to come here? The gossips will have a field day with this.'

'I had no choice, Hugo. I am in real trouble.'

'Oh, God. What now?'

'Money,' Kit said in a hollow voice. 'I lost five thousand pounds to Lady Luce—and she's demanding immediate payment.'

First Emma, and now Kit. Hugo's fraying temper snapped. 'Have you *no* sense of honour? You played with money you do not have. Worse, you did so against a lady. You're a disgrace to the name you bear.'

Kit stood ramrod straight, taking Hugo's angry words as if they were blows.

Hugo's voice rose even more. 'I take it you *don't* have the money to pay her?'

Kit did not move, though he coloured a little.

'Well, do you?'

'No. But I—'

'Don't give me your lame excuses, Kit. We'll finish this bout with the buttons off. You lost a fortune at the tables and now you have a debt of honour that you can't pay. Well? What do you intend to do about it?'

Kit looked his brother straight in the eye. 'I did think to blow my brains out, but I have already brought you trouble enough.'

The intent expression in Kit's face shocked Hugo. He meant it. All Hugo's anger drained from him at the thought of what his rash young fool of a brother might have done. Hugo gripped the back of the chair for support, his mind racing. 'Good of you to think about the rest of the family. I'm sure John will be suitably grateful,' he said with heavy sarcasm. 'Pity you didn't think of us before you set about losing money you don't have.'

Kit still stood rigidly to attention. 'You are furious, Hugo,' he said at last. 'I suppose you have every right to be. I own it was a stupid thing to do. If it hadn't been for Forster—'

'Forster?' Hugo thundered. 'Forster was there?'

At last, Kit hung his head a little. 'Yes. I know I should have left as soon as he joined the table, but I didn't want anyone to think I was afraid to face him.'

Hugo nodded. He knew Forster's ways only too well.

'So I stayed,' Kit continued, 'and played. And when Lady Luce started winning so heavily, he said...he implied that I wasn't man enough to stick at the table when I was losing. After that, I couldn't leave, could I?'

Hugo nodded a little reluctantly. He fancied he would have done the same in his brother's place.

'I was sure I would win eventually. You know I've always been lucky with the cards and the bones. Thought it was just a matter of time. Lady Luce's luck would turn, I would recoup my losses, and nobody would be any the wiser. Especially Forster.'

'But your luck didn't turn,' Hugo said flatly.

'The grasping old witch gave me no chance. I swear I'll have my revenge on her yet. She'd take the

last farthing from a beggar. She must have been keeping count. The moment my losses reached five thousand, she announced that she had had enough for the
night and would retire. Said she expected me to call
on her within the week.'

Hugo found he was still gripping the chair. He deliberately relaxed his hands, one at a time, while he
thought through Kit's story so far. There must be
more. He knew that. He waited in silence for Kit to
resume.

'She refused point blank to give me any chance of
recouping my losses. Said she wouldn't be playing
for more than chicken-stakes for a while.'

'That doesn't sound like Lady Luce at all,' Hugo
said, surprised.

'Transpires that she needs the money to cover her
own losses. For once, her son is refusing to pay—
word is he can't lay his hands on the blunt—so she
is desperate. She would still be received, given her
pedigree…but no one in his right mind would ever
allow her to play again.'

Hugo made to speak but Kit forestalled him.

'You don't need to say it, Hugo. I know I was mad
to play. And for such stakes. Do you think I would
have chosen to come cap in hand to you if I could
have found another way? Believe me, I tried every
other avenue I could think of.'

Hugo went over to the desk and leaned against it,
breathing heavily. 'And you think I might just happen
to have five thousand pounds about me? Kit, you really must be mad.'

This time, Kit refused to meet Hugo's eyes. His

neck was very red above his snowy cravat. 'I thought…I knew John could never raise so much. You were my last hope. I knew you had Emma's dowry.'

'*What?*'

As Hugo's shout of fury echoed around the wooden panels, the door opened.

'Excuse me, I did knock, but—' At the sight of Kit, Emma stopped dead, eyes wide and face suddenly ashen.

Hugo crossed the room in a few strides, taking her arm in a fierce grip and turning her back towards the open door. 'You have no business here, Emma,' he said angrily. 'You will have the goodness to leave us. At once.'

She gasped in protest, but Hugo took no notice. He propelled her into the corridor and shut the door firmly at her back.

Chapter Seventeen

Emma's hand came up to her mouth, trying to stop the cry of anguish that had risen in her throat. Hugo's furious words seemed to be echoing inside her head. No man had ever spoken to her in such a fashion. And this man was her husband.

She could still hear Hugo's angry voice from the other side of the door. This time, he must be berating his brother. The heavy wood muffled most of the sound, but the word 'dowry' was unmistakable…as was the venom with which it was spoken.

Emma fled before she could hear any more.

She found herself in Jamie's conservatory. How had she come there? She did not know. Only that she had been desperate to escape from the sound of Hugo's anger.

She threaded her way through the lush greenery and sank down on to the stone bench. It was shaded, though uncomfortably humid. That was a blessing, she decided. No one would think to look for her here, on such a hot day. She would have time to gather her thoughts, to decide what to do.

A drip of water fell on to her face from one of the huge leaves.

Emma started to laugh. It might as well have been a bucketful, for it had brought her back to reality. *She* could not decide what to do, for Hugo had made all the decisions for her. It did not matter what she thought, or what she wished. Her husband did not see a need to consult her in any way. It seemed he did not even wish to talk to her.

Emma bowed her head. She felt very close to despair. Why did it have to be like this?

The leaf dripped again.

Emma edged along the stone bench to avoid the next drip. The stone was cool under her hand. It reminded her of the seat in the garden at Epsom where this nightmare had begun. And it reminded her of the moment when she had understood that she loved Hugo Stratton.

Did she still? Could she love a man who treated her so abominably?

No.

Yes.

She did not know. Everything was so confused. In this very spot she had seen Hugo kissing Jamie…but she had been mistaken. On the other side of those plants, she had accused Hugo of the vilest conduct imaginable and he had lost his temper. His hard grey eyes had narrowed to furious slits. He had been about to strike her. But he had kissed her instead.

That kiss was the cause of everything.

Hugo was standing by the desk, drumming his fingers on the polished wood. Kit had not moved. He looked like a man about to face his execution.

Hugo glanced towards the door. Emma must be long gone. What had he said to her? He could not remember, but he was sure it had been insulting. He had never known such black rage.

He ran his free hand through his hair and stared distractedly at the wood beneath his fingers. This would not do. Hot words achieved nothing. He needed a cool head to deal with Kit. And then there was Emma...

Hugo trod slowly across to the window. Thank goodness it was not open. It was bad enough that Emma had walked in on them, but if Richard and the others had heard too...

First things first. He forced his thoughts back to his impossible brother. Kit had been right to come to him. Courageous, too. He must have known that Hugo would be furiously angry, but he had not flinched once.

Kit's losses were enormous, a fortune, but it was not his fault, not totally. A more experienced man would have found a way to side-step Forster's malicious insinuations, but Kit, at twenty-two, could not have encountered many of Forster's stamp. Kit's magnificent figure and dashing ways made it too easy to forget just how young he was.

Kit had stayed—and played—to protect the family's good name.

Hugo turned on his heel to face his brother. His mind was made up. Now that he had regained control of his temper, he could clearly see the way ahead.

'You have been a fool, Kit,' he said, without heat, 'but I can understand why you acted so rashly. And, believe me, I *am* glad that you decided not to blow your brains out. Think of the mess it would have left for the servants.'

Kit started, looked searchingly at Hugo, and then laughed in relief. 'Hugo—'

'Don't think you'll get off scot-free, though, for you won't. I'll pay your debts, but there are conditions.'

Kit raised his head a fraction and narrowed his eyes.

'First,' Hugo continued implacably, 'you will give me your solemn promise never again to play for more than you can afford to lose. Not even against Lady Luce.' Hugo stopped, glaring sternly at his brother, but Kit met his challenge, and nodded briefly. 'And second, you will take yourself off abroad for a year or two so that all this madness may be forgotten.'

This time, Kit's nod took a little longer to come. He had gained quite a following among the young bloods of London Society. It was not surprising that he should be loath to relinquish his position there.

'Go to Paris. Or—better still—Vienna. Make yourself useful. I've quite a few friends in both places who would be glad of another pair of hands.'

Kit grimaced.

'I should tell you, I suppose,' said Hugo, trying not to smile, 'that there are…er…other attractions in Vienna, too. It's not as glittering as it was during the Congress, but I believe the social round is quite as hectic as London's.'

'I would go in any case, Hugo, and you know it,' Kit said seriously. Then he grinned. 'But you have just made my penance sound a great deal more attractive.'

They both laughed.

Hugo went back to the desk. He must start to organise the money to pay Kit's debts. And it would have to be taken from Emma's dowry. Kit had been right about that. There was no time to do anything else before Lady Luce's deadline. Hugo drew a sheet of paper towards him and dipped his pen in the standish.

'Hugo, what are we going to do about Forster? He's clearly determined to do you mischief now that he knows you're back in England.'

Hugo felt the black rage beginning to rise again. He forced himself to remain calm. 'The man is a blackguard. And a coward. A great many men died because of him, Kit, and he didn't give a rap. This time, I *shall* find a way to stop him.'

'Careful, Hugo, he's got friends in high places.'

'So have I. Don't forget it was Wellington himself who gave me my majority. And he had the measure of Forster almost from the start. Sent him back to Horse Guards at the first opportunity. Knew he was bound to toady up to the Duke of York, but in London, at least, he couldn't be responsible for any more disastrous sallies like the one at Ciudad Rodrigo. I swore then that Forster would pay, one day, and I don't intend to break my oath. Langley and the others died because Forster sent us to take that impregnable ridge—'

'Against your advice,' interposed Kit.

'Yes, against my advice. But that doesn't make me blameless, Kit. I was experienced enough to know that the attack was unnecessary—and that it would be a disaster. But I wasn't nearly wise enough to hide my contempt for Forster when I warned him not to issue the order. He was furious that a young whippersnapper like me should dare to question his judgement. Almost had an apoplexy on the spot. God, I wish he had. It would have saved all those lives. As it was, the attack went ahead, and more than a hundred good men died, needlessly. Only a handful of us came back. If I had been less concerned about showing Forster that I was the better soldier, I might have made him listen to me. As it was—'

'As it was, it cost you your career. And, if it hadn't been for Wellington's intervention, it would have cost you your good name, too, once Forster started telling the world that you were a coward as well as insubordinate. He wanted you dishonoured, Hugo. I am sure he still does.'

'I didn't *feel* honourable after seeing all my friends die for nothing, knowing I could have stopped it.'

'But you can't *know* that,' Kit protested. 'Forster would never have heeded your advice, even if you'd offered it on your knees. It was his responsibility, not yours, Hugo. He accused you of cowardice just to cover up his own incompetence. He's the coward, not you. He'd run a mile if his own life were in danger. I've a mind to call him out. I could easily find an excuse—'

'No! For God's sake, haven't you caused enough

trouble already, you young hothead? Society already holds you convicted of seduction and gambling away the Stratton family fortune. Would you add murder to the list?'

Kit grinned like a mischievous schoolboy. 'I might miss, you know.'

Hugo snorted in disbelief. 'If you did, it would be the first time.' Hugo had been a first-class shot before his injury, but Kit was even better, and they both knew it. 'Be serious, Kit. Think of the damage you might do—to the whole family—and try to rein in that impetuous spirit of yours.'

'It's no worse than yours, brother.'

'But I have learnt—since Rodrigo—to temper mine, lest it harm the innocent. You must learn to do the same. Look where it almost got you this time.'

'Oh, very well, but—'

'Leave Forster to me, Kit. I will deal with him in my own way and in my own time. I believe I have the right.'

Kit looked mutinous for a moment, but then nodded.

'And, in the meantime, you must pay your debts to Lady Luce and make ready to go on your travels. Come, sit down and have a glass of madeira, while I compose a letter to my bankers. They will be surprised to learn that I am coming up to London...especially as I wrote to them only the other day about what I wanted them to do.'

Kit choked a little on his wine. But then, irrepressible as always, he favoured Hugo with a rueful grin that made him look handsomer than ever. Raising his glass in salute, he said, 'Happy birthday, big brother.'

'Heaven help the ladies of Vienna,' Hugo said under his breath.

Hugo was at first surprised to find that Emma had not returned to Dickon's party in the garden, but then he recalled just how brusquely he had expelled her from the bookroom. He had not given her a single word of explanation for Kit's arrival. And he had not listened to a single word she had to say.

She would be furious. Again. And—this time—she had cause.

He must find her before he left and try to explain. But what could he say?

He made his way back into the guest wing and climbed the stairs to their suite. He could not race up the stairs two at a time, as he had when he was younger, but his self-imposed exercise programme was certainly working—stairs were nothing like the ordeal they had been. He had been looking forward to the move to Lake Manor so that he could start to ride again—in secret. He did not want anyone to see him on a horse until he was sure he could control his mount...and stay on its back. Emma was a remarkably fine horsewoman, and she would have even more cause to despise him if she found he could not stay in the saddle. He would not dare to invite her to ride out with him until he was very, very sure.

His own bedchamber was empty, of course, but it provided the best route to Emma's. If he went in from the corridor, the servants might well see how she received him. They always seemed to be hovering about the guest wing, watching. He had no desire to provide any more food for backstairs gossip.

He hesitated at the door into Emma's room. Was it only a few hours since he had left her there, curled up on the other side of that great bed, as far a possible from her new husband? The very presence of that bed was going to make this interview even more difficult.

But it had to be faced.

He knocked sharply and opened the door, without waiting for an invitation.

The chamber was empty.

The shutters and the windows were open, just as he had left them, but the bed had been made and the curtains drawn back. A heavy wrapper lay across the end of the bed. There was no sign of a nightgown.

Hugo remembered the feel of it—thin, slippery, with long panels of lace at front and back. He wished he had seen how she looked in it, but he had been in too much of a hurry for that. He had needed to feel her naked skin against his own. Had he ripped it? It was possible. It had been such a fragile thing…just like his wife.

This would not do. Nothing could be changed, no matter how guilty he felt. They had to go forward from where they were. He could not apologise for last night—Emma would probably be mortified if he made the slightest reference to that hasty and brutal coupling—but he could certainly apologise for his behaviour in the library.

After a moment's thought, his tactics were decided. It was easy enough to determine what not to say. He could not tell her about Forster. And he would not tell her about Kit's debts. He would simply tell her that he was going to London with Kit; that she was to go to Lake Manor alone. She would probably welcome the time away from him. So would he. While he was not with her, he would not be tempted to break his resolve to stay away from her bed. For that—if only she knew of it—she should be grateful.

Glancing out of the window, Hugo saw that Richard and his guests had remained on the lawn. But Emma was still missing. She must be in the house somewhere—alone.

Time was pressing, but Hugo began a methodical search of all the rooms where she might be found. All were empty. Where on earth had she got to? If she were outside, she would have returned to the party on the lawn. She *must* be in the house. But where?

When the answer came to him, eventually, he groaned. She must be in Lady Hardinge's conservatory, the place where he had attacked her that first time. She had been bristling with outrage then, and she would be so again.

He made his way back downstairs and along the corridor. He looked through the glass panel. There was no sign of her.

He opened the door, not trying to conceal the noise of his arrival. The last thing he wanted was to creep up on her unawares. 'Emma?' he said in a low voice. There was no response. Perhaps he had spoken too softly? 'Emma,' he said again, his voice a little louder.

There was a movement behind the cluster of exotic

plants. They were pushed apart by a petite blonde figure in a pale muslin gown. Against the deep greens around her, Emma looked almost ethereally beautiful. Hugo caught his breath.

She looked at him unwaveringly. Her eyes were as blue as the Spanish sky.

'I am here, Major,' she said.

Chapter Eighteen

That was the last response Hugo had expected. What on earth was the matter with her? Why did she not use his given name? They were husband and wife.

He stood staring at her motionless figure, trying to recall all their exchanges since she had become his wife. She had called him by name at the altar—repeating the words of the chaplain—but he could not remember a single instance when she had done so since they walked together down the aisle. In fact, he could not remember that she had called him anything at all.

Until now.

But that was about to change. Immediately.

'For heaven's sake, Emma. You are my wife, not my lackey. My name is Hugo.'

She nodded coolly in the face of his hot words. 'As you wish.' She did not move.

Hugo forced himself to remain where he was, to keep a distance between them. He moved only far enough to close the door behind him.

'I have had to change my plans, Emma. As a result

of urgent...family business, I must go up to London with Kit. We leave immediately.'

Emma's face brightened. Was she so delighted to be rid of him?

'I will join you at Lake Manor as soon as I can,' Hugo said, trying not to look at her. 'I should not be more than a few days behind you.'

'But I know no one at Lake Manor,' she cried, 'and nothing about the estate. You cannot expect me to go there alone.' Before he could say a word in response, she went on, 'Oh. I see. You are ashamed to have me appear in London, so hard on the heels of the scandal at Epsom. So your solution is to banish me.'

'Nothing of the sort,' Hugo snapped. 'What kind of man do you think I am?'

Her expression gave him his answer. She was hurt; and she thought he was cruel.

'Emma, I cannot take you to London because Kit and I...because Kit and I have business to attend to. And I have no house in London fit for you. I shall be sharing Kit's rooms while I am there.'

Emma sighed. It sounded like exasperation. The expression in her eyes had not softened. 'My father has a London house. He would open it for us if we asked. My Aunt Augusta, too, is always delighted to welcome her family to her London home. And she left for London first thing this morning.'

Hugo waited for her to continue. She was surely about to ask if they might both stay with her aunt. But she said nothing more. In the silence, Hugo realised she was too proud to ask for favours that she feared would be denied. She just looked at him, with hurt in her eyes.

She thought he was ashamed of her. How could he be? She was everything he had ever dreamed of in a wife. A tiny inner voice reminded him that one quality was lacking—she did not love him. He refused to heed it.

'Emma, I promise you I had no thought of banishing you. I merely sought—' He shook his head in annoyance. Excuses would not do here. 'I do not expect to be in London for more than a few days, but if you wish to accompany me—and if suitable accommodation is available with your aunt—I should be more than happy to have you there.'

Emma gave a curt little nod of agreement.

'Then that is settled. Kit and I must drive on today as we planned, but you may follow us as soon as you wish. Will that content you?'

'I will be ready to leave first thing in the morning,' she said promptly. 'May I ask...?' She sounded hesitant. And she was looking at the floor. 'Forgive me, but may I ask about this urgent business? Does it concern me?'

It was the first time she had ventured a question of any kind. Hugo wondered how much she might have heard. Nothing about Forster, surely? She had been long gone before the discussion turned to that blackguard. Kit, then? Possibly. What could he tell her? He could not betray his brother's follies. But neither could he lie to his wife. He had done her harm enough already.

'Kit is going abroad for a time, Emma, and funds

must be arranged before he goes. John is in Scotland, as you know, and so it falls to me, as the next brother, to see to matters.'

Emma blushed fierily. 'A sudden departure, I collect?'

Hugo winced. She thought it was because of her, because of the scandal. He was tying himself in knots, tighter and tighter. And his poor wife, whom he had treated cruelly since their wedding, was being humiliated in the process. She was beginning to look distraught.

Hugo could not stand to see her so. In two strides he was beside her and had taken her in his arms. His resolutions could go hang. 'Emma, it is not what you think. Trust me,' he said in a low voice. He cupped his fingers under her chin and forced her to look up at him. 'Kit's departure has nothing to do with what happened between you. Please believe that. I cannot tell you more without betraying a confidence. I only ask you to trust me.' He gazed into her eyes for a long time, willing her to yield to him. 'Will you do that?' he said at last.

'Of course I trust you, Hugo,' she said immediately, making his heart begin to race. Then she spoiled the moment by adding, 'I am your wife.'

It was too much. He crushed her to him and began to devour her luscious mouth. It was their wedding night, all over again. But, this time, her tiny whimper of protest reached him, damping down the madness that seemed to overtake him whenever he touched her. He dragged his lips from hers and, with an effort, put her from him.

'Forgive me, Emma. That was…uncalled for.'

'As you say. But then—' she stopped, looking up at him through her dark lashes '—I am your wife.'

And this time, she smiled.

Hugo and Kit were together on the step when Emma appeared in the doorway to bid them farewell. She was fully in control now, she was sure of that.

Kit, clearly, was not. The moment Emma appeared, he bowed awkwardly to her and retreated, striding across the gravel to climb into the chaise. Emma did not give him another thought. She was much more concerned about her husband. How would he take his leave of her? He had left the conservatory without another word. He had asked her to trust him—again— but he had explained nothing. And her lips were still burning from his searing, passionate kisses. He desired her still, but he seemed to be fighting desperately to resist his feelings. He did not want to want her. It was all so demeaning.

They would be together again in London. There, they would have a chance to right matters. Or would they? Staying with Mrs Warenne would make life difficult, to say the least. Aunt Augusta was kind, and well-meaning, but she never stopped talking and fussing. She would surely drive Hugo mad. And then there was Kit, too. Would she have to entertain him? If the brothers had such important business to transact, they would certainly be together a great deal. Emma began to think that London was not the solution after all. Lake Manor, for all its remoteness, might have more attractions than she had imagined.

Hugo barely glanced at Kit when his brother strode across to the chaise. Hugo was looking at Emma, and his look seemed very serious indeed. Emma thought his eyes had grown very dark, more black than grey. What was it he saw when he looked at her? If only she knew.

Hugo stepped forward to take Emma's hands in his. He kissed one, then the other, and held them both in his own for a long time, looking deeply into her eyes. Then he leant forward and placed a chaste kiss on her cheek.

'I shall look to find you at your aunt's, in a day or two.'

Emma nodded, but she was still anxious. 'You will join me there, I hope?'

'Of course,' Hugo said calmly. The strong clasp of his hands was reassuring. 'I have no intention of providing any more food for the gossips, you may be sure of that. Take care not to overtax yourself on the journey, my dear. There is no need to rush, you know.'

Something told Emma that there was every need to rush to her husband's side, but it was only a vague feeling. He had told her nothing about the reasons for his haste. That story about arranging money for Kit was not the truth, of that she was sure. Not the whole truth, at any rate.

Hugo was still holding her hands. It felt comforting, and comfortable. She wished he would stay a little longer, so that they might travel together. She was a little afraid of what might happen, though she could not begin to understand why.

The moment lengthened. There seemed to be nothing but Hugo's eyes gazing into hers, and the touch of his hands.

The restless horses broke the spell.

'Goodbye, Emma,' Hugo said softly, with just the suggestion of a smile in his eyes. Then he bent his head and kissed her hands once more, lingering a little over each one. He seemed reluctant to relinquish them.

When he turned to join his brother in the post-chaise, Emma felt as if the pressure of his fingers was still on hers. He had run his thumbs across her palms, leaving an imprint behind like a finger running across velvet. It tingled strangely.

Emma thrust her hands into her skirts. She thought that, if she looked at them, there would be marks.

The chaise started to move. In a few seconds, the horses were speeding down the avenue towards the gates. Soon they would be out of sight.

Emma picked up her skirts and dashed into the house. If she ran, she would be able to catch sight of the chaise from the upstairs window before it turned out of the estate. She was gasping for breath by the time she gained her bedchamber, but she was not disappointed. The chaise was still in sight. Hugo's arm was resting on the frame of the open window, his ungloved hand just visible against the dark wood. And then the chaise was lost to view behind the trees.

She could still feel the warm trail of his fingers across her palm.

Emma opened the connecting door into Hugo's room, hesitating on the threshold. There was no reason not to go in. It was her husband's room. Nevertheless, she felt like an intruder, somehow. This was Hugo's domain. They had never shared it, not in any way. It was a purely masculine room. Even the scents were male—shaving soap, tobacco, a hint of cologne. She crossed to the bed and sat on the very edge, hardly daring to touch. This was where her husband had slept after he left her. If only he had stayed. If he had been there when she woke, things would have been easier between them, surely?

She reached out a hand to smooth Hugo's pillow. Soon, the maids would come to take the bedlinen to be laundered. It would no longer be Hugo's pillow, with Hugo's scent. It would be fresh, and clean, and totally anonymous. He would be gone from her.

Emma lay down on the bed and put her cheek on the pillow, feeling its softness. She could smell the faintest lingering trace of his cologne. She closed her eyes, breathing deeply. For a moment, she would imagine that he was still here, that he was about to come to join her, there on his bed, that he would take her in his arms…that he would tell her he loved her. It was a dream, Emma knew, but such a wonderful dream…

'Emma? Oh, there you are.' It was Jamie's soft voice, sounding a little concerned.

Emma opened her eyes to see her friend's rounded figure standing in the open doorway that led to her own room. She sat up hurriedly, trying to assume a nonchalant pose. What on earth must Jamie think, finding Emma lying on Hugo's bed, eyes closed, fingers stroking the pillow? She would surely think she was run mad.

'I came to ask whether you needed any help. I understand that you plan to leave for London tomorrow.' Jamie sounded neither surprised, nor curious. She was just her usual matter-of-fact self.

'Bless you,' Emma said, and meant it. She did not deserve such a staunch friend. 'I expect we shall be in London for only a few days, and so I shall not need much by way of baggage. If I have Sawyer pack up the rest, perhaps you would be so good as to send it on to Lake Manor?' She rose and followed Jamie back into the other bedroom.

'Certainly I will. But are you sure you may not stay longer in London? Your aunt is bound to press you to remain, especially as the Season is in full swing. I fancy she will wish to parade her newly married niece before the world.'

Emma grimaced. 'I doubt that Hugo would take kindly to that,' she said. 'And what use is a newly married niece if her husband refuses to be paraded at her side?'

Jamie laughed. 'You are quite right. Major Stratton detests being the object of vulgar curiosity, especially now… He is a very private man, I think.'

Emma nodded, but said nothing.

'Emma, will you allow me to give you a word of advice?'

Emma could not look at her friend. She was too embarrassed at the thought of what Jamie might wish to say. But she managed to nod. Jamie was wise, and she had Emma's interests at heart. Her advice would be worth hearing.

Jamie paused, preparing her words. 'I said that your husband is a very private man, Emma. He is proud, too. I think that he is very conscious of his scars and of the weakness caused by his wounds. Richard says Hugo used to be a very active man, never still, always riding out, or shooting, or following some sport or other. It must gall him to be less than the man he was. And it galls him even more—of this I am sure—to think that others might pity him. Especially you, Emma. I think he is afraid that you think him less than a whole man.'

Emma swallowed hard. She could not speak. She nodded to Jamie to continue.

'One of the things I have learned in my own marriage, Emma, is that sometimes it is necessary to take risks.'

Emma looked up in surprise.

Jamie smiled slightly. 'That sounds strange, does it not? I do not mean risks of the physical kind, but risks with your own…your own self-esteem. A proud man will find it difficult, perhaps impossible, to allow his new wife to see his weaknesses, lest she use them to wound him. And if the wife feels the same, then the barriers will never be removed. They will never really be able to talk, or trust, or—'

'But what can I do?' Emma burst out. Jamie's uncanny ability to describe Emma's relationship with Hugo had wiped away any thought of reserve. Jamie knew what was wrong between them. Jamie knew what could be done.

Jamie continued in the same soft, measured voice. 'If the wife is brave enough to expose her own weaknesses first, her husband may learn to trust her enough to do the same. Especially if he loves her.'

Emma shook her head. Hugo did not love her. Jamie was wrong there. He despised her. And she had given him cause. She shook her head again.

Jamie did not pursue the point. 'There is one other thing I must say to you, Emma, though it will worry you, I fear. There is something in your husband's past, relating to his time in the Peninsula. I cannot give you details. Even Richard does not know what happened. I only know that it happened many years ago—and that it worries him still.'

So there *was* something. And it had to do with Colonel Forster, of that she was sure. She thought back to that extraordinary exchange between the Colonel and Kit at the Derby. The animosity had been almost palpable, barely covered by a veneer of politeness. If Richard or Jamie had seen it, there would have been no doubt in their minds about the origins of Hugo's concern.

But they had not seen. They did not know. And it was not Emma's place to tell them. If Hugo wished to share his past with Richard, he would do so, in his own time.

Would he, one day, trust Emma enough to share it with her?

Chapter Nineteen

'Well, my dear, I am delighted to see you. And so soon after your wedding, too.'

Emma nodded politely. Aunt Augusta was at her worst when one had just arrived. The only solution was to allow her to talk herself out.

'I am surprised that the Major permitted you to travel such a way alone, however. Most unseemly.'

Emma could not allow criticism of Hugo, not from anyone. 'But I was by no means alone, Aunt. My abigail was with me and two stout grooms besides. Indeed, I travelled in exactly the same style when I came to you a few weeks ago.'

'Hmph.' Aunt Augusta did not like to be proved wrong. 'When can we expect your husband? I do hope he does not neglect you, now you are both in London, Emma. People are bound to remark on it, if he does not join you here.'

Emma hoped her expression did not betray her. Her aunt had given voice to the thing she most feared. She forced a smile. 'My husband plans to join me here, naturally, but said he would not trouble you until I had arrived,' she lied. 'No doubt he will make an appearance in the course of the day. I have sent word to Kit's lodgings.'

'So that's where he is,' said Aunt Augusta with satisfaction. 'I only hope his presence will serve to curb that wild young man's excesses.'

Emma gritted her teeth, wishing her aunt could be a little less forthright. She did not need to be reminded of the scandal that she and Kit had created.

'Oh, I did not mean you, my dear child,' said Aunt Augusta, stretching across to pat Emma's hand. 'No, indeed. Your brother-in-law's indiscretion at Epsom is all but forgotten now. Have you not heard? He lost five thousand pounds to Lady Luce the very next day.'

Emma gasped. Five thousand pounds was a fortune.

'And Colonel Forster was playing, too, I believe, though his losses were nowhere near as bad as Kit's. I find I cannot like that man, Emma, for all that he is one of the Duke of York's friends. By all accounts, he made very sure that the news of Kit's losses was all over London before breakfast. There is no love lost there, I fancy.'

Emma was well aware of that. She had seen the animosity with her own eyes. But what had possessed Kit to play so high? It was madness. And, of course, he had had to come to Hugo for help. No wonder her husband had been so blazingly angry. He was going to have to use Emma's dowry to pay his wastrel brother's gaming debts.

Was that why Kit was to be sent abroad? And what

of Colonel Forster? What was his role in all this? Emma had instinctively mistrusted the Colonel's motives. He had struck her, on that one short encounter, as a vindictive man—and no true gentleman. She was sure he was not to be trusted, not in any way.

Emma forced herself to pay attention to her aunt's interminable gossip.

'And so Sally Jersey was silenced. I swear it was for the first time in her life.'

'Indeed,' Emma said, wishing that someone would do the same for her aunt.

Her prayer was answered by the arrival of her aunt's butler. He was an old man, slow and rather stooped, but he was still very conscious of his important position in the household. 'Major Stratton has arrived, ma'am,' he began in a pompous voice. 'Shall I—'

'Show him up, man, show him up,' snapped Aunt Augusta. 'There is no need to stand on ceremony with the Major. He is a guest in the house, remember.'

The butler bowed and made his stately way out of the room.

Emma giggled nervously.

'Yes, I know, my dear, but he has been with me for ever. I could not turn him off, no matter how preposterous he has become. It would break his heart.'

Emma nodded. She had not been thinking about the butler. Hugo was downstairs and would appear at any moment. She smoothed her silken skirts and put her hands to her hair.

'You look very well indeed, my dear,' said Aunt

Augusta kindly. 'He will find no fault with your appearance.'

The door was thrown open with exaggerated ceremony. 'Major Stratton to see you, ma'am,' the butler intoned, completely ignoring his mistress's instructions.

Emma thought her aunt muttered irritably under her breath as she rose to greet her guest. Emma rose, too, thankful that her legs were fairly steady beneath her. Her insides had turned over at the sight of him. He was wearing a new blue coat which fitted him much better than those he had worn at Harding. He no longer looked thin. Indeed, he had greater breadth of shoulder than she had remembered. He looked almost normal—tall, straight and strong, the epitome of a gentleman of the *ton*. The only outward sign of his wounds was the scar on his face. Even that was fading. Soon it would be only a thin silvery line.

Hugo bowed elegantly over Mrs Warenne's hand. 'Good afternoon to you, ma'am. I hope I find you well?'

When he moved past Mrs Warenne to greet Emma, she found she was holding her breath. He bowed over her hand, too, but at the last moment, he turned it to place a kiss on her palm. Emma let out her breath in a gasp of surprise.

Hugo looked up into her face and smiled at what he saw there. Then he straightened and placed a chaste kiss on Emma's cheek. 'Good day to you, too, my dear wife,' he said. 'I need not ask if I find you well. It is obvious that you are blooming, in spite of your long and arduous journey up to London.'

'You have a very poor opinion of me, sir, if you think I would find such a journey arduous,' she said, returning his smile.

'*Touché, madame,*' he replied, running his thumb over her palm before finally relinquishing her hand. 'I see that you are as tough as the doughtiest of my soldiers, and that not even the most difficult journey would hold any terrors for you. Beware. I may yet put your mettle to the test.'

Emma's smile widened a little. There was so much warmth in his eyes when he looked at her, and a wicked glint, too, when he teased her. She wished he had not let go of her hand.

Behind them, Aunt Augusta coughed. She was not used to being ignored, especially in her own house. 'I have had a suite of rooms prepared for you,' she said briskly. 'I hope you will both be comfortable.'

Emma knew she had not imagined that slight emphasis on the word 'both'. 'Thank you, Aunt,' she said politely. 'I am sure we shall.'

Aunt Augusta had started talking again, as volubly as before. 'And what of that scapegrace brother of yours, Major? Is he still in London?'

Hugo frowned. Mrs Warenne might be family now, but he did not take kindly to such strictures on Kit, even though he himself was wont to use much harsher language. 'He is well, ma'am, I thank you.'

Aunt Augusta clearly expected him to say more, but his lips were set in the firm line that Emma had already learned to recognise. 'I think perhaps I should like to lie down for a while, after all, Aunt,' she said, rising. 'Especially as we are bidden to Lady Dunsmore's musical soirée this evening. I would not disgrace you by falling asleep during the arias.'

Hugo, too, had risen. Listening to his wife's blatant lies had brought a touch of a smile to the corner of his firm mouth.

Aunt Augusta was not deceived either. 'Get along with you, you little minx,' she said, smiling indulgently. 'And take that husband of yours with you. Show him the rest of the house. He needs to know his way about, now that he's joined the family.'

Hugo bowed and moved to open the door for Emma. No sooner had it closed behind them than he whispered, 'How many days shall we be forced to remain here, Emma? I'd liefer face a French cavalry charge, I think.'

Emma tried not to smile. 'It all depends upon you, sir. I can be ready to leave for Lake Manor as soon as you give the word. Or for anywhere else you should choose.'

'You tempt me, Emma, you tempt me greatly. I should dearly like to carry you off to Paris, or Rome. Never mind. Lake Manor it shall be.' He glanced back at the door with obvious distaste. 'And our deliverance shall not be long delayed, I promise.'

The attractions of Lake Manor were growing by the minute.

Emma had no intention of dragging Hugo all over the house. He would find his way perfectly well by himself. It was only when they arrived at the door to her room that she realised where they were. Heavens, she had brought him straight to her bedchamber. With a quick change of direction, she led him a little further along the corridor and opened the door to a small sitting room. 'Aunt has been most generous, as you see. We have this private sitting room as well as the two bedchambers. Mine is through that door.' She pointed. 'And yours is over there.'

'Splendid,' Hugo said, surveying the comfortable room. When Emma moved towards her own bed-chamber, he strode across to open the door for her. Then, without a word, he went to the sofa and threw himself down on it, closing his eyes and stretching out his long legs with a sigh of relief. Emma watched from the doorway. She fancied she had seen a hint of a limp when he was climbing the stairs. He was tired, clearly. Rest would do him good. She wondered what he had been doing since his arrival in London—apart from dragging Kit out of a very expensive hole. She paused, her hand on the doorknob. 'Would you like some tea? I can send for some if you would like.'

He rose to his feet immediately. 'Forgive me for my rudeness, Emma. I thought you had gone through to lie down.'

'Oh, no,' she replied airily. 'That was only for Aunt Augusta's benefit. I am not in the least tired, as I told you.' It was clear from the tone of her voice that she thought her husband was the one in need of rest.

'You wretch, Emma,' he said with a rueful grin. 'Your face betrays you, you know. Yes, I am tired, but I shall survive, never fear. A cup of tea would revive me wonderfully, I am sure—always provided you remain to share it with me.'

Emma did not attempt to engage in a battle of wits. Hugo was too tired—and she was too unsure of how a wife should behave, especially when they were alone like this...

She crossed to pull the bell and then sat in the chair by the fireplace, so that Hugo would feel able to resume his place on the sofa. Neither spoke again until the tea had been ordered.

'Do you—?'

'Shall I—?'

Both stopped in mid-sentence, laughing awkwardly. From his lazy position on the sofa, Hugo waved an indulgent hand. 'After you, *madame*.'

Emma resisted the urge to repeat the gesture to him. The young man she had known all those years ago had dearly loved a jest, even at his own expense, but the man she had married was not the same. His experiences—whatever they had been—had changed him greatly. She said simply, 'Do you accompany us to the soirée this evening?'

'I fear not, Emma. I am...engaged to Kit. Our business is not yet completed.'

It was a strange sort of business that took place in the hours of darkness, in Emma's opinion, but she refrained from saying so.

'As I said, your face betrays you, my dear,' Hugo said with a wry smile. 'But, truly, I must be with Kit this evening. It cannot be avoided. Our engagement is for later, however, so I could certainly escort you to Lady Dunsmore's and stay for an aria or two. That should silence the wagging tongues. And when I leave, you may tell the tabbies that your husband has absolutely no ear for music and takes to his heels at the first opportunity. A sad case, indeed.'

The arrival of the tea tray intervened to save Emma's blushes. She was sure she would never say anything so insulting, even in jest.

She made to pour but stopped, the silver pot poised over his cup. 'I'm afraid I do not remember how you take your tea.'

Hugo made a face. 'Good grief! What kind of a wife have I saddled myself with?'

This time she was prepared to respond in kind. 'One who will put five spoons of sugar in your tea, if you do not speedily enlighten her.'

'Aargh!' he cried, falling back on the sofa with his hands to his throat. 'My wife has poisoned me!'

Emma threw him a speaking look, replaced the pot and picked up the sugar basin. 'One,' she said menacingly, dropping a spoonful into his cup.

'Spare me!' he cried, grinning like the madcap boy he had once been. 'Save me, fair princess, from the hands of the wife who would murder me!'

'I collect that means only one sugar, Major,' Emma said demurely, pursing her lips to stop herself from responding to his infectious grin. She finished pouring his tea and rose to take it to him.

He was on his feet in an instant. She had not known he could move so fast. If there had been a limp earlier, it certainly did not prevent him from moving his limbs as much and as fast as he wished.

'Emma…' The laughter was gone from his voice. He sounded serious, almost angry. What could be wrong?

'Is something the matter, Hugo?'

He smiled, satisfied. 'Not now,' he said, taking his cup from her. 'Not any more.'

Emma returned to her seat to pour tea for herself. Now was the time. He seemed to have relaxed with her. 'Hugo, will you tell me about your time in Spain?'

'No, my dear, I think not.'

'But you used to write such wonderful letters— Oh! Now I remember.' Emma puzzled over her disjointed recollections for a second. The memory of Hugo's letters had been dancing round at the back of her mind since the day she had first seen him again, but until now it had refused to be caught. Now she grasped it, firmly. 'Those wonderful letters you used to send to Richard every month or so, telling him all about your adventures. When you described your arrival in Portugal, the colours, the noise—I could almost taste it.'

'Richard let you read my letters?' Hugo was troubled to think of it. He could not remember how much he might have said. He was sure they had not been fit for a lady's ears.

'No. But he used to read them aloud to me. Well…parts of them.' Emma smiled at the recollection. 'It all sounded so magical, so different from our humdrum life here in England. I think Richard envied you.'

Hugo grimaced.

'And then the letters stopped.' Emma looked questioningly at her husband. He seemed bleak and distant. 'Richard said you must be too busy to write. Responsibilities and so on. But it wasn't that, was it?'

'No,' Hugo said, refusing to elaborate.

Sensing his withdrawal, Emma did not press him further. She reverted to her gay, light-hearted Society mode. 'And then I went to stay with Aunt Augusta— to be finished, you understand—and I saw Richard much less often. He said you did write—occasion-ally—but he never read your letters to me any more. I missed them. I thought I knew you so well, and then, suddenly, you weren't there any more.' She blushed. 'Oh dear, how childish that must sound. I—'

'It sounds much kinder than I deserve, Emma,' Hugo said wonderingly, 'and I thank you for it. I suppose I should have known that Richard was shar-ing my letters with you. He spoke of you so often in his own.'

Emma was blushing even more now.

'I used to laugh at his tales of your antics. That was all before your aunt turned you into a fine lady, naturally.'

Seeing Hugo's indulgent smile, Emma longed to ask why he had stopped writing, but decided against. It was clearly a very sensitive subject. She had no wish to undermine their new-found rapport. 'Perhaps it is as well that you both stopped writing regularly. You would have been thoroughly bored by anything Richard said of me after I came to live with Aunt Augusta. It was all very tame and insipid, I fear.' She smiled teasingly at him. Would he respond?

Hugo smiled too. 'I take leave to doubt that, my dear.'

'I declare, you seek to insult me, sir,' Emma said

in mock outrage, throwing him a wicked look from under her lashes.

It was too much. He went to her and pulled her roughly into his arms. 'Now that, my dear wife, is something I would never do,' he said huskily, bending his head to touch her lips with his own.

It was a gentle, teasing, tantalising kiss, quite unlike anything he had done before. Emma's whole body responded. Her belly turned to hot, churning liquid, the warmth spreading rapidly up into her breast and down into her thighs. This time she could not remain passive; the feelings were too strong. She leant into him, sliding her arms around his neck, and responding to his lips and his tongue, first shyly, then passionately. Hugo's response was immediate. He pulled her body hard against his own, one hand behind her head, the other gliding down her back. The kiss went on and on. It was terrifying how he made her feel.

It was magical how he made her feel.

At last, Hugo pulled away from her, breathing rapidly. Emma herself was gasping for breath, gazing at him wide-eyed. She did not begin to understand what had happened to her, but she knew she had behaved like a wanton. What would he think of her? She could feel the flush rising on her neck. She turned to flee to her room, but Hugo was before her.

Taking her hand gently, he said, 'Emma, there is nothing to fear.' He raised the hand to his lips, kissing it with exquisite courtesy. 'I have upset you. I apologise. But pray believe that I would never hurt you. You have no need to run from me.'

Emma turned away. She was afraid of what she might see in his eyes. And she knew his words did not excuse her appalling behaviour.

'I will go,' Hugo said quietly. He sounded strained. 'I had hoped you would come to accept me, but I can understand how difficult it must be for a beautiful young woman like you, forcibly married to such a wreck of a husband. Perhaps, in time—'

Guilt engulfed Emma. Her eyes filled with tears that threatened to well over at any moment. She did not want him to see—but she must not let him leave like this. She steeled herself to reply. 'You are wrong, Hugo,' she said in a low voice. 'I am not afraid of you. And you are not—' Her hands were shaking now. She clasped them together in an attempt to hide her emotions from him. In a whisper she continued, 'But I *am* afraid of the way you make me feel.'

Chapter Twenty

In the sudden silence, Emma swallowed hard. What had she said? She must get away from him; she must be alone. Head bowed, she made for the door.

Hugo reached the door in a few strides and pulled it closed. Then he leant back against it, looking intently at her. His arms hung loosely by his sides. He made no move to touch her. A great surge of anger had coursed through him at the thought that he had hurt her, but now, seeing her tears, and hearing her words, he felt only joy. She must be made to believe him now. 'You have no need to be afraid of anything, my dear one,' he said softly, willing her to look at him. He opened his arms to her. 'Come,' he said. 'Let me show you it is true.'

Emma looked up at him then and walked into his embrace without pause for thought. He held her tenderly for a long time, not attempting to kiss her again. She felt warm and protected.

At last, Hugo bent to kiss her tear-streaked face. 'Do not weep, Emma. I promise you there is no need.' He held her gently, hesitating. The moment was too special to be spoilt by allowing his passions to rule him. He desperately wanted to make love to her, but she must be willing, totally and completely willing. He would not repeat the brutality of their wedding night.

He could not find the words to ask her. Instead he began to plant tiny kisses on her eyelids, her cheeks, the corners of her mouth, the side of her neck. When he began to nuzzle her earlobe, she groaned, tightening her arms around him.

'Emma, my dearest, I want you so much,' he said huskily, 'but I am afraid to frighten you with my desire. If you want me to, I will stop. You have but to say the word.' In truth, he was not sure whether he could, especially if she continued to respond to him like this.

'I…' Emma's voice was barely audible. She tried again. 'I am not afraid, Hugo. I do want you to…' She could not say the words, but her blushes told him everything.

'Oh, my beauty,' he said, awe in his voice. 'My sweet, wonderful wife.'

She was blushing so much that she looked to be on fire. This would not do. He must help her through her embarrassment.

He turned to the door that led to her bedchamber, the bedchamber they would share. 'Emma, my dear, I believe I have been remiss in my duty.' Good. Now curiosity was overcoming her embarrassment. 'Is it not a fact that a husband should carry his new wife over the threshold into their new life? And have I not failed?'

'But you cannot,' she said at once. 'Your wounds…your weak arm… Hugo, I am no lightweight, in spite of my lack of inches. Do not attempt it, I beg of you.'

'Am I to understand that my wife has no faith in her husband's ability to perform his duties, ma'am?' he said, trying to assume the kind of voice he used to lacerate an incompetent subaltern. 'You try my patience, wife, indeed you do.'

Clearly, he was not as good an actor as he thought, for his wife was laughing up at him. 'You, sir,' she said archly, 'are a fraud. But, none the less, I beg you will not attempt it.'

'Coward,' he said, laughing with her now. 'Why should I not? For who is there to see, apart from my faithful wife? And she, I know, will not betray me if I should fail, even though she has my permission to upbraid me roundly if I should drop her on the floor.'

Emma shook her head in wonderment, laughing still. It was such a little thing, but the thought that Hugo would trust her to see his weakness was a prize to be cherished. 'Since you are determined, husband, I must obey you. Did I not take a vow to do so?'

Hugo kissed her soundly to seal their bargain. Then he opened the door to her bedchamber and took his stance by the threshold. 'Put your arms around my neck, Emma,' he said crisply, 'and do not let go, whatever happens. This will be something of an experiment…'

Emma did as she was bid. Hugo put his weaker arm around her waist, then bent and slipped his strong right arm under her knees. With a sharp intake of breath, he lifted her from the floor and stepped through the doorway into the bedchamber. He had done it. But it was not enough. It was but a few more steps to the bed—and that was where he should deposit his lovely burden.

After two more steps his hold was weakening.

'Hugo, put me down,' Emma cried.

He took one more step and catapulted them both on to the huge bed in a tangle of arms and legs. Emma lay almost crushed beneath him.

'You did it,' she said, as soon as she had caught her breath. She tightened her arms around his neck. 'And see what an obedient wife I am become—I did not let you go for even a second.'

It was true. And she was laughing up at him, her eyes like huge pools filled with summer sky. She was beautiful. And she was his laughing, willing wife. He lowered his lips to hers, to begin the long, slow, and infinitely delicious task of arousing her passions.

The first knock barely registered with Hugo. But the second knock was louder, more insistent. He raised his head and glanced towards the open door to their sitting room. There was no one there.

The knock came a third time. Someone was in the corridor, and knocking urgently at the door to his own bedchamber. Damn! Damn! Damn! He pushed himself up and swung his body round to put his feet to the floor.

Emma opened wide, unseeing eyes. 'Hugo?'

Again that strident knocking.

She had heard it now. And she clearly expected that someone would walk in on them at any moment.

Hugo took her hand and squeezed it. 'It is nothing, my sweet,' he said reassuringly. 'Someone is a little impatient to find me, that is all. Give me a moment, and I will send him away with a flea in his ear.' He looked down at her. She was so desirable that his whole body ached for her. 'Stay there,' he whispered. 'I shall be but a moment.' He made for the door, mechanically straightening his cravat.

In his own bedchamber, the knocking had continued. Hugo wrenched open the door. 'What the devil is the meaning of all this noise?' he cried angrily, and then stopped in surprise.

Trouble.

'Oh, God,' Hugo said wearily, 'what is it this time?'

Kit said nothing, merely glancing warily up and down the corridor.

'I suppose you'd better come in,' Hugo said, turning away and leaving his brother to shut the door behind him. Hugo himself was more concerned to ensure that the door to the sitting room was securely closed. It would not do for Emma to hear anything that was said.

Emma kept her eyes closed and desperately tried not to think. Thinking would get in the way of feeling—and feeling was blissful. He wanted her. When he touched her, she burned. When he kissed her, she longed to melt into him, to become part of him. In a moment, he would return, and he would start to kiss her again...

She felt her limbs sinking weakly into the soft bed.

It was a kind of lethargy—and yet every fibre of her body was tingling in expectation of a resumption of his touch. He had the ability to bring her alive, as she had never been. She let out a long, contented sigh and snuggled deeper still. Time together—alone—was the answer to their problems. She was more than ready to let him see her weaknesses, if only he would show her that he did not despise her. And surely he could not? Not now. Not the way he had touched her.

She began to relive the last few minutes, the kisses, the laughing words, the joy of being carried in his arms. She would keep those pictures in her heart for ever, she told herself, trying hard to remember exactly how his brow had furrowed with the exertion of carrying her across the threshold. He was much, much stronger than she had thought. Much, much stronger...

The effort of focusing her mind was becoming increasingly difficult. She had forgotten how tiring a long carriage journey could be. Perhaps Aunt Augusta had been right. It would not matter if she took just a little nap. Hugo would be sure to wake her when he returned...

'No, ma'am,' said the abigail, white-faced, 'that is exactly what the Major said. He made me repeat it twice before he left with the other gentleman.'

Emma rose from her chair and began to pace. It could not be true. He had promised. 'Tell me again, Sawyer,' she said sharply.

'The Major said to tell you as how he had been called away on urgent business. He would try to return to escort you to Lady Dunsmore's, ma'am, but you were not to delay on his account if he did not arrive in time.'

'I see,' Emma said unhappily. What could be so urgent, so important, that he could walk out on her without a word? That was not the act of a caring husband. She felt an overwhelming urge to throw something, but she managed to resist. The ornaments in this room belonged to her aunt.

'Oh, and he said to give you his apologies, ma'am. I forgot that the first time.'

'Thank you,' said Emma quietly. That was some small consolation, though hardly enough to make up for her shattered dreams. She was desirable, but her attractions appeared to rank well below a casual summons from one of his male friends. She was clearly insignificant in Major Hugo Stratton's world. He had paused only to change his dress, and then left without a word.

It would not do to let him see how much his neglect had hurt her. She had shown him weaknesses enough already. Tonight, she would show him the practised lady of the *ton*, at home in the most exalted company. He would not be *allowed* to despise her. She would show him…

But would he condescend to appear at all? Emma swallowed a very unladylike curse.

'You had better make a start on my hair, Sawyer,' she said, moving calmly to sit down at the dressing-table. 'Something fairly plain, please. Tonight I shall leave the froth and feathers to the singers, I think.'

* * *

Hugo arrived back at Mrs Warenne's house just as the ladies were on the point of leaving. The carriage stood at the open door. He could see shining silks and flashing jewels in the hallway beyond.

He took the steps two at a time, something he had not even dared to try until now. But there was no time to savour the moment. Emma was standing a little way behind her aunt—and looking daggers at him. Her anger only served to enhance her golden beauty. She was wearing a simple low-necked gown of old gold silk and her shining hair was severely dressed in a knot on top of her head. Her only jewellery was a pair of topaz earrings and the plain gold wedding band he had put on her finger.

He was still relishing the sight of her when her aunt interrupted, tapping him on the arm with her folded fan. The purple feather on her elaborate turban wobbled precariously with every movement. 'We had all but given you up, Major.'

'My apologies, ma'am,' he said immediately, with a polite bow. 'It was not my intention to have you wait.'

'No,' said Mrs Warenne sharply, 'but you knew very well that we were agreed it would be best for you and your wife to arrive together.'

Hugo nodded. There was nothing he could say. Out of the corner of his eye, he could see that Emma was enjoying his discomfiture. That did not bode well for the rest of the evening.

'I can see that there is no time to be lost, ma'am,' he said with a grim smile, offering his arm to Emma's aunt. 'May I escort you to your carriage?'

Mrs Warenne looked suspiciously at him, but apparently saw nothing amiss. She allowed him to help her down the steps and into the carriage. Emma followed, unescorted. When Hugo turned to help her down the steps, he found that she was already beside him on the flagway. He held out his hand to help her into the carriage.

'Thank you,' she said, in a cold, polite voice. He might as well have been a servant, for she did not look at him. The pressure of her hand on his was so fleeting that he could not be sure she actually touched him. She took her seat beside her aunt and started to make conversation as if he did not exist.

And with all three of them in the carriage, it would be useless to attempt any kind of explanation. Hugo swallowed his burgeoning anger and took his place in the carriage opposite the ladies, allowing them to monopolise the conversation throughout the short journey to Lady Dunsmore's.

'Ah, here we are at last,' said Mrs Warenne, for all the world as if they had been travelling for hours. She looked at her niece sitting rigidly alongside her. 'I think it would be for the best if you were to go in on the Major's arm, Emma,' she said decidedly. 'No need to wait for me. The footman will help me down.'

'As you wish, Aunt,' Emma said in a colourless voice.

Hugo wanted to shake her. She was behaving like a spoilt child. Just give him a moment alone with her...

He alighted first and reached up to offer his hand to his wife. She fixed her gaze on a point over the top of his head when she put her hand in his. Hugo caught her fingers and squeezed sharply, surprising her into looking directly at him. 'Emma,' he said in a warning whisper, 'remember how important this is.'

Her eyes widened. She gave the tiniest nod.

Hugo gave a sigh of relief, tucking her gloved fingers under his arm while he led her up to the entrance. With his free hand, he gave her an encouraging pat. 'Smile,' he said softly.

Smile.

Emma groaned inwardly. She was to be put on show, as she had been on her wedding day. The slightest chink in her armour, and the tabbies' claws would reach in to tear her flesh. She straightened her back even more. It would not be allowed to happen.

One step at a time.

Smile.

Chapter Twenty-One

The interminable aria was followed by warm applause—much too warm, in Hugo's opinion. The tenor had definitely been straining a great deal to reach his top notes, and at least one of them was decidedly flat. Hugo would be glad to leave.

He looked down at Emma at his side, engrossed in polite conversation with her other neighbour. He would not be glad to leave her like this. She was still bristling with anger. He could almost feel it sparking out across the gap between their bodies. The laughing, willing wife who had lain in his arms had been supplanted by a hissing cat, ready to scratch his eyes out the moment he said a word to her. It was almost impossible to believe that these were two aspects of the same woman. She was desirable, delightful—and utterly exasperating. She made him furious. She made him ache for her. She was driving him mad.

He did not see what else he could have done. There had been barely time enough to change into evening dress—and certainly no time to write a note to her. There would have been time—just—for a kiss and a few words, but when he saw her so peacefully asleep, her cheek pillowed on her hand, he could not bring himself to wake her. He had even resisted the temptation to stroke the peach-like bloom of her cheek.

And in the end it had been for nothing. They had not found Forster, or any useful evidence against him. Kit's supposedly infallible source of information was as unreliable as all the others. So far, they were making no headway at all. Their carefully crafted plans for dealing quietly with the blackguard colonel might have to give way to more direct action, unless they could find an opening very soon. Forster's rumours were beginning to be repeated in the clubs; they had to be scotched. Perhaps tonight they would find the lever they needed? At least they knew that Forster could not fail to appear this time, since he himself had issued the challenge to the assembled hazard players. Everyone had agreed to return to the table to give Forster a chance to recoup his losses.

In the interval between the arias, Hugo rose and extended his hand to Emma. 'My dear,' he said politely, 'I have to leave now, as you know. Will you walk with me to the door?'

Emma looked first at Hugo and then at his outstretched hand. She had no choice. She could not possibly refuse her husband's request in front of all these witnesses. He obviously knew it, too.

'Of course,' she said, rising. 'Excuse me for a few moments, Mrs Gray. I hope to return before the music restarts. It would be a pity to miss such splendid entertainment, do you not think?'

Emma's neighbour nodded her agreement. Hugo

took her hand in his and led her out into the hallway where he bent and whispered in her ear, 'Emma, you lie with such conviction, you should have been on the stage. You would have made a fortune.'

'Thank you, sir,' Emma said bitterly. She should have known he would wish to take her to task. He was the one in the wrong, but he would surely put the blame on her. 'I take it there was something more you wished to say to me?'

Hugo straightened as if he had been stung. 'Indeed there was,' he said sharply. 'It was this. Whatever may be wrong between us is a private matter. It is not to be spread around London as a result of your childish behaviour.'

Emma gasped.

'Think, Emma. Think of the impression you are creating and the gossip you are giving rise to. You are supposed to be a new—and happy—bride, but you have spoken hardly a word to your husband all evening. You hold yourself aloof in the most obvious way. You smile—I grant you that—but a painted smile would be more natural than yours. You look, for all the world, like a martyr going to the stake.'

'Have you quite finished?' Emma hissed. She was having difficulty controlling her temper.

'For the moment,' Hugo said crisply, beckoning to the footman to bring his hat and cane. 'We will discuss this in the morning, Emma, when we have both cooled a little. And, in the meantime, I would strongly counsel you to have a care how you act. A lady's reputation, once lost, cannot be regained.'

Emma bit back the words that rose to her lips. The

servant was watching them with barely concealed curiosity. She could not afford to insult Hugo in public, however much satisfaction it might give her.

Hugo bent over her gloved hand for a moment, before leaning forward and gently kissing her cheek. 'Goodnight, my dear,' he said, loudly enough for the servants to hear. 'Forgive me for deserting you but, as you know, I have an engagement that cannot be broken. Do not wait up for me. I may be very late.' He smiled at her. It was a crooked smile. And, as he smiled, the steely hardness melted from his eyes. He leant forward once more. 'Sleep well, my dear wife,' he whispered. Then he was gone.

Emma stood for several moments staring at the door. Her face was beginning to ache from the effort of maintaining that fixed smile. She allowed her muscles to relax. No one would think it surprising if she ceased to smile, having bade farewell to her husband.

She needed to be alone. She needed to think.

She strolled back along the hallway, bypassing the door to the music room in favour of a small, empty saloon with a bay window. She pushed her way behind the drawn curtains and looked out into the street, trying to catch a glimpse of Hugo's tall figure. Too late. He had gone to keep his engagement, whatever it was. He had left her here to mend her reputation as best she might.

She stroked the plush velvet with the back of one hand. How very soft and sensuous it felt, to be sure. It reminded her of the way Hugo had stroked her skin—with a touch so light and gentle that it was as if a butterfly had settled there.

She continued to stroke the pile in a long sweeping motion. It was almost hypnotic. She wanted to close her eyes and sink into strong, loving arms—Hugo's arms. It was no use trying to stoke her anger. It would serve only to make things worse between them, when—if she were to admit the truth—she wanted things to be as they were before that cursed knock on the door. She wanted—

Footsteps on the wooden floor interrupted her thoughts. She shrank back against the wall, hoping that her presence would not be noticed. How could she explain herself, if she were found hiding behind the curtains in an empty room? It would have the appearance of an assignation, and with Hugo now gone— It did not bear thinking about. She held her breath.

'Thank goodness for a little peace,' said an elderly female voice. 'What on earth persuaded Amelia Dunsmore to hire that man? He must be the worst tenor in London.'

'She doesn't know the difference,' drawled a younger voice. 'Never did have the least ear for music, y'know. Thinks musical evenings will enhance her standing.' She gave a very unladylike snort.

'I was surprised to see the Strattons here,' said the older woman. 'Were not you? She always was a pert little madam, I thought, but to walk in here on her husband's arm, as though it was the most natural thing in the world... I didn't think even *she* would have the gall to do that. Still, I suppose we should be grateful she didn't arrive with the brother in tow as well.'

The younger woman laughed nastily. 'Kit is to be sent abroad, by all accounts. Major Stratton apparently made that the price of clearing the young man's debts. And, of course, it will also ensure that Kit is kept well away from the new Mrs Stratton. He's no fool, the Major.'

'He may be no fool, but...' The voice was lowered to a conspiratorial whisper. 'The latest *on dit* is that he's nothing like the hero he purports to be. Had you not heard? When he was in the Peninsula, he was all but cashiered for insubordination and cowardice.'

'*No!* Surely not? We would all have known, long before this.'

'Apparently it was hushed up. Wellington himself did not want it known. He must have some distant link with the Stratton family, or something of the kind. It was all put down to a misunderstanding. The officers were transferred.'

'Then Emma Fitzwilliam is well served,' hissed the younger voice. 'She deserves it, after queening it in Society for so long, and tempting all the eligible young men away from young ladies of much better pedigree.'

'You are probably right, my dear. And I am sure your daughter will receive several eligible offers this Season. She looks remarkably well, especially now that you are dressing her at Célestine's.'

A male voice intervened. 'Excuse me, ladies. Lady Dunsmore asked me to tell you that refreshments are about to be served. Will you come this way?'

Slippered footsteps retreated. There was the sound of a closing door.

Behind the curtain, Emma sagged against the wall, her clenched fist hard against her quivering lips.

It was not true!

She wanted to throw open the curtains and scream the words after those wicked women. It was not true! Hugo Stratton was no coward. He had almost died at Waterloo, while Forster—his accuser, without a doubt—had sat snugly in Horse Guards, resting on the patronage of his royal crony.

She would have to tell Hugo what she had heard. He had to know what was being said of him. But how could she? He was already furious with her for behaving like a spoilt child. And he was right. She had done exactly that. If only she had known...

She must make amends. She must help Hugo.

Pulling aside the curtain, she went back into the room and made for the door. There would be no more eavesdropping. She must do what she could to retrieve the situation, here and now. She could not defend Hugo's honour against his malign accusers, not yet at least, but she would show those harpies that she was happy—aye, and proud—to be Hugo Stratton's wife.

'I still can't understand what possessed you to do such a thing, Hugo. We could have found another way, surely?'

'Keep your voice down, Kit. It's after four in the morning. Do you want to wake the whole household?'

Kit gave his brother an exasperated look, but allowed his voice to sink to a whisper. 'If only you had told me what you meant to do. Why couldn't you let *me* challenge him? I am younger and fitter than you are, and a better shot, besides.'

'And you have no real cause. He would have refused to fight you, you know. He's so much older than you are that it would have seemed perfectly proper. Against me, on the other hand, he had no such excuse. Some of those around the table were well aware of the vile rumours Forster has been spreading. He had no honourable way of avoiding my challenge. He would have been ruined, and branded a coward himself. That might have been justice, but he was not fool enough to do it. No, Kit, I had to be the one. I am the target of his lying tongue. And I am the one who has comrades to avenge.'

Kit shook his head despairingly.

'You can procure another second today, I take it?' Hugo asked. 'I could send to Richard, or one of my other friends, but it would only lead to delay. We must have this speedily resolved, before even worse rumours start. Emma has suffered enough. She would be totally humiliated if Forster's rumours were added to the gossip over our marriage. I could not let that happen, Kit. Let it be tomorrow morning, and early.' He laughed wryly. 'I would happily let Forster sweat, but I don't want him to have too much time for sword practice.'

'Good God, Hugo, surely not swords? He would truly have you at a disadvantage then. When was the last time you used a sword?'

'I'm not as weak as you imagine, Kit, though I'll own I'm not in practice. If he chooses swords, I'll have to rely on remembering all my old skills and hoping my body will respond to the challenge. My sword arm is still strong enough, I think.' He paused to look assessingly at his brother's worried face. 'But, on reflection, I fancy Forster will choose pistols. He's not man enough for cold steel. Too protracted. Too many chances that I might kill him. And he'd have to be prepared to look me in the eye, which isn't his style at all. With pistols, we keep our distance. And I have only one shot.'

'You won't miss?'

'No. I won't miss. Langley and the others will be avenged.'

'Good. Though a quick death is better than he deserves.'

'You're too bloodthirsty, Kit. I shan't kill him. I would have—before—but not now.'

Kit looked hard at his brother. 'But—' he began. He stopped, frowning. 'No. It is not for me to say. You will do as you think fit.'

Hugo smiled. Kit was learning, at last.

Kit cleared his throat. 'Forster will kill *you*, if he has the chance, Hugo, whether it's swords or pistols.'

'I know that. And he's not above a trick or two, either, if he thinks it might help his cause. I look to you to watch my back. Believe me, I have every intention of coming off with a whole skin. I've wasted enough time playing the wounded soldier. I have better things to do, now.'

Kit grinned knowingly but said nothing.

'I need to change—and wash away the smell of Forster.' Hugo grimaced. 'I will join you at your lodgings as soon as I can. You can give me an early break-

fast, before you go to settle matters with Forste[r]
seconds. And then you can give me a little practi[ce]
if Forster does decide for swords. We'd have to f[ind]
a quiet spot, I suppose, since it's Sunday?'

'I think I can find somewhere suitable, broth[er]
though I am sure it won't be needed. Leave eve[ry]
thing to me.' With a breezy wave, Kit left to ro[ut]
out a fellow second.

Hugo sighed at the closing door. He had [not]
planned for this at all, though Kit seemed to belie[ve]
that he had. He had known at once, from the reactio[n]
of the players round the hazard table, that Forste[r's]
ready tongue had already begun to accuse him of [un]
speakable things. The gentlemen were clearly cha[ry]
about being seen in the company of a man who h[ad]
been branded a coward by his own commanding [of]
ficer. When Hugo had reached for the dice, the ge[n]
tleman on his left had pulled his hand away as if [it]
had been burnt. Hugo had known—then—that he h[ad]
no choice but to force a challenge on Forster—ev[en]
if he died as a result. That was certainly possible. [For]
all his show of confidence to Kit, Hugo knew t[hat]
Forster was likely to choose swords. If he did, Hu[go]
would be at a severe disadvantage. Unless he co[uld]
bring the duel to a very speedy conclusion, he w[as]
bound to lose, for he was not strong enough to end[ure]
a lengthy contest.

His sweet Emma would be a widow before she h[ad]
really become a wife.

Chapter Twenty-Two

Emma lay on her side, staring out through the open curtains towards the garden. The sun was up long ago, but her husband had not returned. Surely she would have heard something if he had? She had deliberately left open the door to their sitting-room, in hopes that he would see and come to her. There were so many things she needed to say to him—that she believed in him, that she loved him…that she was sorry for her appalling behaviour.

She had lain awake, waiting, but he had not come.

The sound of distant bells reminded her that it was Sunday. She rose and went to the window. It was a beautiful day. And they must go to church. Would Hugo return in time to accompany them? He had said he would speak to her this morning when his temper had cooled—and hers, too. He had known perfectly well that she was furious with him. Had he known why? Possibly not. In any case, her reasons were petty and insignificant now, in the light of Forster's nefarious accusations. She shuddered at the thought of what the man might yet do, for he was clearly out to ruin Hugo.

Emma told herself sternly to stop thinking about Forster. Spinning ever more fantastic possibilities would only serve to heighten her own fears. She must concentrate on what she could do. She could outface the gossips, just as she had done at Lady Dunsmore's last night, and she could show Hugo that she believed in him and would do her utmost to help him...if he would let her.

Oh, if only he would come home.

Tightening the belt of her heavy wrapper, she crossed into the little sitting-room and put her ear to the door of Hugo's bedchamber. No sound at all. If he was there, he must be asleep.

She put her hand on the doorknob. The polished brass was cool and slippery to the touch. It needed a firm grip but her palm was damp. She rubbed it vigorously on the side of her wrapper, grasped the handle firmly, and opened the door.

The room was empty.

All the curtains were open. The bed had not been slept in. Emma wandered slowly into the room, touching first the table by the bed, then the hangings, then the bedpost. If only he would come home to her.

She sank on to the bed, listlessly surveying the rest of the room. Hugo's valet was clearly not up to his work, for he had left some of his master's clothes draped over the back of a chair in thoroughly haphazard fashion.

Evening clothes.

Emma flew across the chamber. She had to be sure

There was no room for doubt. These were the clothes Hugo had been wearing at Lady Dunsmore's last evening. He must have returned at some time during the night, changed his dress without even calling for his valet, and left again. Without a word to his wife.

She ran her fingers over his crumpled cravat. Where was he? What was going on? An involuntary shiver shook her frame. It was Forster. The business that Hugo and Kit had to attend to so urgently—it was Forster.

And it was very, very dangerous.

Hugo had now spent at least half an hour pacing up and down in Kit's rooms. What the devil was keeping them? It was only a simple matter of agreeing the hour and the place—and the weapons. There was no point in wasting their breath over attempts at conciliation. That was impossible.

Hugo had hoped to be in time to escort Emma to church. He knew she would need his support.

Emma. His wife—who might soon become a widow, especially if Forster chose swords, as he was surely bound to do. Hugo must write a letter to leave behind for Emma. And now was as good a time as any. She was amply provided for—his will had been made at the time of their marriage—but he could not desert her with no word of explanation. That would be unspeakably cruel.

He sat down at Kit's untidy writing table, eventually finding the materials he needed. What could he say? The ink dried on his pen as he gazed at the blank

wall. How could he tell his wife of less than a week
that she was become a widow because of something
that had happened all those years ago, because of men
who were long dead and buried? Was he to tell her
that he loved her, but that love alone was not enough
to prevent the duel? No. He could never tell her that,
though it pained him deeply to know that she was
bound to think it. Would she ever believe that he had
cared for her at all?

There was no way out of that impasse. He must
simply stick to the bare facts.

Swiftly, he wrote an account of what Forster had
done—and might still do. God willing, she would understand that he had had no choice.

'I go to avenge their honour, and my own,' he
wrote, concluding his recital of Forster's iniquities. '
ask you to forgive me for my failure to return to you
To do so was my greatest wish. Your loving husband
Hugo.'

Kit came in just as Hugo was putting the sealed
letter safely in an inner pocket. It was as well that he
knew nothing of it, Hugo thought. With the confidence of youth, Kit was certain his elder brother could
not lose. Hugo—older, and much more experienced
in the ways of men—was not so sure.

Hugo rose, grateful to find that his heartbeat was
as steady as ever. His fears were for Emma, not for
himself, but for her those fears were very real. If he
should die, his widow would be at the mercy of Forster and his cronies, who would do their best to ruin
her, too. That thought terrified him. It must not be
allowed to happen.

In two strides he was at Kit's side and had laid a hand on his shoulder. 'Kit,' he said urgently, 'if I should fall, *you* must protect Emma from Forster. You must give me your word on it, Kit.'

Kit grinned. 'You have it, Hugo, but there is no need. It is pistols.'

Hugo's jaw clenched. Surely not?

'Why do you look so surprised?' said Kit. 'You yourself predicted it. The man has not the stomach for a long drawn-out fight. Indeed, I am not convinced he has the stomach for any fight at all. We did not see the man himself, of course, but his seconds seemed decidedly uncomfortable about something.'

'That is of no moment. Come. Tell me what you have agreed. Is it for tomorrow?'

'Yes. At five o'clock,' Kit said, and then proceeded to detail the rest of the arrangements. 'Now it only remains for me to ensure we have a surgeon on hand. I shall do that this morning.'

'Good,' said Hugo curtly. 'Now, I must go. I am already late. You will have the carriage at Mrs Warenne's in good time tomorrow?'

Kit nodded. 'You may rely on me.'

'I know that,' Hugo said sincerely. He gripped his brother's hand fiercely for a moment. 'And I thank you.'

It took too long to find a hackney and too long for it to thread its way through the traffic. All the inhabitants of London seemed to be out upon the streets on this Sunday morning.

He was too late. Emma and her aunt were long gone.

Hugo made his way impatiently to the church, but
the service was well under way. He could not interrupt by arriving so late. That would cause even more
scandal, more trouble for Emma. He would wait until
she came out and then join her as if it were the most
natural thing in the world.

He paced up and down St George Street for what
seemed like hours. Why was it that, on this day of all
days, the service had to go on so long? The sermon-
ising should have been over hours ago. He paused to
gaze at the grand doorway of St George's, willing the
service to end. His gloved hand gripped the railing
ever more tightly, as if he were trying to snap it to
relieve his frustrations. They had so little time left.
They needed to be together.

The congregation began to emerge at last, most of
them stopping for a few words with the vicar. Where
was Emma? He scanned the crowd for her petite
blonde figure. Perhaps she was not here at all? Perhaps her abigail had mistaken the church?

This would not do. He marched across the street
and up the steps, forcing his way through the chat-
tering worshippers. Emma and her aunt were just
emerging from the gloom, hidden behind two elderly
ladies who were so large that they almost overflowed
the aisle.

Emma's face lit up when she spied him. She was
not yet close enough to speak, but she smiled, a wonderfully tender smile such as she had never before
granted him. She was surely telling him he was forgiven—and more, too, perhaps?

Hugo held out his hand and waited for her to come

to him. She did so without a word, smiling still as he tucked her hand under his arm and possessively placed his gloved fingers over hers. He gazed down at her glowing face. There was nothing to say. It was enough to have her touching him, looking up at him with that soft gleam in her azure eyes.

'You are late, Major.'

Confound it! The impossible aunt! For a moment, it had seemed as if he and Emma stood alone on the step. But that was an illusion. Reality had intruded, like a blow, in the shape of Mrs Warenne.

'Good morning, ma'am,' Hugo said, bowing quickly so that she would not offer her hand. He had no intention of letting go of his wife for even a second. 'I am afraid I was unavoidably detained. Pray accept my apologies.'

Mrs Warenne nodded an acknowledgement and launched into a description—in excruciating detail—of the glories of the service he had missed.

Hugo closed his eyes for a second and took a deep breath in an attempt to control his urge to strangle the woman. He wanted...he needed to be alone with his wife, but her aunt seemed determined to prevent it. Now she had finished talking about the sermon and was laying out plans for the rest of their day. Had she no understanding at all?

It seemed not.

'Ah, here is the carriage at last,' she said. 'Where was I? Ah, yes. I had thought that, since we have no engagements this evening, we might dine quite informally and have a little music afterwards. Emma may sing for us. She has such a beautiful voice. Do you know, Major, that, until she came to me at sixteen, she had had hardly any training at all? Most remiss of my brother. And I told him so, in no uncertain terms. However, I soon put matters to rights. It was only a question of finding the best London masters and, naturally, I knew exactly how to do that.'

Hugo felt a gentle pressure on his arm. He looked down at his wife. She was smiling politely now—her company smile—as she listened to her incorrigible aunt, but the expression in her eyes was eloquent. He could read rueful laughter and resignation...and something deeper, something almost hidden. Was it longing?

If only the blasted woman would vanish off the face of the earth. He needed to be alone with his wife. And she with him. He could read that in her eyes. It was almost as if Emma knew how little time they had left.

'At last,' said Aunt Augusta, sinking into a crimson damask chair. 'What an incredibly boring day we have had, to be sure. With no engagements, it is difficult to know how to pass the time, especially on a Sunday. Do you not agree, Emma?'

Emma acquiesced politely. What else could she do? Hugo had spent the whole day at her side but they had barely had a moment alone. Aunt Augusta had hovered around them like a persistent wasp which could not—unfortunately—be swatted.

'Will you play, Emma? I am sure the Major will not linger over his port when there is no male company.'

Emma rather fancied that Hugo might enjoy the blessed silence of a few moments alone with a glass of wine, but she was proved wrong. The door opened to admit him before she had played more than a few bars. She smiled at him, willing him to come to her. He could pretend to be turning her music, surely?

'Ah, there you are at last, Major,' said Aunt Augusta acidly. 'Do come and sit here by me, so that we can both appreciate Emma's talent.'

Emma's fingers fumbled the notes.

'Good gracious, Emma, what is the matter with you? I have just been telling your husband what a fine player you are, too. Perhaps you would like to start again.'

It was a statement, not a question. Emma was sure she must be as red as her aunt's chair. To cover her embarrassment, she busied herself with choosing a different piece, something loud enough to cover even the worst of her aunt's carrying voice.

She began to play, without bestowing so much as a glance on either of them. She did not dare. She forced herself to concentrate on the difficult phrasing of the sonata and when she reached the *fortissimo* passage, she fairly pounded the keys in her frustration. If only they were at Lake Manor, or at Harding…or anywhere else but here.

The gentle slow movement calmed her. She could hear Hugo's deep voice talking quietly to her aunt. What could he be saying?

The final lively movement was soon over. Hugo rose from his seat, applauding, and came across to the instrument, closely followed by Aunt Augusta. 'I

have prevailed upon your aunt to play for us, Emma,'
he said, smiling at her in the strangest way. 'I should
like to try—here, in the privacy of Mrs Warenne's
drawing-room—whether I can learn to waltz again.
Will you honour me, my dear?' He held out his hand.

Emma sat, frozen, staring up at him in disbelief.

'Come along, my dear,' said Aunt Augusta sharply.
'If you do not give up your place, I shall dance with
the Major myself, you know.'

Hugo bent down and took Emma's hand from her
lap, gently raising her from the stool. 'You do not
object?' he said very softly.

Emma closed her eyes and shook her head.

'Good,' he whispered and pulled her into his arms.
He turned towards the instrument. 'When you are
ready, ma'am?'

Aunt Augusta began to play a waltz, marking the
time rather too strongly. Emma wanted to focus on
helping Hugo, but her feet seemed to be weighted
with lead. His hand was burning its way through the
back of her gown, and that familiar heat was starting
to uncoil in her belly.

Hugo bent his head so that his lips were close to
her ear. 'I know I am much in need of practice, my
sweet wife, but I begin to think that you are no better.'
Emma could hear the thread of laughter in his voice.
'Shall I dance with your aunt instead?'

His light-hearted mockery almost made her laugh.
She steadied herself. She must try to ignore his touch.
She must mind her steps.

She tried to concentrate on his cravat. That seemed
to work rather better than looking up into his face.

Hugo's grey eyes, full of teasing mischief, were like to be her undoing.

He had begun a little stiffly, but now he was starting to move with much greater ease, guiding her deftly into turns and reverses. He had obviously been a very good dancer, before. With a little more practice, he would be the equal of any of her cavaliers.

When the music ended, Hugo let her go, bowing formally. Emma automatically sank into a curtsy.

Before Aunt Augusta could say a word, Hugo smiled generously at her and said, 'That was splendid, ma'am. You play quite delightfully. But one waltz has simply proved how much I am in need of practice, as you, with your unerring eye, will certainly have seen. I should disgrace you by daring to step on to a dance floor as I am. Might I prevail upon you to play just one more waltz?' Aunt Augusta was so flustered by his compliments that she nodded without speaking. Emma was astonished.

Hugo held out his hand to Emma once more. His face wore a look of studied innocence. His eyes were laughing.

They had barely begun this second waltz when he whispered, 'After this, I think we should retire to our suite, do not you?'

Emma stumbled, but his strong arm steadied her.

He grinned wickedly at her. 'I am minded to continue our practice upstairs—alone.'

Chapter Twenty-Three

'**W**ill you honour me, *madame*?' Hugo held out his hand.

Emma stared at his fingers in amazement. She could not move another inch. It had taken all her courage to accept his invitation to accompany him upstairs at such an early hour. Hugo had delivered his proposal with every appearance of innocence, but Aunt Augusta had not been deceived. Emma could still see the look of distaste on her aunt's face, as if she had just been confronted by a bad smell.

Hugo closed the space between them, took Emma's right hand in his left, and pulled her towards him.

Emma felt suddenly very shy. 'Wh-what are you doing?' she stammered.

'Exactly what I said I should do. Practising the waltz,' he said with maddening simplicity.

Emma gasped, but it was too late. Her husband had started to dance her round their little sitting room, steering expertly between the chairs and tables and humming a waltz all the while. It was absurd. It was childish. It was heaven. She had been longing to be held in his arms and to be alone with him. Now, at last, it was happening. A bubble of laughter rose in her throat, demanding to be liberated. This was what she had ached for since the moment he had stretched out his hand to her on the step of the church. She let her laughter peal out, joyous as Easter bells.

Hugo stopped humming long enough to say, 'I hope you are not making mock of my singing, wife. I know I am not your equal, not by any means, but I believe I can hold a tune.' He did not wait for a response. Waltzing required music. He resumed his humming.

He really had a very fine voice, Emma decided, a baritone as rich and as warm as thick, dark chocolate. Without quite knowing when she had begun, she found herself humming in harmony with him, blending her voice with his. To Emma, it sounded as if they had been made to sing duets together.

When Hugo put his lips on the topmost curve of her ear, Emma's humming stopped abruptly; she gasped in response to his warm breath on her face. The feeling was amazingly seductive, even though he was barely touching her. It felt as if his humming was vibrating every inch of her skin. A shiver ran down her spine. The tiny hairs on her arms prickled in response to his nearness. Hugo seemed to sense the change in her, for he pulled her even closer, holding her so that their bodies touched from breast to thigh. She could feel the hardness of him against her belly and his chest crushing her breasts into her ribs. Her heart was beating very fast, knocking so strongly that he must surely be able to hear it. Could he not see what he was doing to her?

Hugo continued to waltz, supporting Emma with his strength, pulling her ever closer. And he continued to hum until her whole body was quivering like the strings of a harp, plucked by a master's hand.

Slowly, delicately, he began to undo the buttons on the back of her gown. She felt his fingers moving on her. She knew he was timing each move with the steps of the dance. She found she was waiting eagerly for every touch, for it was taking them closer to something she knew she desired, perhaps as much as he.

Hugo continued to hum and to guide her through their sensuous waltz until every button had been undone. A little pressure on the neckline of her gown and it would fall to her feet. Emma closed her eyes, leaning in to him. She felt such love and longing. She wanted to look into his eyes, to see her own emotions mirrored there, but she did not dare. She could not bear to think that they might be absent. Hugo's humming moved down the curve of her ear to her earlobe and thence to the line of her jaw. And still he continued to waltz. She no longer knew where she was—except that she was floating.

When at last his lips touched hers, she let out a little groan. Now the music must stop. Now he would stop waltzing and kiss her properly. Her lips parted of their own accord.

But she was wrong. Even as his tongue slipped teasingly between her lips, the music continued from somewhere in his throat. And he was still whirling her round and round. She had to stop him. She would go mad with frustration if she did not stop him.

With a cry of protest, she wrested her hand free and flung her arms around his neck, returning his gentle kiss with a passion so fierce that it frightened her. She did not know what she was doing or why, only that she must find a way of showing him what she felt, even at the risk of repelling him with her behaviour.

The answering moan, deep in his throat, was eloquent, as was the way his hand skimmed down her back to press her hard against him. He drew his lips away from hers to whisper, in a voice so husky that she barely recognised it, 'Emma, you are like to drive me mad.'

So he felt it, too. Why, then, had he stopped kissing her?

She opened her eyes. They were in her bedchamber. She did not know how they had come there. And the shutters were closed. For a moment, she was blind in the sudden gloom. She could barely see his face, though she knew instinctively that his eyes were gazing into hers. As her eyes became accustomed to the dark, she had a fleeting fancy that he was studying her face, as if trying to carry away her picture, but then he smiled down at her and she forgot everything but the joy of being in his arms at last.

When he put his hands on her shoulders, pushing the neckline of her gown aside, she held his gaze bravely. There was nothing to blush for. Not now.

Obedient to his touch, she let her arms slide down
to her sides. With the softness of a lover's hand, the
gown whispered over her skin to pool at her feet.

Hugo stood transfixed, looking at her as if he had
never seen anything so beautiful. Then he crushed
her fiercely to him, kissing her with such desperation
that she thought she was about to be consumed. She
tried to speak, but it was impossible. His mouth was
too strong, too insistent. Without another thought,
she gave herself up to him.

The noise of her chemise tearing seemed to come
from a long way off. She barely noticed it. All her
being was focused on returning his passion, kiss for
kiss, and pushing aside his clothing so that she could
put her hands on his naked body, and make him
share the tremors that were beginning to torment her.
'Hugo,' she groaned into his mouth. 'Hugo, I love
you.'

He stopped kissing her. He stopped breathing altogether. Then he swung her naked body into his
arms and on to the bed as if she weighed no more
than thistledown. She cried out at the loss of his
touch, but in seconds, it seemed, he was beside her
again, and as naked as she.

He put his hand on her cheek, turning her to face
him. 'Emma, my darling wife,' he began throatily.

It was too much. She did not care what was to
come. She would endure any amount of pain to have
his kisses, his touch. She needed them now. 'Kiss
me, Hugo,' she said desperately. 'Please.'

He could not resist the longing in her voice. She
loved him. And she wanted him. This time, he would

show her how it should be between lovers. This time, it would be for her alone.

He began to kiss her delectable mouth, not frantically now, but with controlled passion, fierce and tender by turns until she was moaning with desire. His own cravings he ruthlessly suppressed, even while the glories of her body under his questing hands painted pictures of wild abandon in his mind. He would not give in to their call, not until his wife—the woman he loved—was mindless with need.

Emma's hands were roaming over his body, stroking his hair when he took her proud nipple into his mouth, scoring her nails down his back when he pulled her beneath him at long last, cupping his buttocks to urge him on. This time, she did not flinch when he entered her, but welcomed him with a deep sigh of longing fulfilled. It seemed to echo through his whole being. He held himself very still, in wonderment.

'Don't stop!' she cried. 'Please!'

Hugo's hard-won control was snapped by that single word. He began to move within her, urged on by the passion of her responses. He needed to give her the fulfilment she sought but he was losing control, he could not hold back, he had to—

Emma gasped for breath as the shudders began to rack her body.

Hugo let go at last. And, as he reached his own climax, he heard a strangled voice which sounded somehow like his own. It was surely inside his head. And it was saying hoarsely, over and over, 'I love you.'

Hugo stood looking down at his sleeping wife, trying to absorb every detail of her beauty. If he was to die this day, he wanted her face to be the last picture in his mind, and her name to be the last word on his lips. He closed his eyes for a second. Yes, he could still see her image, her golden curls spread over the pillow in disarray, her lips a fraction open as if in invitation of his kisses, her breast rising and falling with each slow breath. In his mind, her eyes were open and filled with love—eyes as blue as the Spanish skies.

He must leave.

He took one last look at Emma. She slept peacefully, a picture of innocent yet seductive womanhood against the tumbled evidence of their passion. He would not have believed that she could respond to him as she had. Under her chaste exterior, he had uncovered a woman as sensuous and as bewitching as the goddess of love herself. He could not leave without one more touch.

He dared not kiss her lips, lest she wake. Instead, he leant across the bed to place a tiny kiss on her cheek. She moved a little in her sleep, making a faint sound in her throat. It was like an echo of the cries of pleasure that his love-making had drawn from her last night.

'I love you, Emma,' he said in a low voice, willing her to understand even though she slept. 'I love you. Forgive me.'

He went out quickly then and regained his own bedchamber before the sight of her could break his resolve. He had been on the point of taking her in his arms and kissing her until they were both lost in passion all over again.

He closed his door firmly but he could not bring himself to turn the key in the lock. He could not shut her out, even today.

His valet had already brought his shaving water and was laying out his clothes—dark, unostentatious garments to make him less of a target in the early light. 'Thank you,' Hugo said quietly. 'I shall not need you now. Go downstairs and watch for my brother's arrival. Make sure he does not wake the house.'

The valet nodded grimly and left.

Hugo began the methodical business of readying himself for what might be his last day on earth. He was not afraid. His resolve was unshakeable. He was determined that Forster would suffer for what he had done, but he would not kill the man, much though he deserved it. Emma could not be married to a murderer. No. Forster would be scarred, and preferably for life. And he? That would depend on Forster's nerve, and Forster's skill with a pistol.

Hugo straightened his dark coat and sat down at the little table by the window where he had placed his letter to Emma. The black ink of the superscription stood out starkly against the white paper—*To my wife, to be opened only in the event of my death.* He took it in his hand, remembering the words he had written. He could not leave her like that.

A soft knock was followed by the return of his
valet. 'Sir,' he said, 'your brother is waiting for you.
I am to tell you to hurry, he says. If you do not leave
now, you will be late.'

Hugo waved him away with an impatient hand.
'Tell him I will be there presently.'

He opened the letter and reread what he had written. It was just as cold and stiff as he had thought.
He should write another. But there was no time.

He hunted around for a usable pen and dipped it
in the ink. There was no time to compose fine words.
He must write what he felt and hope she would understand.

'PS I do not have time to write again. This short
postscript must suffice. Emma, my love, my darling
wife, it grieves me not to be able to look into your
eyes as I say this farewell. I love you. Believe that
whatever else you may not believe. Your love goes
with me, my most cherished possession. I beg you
to try to forgive me for deserting you. It was not for
want of love. God bless you, always. H.S.'

The door opened again just as he finished those
few lines. 'For God's sake, Hugo,' hissed Kit. 'You
must come now!'

'Yes,' said Hugo, rising, and trying to refold the
letter into its existing creases. Where were the wa-
fers? He cursed. The more he tried to hurry, the
clumsier he seemed to become.

At last he propped the letter on the table where
she would find it—if he did not return. Kit was
standing in the open doorway, beckoning urgently.

him. With a final glance in the direction of the sitting room and his sleeping wife, Hugo hastened out.

But he closed the door too hastily. The sudden draught caught the letter and carried it to the floor where it lay, face down, concealed by the shadow of the chair.

Chapter Twenty-Four

It was a strange morning, its atmosphere almost uncanny. Hugo could not decide why he felt so detached from everyday reality. For a man who was going to face death, he knew himself to be unnaturally calm.

He looked out across the expanse of the park as they drove by. There was something peculiar about the way the early morning mist hugged the ground, obscuring all but the tallest trees. The treetops seemed to be floating, disembodied, beneath the bloody orb of the sun. Was it an omen? He refused to believe that it could be. Forster, too, must be seeing the same baleful image. Its message could as easily be for him.

It was a long time since Hugo had been about so early. In Spain, there had been many a day when he had risen at first light, but the dawn chorus was never like this. He found it hard to believe that London could be home to so many songbirds, even in early summer. Like the mist, the sound seemed magical. Was it just his own heightened senses drinking in the beauty of his surroundings for, possibly, the last time?

He smiled to himself. No. It was not any morbid

fascination with his last day on earth. It was joy: joy that his wife, his Emma, was in love with him; joy that she had found fulfilment in his arms; joy that they had been able to share their passion at last, even though for only one night.

But there would be other nights. He was almost sure of that, now. Emma's love made him feel armoured, almost invincible. He must survive to return to her.

At his side, Kit was silent, giving all his attention to his horses. There was little traffic at such an early hour, but it was vital not to be late. Blessing Kit for his understanding, Hugo leant back against the soft leather and closed his eyes. He would allow himself a few moments to dream of Emma. And then he would bury every vestige of emotion deep within himself, to prepare for this meeting with his mortal enemy. He was determined to be cold and implacable. Forster had as good as murdered Hugo's comrades. Such a man deserved no mercy at all.

By the time they reached Paddington Green, the sun would have begun to burn off the mist. There was yet time. By five o'clock, they would surely face each other in bright, dazzling daylight.

Emma stretched contentedly but did not wake. She was not dreaming. Waking or sleeping, she now knew that she had no need of dreams, for the man she yearned for was the man she had married. He loved her, and he had spent the night teaching her the joys of love between husband and wife. He had shown her that physical love could carry her to a place of wonder and ecstasy. And he had let her see that she had more power over him than she could ever have imagined. When she touched him, his body responded, just as hers responded to him. He was powerless to control his hunger for her. And he was proud of his own weakness, confessing it to her between kisses that drugged her senses. She had conquered him, he told her, and he was more than willing to yield.

She moaned a little, remembering. Soon she would wake and turn to him. He would be waiting for her. And he would respond.

Hugo paced up and down, impatiently slapping his thigh with his gloves. His seconds were here. The surgeon was here, standing apart in his rusty black coat. But there was no sign of Forster.

Kit made his way to his brother's side and put a hand on his arm. 'It still wants five minutes to the hour, Hugo. He is bound to appear. He would be branded a coward, else.'

Hugo was in no mood to be placated. He shrugged off Kit's hand and resumed his pacing without a word.

Kit merely shook his head and walked back to consult with his fellow second.

The bell of St Mary's began to chime the hour. Hugo looked up, listening. One. Two. Still no sign of Forster. Three. The distant sound of galloping horses broke the stillness.

On the fifth stroke, a closed carriage appeared through the trees, drawn by steaming horses. Forster had arrived.

Hugo nodded towards his seconds and resumed his pacing. There was nothing for him to do until they had examined the weapons and marked out the ground. Kit would come for him when all was ready. Hugo strode away from the little group. Twenty-five paces, he thought, counting. Then he would turn and take twenty-five paces back. It seemed appropriate. They would face each other at just such a distance.

He turned, still counting. One, two... What on earth was going on? The seconds were conferring in considerable agitation. There was still no sign of Forster. Hugo supposed he must still be in the carriage. Stupid man. His muscles would be cramped from sitting. Not the best preparation for a duel, even if it was not to be swords. Eleven, twelve...

The seconds had begun to pace out the ground at last, taking care to ensure that neither protagonist would have the morning sun in his eyes. The bloody orb was gone now, as was the mist. A slight, fresh breeze had arisen, stirring the trees like a whispering voice. The sky was as blue as Emma's eyes and the sun was as gold, as dazzling, as her hair. Hugo swallowed hard and banished her image. Not now. He dare not think of her now. Later. When it was over.

Kit came to meet him and lead him to his place. Forster had still not emerged from the carriage. Kit touched Hugo on the arm. 'Forster's second will drop the handkerchief,' he said. 'I will—' He broke off. Forster was climbing down from the carriage at last. 'Good God!' Kit exclaimed. 'I'm not having that!' He strode off towards the other seconds, indignation clear in the set of his shoulders.

Forster was dressed, like Hugo, in a plain dark coat.
But, while Hugo's head was bare, Forster had covered
his with a close-fitting black cap, such as might be
worn by an elderly invalid, crouching by the fire to
keep warm.

Hugo could hear Kit's angry voice though he could
not make out the words. There was no need. Kit
would certainly be accusing Forster of ungentlemanly
conduct, covering his head to make himself less of a
target. The exchange would not last long. Hugo
smiled grimly. He had complete faith in his brother's
ability to carry his point.

He was right. Forster's seconds had begun to remonstrate with their principal even as he chose his
pistol. And Kit was walking across the grass, carrying
the remaining pistol by its barrel.

Hugo took it, checking it mechanically. It was
primed and cocked. He let his arm hang by his side,
pointing the pistol at the ground, feeling the weight
of it. Not long now.

Kit gave him one long, meaningful look and
walked calmly back to his place.

Hugo took his stance, his right shoulder and arm
towards his opponent, his body sideways to make the
smallest possible target. He looked towards Forster.
The man had his pistol in his hand now, but had still
not uncovered his head. He was arguing with one of
his seconds in a low angry voice. The second seemed
to lose patience. He reached up and pulled off the
cap.

Forster's cry of anger echoed round the green. His
brown hair was white.

No one moved. Everyone was staring at Forster. It was impossible, surely? Except… Hugo smiled grimly to himself. Fear was the answer, of course. Forster's seconds had obviously had to drag their man to this meeting. He was such an abject coward that his hair had turned white overnight at the prospect of facing Hugo along the barrel of a pistol. No wonder he had tried to conceal his hair. It was the badge of his shame. And now, all London would know it.

'Get on with it.' Forster's angry shout, and the accompanying curse, carried clearly across the field.

The seconds moved to their places. The doctor turned his back. The handkerchief was raised.

Hugo fixed his gaze on his target. The pistol hung heavy in his hand. In a moment, the handkerchief would fall, he would raise his pistol and—

The ball reached him almost before he heard the sound of the shot.

Forster had fired before the signal!

Hugo was stunned. He could hardly believe it, even of a man like Forster. He stood motionless, watching the shocked reactions of the others as if they were actors on a distant stage. The turf between them now seemed to stretch for miles. The seconds at the far end were closing on Forster, shouting in angry voices. Kit looked ready to kill the man with his bare hands.

But the second with the handkerchief was rock steady, as if such perfidy was an everyday occurrence. 'Stand back, gentlemen,' he called loudly, looking sternly first at Forster and then at Hugo. 'I am about to begin.'

Silence.

The handkerchief fluttered to the ground, swirling a little in the breeze.

Very slowly, Hugo raised his arm and levelled his pistol. Forster had not dared to move from his place. His shaking was clearly visible at twenty-five yards. His white head shone like a beacon.

A fly settled on Hugo's forehead and started to crawl down towards his eye. Hugo cursed silently and reached up to brush it away with his free hand. But there was no fly. It was blood, trickling down his face. Blood! He must have been hit. And yet he had felt nothing but the wind when the ball sped past him.

He narrowed his eyes and took a bead on Forster's white head. The man seemed to be trying to cower away now. It would be so easy to kill him, to rid the earth of a proven coward.

But he had promised not to make Emma the wife of a murderer.

He gradually lowered his aim, pausing at Forster's belly. No, that too would probably kill him...though gratifyingly slowly. His legs, then? A shattered knee would leave him crippled. Hugo knew exactly how it felt to be pitied and despised as less than a whole man. Forster, coward and blackguard, had never been a whole man. It would be simple justice to let the world see it at a glance.

His finger was almost on the hair-trigger. It would take only the slightest pressure. Hugo took one last look up at the sun and the sky, and fired.

Emma sat up in bed with a start. She had been dreaming, and—

She was alone.

No! Not again! He could not have left her again!

She sprang out of bed, forgetting her nakedness until forcibly reminded by the cool morning air on her skin. She dragged her wrapper around her body, fumbling with the fastenings.

She needed to be able to see. This gloom was almost oppressive.

She flung back the shutters. Sunlight streamed in, temporarily blinding her. She found there were tears in her eyes.

She wiped them away impatiently. It was only the sudden glare. She was not crying. She would not cry.

It was a beautiful day. And he had left her.

She leant wearily against the shutter, gazing out across the empty square. Nothing moved. It was much too early. The solid wood pushed into her arm, as if trying to remind her of its presence. Mechanically she folded the shutters back into place. Someone had undone them last night, closing them so that her bedchamber would be dark when she came there…in her husband's arms. Someone knew she preferred the dark, even though her husband did not. Someone… Hugo?

She ran her hand caressingly down the smooth wood. There was no need of darkness now. If Hugo preferred the light, she would not deny him. Not now. There was nothing she could deny him now.

She had to find him.

He must have gone back to his own bedchamber, his own bed. She would find him, tell him… She took a deep breath and made for the door. Yes, she would tell him that she wanted—needed—him to be beside her when she awoke. She trusted him completely. She would tell him that, and more. She was no longer afraid.

The sound of Hugo's shot broke the stillness. He remained absolutely still, his contemptuous gaze still fixed on Forster, his arm still pointing at his target. Then he threw the pistol to the ground. 'Killing is too good for you,' he said venomously, turning to walk away.

The snarl sounded like a wounded beast, but it came from Forster's lips. Hugo continued to walk. He would not deign to look back at such a man.

Behind him, he heard the scuffling sound of several pairs of running feet on the grass and then Kit's voice, crying out in anger.

Hugo turned.

Forster was face down on the ground, only ten yards away. And Kit was on top of him, wrestling with him for possession of a small silver pistol.

Hugo strode back towards them, ignoring the fact that the pistol was meant for him. The other seconds had almost reached the pair on the ground but Hugo calmly held up a hand to stop them from interfering. He could deal with Forster without any help from anyone. He bent to wrench the pistol from Forster's grasp.

Kit leapt to his feet, automatically brushing grass and dust from his coat. His features were grimly set.

Hugo smiled down at the wicked little pistol in his

hand. 'I do not think it is safe for you to carry a loaded weapon, Forster,' he said, taking aim.

A third shot rang out.

'It throws a trifle left,' Hugo said nonchalantly, dropping it.

The bullet had hit the same tree as Hugo's pistol shot, but some two inches to the left. Forster's seconds gazed at Hugo in awe. Then they looked down at their man, and their expressions changed to disgust.

'Come, Kit,' Hugo said, putting an arm round his brother's shoulder. 'We have nothing more to do here.'

Kit grinned. 'He could have killed you, you idiot,' he said.

'Oh, I doubt it,' replied Hugo. 'You seemed to be getting the better of him. I had every faith in your ability to subdue him.' He threw a quick glance over his shoulder. Forster had been dragged to his feet and was being propelled towards his coach. 'I must say that your technique leaves something to be desired, though, Kit. I'd take some boxing lessons if I were you.'

Kit choked. 'I'll have you know, brother—'

Hugo stopped in his tracks and turned to face his brother. 'You don't have to say it,' he said quietly. 'You saved my life, and we both know it.' He gripped Kit's hand. 'And I *am* grateful.' He paused. A wicked smile tugged at the corners of his mouth. 'I suppose you expect some kind of recompense? Like calling off your banishment, perhaps?

Kit punched Hugo's shoulder with his free hand. Oh, you can do so if you like,' he said airily, 'but I fancy I shall go in any case. I have a notion I am going to enjoy Vienna.'

The curricle was taking much too long to get back to town. 'For God's sake, can't you go any faster?' Hugo said impatiently. 'Let me drive.'

'No,' said Kit. 'You are in no fit state to do so. And you know perfectly well that even you could go no faster, unless you were prepared to mow down all these people.' He nodded in the direction of the thronging traffic on the road, now that London was up and about its business. 'You would do better, Hugo,' Kit went on kindly, 'to do something about all that blood. Emma will have a fit if she sees you like that.'

Hugo blanched. He had not stayed to allow the doctor to tend his wound. It was only a scratch, but it was still bleeding sluggishly. He took out his handkerchief and rubbed it vigorously across his forehead.

'There's blood in your hair, too,' Kit said, glancing sideways at him.

'Thank you,' Hugo said politely. 'I think I can manage.' Then he laughed ruefully. Now he could feel the crease where the ball had grazed his forehead and his scalp. 'I shall probably have another scar, right alongside the sword-cut. Poor Emma. What a pitiful specimen of a husband she has taken, to be sure.'

Kit shook his head in mock despair. He was laughing, too. 'I am sure Emma knows that she had the best of the bargain,' he said. 'You will make a much better husband than I—provided that she will let you near her after this.' He gestured towards Hugo's bleeding head. 'She is bound to find out now, Hugo. What will you tell her?'

Hugo was no longer laughing. His hand stilled, holding the handkerchief over his wound. 'The truth, perhaps. Or...' He shook his head. 'I don't know. I...I'll know when I see her. For heaven's sake, Kit, can you go no faster?'

Chapter Twenty-Five

Emma was standing in Hugo's bedchamber, staring hopelessly at the empty bed. Hugo was gone. The bed had not been slept in. It was just as before.

She could not bring herself to go near it. She could not touch it. She felt hollow inside. She had given her heart into his keeping, she had trusted him, and he had left her without a word. Where had he gone?

Terrible, wicked thoughts rose in her mind. She did not have the strength to fight them off. He was leaning over the gambling table, staking her fortune on the turn of a card. He was clasped in the arms of a faceless harlot, groaning with pleasure. He was...

Her knees started to buckle. She ought to sit down. The bed was nearer but it repelled her. She stumbled towards the window, holding on to the back of the chair for support. She noted, absently, that the writing table was strewn with papers. How strange. That did not seem like Hugo at all. Her husband was a methodical man. Her husband...

Her husband had left her alone.

She needed to sit down. Just for a moment. Then

she would go back to her own room and prepare to face the day.

With shaking hands, she pulled the chair out a little way and sank gratefully on to it. She leant forward, pushing aside the jumble of papers to make room for her hands. She clasped them together, and closed her eyes. She pulled her knees together to stop them shaking.

There was something on the floor, under her bare foot.

It was a letter. And it was half open.

She bent down to pick it up. It had been clumsily folded, and the wafer had not stuck properly. She started to put it away from her. She could not read someone else's letter.

Her own name shouted up at her from the page.

With white, shaking fingers she spread the crackling paper and began to read. Hugo and Forster. Hugo branded a coward. All those men dead. She could hardly bear to read on. When she came to the end of his explanation, she was suddenly cold with fear. Hugo had gone to fight a duel with Forster. For the sake of a hundred dead men who must now be nothing more than bones. Why? Nothing could bring them back. Why must it be Hugo? The cry screamed through her head. He had gone from her. And he might never return.

She could hardly bring herself to look at the paper again, but she knew there was more. Tears were pouring down her face. She could barely make out the words.

It was difficult to decipher the last few lines. They

must have been written in a great hurry. She wiped her eyes, trying to focus. And then she saw what he had written.

A great sob rose in her throat and burst forth. She crushed the letter to her breast, holding it as if it was the most precious thing she had ever owned. Then she smoothed it out again, desperate to reread those last, loving words. He loved her. And he had gone. At any moment, some servant would knock at the door to bring her the news that he had fallen, dead of a murderer's bullet.

She looked towards the door to the corridor. Silence.

She rose, still clutching the letter, and moved across to the bed. Hugo's blue silk robe lay across it. She reached out, touched it. Then, overcome with the horror of her loss, she seized it and hugged it to her, breathing in his scent.

It was all she had left of him.

A soft knock on the door to the corridor sent a shiver of terror down her spine. She heard a voice say something, but the words did not register. She recognised that voice. It was Hugo's valet, come to tell her. She must be strong. She must not disgrace his memory.

She turned towards the opening door.

'Emma!'

This voice came from behind her, from the door to the sitting room. It sounded like Hugo's voice. But that was impossible, wasn't it?

She turned, saw, and sank to the floor in a dead faint.

Hugo rushed across to catch her, but he was too late. He knelt to take his wife in his arms. She was deathly pale. He was not sure that she was breathing.

His valet seemed to appear from nowhere. 'Sir,' he began, 'I came to see if you wanted—' He broke off at the sight of that white face. 'Shall I fetch madam's abigail?'

'Out!' Hugo cried furiously, raising his eyes from Emma's face for only a second. 'Leave us!'

The valet scuttled for the door.

Hugo pulled Emma into his arms and swung her from the floor. He felt as if he had the strength of ten as he carried her across to his bed and laid her tenderly on top of the covers. His precious wife. She must come back to him. She must forgive him.

He prised his robe from her grasp but, when he tried to take the letter, he could not. She held it fast. How cold she was. He put his hands over hers, willing the warmth from his own body into her freezing fingers. It was not enough. He pulled the covers out from the far side of the bed and wrapped them round her. She was shivering now. And her eyes were still closed.

It was not enough.

He dragged himself out of his coat and tore off the rest of his clothing, ignoring the sound of ripping cloth and popping buttons. Then he slid between the covers and took her in his arms. Still, it was not enough. He slid his hands down her silken wrapper until he found the belt. He pulled it apart and drew her naked body into his, covering her with his limbs. At last, her shivering began to wane.

He put his lips to her ear. 'Emma,' he whispered, 'Emma, my love, my darling, come back to me.' He dropped a tiny kiss on the corner of her jaw. 'Emma—'

Her eyes flickered and closed again. She pushed even closer into his warmth.

'Emma? Emma, speak to me.'

'No,' she said, whispering into his chest. 'I can't. I just want to feel you holding me, to know that you are safe.'

He could feel her tears on his skin. And the stiff paper of his letter was digging into his ribs. He eased it out and threw it on the floor, wondering how it was that she had come to read it. He would ask her. Later.

Her tears seemed to have stopped. She was feathering tiny kisses across his chest. When she reached the long scar, she continued her trail, down towards his belly. The hairs on the back of his neck were standing on end. It was too much. He groaned in dismay as his body began to heat even more. They were much too close. Now was not the time.

He made to put her from him, to leave her to recover from her swoon, but she would not let him go. The moment she felt his withdrawal, she clung to him with more strength than he would have thought possible from such a tiny frame. 'Emma, let me go,' he said gently, trying to remove her fingers from his arm. 'You need to rest now, my love. I will come back later, I promise.'

She lifted her head from his burning skin and fixed him with a stern glare. 'What I need *now*, Hugo Stratton, is you,' she said decisively. He had left her once already this day. She would not permit him to do so again. She lowered her head and began to flick her tongue over his skin, moving slowly down his body. When she reach his navel, he groaned with pleasure. She smiled against his skin and kissed his flat belly.

'Now, Hugo,' she commanded.

'Hugo, are you awake?'

'No.' He gently pulled her closer, so that her back and bottom curved into his body and she could feel his legs caressing her all the way down to her toes. It felt heavenly to be so loved. He had slept with his arm encircling her waist, but now he slid his hand idly down on to her belly. She turned into him, before he could divert her yet again. She had to tell him.

She touched her hand to his new wound. It was not serious, though there would probably be a scar. Another scar. She ran her finger down the silver line on his face, from forehead to chin, then placed her palm gently over his cheek. She had explained about the letter. That was simple. She had apologised for her hot, hurtful words when he came to her in the garden. But there was something more he had to understand, something much more important. 'Hugo, that night in the garden, I—'

'Hush. I know you did not go willingly into Kit's arms.'

'But I did.'

Hugo went very still under her hand.

'I thought it was you.'

The stillness vanished in an instant. Hugo rolled over, taking her with him, so that she lay on her back and he could look down into her beautiful eyes. They were wide and loving and honest as they gazed up into his. 'I don't understand,' he said softly, the question clear in his voice.

'I thought I was alone. I was daydreaming, I suppose. It was such a magical place in the moonlight, so still, so exotic. I was dreaming that the man I loved would appear out of the gloom and sweep me into his arms. And when Kit appeared, I opened my eyes and...it was you I saw. It sounds so strange, now, though you are quite alike, I suppose...'

Hugo stroked her cheek lovingly. 'Mmm?'

'And then he kissed me and, in that moment, I knew it was not you.'

Hugo laughed deep in his throat. 'Kit would be mightily displeased if he ever learned that. He thinks himself the most accomplished of lovers.'

'Oh,' said Emma, blushing. 'I...oh, dear...'

'Do you know, wife,' said Hugo huskily, trailing his fingers down her throat and on to her breast, 'you are quite delightful when you blush. It starts on your throat, here—' he kissed the spot '—and it rises into your cheek, here—' he kissed that spot, too '—but, at the same time, it travels down to—' He began to feather kisses down her neck and on to her breasts both now thoroughly rosy. 'Whenever I see you blush in company, I shall know that, under your gown, you are blushing too—in places that are reserved for me alone.'

'Hugo,' said Emma in a constricted whisper, 'how can you say such a thing? I shall never dare to look at you in company if that is what you are thinking. I shall do nothing *but* blush.'

'Mmm,' he said teasingly. 'I shall look forward to that.' He eased himself between her thighs and began to kiss her breasts in earnest until she moaned in response. Lifting his head, he said, 'I shall be thinking of things much, much more exciting than mere blushes, my love. And I dare say that—eventually—you will become accustomed.'

She tried to hide her face in his shoulder, but he rolled over on to his back, never letting go of her for a second. He lay back on the pillows and laughed up at her as she tried to push herself out of his embrace. She could not look at him.

'By the bye, wife, I have received a letter—from the Duke.'

'York?' said Emma, turning back to him in horror. His Royal Highness was Forster's patron. And Hugo had just ruined the man.

'No. Wellington,' Hugo said with a grin of triumph. 'He wrote to felicitate me on my marriage. He hopes to make the acquaintance of my lady wife at an early date.'

'But he already knows me,' protested Emma 'He has met me on several occasions.'

'Ah, but he has not met Mrs Stratton, my love. You forget, perhaps, about the Duke's reputation with the ladies. You may have been safe from him when you were an innocent young débutante, but now that you are married, he will consider you fair game.'

Emma eyed him suspiciously. 'And will you challenge him to a duel, too?'

'That depends,' he said, trailing his fingers round the top of her arm and then down to rest on the underside of her delicate breast. 'Were you planning to give me cause?'

Two could play at that game, Emma decided, trying to ignore the way her breast was settling heavily into his hand. She poised the tips of her fingers around his nipple and squeezed, just a fraction, so that her fingernails tightened into his taut flesh. His intake of breath was satisfyingly sharp.

'Not immediately,' she said.

Epilogue

Jamie looked up at Emma with eyes shining with happiness, in spite of her obvious exhaustion. 'Are they not beautiful, Emma?' she said.

Emma shook her head in wonderment at the two tiny babies cradled in their mother's arms. She knew she had witnessed a miracle. She felt very close to tears. 'They are, indeed. Truly beautiful, Jamie. Richard will be so proud of you.'

At that moment, the bedroom door was thrust open to admit Richard, followed by the Dowager, and the nursemaid. Emma was decidedly *de trop*. With a softly murmured 'congratulations' to Richard, she quietly left the room and made her way downstairs to the garden.

Hugo was pacing up and down on the terrace, for all the world like the expectant father. He turned at the sound of the opening door. 'Emma! What has happened? The servant could not say.'

Emma smiled joyfully at him and saw the strain disappear from his face in a moment. 'Richard has a son. And a daughter. And Jamie is very well. I am no longer needed.'

Hugo inspected his wife for signs of fatigue. She had not left Jamie's side since labour had begun, hours and hours ago. And there was a smear of blood on the side of her gown, where the apron had failed to protect her. He put a sustaining arm around her waist and pulled her close.

'Are you very tired, my love?' he asked.

'A little, I admit, but nothing compared with Jamie. She was wonderful. So brave.' Emma remembered Jamie's hours of pain. It had been frightening at first, but Jamie had never complained. In a moment of calm, she had taken Emma's hand and told her that she did not mind the pain, for each spasm brought her nearer to the moment of birth. And now that Emma had seen that miracle with her own eyes, she had begun to understand.

'Poor Richard was wearing a track on the flags,' Hugo said. 'And he was cracking his knuckles incessantly all the while, too. I've never seen him do that before. When I mentioned it to him, he had no idea what I was talking about. He looked at me as if I were quite mad.' Hugo shook his head, laughing. 'I might have expected such a reaction in a first-time father, perhaps, but he's done it before—'

'Not with twins, Hugo. That was always going to be more difficult for Jamie. You must see that?'

Hugo led her across the terrace and down on to the lawn before he answered. 'I do not seek to make light of the matter, believe me,' he said, seriously. 'The problem is, we men feel quite helpless at times lik this. I know that Richard longed for another child, but his first thought was always for Jamie. I hate to think what he would have done if—'

Emma put a finger across his lips. 'Hush,' she said softly. 'Do not say it. Everything is well.'

They strolled across the lawn in companionable silence until they reached the ancestral oak.

Emma looked up into its branches. Autumn was late. The leaves had not yet begun to turn.

'You know, when I was a child, I probably climbed this oak as often as I climbed my own. If I sat very still, the birds would sometimes start to sing again, forgetting I was there. I used to watch the sunset through the branches and conjure up a magical, musical kingdom where everyone obeyed my slightest command.'

Hugo laughed. 'You always were a little madam, or so Richard told me in his letters.' He bent and kissed her, slowly and thoroughly. When he raised his head again, her skin was pink and her eyes were glowing with love.

'That reminds me,' he said with a sly smile. 'A letter arrived this afternoon, from Kit.' He reached into his pocket and drew out the folded sheets.

'May I read it?' Emma asked, stretching out her hand.

He flung his hand high above her head, taking the letter well out of reach. 'Absolutely not,' he said, with mock severity. 'Think of how your delicate sensibilities might be outraged by what he has to say about is…er…adventures. It did not take him long to tire of the delights of Paris. He has been in Vienna these

last four weeks. And it seems he is already…
er…making his mark.'

Emma looked quizzically up at him.

'It appears that the ladies of the Austrian court are
quite as dazzling as any to be found in London, or
Paris. And—' he opened the letter to remind himself
of its exact contents '—rather more amenable, according to Kit.' He refolded the letter and restored it
to his pocket. 'More than that, I dare not tell you.
Kit's letters shall be treated like mine to Richard—fit
for a lady's ears only if savagely censored.'

Emma leant into his warm, strong body, tilting her
head back against his shoulder so that she could look
up into his face. He smiled down at her. The scar was
a thin silver line now. It made his smile a little twisted
on one side, but she had long ago decided that it was
an endearing mismatch. Hugo's face was full of character when he smiled—especially when he smiled at
his wife as he did now.

'What are you thinking, my love?' Hugo said quietly, starting to run his free hand delicately up and
down her spine.

She shivered in response. She could see in his eyes
that he was deliberately trying to arouse her. They
would have to go inside soon or else—

'Mmm?' said Hugo, fixing his eyes hungrily on her
mouth.

'I was thinking, sir, that though Kit is a rake and
may never be redeemed, his elder brother is but little
better.'

'Indeed?' Hugo was trying to sound severe, but the
mischievous glint in his eyes gave him away.

'Indeed, sir. A few years abroad may do wonders for a young man like Kit, but you, at your age—I fear you are beyond redemption.'

'I see,' said Hugo, beginning to nuzzle Emma's neck. 'Well, in that case...'

Emma felt the familiar thrills running through her body, making her belly heat and her skin yearn for his touch. The months of marriage had made no difference at all to Hugo's effect on her, except perhaps to make the feelings, and the pleasure, more intense.

'Hugo, may we not go inside?'

He laughed against her skin but went on planting those tantalising little kisses on her neck, exactly where he knew they would create havoc with her senses.

'Hugo, you wretch! Think who may be watching.'

'No one, my love. They are all concentrating on the new arrivals. Nobody would notice if I took you round behind this ancient oak and—'

'Don't you dare, Hugo Stratton!' Emma exclaimed. 'I declare, you are quite as bad as that brother of yours. You take a woman in your arms, and—'

'And if that woman is my beautiful wife, I am lost.' He drew her back towards the house. 'But I admit that a feather bed is rather more comfortable than this damp lawn.'

When they reached the terrace, still walking arm in arm, a tiny wail broke the silence. 'Ah,' said Hugo, 'I hear the sound of a godchild.'

'Hugo! Has Richard asked you to stand as godfather?'

Hugo nodded. 'I think he believes I am in need of

a little practice,' he said teasingly. 'He says that I was excused on the last occasion only because I was dead.'

Emma giggled. 'You, sir, are quite preposterous.' She paused. 'On the other hand...Richard is quite right. You do need the practice.'

'Emma?'

She hid her face in his waistcoat, feeling unaccountably shy. At last she said, so low that he could barely make out the words, 'You will have a few months to practise, Hugo, but only a very few, I'm afraid.'

'Emma! For heaven's sake, tell me!'

'You will be a father, too, Hugo. In the spring, I think.'

Hugo gave a soft whoop and lifted her off her feet, whirling her round and round until she was quite dizzy and breathless.

'Hugo, put me down.'

'No—why? I have you, and I mean to keep you, my darling, wonderful wife.'

Emma ran her hand over his dark shining hair. 'I have no intention of trying to escape,' she said softly, offering her lips for his kiss. 'My one, my only love.'

* * * * *